I0690400

The Barlows

A story of
Appalachian Folks

A novel by
Peggy Poe Stern
Moody Valley
Boone, North Carolina

Published by
Moody Valley
475 Church Hollow Road
Boone, N C 28607
moodyvalley@skybest.com

Cover painting by Peggy Poe Stern
Cover design and first edits by David K. Stern
Edited May 10, 2019 by Pamela Baldwin
Published June 23, 2019
ISBN: 978-1-59513-070-9

Dedicated to
Appalachian Folks

Chapter 1

~~~~

A cold sweat gathered on Catalena's skin as she gripped the steering wheel. She didn't want to move a muscle, was afraid to draw a breath. She was scared out of her mind. Her overwhelming fear of heights had her feeling paralyzed.

A sheer rock wall towered on the left side of the vehicle with a cliff of dizzying proportions dropping straight down on the right side. It reminded her of the Road of Death in North Yungas, Bolivia where hundreds of people die each year driving the road. She had driven that road once, and only once, on a motor bike. She shook for two days afterwards and promised herself she'd never get into such a situation again, and here she was, reliving the fright.

How did she manage to get herself into such a situation?

More important, how was she to get out of it? No way could she back up the Jeep on that narrow strip of road without going over the edge. She was almost as terrified of driving forward.

"Stop it!" she demanded of herself. "Get a grip. Don't be cowardly."

She had obviously taken a wrong turn several miles back. The map of *Back Roads of the High Country* showed a decent road crossing over a mountain with spectacular views. The road appeared safe when looking at the map. The author of the book and map stated he traveled this road for sheer pleasure when he visited the mountains of the North Carolina.

The word *sheer* brought a lump to her throat and unwanted tears to her eyes. It was a *sheer* drop down the mountainside.

She had convinced herself facing her fear by traveling that road might be the cure for her fear of heights, but it hadn't worked. If anything, her fear was worse.

Traveling this rough, narrow, semblance of a road was not what she had intended. She had obviously taken a wrong turn somewhere, which would have been easy to do in the maze of backroads.

"I don't believe this," she said, hoping the sound of her own voice might give her comfort. "I never allow myself to get lost." Not even when visiting her father's relatives in Arizona, or going with her mother to Chicago, or all the other places she had traveled. It was a fact she was good at reading maps and finding directions even in remote out-of-the-way places.

What had been a narrow excuse for a paved road had turned into gravel, then the gravel turned into a dirt road for several more miles, and now it was nothing other than a narrow goat path. Stupidly, she kept going forward hoping to find a place to turn around. It hadn't happened.

She was now trying to force her meticulously restored Willys Jeep her grandparents once owned to maneuver forward without going over the cliff's edge. The Jeep had been a gift from her grandmother before she died.

Surely, there was a turnaround somewhere ahead, but she wasn't finding it. She tried to ignore the nagging possibility that a turnaround didn't exist. If she attempted to back up, it would surely be to her death. She couldn't back up worth a lick. Luck might get her ten feet before going over the edge and tumbling down the cliff. There wasn't more than eight inches of space from the Jeep's right tires into nothingness. The Jeep was already hugging the rocky left-hand side so closely the mirror had gouged a furrow in what little dirt covered the rocky side of the mountain. The mirror had broken sometime back and was now hanging down.

The situation was downright terrifying to put it mildly. She pulled her cell phone from her purse. "Oh crap!" No signal.

But whom did she plan on calling? The man who drew the map or perhaps 911?

She knew what was behind her but couldn't see what was up front for the foliage of a sudden crop of giant weeds growing in the goat path. She took a deep breath, shut her eyes for a moment, and called herself a few appropriate names for not turning back when the gravel road turned into a dirt road. Now, there wasn't a road but a path little more than the width of the Jeep tires.

Now what?

"Get out and walk the path before you drive any farther," She spoke the words out loud. Good idea except for a thing or two. The left door was against the bank of the mountain and could not be opened. She couldn't crawl out the window because the rocky bank was only her hand's width away. She swallowed hard, scooted across the seats, and opened the passenger side door.

She couldn't stop herself from letting out a shriek as the door swung open. The scene was almost as breathtaking as looking out of an airplane window at the miniature landscape below. Below was a rocky gorge with straggly trees and a stream of water running through it.

She considered herself a strong and capable woman who could do anything – almost. The one thing she hadn't been able to force herself to do was jump out of an airplane. She didn't trust a parachute to open, plus her terrible fear of heights – the fear had a powerful grip on her right now.

Her eyes focused on the sheer drop into glistening water hundreds of yards down into a gorge. Lightheadedness took over as fear sent icy chills through her body. Those same icy chills filled her stomach causing her heart to thud wildly against her chest. *Panic attack,* she told herself and tried to reason with her fear.

The fear was winning.

She couldn't force herself to step out the door and feel for the meager inches of rock between the Jeep's tires and the cliff's edge. Carefully, she pulled the door closed and scooted backward. It felt much safer inside the Jeep than looking down into the gorge.

"Grand Canyon, you've got competition," she mumbled, attempting to regain her calm. She had once ridden a donkey down into the Grand Canyon to prove to her father she could do it. Here she would need wings to safely get to the bottom of this gorge. Colorado's Big Horn Sheep would have found this cliff impossible. Even the best of rock climbers would be greatly challenged by this sheer rock wall.

The narrow Jeep had a canvas top and a tailgate. She climbed between the front seats into the back, unzipped the canvas flap and climbed out. Once her feet were on solid ground. she congratulated herself for driving something she could climb out the back.

So, what was she to do now? Walk back down the road a zillion miles until she came to a house and found help in backing out of this place? She remembered seeing a house right before the gravel road ran out. More correctly what she saw was smoke rising through the trees. It was only reasonable to assume the smoke was coming from a chimney attached to a house. Being this far into the mountain backwoods, she wasn't sure about the house. Worse, she wasn't sure about who, or what, lived in the house. She recalled reading the book "Deliverance". She had assumed the book was extremely exaggerated, but what if it wasn't?

That, plus confess to a stranger she was too afraid to back a Jeep out of what she had gotten herself into wasn't appealing. She had enough foolish pride to rely on her own capabilities. The alternative was to walk forward and see what was in front of the Jeep. Hopefully, if she stomped down the weeds enough not to blindly drive off the narrow goat path, she would find a place to turn around. Or at hopeful best, be able to continue over the top of the mountain and drive down the other side. It appeared she was getting ready to crest the top of the mountain when the weeds became so thick, they blocked the view.

And just how could she manage that?

She reminded herself again there wasn't more than inches of room on the passenger side of the Jeep and tried again not to dwell on being petrified of heights. The weakness was something she hadn't been able to purge no matter how hard she tried. At least it was somewhat a benign fear, one that didn't control her life. She'd been told a lot of people had the same fear, especially women.

She forced herself to stop dwelling on her fear long enough to wonder who had carved out the goat path in the side of the rocky mountain. Must have been one of the lumber companies she had briefly read about. Whiting Lumber Company came to mind. This whole area had been timbered many years in the past. She didn't see how it could have been profitable timbering this mountain. From the looks of the remaining trees and plants, it was only stunted, crooked trees that grew out of rock crevices. It didn't appear a few hundred years would have been enough time to change the plant growth.

Now, how to get from the back of the Jeep to the front? She looked the Jeep over. There was only one way. She managed to crawl over the canvas top but was not pleased with the way the cloth top now sagged. Her weight had popped a few of the snaps. Nothing ripped, at least she hoped it hadn't. She took pride in her newly restored Willys Jeep. Not many still existed, and certainly not one in prime condition such as this one. She slid onto the hood and jumped down on the road.

One thing was for sure, nothing had stunted the weed growth in the path. Obviously, these weeds didn't require much soil to grow tall and thick. Sunshine was surely enough. There could be few natural nutrients in the rocky ground. Without doubt, those weeds were tough and had roots that drilled their hold into almost solid rocks.

She grabbed hold and discovered she couldn't easily pull them up. Stomping them down took a lot of work. At least the path was still wide enough to drive on. She was glad she drove the Jeep and hadn't chosen a rental vehicle for this trip, but then she would not have tackled the goat path in anything with a wider wheelbase.

After what seemed like hours of stomping weeds, she finally reached the top of the mountain. Tears of relief stung her eyes as she realized the ground flattened out and widened. There might be just enough room for her to turn the Jeep around if she did something like a fifteen-point turn-around. She stomped a few more weeds until she could see down the other side of the mountain. There was no longer a goat path. That side of the mountain was solid vegetation. No path and no place for the Jeep to travel unless she tried to excavate a path through woods and laurel hells down the steep incline. At least the wooded area wasn't a continuation of the rock-faced cliff.

Turning around was the logical thing to do. Problem was, if she managed to turn around, she would be sitting on the cliff side looking down the drop-off into the gorge. There would be no closing her eyes and trusting a donkey to get her safely to the bottom.

How did she get herself into such an unpleasant situation she questioned again? Wasn't it only a couple of hours ago that she had finished a delicious, relaxing meal at a restaurant near the hotel where she was staying? Right now, it seemed like a lifetime ago.

She tried to make herself angry for being foolish enough to allow herself to drive up this goat-path of a road. Anger would be better than the shakes. Plus, anger just might give her the courage needed to drive back down the goat path.

She climbed to the highest spot on top of the mountain and took time to sit down on a rock underneath a tree in hopes of calming herself enough to overcome the renewed bout of shakes brought on by the thought of driving back down the goat path. It was going to take determination and nerves of steel for her to turn the Jeep around and drive out of this place. Her nerves of steel had momentarily gone limp. She was going to need a self-delivered pep talk along with a good dose of anger to get her spine back in place.

She prepared the best she could, while trying to ignore the fact her body was already in a cold, clammy sweat.

"Dummy, if you drove up the path, you can drive down the path."

Yeah, right.

"Sure, you can do it," she declared, hoping she could make herself believe her words.

She assured herself there was nothing more encouraging than hearing her own voice saying she could do something she didn't want to do.

"I'm determined to do this," she added, but, at the moment, her determination wasn't enough to brag about.

If she was too much of a coward to turn the Jeep around and drive out of this place, she could always walk out, which just might take hours if she didn't make a misstep and tumble down into the rocky gorge.

She let out a spiel of several bad words and barely refrained from continuing to sit in the shade of the nice stunted tree to wait for some gentleman to show up and rescue her – even if it did take a few years to happen.

"Crap, Catalena Gallaher. You're going to turn that Jeep around and drive down that goat path. What you drive into, you can drive out of," she said with determination she wasn't feeling.

Every step she took back down the goat path toward the Jeep was made with pure grit. She was determined not to let fear of heights, or the narrowness of the goat path, defeat Catalena Gallaher. She *would* turn that Jeep around and then keep her eyes straight ahead without ever looking out the side window at the sheer drop into the gorge. She would no longer permit herself to tremble the way she was now trembling.

She was also determined to ignore her trembling as she climbed on the hood and over the cloth top feeling it sagged more than the first time as more snaps give way. Her feet hit the ground, and she stood in the road for a moment, clenched her teeth, and forced her foot to lift enough to step on the back bumper. Her shin painfully hit the metal as she climbed over the tailgate, squeezed between the seats, sunk into the driver's seat, and turned the key still in the ignition, while actually hoping the Jeep wouldn't start.

"Oh Crap!" she mumbled as the engine turned over on the first crank. She'd now have to continue up the goat path even when she was hoping for an excuse not to drive another foot.

Catalena held her breath as she eased the gas pedal down. The Jeep moved forward over the tangle of weeds she had stomped down. The narrow goat path ahead appeared to be just as solid as the rest of the rocky goat path. Maybe even more solid because the rocks were bigger and overlapping each other.

Stop! Some kind of warning screamed inside her head. *Don't go any farther*!

She took her foot off the gas pedal for a moment, but then ignored the mental warning. Reason told her she couldn't sit in the Jeep until she died of thirst and starvation. She then asked herself what kind of person would go on a back-road trip without taking along food and water? The kind of person she had always been was the answer.

She put the Jeep in low gear and pressed on the gas petal, holding her breath as the Jeep moved forward easing onto a rocky surface that appeared to be solid. The rocks shifted at the weight of the Jeep. The right front wheel began to slowly sink downward as the rumble of falling rocks filled the Jeep. Other rocks gave away as the Jeep went into a fast, death plunge downward.

Realization hit Catalena hard and fast.

She was going to die any second now!

Would there be much pain?

When it was over, would she know she was dead?

Chapter 2

~~~~

George Barlow took for granted he was young and strong. He was also gorgeous, but the gorgeous part didn't come into play as far as George was concerned. It did come into play with girls as well as a few young women. He was used to being admired and sought after by the opposite sex. That was why he had developed his *run-away from 'em* technique to perfection. It added a challenging dimension to their chasing of him, which he enjoyed or ignored at will.

If George ever fell into acting as though he was gorgeous, his older twin brothers were there to quickly dissuade him of such foolishness. Actually, the three brothers looked a lot alike, although the twins had a more rugged type of rough and ready appearance. George was smooth muscled with peach fuzz on his chin and upper lip instead of the full mustaches his brothers had. George also had flashing laughter glowing from his eyes that mimicked his uncle's

All three brothers had the Barlow black hair, dark eyes, and tall, broad shouldered build. The twin boys had a solemn, almost forbidding quality that George lacked. They retained a lot of the early mountain qualities of the Cherokee and Muskhogean Indians, along with the Irish, Scottish, and English people who had settled the area, that the younger George had failed to acquire.

His different outlook on life could be the result of teachers arriving from outside the area who brought in new thoughts and culture to the younger generation. Then, there was also the

influence of his Uncle Homer who took on the raising of
George as his priority.

Rob and Bob Barlow were as slippery as eels as far as
women were concerned. Neither of them had allowed
themselves to get caught in the marriage trap. George planned
on being just as wise as his brothers where the opposite sex
was concerned.

His three sisters were already married, and that included
the one who was only a year older than him. But early marriage
was all right for girls. They had nothing better to do with their
lives other than get married and have a bunch of children. Girls
seldom went beyond high school.

There wasn't enough money on the whole mountain for
more than a high school education. Most kids in the area were
lucky to get in a full twelve years of schooling, even now in
modern times. Take that bunch of Kormans who lived on the
back side of the mountain. Most of the Kormans dropped out
of school by the time they reached sixteen. George almost felt
sorry for them. Not a one of them realized the value of an
education or much of anything else that was worthwhile.

At a few weeks short of eighteen-years of age, George was
thinking about his future and hoping for a college scholarship.
He thought he was lucky his mother started him to school when
he was seven instead of six years of age. It gave him another
year to decide what he wanted to do with his life after high
school. He needed a way to earn cash money if he was to get
away from home and go to college. Working for his brothers
on Saturdays wasn't a high-paying job, but it would help
toward his college fund.

George had always known he could never compete with his
brothers. It was one of the reasons he developed his own
personality totally opposite of theirs. He took back after his
uncle, Homer Barlow, in many things, especially where his
uncle's sense of humor was concerned. Just like Uncle Homer,
if something struck George as funny, he leaped on it and was

ready to ride it to the finish line. George found humor was the next best thing to salvation.

George's mother, Mazy, claimed his Uncle Homer was so full of bull crap he was a good man to keep in the garden.

Homer often told a story about his wife's great uncle, Hadley, who was noted to have been one of the meanest men alive. The uncle lied, fought, stole, and killed everything in sight. When Hadley finally got caught and sentenced to hang, the sheriff led him onto the scaffold in front of the gathered crowd and said, "Okay Hadley, any last words you want to say before we hang you?"

"Shore is," Hadley called out. "This here hanging is gonna be a lesson to me that I won't forget in a hurry."

George was coming out of the house as his Uncle Homer came into the yard from the barn. Homer's eyes widened as he looked at George. He pushed his sweat-stained hat far back on his head in a bewildered manner.

"Lord have mercy! What in the name of tarnation do you think you're wearin'?" Homer asked George in complete befuddlement.

Delight came to George. He could think of nothing more fun than to antagonize his uncle, which wasn't easy being Uncle Homer had a lifetime of experience in aggravating.

"I've taken up jogging. I'm on the cross-country running team this year, as well as on the wrestling team."

"What's exactly is jogging? Is that what they call strippin' down necked and wearing a girl's skirt?"

"No, I'm not naked, and I'm not wearing a skirt."

"Come danged close to being naked, if you ask me. One thing's for certain, I wouldn't be wearin' my sister's little plaid skirt if I was you, being you're supposed to be a man and all. Well, pert near a man that is."

Homer couldn't resist adding the *pert near* part even though George looked manlier than any man he'd ever seen, except for his two brothers. The boy had taken up lifting weights when he was around thirteen. Had to muscle up to hold his own with his brothers. Those two were wiry with rippling muscles and as strong as bull elephants. Had to be strong when they'd spent their entire lives sawmilling. He'd seen them lift a truck out of a mud hole all by themselves, not to mention the logs they man-handled every day except on Sundays.

"This is called a kilt," George informed his uncle.

"It shore enough looks kilt on you. If your brothers catch you wearing that skirt, you'll be the one who gets kilt."

George lifted his chin and let out a good-natured laugh. "This isn't a skirt. It's what our Scottish ancestors wore. Our schools marching band has agreed to wear it at the Highland Games to celebrate our Scottish heritage in July. Our instructor said we've got to get in a lot of practice in wearing it, so it'll feel natural."

"Bull hockey. All that thing's good for is to allow your boys to breathe a little. Makes me want to take a peak up your legs to make sure you've still got your boys, being you're wearing a skirt. They could have hauled off and dried up on you since I strapped diapers on your rump." Homer bent his head to take a peak. "Your brothers would fight a grizzly bear afore they'd strap that little skirt around their hindquarters, much less parade around where a body could see 'em in it."

"I've still got my boys," George assured him, undisturbed by his uncle's remarks, or his looking under the kilt. "I'm going to wear this kilt while I jog to the top of Nowhere Mountain. I need to get the feel of it. Like I said, I don't want to act self-conscious wearing it at the games. Besides, it's airy enough to keep down a lot of sweating."

"Heck fire, boy. Don't you know gnats will get up that skirt and eat you alive? If that ain't bad enough, you'll have to run for your life if a man sees you wearing that thing. If I wasn't so confounded old, I take you on right here and now and strip that thing off you afore some woman sees you and laughs herself to death."

George flipped up the edge of the kilt at his uncle, exposing a good length of muscled leg. "Want to jog to the top of the mountain with me?" George offered with a challenging grin.

"Hell, no."

"Guess that goes to show Mom's a big fibber."

"What're you talkin' about, boy?"

"She always claimed you'd chase anything in a skirt."

~~~~

Homer didn't chase George far until he got winded and had to set down on a log to rest a spell. It was while Homer was sitting on the log huffing in lungs full of fresh mountain air that he heard the kabooming sound of an explosion. The noise rose and vibrated off the mountains in a resounding echo. He wasn't sure where the sound came from, but he figured George might be headed in the right direction to come upon what happened. He forgot about being winded as he jumped up and cut across to the old logging road on the far side of the mountain. He knew something was bad out of place when he saw the tire tracks in the old, narrow road.

Homer had an idea those confounded Korman boys had been growing 'em a little wacky weed on top of old Nowhere. Guess those Kormans and whoever left the tire tracks had encountered each other. It sounded as though it had not been a pleasant union.

But then, he'd seen the Korman boys leave out long before daylight. He figured they were taking their crop off somewhere to sell it. He didn't approve of what the Korman boys were doing, but a man learned it was best to mind his own business and allow others to do the same. Besides that, it was about the only way those Korman boys had of bringing in a dollar to help feed and clothe the lot of them.

One thing was for sure about those Korman women. They had a way of producing children like a bunch of horny goat weed eating rabbits. If those Korman boys had a lick of sense, they'd be gathering that horny goat weed to sell instead of that illegal weed. Even he knew that new stuff advertised as Viagra had to be derived from horny goat weed, and the mountains were full of the heart-shaped weed.

Trouble was, that crazy boy would hear the explosion and cut through the woods to the logging road, see those tracks, and follow them to where the trouble was. Where the devil were Rob and Bob when a man needed them? Reckon whatever happened now would be left up to George and him. Thing was George would get to where the explosion took place a long time before he could. At least he'd be bringing up the rear, and he always carried a pistol tucked away in his bibbed overalls just in case the need ever arose.

Unless he missed his guess, those Korman boys had grown suspicious that some kind of law enforcement might get wind of their farming operation and drive up the old logging road even when it was so narrow a vehicle couldn't go far unless it was one of them four-wheeler things. Knowing the Korman boys, they would take great pleasure in rigging up some kind of trap that would tumble a four-wheeler off the cliff and down into the hollow. It was possible that was what happened, and the vehicle's gas tank exploded. What if a body or bodies were down in the gorge burning to a crisp right now? That would be the beginning of a dang-blasted heap of trouble.

Stupid, ignorant bunch of Kormans. Growing weed was one thing, but killing somebody was entirely different. Law would be all over them if their own men were injured or went missing. And before long, George would be right in the middle of the fracas before he could reach him. That boy would run head-long into the middle of a dog fight. He had no sense of self-preservation. Why, he wouldn't keep himself out of a vat of hog manure while knowing he'd come out stinking.

A sharp pain shot though Homer's leg and back. Danged his old-aged crippled up body. He simply couldn't move as fast as an eighteen-year old no matter how hard he was trying. Again, he wondered where Rob and Bob were when they were needed. He was near scared senseless that they would definitely be needed.

~~~~

George hadn't jogged far when he heard the explosion and headed toward the noise as fast as his legs could run. By the sound of the explosion, something mighty bad had just happened. His first thought was that his brothers had an accident and were in some sort of trouble, but what would they doing on top of Nowhere Mountain? But then they might not have been on the mountain. Sound was tricky. It rose upward and bounced from mountain to mountain in multiple echoes. The explosion could have come from down in the gorge instead on top of old Nowhere.

He headed for the logging road to see if it could give him an indication of what was going on. Sure enough, there were fresh tire tracks climbing upward, mighty fresh tracks at that. One thing was for sure, those tracks weren't made by his brothers' logging truck – but they were sure enough made by some unlucky person. Whoever it was most likely needed help bad, be it a no-account Korman or somebody else. He didn't hesitate as he tried to make his legs pump even faster.

Chapter 3

~~~~

Shards of pain were everywhere. The pain burned, throbbed, and ached as it tried to force Catalena to open her eyes. She didn't want to do it. The best thing for her was the darkness. It held relief from the pain as well as the thing she realized was a surging panic. Something horrible had just happened and she didn't want to know anything more about it. Yes, the blackness was a good thing if she could just make it stay with her, but flashes of intruding light prodded her awake like a sharp knife.

"Good Lord in heaven!" The words floated down from above and penetrated her semiconscious mind.

Dead, she thought. *I'm dead* – and being dead hurt like shards of glass shooting through her flesh.

Somebody was talking about the Lord and heaven, but she was far away from the voice. She wanted the voice to shut up and let her go back into the painless darkness that she was trying to hold onto.

"Hang on," the voice hollered loud and clear as though she might be hard of hearing. "Don't move an inch. I'll figure out how to get to you."

It was a young man's voice. He must be one of God's angels trying to help her reach the tunnel of light that opened up into heaven. She had always imagined that dead people automatically floated upward toward a bright light, but maybe not. Maybe angels came to help with the crossing over process.

Catalena tried again to open her eyes and succeeded slightly. Oh dear, she certainly didn't want a bright light. Bright light brought pain hammering in her head. She definitely wanted to remain in the easing darkness for a while longer, but she feared it was not going to happen. The best she could do was keep her eyes closed and not move in the slightest. Even taking a breath was painful.

Breath? Painful? Did a dead person breathe? Could a dead person feel pain? Cell memory, she concluded. She was dead and reliving the cell memory of such things. People were said to still be able to feel an amputated leg long after it was gone. It only made sense that she would be able to feel pain as if she were alive.

Dang blast and confound it! Lightning bolts of pain shot through her again. She was being picked up bodily and it hurt like blazes. "Put me down," She demanded in a very weak voice.

"Can't," came a voice close to her ear. "There's barely room for my feet. There's no way I can walk on this ledge if you're lying on it. Besides, we've got to get on solid ground mighty fast. These rocks are about to give way. If they do, we'll both be goners for certain."

Catalena made a feeble attempt to force him put her down, but her effort to move made the shards of pain worse.

"Stay as still as a mouse. If you struggle, I might lose my balance and we'll both tumble off the ledge into the gorge. Like I just told you, we certainly don't want that to happen."

Those words brought back terrifying fear. She didn't dare struggle.

"Good girl," he soothed. "Good girl. Stay still a little while longer. We're doing great. Just a little farther and we'll both be safe and sound."

Catalena listened to the sound of that voice, needed it. She wanted to hold onto his soothing voice along with the darkness. There was safety in both.

"Don't know why in the dickens you'd be driving on that old logging road, but you're lucky to have landed where you did. Hope you were the only one in that vehicle. Don't know if you were thrown out or if you jumped. It would be my guess you jumped out when the vehicle started to turn over. Good thing you did. Things don't look too good down there in the gorge. At least I found you before you moved enough to fall off the ledge. Don't know how badly you're hurt yet. You're bloodied up a little but at least you're breathing pretty good and not screaming in pain. I'm guessing you're not hurt bad, just shook up a whole lot, I'd say," the voice nervously rambled on.

Catalena couldn't stop her eyes from opening again. She had to get a look at who that voice was coming from. What she saw didn't look anything like an angel.

"Who are you?" She tried to ask, but her words must not have come out loud enough for him to hear, for he continued talking.

"Aw, thank the Good Lord. I've got us on solid ground. Dang near wet myself a few times there. Thought that ledge was gonna crumble out from under my feet for certain. Your weight and mine together caused the ledge to break off in several places, but we made it. I've got to lay you down now so I can see how badly you're hurt. Can't tell if anything is busted while holding you in my arms."

Pain shot through her as her flesh touched the hard ground. With great relief, she felt the darkness taking over again.

~~~~

"What the dickens happened?" Homer managed to wheeze out as he came upon George kneeling over the roughed-up body of a girl. Relief flooded him as he realized there were no Kormans and no law to be seen. George wasn't in that sort of danger, but something had gone bad wrong for somebody.

"It looks to me like a vehicle tried to turn around and didn't make it," George answered.

"I already gathered that much from the tracks left on the ground. What happened to the girl? Where did she come from? Can you tell if she's hurt bad?"

"I think she must have jumped from the vehicle as it went over the cliff. I found her crumpled up on a ledge about fifty feet down from the logging road."

"How did you get her up here?"

"Wasn't easy. I had to climb down and go around those big rocks and then walk on that little ledge down there."

"Dang!" Homer said as he looked where George pointed.

"Dang is right. My knees haven't stopped trembling yet."

"Fifty feet down had to be a hard drop," Homer said, as his stomach muscles clenched. A big cat would have had trouble walking on that ledge much less George carrying the girl. It was pure luck they both weren't down there in the gorge dead. If that had happened, Mazy would have never forgiven him for not looking out for her baby boy – not that she'd ever forgiven him regardless. But then, a body needed someone to blame when things went wrong.

"It would have been a rightful shame if you died while wearin' your sister's little skirt," Homer said as he looked down the cliff at the burning vehicle on the bank of the river that ran through the gorge down below.

George ignored that remark.

"One thing's for certain, if there was anybody left in that vehicle, it's done too late for 'em," Homer said. "Looky down yonder. Your brothers have arrived, and they are getting out of the truck to check things out." Homer whistled through his teeth and waved his arms above his head to signal he had things under control on top of the mountain.

One of the brothers gave the same signal as the other dipped water from the river in a rusty bucket and tossed it on the burning Jeep.

"Must be Bob with that bucket. He'll be bound and determined to put the fire out. That boy never learns. He might as well stand back and watch 'er burn. If somebody is in there, it's done too late for 'em. If the drop didn't kill 'em, the fire did." He turned away from the cliff. "Is she hurt bad?" he asked again. "Let me have a look at her."

George moved back from hovering over her and said, "From what I can tell, there's nothing broken. Don't know about internal injuries. She's got a lot of scrapes and cuts, but they're not bleeding hardly any."

"She was knocked unconscious," Homer said with concern. "That's not a good sign."

"Yeah, but she talked to me before I laid her down on the ground. Do you suppose she just fainted?"

"Yeah, that's probably what happened. Seeing you in that skirt would do it to a woman. What did she say?"

"She told me to put her down."

"Yeah, she got a good look at you all right. Was that all she said?"

"Her mouth moved some, but that's all she said. What do you think? Is she going to be okay?"

"She's all right, from what I can tell, but she's got a goose-egg of a knot on her head," Homer said as he moved his hand from her head and lifted her eyelids. "Her pupils are both even and respond to light, which is good. I just don't like the fact that she blacked out. Reckon your maw can tell more about her condition than we can."

"Do you think it'll be okay for us to carry her home, or do I need to run and fetch Maw?"

"Take a lot longer to get your maw up here than it will to carry the girl down the mountain. I reckon the girl will be all right if you carry her right gentle like," he said, trying not to convey the concern he was feeling for the girl. No need to worry the boy unnecessarily, or to bring Mazy up here to see where her boy had walked on the ledge to save the girl. Mazy would plain go berserk. "Ask me, it was seein' you in nothing but that skirt what blacked her out. When I first got an eye full of you, I come close to doing the same thing and there ain't nothing wrong with me," Homer added.

"That's a matter of opinion," George couldn't resist saying.

"Yeah, it's my opinion, and mine is the only one that counts for anything."

Homer really did hate the kilt, but George was good at ignoring his uncle, considering how much practice he gotten through the years. Homer always treated George like he was the only chick and Homer was the mother hen. Homer knew George both resented and appreciated the way he always tried to look out for him.

What Homer hated most of all was losing the strength he used to have when he was a younger man. Both he and George remembered the time when Homer could lift a hundred-pound sack of corn with his teeth. Folks claimed Homer Barlow was the strongest man in the mountains. Now, Homer felt himself to be less than a man, and that kind of hurt went bone deep, but Homer tried not to show his disappointment in himself.

"You might be strong enough to cradle a little thing like her in your arms if you stop and rest right often. At least it'll all be downhill going. As for me, I'm plum whupped by rushing all the way up this mountain and most likely won't be able to spell you none. Old age is wicked, boy. Mighty wicked on a man."

Homer watched as George bent down and eased his arms under the young woman. He lifted her up with a grunt and headed down the logging road followed by Homer. They hadn't gone far when Homer looked over at George trying not to struggle under the girl's weight. Dead weight was a lot harder to carry than live weight. It hadn't taken long for George to show the strain of carrying her, while her body gravitated downward. Homer longed to take the girl from the boy's arms but all he might be able to do was take the boy's mind off her weight for a few moments.

"Do you reckon she's really a brunette or do you suppose she's a natural blonde?"

"What are you talking about?" George wheezed out.

"Just wondered if she's the one who drove the jeep up that loggin' road."

"What's that got to do with her hair color?"

"Hair color tells a lot about a person, you know. There was this brunette who went to the doctor complaining that every place on her body ached.

"Show me the places that hurts you', the doctor told her.

She touched her head and hollered. She touched her knee and hollered. Same thing happened when she touched her stomach and chest.

"See, I hurt all over,' she told the doctor. "There's not a place on me that doesn't hurt when I touch it."

"Humph, I see all right,' said the doctor. 'You dye your hair, don't you?'

"Amazed at the doctor's insight, she said, Why yes, I'm a natural blonde."

"That's what I thought,' he told her.

"The woman gave him a puzzled look. What does my hair color have to do with my pain? asked the woman.

"You've got a broken finger, the doctor told her."

George shook his head and grinned at his uncle, but his grin was short-lived. Carrying the girl was something he wasn't used to doing. It was harder than off-bearing at the sawmill. Her unbalanced weight was straining his arms and back muscles something awful. He had to set down with her for a while. He backed up to a rock and eased himself down with the girl still in his lap. He couldn't get much relief. He had to hold onto her, so she didn't fall off his lap.

George tried to take his mind off the injured girl as he watched Homer shuffle his feet on the rocky logging road as though he didn't know what to do next. Like usual, when Homer found himself in a fix, he started talking faster. Finding the injured girl was definitely troublesome for all three of them.

"Lord, lord," Homer said as he frowned. "She's a right pretty little thing. Makes me wish I was back your age and had her in my lap, but Father Time won't allow a man to go back and relive his youth. I can tell you that folks would do things a lot different if it were possible. About all an old man has left to him are his memories, which will eventually leave him, too. I reckon there's a reason for old age. It's to make a man not mind dying."

George watched a sadness come to Homer's face as he stood there thinking and talking. Homer had made a lot of mistakes in his past that still haunted him. Sometimes he was overly pushy in trying to keep George from making similar mistakes, but as his uncle often said, a boy needed to make mistakes if he was going to learn from them. Mistakes were the best teacher a body could have.

"Did I ever tell you about the time old man Jenson sold his cattle and had a little cash money in his pocket. He wanted to do something special for his wife, so he went into one of them fancy lingerie stores in town to buy his wife one of them brassieres? Claimed he'd always wanted to see a real, live woman wearin' one of them things he'd seen in the Sears and Roebuck catalogue. He went into the store having no idea they came in different sizes, but the sales lady was doing her best to help him out.

"You don't know what size your wife's breasts are?" the sales lady asked.

"Nope, old man Jenson told her as his face turned as red as a tom turkey's waddle".

"Are they the size of a grapefruit,' the sales lady asked him."

"Smaller."

"The size of oranges?"

"'Smaller.'"

"Eggs?' She finally suggested."

"Yeah, that's it. Fried eggs."

George cringed.

"Now, every time I see old lady Jenson I can't help thinking of fried eggs. Has just about turned me against eating fried eggs, and that's a fact."

Grapefruits, George thought as he glanced down and couldn't help feeling ashamed of himself for daring to look at the injured girl in such a way. He hoped Homer hadn't noticed.

"Let's just hope she stays knocked out until you get her to Mazy. Otherwise, she'll never be able to get the horrible image outta her mind if she comes around looking at your naked chest," Homer told him. "It's time you started growin' you some hair on there, boy. Hain't never seen a Barlow man what didn't have a hairy chest."

George paid no attention to his uncle. He expected to continue listening to such nonsense for many years to come. Actually, his uncle's ramblings kind of helped ease the tension he was feeling. He'd never been sure what spouting all that nonsense eased in his uncle, but he supposed it was a help to him in some sort of way, otherwise he'd shut up.

George gathered his legs beneath him and forced himself to stand up with the girl still in his arms. It was like doing squats with weight. If it hadn't been for the seriousness of the situation, he would have enjoyed having the girl in his arms. Lifting the young woman sure beat the heck out of standing up holding one-hundred-pound weights across his shoulders. Thing was, holding weight in front of him instead of across his shoulders tended to strain his back muscles in an unaccustomed sort of way.

When George stood and got the girl's weight balanced and was walking again, Homer continued his story.

"They say Mrs. Jenson was as mad as an ole wet settin' hen when old man Jenson gave her the brassiere. She was in such a fury that a woman who happened to be visiting from down off the mountain asked if she was considering divorcing him.

"No, I'm not,' she told the nosy woman firmly. 'We don't believe in divorce here in these mountains, but I am considering killing him."

~~~~~

Mazy was in the kitchen building up the fire in the kitchen cook stove to get it hot enough to cook supper. It took a mighty lot of cooking to feed her men. If Harm was alive, he'd be so proud of his boys he'd have popped his shirt buttons off. Rob and Bob were so darned handsome it almost hurt her eyes to look at them. They were the spitting image of Harm when he was their age. Looking at them made losing Harm even more painful.

Oh, how she had loved that man of hers – and still did.

Harm had been dead ten years this past winter, but it seemed like yesterday. Sometimes during the night, she still reached out her hand hoping to feel him beside her.

Occasionally, another woman would ask her why she didn't marry again. The answer to that question was easy. She could never love another husband the way she still loved Harmon Barlow. Someday when her trial here on earth was over, she knew she'd be able to go to him, and he'd be waiting for her with open arms.

Until then, she had their three daughters and their three sons who were Harm made over. To be honest, George only looked like Harm. He took his personality after Homer Barlow, Harm's older brother. She hated that. Not that Homer wasn't a fine man and all, for he was. She simply couldn't stand the mouth on him. If he had worked half as much as he talked, he would have been a very wealthy man by now – not that Homer wasn't a hard worker, which he was. He was simply a bigger talker than a doer. She often wondered if the man talked in his sleep, but she had never been interested enough to find out by asking Betsy before she died. She never figured out why Homer married Betsy in the first place. She's always been a sickly, skin over bone, sort of woman, but Homer was devoted to her. The fact that they never had children of their own beared down hard on Homer. She supposed that was why Homer devoted so much time to Harm's boys.

Harm and Homer were sawmill men. They bought forestland, timbered it, and made a fine living until they loaded the two-ton lumber truck high with huge, heavy oak logs. When they were cinching the chains tight, a standard broke and the logs tumbled. Harm was killed and Homer crippled.

Rob and Bob were now sawmill men, and she worried herself gray-headed about those two boys. Sawmilling had too many quick and easy ways to get a man killed. George was now off-bearing at the sawmill on weekends, and she was a nervous wreck, but George loved it. Lifting the heavy green lumber not only gave him a little money, it added to those muscles he was so proud of displaying. Leave it up to the young to put their priority on foolish things. Youth and good sense didn't go together, but then the youngsters of today were determined to learn the hard way. In her opinion, God had given youth a whole bunch of guardian angels to keep them safe. Otherwise, the human population would decrease rapidly.

Like Homer, George loved to play and joke around. Had George not been the class valedictorian, she might have worried about his educational intelligence. Had not every ounce of him oozed manliness, she might have worried about his masculinity. It wasn't good for a boy to grow up without his father's influence and guidance. Although he was unusually sensitive, there was really nothing feminine about George. Yet many of the things he came up with stumped her and infuriated his brothers. If only Homer didn't think George was a never-ending source of entertainment and encouraged his foolishness, George might be more serious minded.

Mazy suspected George was the way he was because his brothers weren't. Her youngest strived to be one of a kind – an individual. He didn't want to be like his older twin brothers. "Two of a kind is enough," he'd say when she asked him why he couldn't be more like his brothers. "I plan on becoming the cream of your crop," he'd say and then laugh at her irritation.

While she was cooking supper, she stepped out onto the kitchen porch to get another armload of stove wood. Her breath caught in her throat. She couldn't believe she was seeing what she thought she saw. In the gloaming light of the evening, it appeared George and Homer were hoofing it toward the house in a near run – and George looked naked – except for the girl he carried.

Mazy had seen a lot in her time but such a sight as she thought she was seeing, she never expected. The girl's legs and arms were flopping, as were her head and long brown hair. She was out cold and appeared to have been roughed up considerable. The first thing to hit her mind was that the girl had been caught out in the woods by that bunch of no-account Korman boys. There wasn't a decent one in the bunch. George was heaving for breath and his hair was wet with sweat. He had evidently carried her a long way even though the girl was slender and didn't look to be much heavy.

Homer picked up speed and got in front. "Mazy, gal, toss an old quilt over the extra bed. George needs a place to lay her down. He's worked up a powerful sweat, and he's just a minute short of droppin' her."

Mazy didn't hesitate. She had the old quilt on the bed by the time George carried the girl into the bedroom. He eased her down with the greatest of care. "Thank goodness. I was about to give out," he said as he sucked in a great big breath of air, stretched his back muscles, and shook his arms to get the blood flowing again.

"What in the name of tarnation is going on?" Mazy demanded as she looked from the girl to George with her eyes as large as fifty-cent pieces. Seeing her youngest son carrying a passed-out, strange girl was something she'd never expected to see during her lifetime.

Homer Barlow gave her the saddest of looks. "See what happens when you allow your baby boy to put on his sister's little skirt."

Mazy had no idea what he was talking about, but she ignored him just the same. "George?" She questioned in a shaky voice as she looked the kilt up and down. She believed in getting an answer to her question before she asked another question.

"Found her on top of Nowhere. The vehicle she was in tumbled down the cliff. She must have jumped out at the last moment and hit her head on the rocks."

"What was she doing way up there?"

"Have no idea," Homer answered

"How in blazes did a vehicle get up there anyway?"

"Had to be driving a narrow wheelbase vehicle," George told her.

"Why are you wearing such as that around the house?"

"Beats me," George told her. "Can you tell if she's hurt bad? She spoke to me before she passed out, but that's been a good while ago."

George's question snapped her into action. "Homer, go dip me up a pan of hot water. Bring soap and a washrag. George, for goodness sakes, take that thing off and put some decent clothes on. Wearing *that thing* is plain silliness. Highland games my foot. I hope Homer burns *that thing*. It's disgraceful."

George left the room to put some clothes on and to hide *that thing*. He knew Homer would burn his newly acquired kilt if he got the chance. So might his mother.

Chapter 4

~~~~

Bob stood in the edge of the river carrying buckets of water and tossing it on the fire until Rob grabbed hold of the bucket and flung it as far as he could.

"All you're doing is scalding yourself from the steam. Stop throwing water on the flames and let 'er burn out. We've got no choice in the matter. That fire can't be put out with an old rusty bucket," Rob told his brother. "Wouldn't change a thing if it could be put out."

"Somebody might be in there," Bob looked where the bucket was bobbing up and down in the river and considered chasing after it as it floated away. He did hate to lose a pretty good bucket even if it was old and rusty.

"Could be, but a little water won't make any difference. If there's somebody in there, they're already as dead as they'll ever get."

Bob knew his brother was right, but he was the kind of man to fight what he didn't like, and he certainly didn't like to see somebody dead or a little Jeep burn if he could stop it.

"How did that thing get all the way on top of the mountain?" Rob questioned as he looked up the high cliff of almost solid rock. "Couldn't have picked a worse place to go off," he pushed his hat back on his head so he could get a better look at the top of the mountain. "Do you suppose that bunch of Kormans has anything to do with this?"

"Saw some of them heading out before daylight this morning. I'd say they're still gone," Bob said as his gaze followed his brother's up the mountain.

"Being gone doesn't mean they have nothing to do with this," Rob nodded toward the Jeep. "Know anybody around here who owns a little Willys Jeep? Don't see them much anymore."

"Nope," Bob said. "Whoever owned it made a bad mistake. For one thing, those little fellows turn over easy, and for another, if it had a wider wheelbase, it wouldn't have made it up the old logging road." He looked up the rock cliff with searching eyes. "Don't see a body hanging on a ledge anywhere, do you?"

"Doubt the driver was that lucky. How do you know someone drove it up the logging road?"

"How else would it have gotten all the way up there? It sure didn't fly."

"Right," Rob said. "Do you think Homer found something up on top?"

"Could have. He appeared right excited by the way he was waving his arms. Plus, he disappeared mighty quick instead of standing there watching the Jeep burn like he'd normally do. Think we should head home or stay with the Jeep?" Bob asked. "We don't want fire to get out and burn up all creation."

"It's not likely fire will get out considering what side of the river the Jeep landed on. There's not much vegetation over there. Too bad it didn't roll another time and land in the water. Might have saved the tires," Rob said in his common-sense way.

"Fire jumps really easy, and it's summer. Dry season and fires don't go well together," Bob made a point of saying.

"The fire is burning down, but it'll take a few hours before it cools off enough for us to poke around in the ashes. If somebody's in there, they won't mind waiting a while."

Bob gave the burning Jeep a bewildered look. He didn't agree with that, nor did he like leaving something unfinished and this was certainly unfinished. At the very least, he wanted to know if somebody was still inside that thing. It didn't seem right to walk away if there was. A person shouldn't have to die alone.

Bob waded out of the river and got as close to the Jeep as the heat would allow and did his best to see if a body was trapped inside the burning hunk of twisted metal. The seats and insides had already burned but the tires were still bubbling and popping – and would be for a while. There wasn't a thing he could do. With a feeling of helplessness Bob crossed back to his brother.

"Can't tell a thing," Bob said.

"Don't smell burning flesh. Just the stink of your singed hair."

"Wouldn't. The smell of burning rubber overpowers everything else."

"Odd isn't it, how you can hardly recognize what the Jeep is after it tumbled down that mountain and burned. Looks like a big crunched-up tin can. Let's go," Rob told him. "Nothing we can do here for a while. Homer might know something about this. Besides, Mom could have heard the explosion and thought it was us. You know how she worries."

Bob still didn't want to leave the scene of an accident, but Rob was right. There was nothing they could do here until the fire burned out and things cooled off. They had best go home and find out what was happening on that end.

Most likely Homer knew more answers than they did. Homer tried to keep his thumb on the pulse of everything that happened on and around Nowhere Mountain. And that included them.

Chapter 5

~~~~

After George and Homer filled Mazy in on what had happened, she ran them out of the bedroom so she could wash and check the girl for injuries and broken bones. If the girl had been properly dressed, she wouldn't have gotten as many cuts and scrapes from rocks. She never liked seeing girls wearing those little shorts and tank tops that exposed their upper chests while barely covering their navels.

Of course, her daughters claimed she was always too strict and old fashioned. To her way of seeing things, modesty wasn't old fashioned, and being too strict was far better than being too lenient. Being a strict mother was wise and appropriate. A girl didn't have to show everything she had for a boy to know she had it.

One thing was for certain, this girl wasn't from around here. Her fancy tennis shoes and clothes looked too expensive, as did the gold necklace she had around her neck with the name Lena engraved on it. Mazy slipped the necklace off and placed it under some clothing in the dresser for safe keeping.

The girl's hair had obviously been styled, and the girl herself had that well-cared for expensive look about her. It was odd how a rich girl could look so much different from a country girl even when she was laying on a ragged quilt on an old bed passed out cold. This girl even smelled like money with soft, well-cared for body and hands.

The difference between city girls and country girls was not all that was bothering her. The girl was unconscious and had

been out for a while. It had to take George a good hour to walk
down the logging road even with his long-legged stride. He
said he'd had to stop and rest about every half-mile. That meant
the girl had been unconscious for at least an hour or more. Not
a good sign considering the knot she had on her head.

She heard the twins' big truck grinding up the road at a
right fast speed. Rob usually drove the truck and never pushed
it. Rob was the cautious one. He thought ahead and never acted
on impulse. For him to be going fast meant he already knew
something about the girl. She grabbed another quilt and
covered the girl to her chin. She didn't want her boys seeing
that much flesh in or out of bed, and she knew both Rob and
Bob would have to take a look at the girl or die trying. She
would need to find one of her cotton gowns to put on the girl,
but she only owned the one good gown plus a ragged one, both
of which would swallow the girl. The ragged one wasn't fit to
put on the girl, and she didn't want to give up her good one.
She wondered if either of her daughters had left clothes behind
that might fit this skinny little thing. She'd have to look in her
rag bags.

Mazy rushed out of the bedroom to see if she could find
one of her daughter's old cotton gowns. She wanted to get it
on the girl before she came around. She found an old gown
belonging to Willa, her youngest. Willa had always hated that
gown. Claimed it made her feel like a drab, old granny woman.
Exactly how that pretty young thing in the bedroom needed to
look. She didn't want to take any chances that her boys would
be tempted in any way. Mazy went back into the bedroom and
turned the wooden button that served as a door lock. When
Harm built this house, he saw no reason for fancy door locks
when wooden buttons would do the job.

"My goodness," Mazy gasped as she removed the girl's
tank top and shorts. Never in her entire life had she seen such
fancy underwear - not even in the Montgomery Ward catalogue
she used to get in the mail. Mercy, she could see right through
the little scraps of lace, and what she saw turned her face red

even when no one was around. It was obvious this girl hadn't received a proper upbringing, or she would not have been wearing clothes that were so revealing of her private parts. Some things were meant to be concealed, not flaunted.

She would have given her girls a good whipping if she ever caught one of them wearing such as that. Mazy didn't know if she should take them off or leave them on the girl. Since she didn't have anything else for the girl to wear, she decided little bits of lace adding additional covering was better than nothing at all. She'd have to cut and sew the girl flour-sack underclothes if she didn't wake up soon. The way this girl was put together was assurance that her boys would get their eyes full even with the lace underwear covered by a cotton gown. What was the world coming to when girls dressed such as this? What had happened to modesty in the younger generation. It was a flaunting shame and disgrace.

Once Mazy had the girl dressed, she wasted no time hiding the shorts and top between the mattress and box springs. After she had them hid, she thought maybe she should have left them on the girl and put the gown on over the top of them. But no, once the girl came around, she'd take off the gown and wear the shorts and top where her boys could see her. Better she hid those disgraceful clothes right off.

~~~~

Rob and Bob got out of the truck in their slow purposeful strides. Homer and George were sitting on the front porch in twin-bottom chairs, leaning against the wall. George appeared jumpy, but Homer was calmly whittling on a stick of wood with his Hawksbill Barlow knife.

"He don't seem overly excited," Bob said.

"Nope."

"Guess that means the driver of the Jeep burned up."

"Could be."

"George keeps glancing toward the door though," Bob added.

"Yeah."

"Why do you think that is?"

"Maw's patching up the driver of the Jeep," Rob told his brother. "George wants to know how it's going."

"I hope that's it. I'd hate for the man to have burned. Think Homer and George carried him all the way down the mountain? Even between the two of them that would be tough toting especially if the man was of any size."

"We could ask," Rob suggested.

Bob got a couple of steps in front of Rob. He had always been the one with the most unanswered questions. Rob was the one who had a knack for seemingly knowing answers in their simplest form.

"Took you long enough to get home," Homer told them as they stepped up onto the porch. A frown of concern came to his face. "Anybody burn up in the explosion?"

"Don't know," Bob told him. "The fire was too hot for us to get near enough to tell. What do you know about this?"

"Precious little, and you?"

"Same," Rob answered. "Find anybody?"

"George did."

The look that came to George's face both puzzled and intrigued the twins.

"Finders keepers," George was quick to tell them. "I've already claimed the prize. You two have to stand back and eat your hearts out."

Homer had to grin. "Yeah, baby boy there has got first dibs in on you two this time."

"What are you talking about?" Bob wanted to know.

"Sure is a pretty little thing," George said. "I found her and I'm hoping Mom will let me keep her, being I've always wanted one just like her."

"He aims to keep her as a pet," Homer added. "Not sure Mazy's gonna let him do it, mind you."

"You found a dog?" Bob questioned.

"Nope? She shore hain't no dog," Homer grinned from ear to ear. "Far from it."

"She?" Rob questioned.

"Yeah, your baby brother found him a girl on top of that mountain and toted her all the way home. I'm betting your maw won't allow him to keep her, but he's shore enough got high hopes."

"Jeep driver?" Rob asked, ignoring Homer's foolishness.

Homer became serious. "We think so. George found her about fifty feet down on a little ledge. She'd evidently jumped from the vehicle as it went over. The way I figure it, she had to be on the driver's side. If she'd been a passenger, the vehicle would have rolled on top of her when she jumped."

"Makes sense. Was she hurt?"

"Some. Don't know how bad. Mazy's lookin' after her," Homer answered Rob. "George said the girl spoke to him right before she passed out cold. Hadn't come back around by the time we got here with her."

"Who is she?" Bob asked.

"Never seen her before," Homer told them. "Fancy lookin' little thing. Smells like money if my nose and my instincts are still working right. Wasn't dressed like someone from around here, kind of slender-bodied with a mighty nice tan going for her. If I was to take a wild guess, I'd say she got herself lost. You know how easy it is to miss the road leading over the mountain into Tennessee."

Rob leaned against the porch rail while Bob sat on it.

"How old?" Rob asked.

"Oh, eighteen to twenty-five," Homer said. "It's kinda hard to tell when a woman has been able to keep herself up real nice like."

"She looks more like eighteen," George was quick to tell them.

Homer grinned. "He hopes she's his age."

"Let's go take a look at her," Bob said.

"If I was you two, I'd wait until your maw says you can go in. She's washing the skinned places on the girl and seeing if she's been hurt bad."

Rob looked Homer in the eyes for a moment. "Accident?" Rob asked in his direct, no nonsense manner.

"On her part, I'd say so. Like I just said, my guess is she took a wrong turn somewhere."

"The Jeep was an older model Willys that's hard to come by. One of the small ones like used to be made. Narrow wheelbase. What did you read on the ground up there on the ridge?" Rob asked, knowing Homer would have read the Jeep tracks along with all other signs. Reading the signs came natural for a mountain man like Homer.

"Korman boys had been up there again. Set those rocks where anything with weight would tumble down the mountain."

"We'll mosey up that way come morning," Rob said. "Reckon there's no big hurry."

"Morning would be best." Homer expected Bob to rush into the house to investigate the girl, but it was Rob who surprised him. After a few minutes of silence, a troubled look came to Rob's face. He headed for the door and went inside letting the screen slam so his mother would know he was coming. Mazy recognized his footsteps and opened the bedroom door as he reached for the doorknob.

"Mom?" he questioned.

"Still out cold."

"Know her?"

Rob went the rest of the way into the bedroom followed by Bob. He looked down at the girl's face and shook his head. "Nope, she's a stranger."

"My gracious," Bob was quick to say. "She's a baby. Can't be a day over eighteen."

"Maybe, maybe not," Mazy said. "I'm inclined to think she's older than she looks. One thing's for certain, she's a young thing who ought to be with her mother instead of driving around all by herself. What business does a single girl have driving up that old logging road all alone?" A scared look came to Mazy's face. "She was alone, wasn't she?"

"From what we can tell."

"How do you know she's single?" Bob asked.

"She's not wearin' a wedding band. What do you boys know about this?"

"An old timey Willys Jeep rolled down the rock cliff from the top of Nowhere Mountain," Bob told her. "My guess is that it belonged to her."

"Burned to a crisp," Rob added.

Mazy nodded. "Anybody in it?"

Rob shook his head. "I don't think so."

"We'll know more when the Jeep's had time to cool down. It's still burning," Bob told her.

"What happen to your eyebrows and mustache?" she asked when she looked Bob in the face.

"Got a little too close the burning Jeep and they singed a little." Bob lifted his hand but didn't touch his tender skin.

"Son, will you ever learn patience? You gotta remember not to rush in where there's danger," Mazy told him for at least the hundredth time.

"I know," Bob agreed, but he was the rushing kind.

"What about her?" Rob asked. "Shouldn't we be driving her to a hospital somewhere?"

"She doesn't appear to be hurt much. Just a bump on her head along with a few scrapes and scratches." Mazy had been thinking about taking the girl to the hospital and then decided it might be best not to do such a thing. Something was warning her this girl would mean trouble for everyone if a hornet's nest was stirred up because of her wrecking. Folks around these parts minded their own business. They almost never went to hospitals or reported anything to the law. Live and let live was always the best policy, and one Mazy tried to go by.

"I don't know what to do," she admitted. "I need to talk to Homer."

Bob frowned and Rob pushed his hat back on his head the way he did when he was puzzled.

"Why would you need to talk to Homer?" Rob asked. Talking to Homer was something she seldom did, taking advice from Homer was foreign to her.

"Several reasons."

"Such as?" Rob persisted.

"First off, we don't need the law comin' in here and stirin' up trouble for folks."

"Are you talking about the Korman boys?" Bob asked.

"Partly."

"And the other part?" Rob eyed his mother as he waited for her answer.

"It's just that I'd rather wait until the girl wakes up so she can tell us what she's doing here. A body never knows why some stranger shows up. When they do, it's for a reason."

"It's like Uncle Homer said. She took a wrong turn and got lost." That explanation seemed the most reasonable to Rob, but his mother was the over-cautious kind. Bob took back after her in that way.

"What would a fancy girl such as her be doing in a place like this? Furthermore, if she was lost, wouldn't she have turned around when she reached the logging road instead of being determined to keep on going until she reached the top of the mountain? I want to know some of the answers before we make any kind of rash decision," Mazy told them. "That's why I think we should wait until she comes around before we grab her up and rush to the hospital. All she's got is a knot on her head and a few scrapes and bruises. You boys have had the same things time and again," she reasoned.

Bob nodded. Those Korman boys would need a good day or more to get that mountain cleaned up before the law came to investigate an accident. If worse came to worse, they could claim they didn't know about the accident or the girl for a few hours longer.

Another thing that bothered Mazy was the way the girl was so sparsely dressed. If the girl couldn't tell what had happened to her, the law might somehow blame her boys for the girl's roughed up condition. After all, that was the first thing she thought about when she saw the girl, except she blamed it on the Korman boys. That bunch had always been quare in the head.

Sometimes the law in these parts was known to seek out a scape-goat to make themselves look good, and she didn't want her family involved.

She'd heard stories about the law that made her blood run cold and didn't want to take a chance on her boys getting accused of something they knew nothing about. A mother had a responsibility to make sure her children were safe. Just like the girl's mother should have done for her daughter – and hadn't.

In her mind, she could already hear Herbert Waddell, the sheriff, claiming the girl got lost and her boys took advantage of the situation, shoved the Jeep down the cliff and made up a story. Waddell hated the Barlows even more than he hated the Korman clan. The Barlows were hard working honest people who were always striving to better themselves. Waddell couldn't take that. He preferred everyone on Nowhere Mountain to fall in the no-account, trash heap. The one good thing about Waddell was that he was the biggest coward who ever drew breath. He had no objections to staying away from Nowhere Mountain but bringing in problems that involved an outsider could change things.

There was that family of Hordlys who lived up the ridge from the Kormans. They had two boys, the youngest of which ran with the Korman's teenage boys. There was no telling what kind of trouble they got into. The girl could have been trying to find where the Hordlys lived. She was too fancy and well cared for to be trying to find one of the Kormans, but it was hard to tell what kids did nowadays. Most likely she was heading up the mountain to purchase what those Kormans grew.

Yes, it was best to wait until the girl woke up and talked before they did anything.

George came in the bedroom followed by Homer, over-filling the little bedroom.

"I do declare," Homer said. "She sure did clean up right nice. All soft and helpless looking laying there in that bed. Even at my age, I'm longin' to pick her up in my mouth and carry her home like I'm a mother cat and she's a kitten."

Mazy slapped him on the arm with real aggravation. How dare he say something that might put ideas in her boys' minds? "If you can't watch that mouth of yourn, you'd best leave. I'll not have talk such as that in my house."

Homer was not the least bit intimidated by Mazy. "I'll keep it shut, depending on what you've cooked for supper."

"Oh, my goodness. I plum forgot about supper." She turned as though she was going to rush to the kitchen and then turned back. She didn't want to leave the girl with all the men in the room. She had obviously become flustered by the shock of all that was happenings to have forgotten about supper.

"Want me to fix supper for you, seein' how you're busy and all?" Homer asked.

"You can't cook."

"How do you think I've been keeping myself alive since my Betsy died? Besides, we both know these boys will eat anything that don't eat them first."

"You survive by eatin' here," she informed him. "And my boys are used to eatin' food that's well prepared. You and everybody else know what a fine cook I am."

He had no argument with all that. "In that case, I don't reckon it would hurt for us to all clear outta here and let the girl rest a spell. She'll come around after a while," Homer said, taking pity on Mazy's momentary confusion.

He'd known Mazy since the day she was born and understood her completely. As for the girl, he was concerned about the fact she was still unconscious, but there was little he could do about it other than give her time.

Homer and the twins left the bedroom for the porch. "Reckon we got time to mosey up to the top of Nowhere before Mazy has supper cooked? If we don't go now, it'll be too dark to see much after we eat."

"No way to get up there in a hurry," Rob pointed out. As he'd thought earlier, morning might not be soon enough. A lot of things could be changed overnight, but those Kormans were on the lazy side.

"Mom will skin our hides if we're late for supper," Bob added.

"Sure would like to get a look at things while they're still fresh. What did you see, Homer?" Rob asked his uncle.

"Lots of rag weeds growing as camouflage. Looked to me like the Kormans had already harvested their main crop. Saw a few inch-high plants growin', but nothing major."

"Did her Jeep go off naturally?" Rob asked just to make sure.

"Nope. Looked to me as though they'd placed the rocks intentionally," Homer repeated what he'd earlier said. "I'm thinking they set a trap for whoever might come investigating."

"They planned on killing somebody," Bob said as anger built. "They tried to make it look like we were to blame since the trap was set across the boundary on our land."

"Appears that way to me," Homer told them. "But I'd like for both of you to take a look and verify my way of thinking. Don't see why they'd set a trap for the girl. It must have been for the law, or one of us."

"Or some innocent person who happened to drive up that road in a four-wheeler or a narrow wheelbase Jeep like the girl did."

"Is it time to do something about that bunch of Kormans?" Rob asked.

"Could be, but I'm not exactly sure what," Homer said. "Reckon I'll have to do some powerful thinking on it for a while. They've gotten way too cock-sure of themselves lately. That's because there're so many young bucks in the bunch. The girls, well, I feel right sorry for them. They lead a pitiful life, if the truth be told. Markum, the old man of the bunch, wouldn't cause nearly as many problems if he didn't have his three boys to do his bidding. Not to mention there is also their Rainey cousins who are just as bad if not worse."

Chapter 6

~~~~

Homer got up early, ate a chunk of cornbread with butter and goat's milk, and then went outside to milk the goat he had named Nanny. The sawmilling accident had not only damaged his legs; it had damaged his stomach until his food had trouble digesting properly. Goat's milk was about the only thing that gave him some relief from the ever-present indigestion. The milk had a creamy texture to it that coated his stomach and gave him a little ease.

He'd tried to get Mazy to let Nanny graze with her cow and milk Nanny for him, but Mazy had flat-out refused. She claimed goats were dirty animals. He tried to explain how particular and prissy his little Nanny really was, but it did no good. Mazy had preconceived notions about goats and nothing or no one on God's green earth would ever change that woman's mind about anything once she'd set it.

The fact that the Kormans had goats was another factor in Mazy hating the animals. In Mazy's mind nothing good ever came from a Korman, and he was inclined to agree. You simply couldn't get good out when nothing good was ever put in.

Once a year, in order to keep his Nanny producing milk, Homer took her across the hill to where the Kormans' goat herd ranged and found a Billy. After Nanny weaned her babies, he added them to the Kormans' herd. They never complained about the arrangement, and he didn't either.

Homer had gone to the stock sale to purchase Nanny. She was an American Alpine, while the Korman herd was a mixture of everything. He figured the yearly goat he added to the herd was an improvement. Over the years he had seen a couple of grown goats resembling Nanny, but mostly he figured his goats went to their table.

After he had finished with his morning's work, he headed toward the top of Nowhere Mountain. His legs ached and creaked, but he paid them as little mind as possible. A man wasn't much of a man if he gave in to what bothered him. It always took him several hours to un-stiffen from a night of rest. At least, it was a fine morning to be out and about. When winter cold set in, he'd be popping aspirins like they were sugar-candy.

Rob and Bob were sitting on a big rock waiting on his arrival. They stood when they saw him.

"Things up here look a little different from yesterday," Homer told them. "Reckon the Kormans are night workers." It always amazed Homer how those Kormans would work like the dickens in doing something dishonest, but they wouldn't work a lick at an honest day's work that would pay them more.

"What's changed?" Rob asked.

"No little pot plants growing in the weeds. Not even a sprig of greenery on the ground, and those deliberately laid rocks that were still here yesterday have all been pushed down the mountain."

"Could they have fallen down on their own accord?" Bob asked.

"Nope. The Jeep took the loose rocks down. The remaining rocks and limbs used to set the trap have been deliberately pushed down the mountain during the night."

Homer stretched his stiff muscles and looked toward the woods where the laurel hells grew thick. He didn't figure they'd set the trap for one of them. Barlows could spot a trap in a second.

"Come on out of there, boys. I know you're still in there. We need to do us some talking just in case the sheriff shows up. You made a bad mistake when you set that trap, especially when you put it on Barlow land."

There wasn't a sound or a movement from the woods, but the silence didn't fool Homer. He'd been raised with that bunch of Kormans and knew their ways.

"Come out right now or we'll leave it to you. We're trying to help you out for your own good. It was a girl who got lost and drove her Jeep up here instead of the law. You're lucky she didn't die. If she had, the law would be all over this mountain for certain. As it is, we're trying to see that don't happen. There's not a one of us who wants Herbert Waddell messing around on this mountain, or anybody else for that matter."

The Barlows waited in silence, but there wasn't a sound.

"Fine," Homer hollered as if he was fed-up with the whole thing. "Hide in the laurel hells and have it your way. Come on boys. Let's leave 'em hiding in there. Don't much care what happens to them. They'd best stay off Barlow land from now on."

Once Homer had hollered, he, along with Rob and Bob, headed off the mountain.

"Now what?" Bob asked once they were out of the Kormans' hearing.

"Looks like we'll have to build a fence on our property line to keep the Kormans off. That girl wrecked on our land, and we can't prove it was the Kormans instead of us who set the trap."

Homer had lived here all his life and he hated to think things had come to the point where fences had to be built to keep neighbors off. Times had changed. Instead of respecting what other people owned, jealousy ran on a rampage. If the Kormans didn't own something they tried to forcefully take it. If that didn't work for them, then they tried to destroy it.

"Doesn't it make us look guilty by not reporting the accident?" Bob asked.

"Depends," Homer said. "Those Kormans don't know it, but they did us a favor by shoving their trap down the mountain. It now looks like the girl wrecked all on her own when she was trying to turn the Jeep around. We ought to be watching our land better," Homer added. "I'll buy the fence material if you boys will put it in. We'll also put in a gate at the beginning of the loggin' road just to make sure nothing like this happens again."

"Yeah," Rob said. "It's better to be safe than sorry."

"Those Kormans will squall like a stuck hog," Bob said. "They've been driving their four-wheelers on the road."

"Don't matter. It's our land, not theirs. They got no rights to the old loggin' road. The girl wrecking is reason enough for us to do something."

Chapter 7

~~~~

Markum Korman raised his head up from where he lay in the laurel hell. He had covered himself in fallen leaves. He knew how to hide by covering himself in leaves, twigs and whatever debris that was lying about– bury into the ground as much as possible. People tended to look at their own eye level instead of ground level. They seldom if ever looked down into a hole.

"Are they gone?" Darnell whispered without raising his head. Darnell was the cautious one, or maybe he was simply a coward. What he regretted right now was letting his pa catch him and force him on the mountain before he could disappear.

"Yeah, I reckon they are," Markum told him.

"Can we get up now? My britches are full of leaves and they're itching me," Alvin, the complainer, said. Nothing was ever satisfactory for Alvin. He was sure life always had it in for him.

"Hell, yeah. Might as well stand up. All this talkin' tells 'em where we're at anyhow, you dumb asses," Markum made a point of adding.

"Thought you said they was gone," Kimbell chimed in. Kimbell was the *tell me exactly like it is* person. Actually, he couldn't understand a thing being told to him. Some folks thought he was rather slow in the head as well as in body. Kimbell was the fat baby of the brothers – more lazy than spoiled.

"I'm sick and tired of them Barlows messing in our business," Markum ranted. "We need to figure us out a way to get rid of that bunch. We're the ones who use this mountain, they don't. Users keepers, so it rightfully belongs to us."

"They could have an accident like that person driving the Jeep already went and done," Alvin said. "Did he say it was a girl? Did he say she didn't die? Don't see how anybody could come out of that burned piece of tin and not be dead."

"Don't know, don't care," Markum told him. "We've got to look out for ourselves. Them Barlows have always taken advantage of us, and I'm not gonna put up with it any longer. That damned Harmon Barlow stole land that rightfully belonged to us, and I intend to get it back. It's been in our family for a hundred years."

"How do we aim to do it?" Darnell asked. "It's best not to get in a fist fight with those twins. They're meaner than a timber rattler."

"We don't have the money to fight 'em in a court of law," Markum said, "but I reckon I know who has."

"Who?" Pudgy Kimbell was quick to ask. If anybody had money, he was ready to befriend them until it was all gone.

Markum gave his youngest son a bewildered look. "Who? You dumb ass. Do you know anybody around here that has money?"

"Only them Hordlys, but he's not from around here." Kimbell hung out with their youngest son off and on during the summer. Densley Hordly bought weed from him before the rich twerp's uncle, Enrick Rainey, taught him how to grow it.

"Don't matter where Nickle Hordly is from, he's here now," Markum told him. "And he claims to have lots of money."

"They're them half-backers, Pa," Alvin had to get his two-cents worth in. "You've always hated them half-backs worse than the Barlows."

"Don't mean we can't use 'em against the Barlows. You know how stupid and greedy half-backers are. They think they're hot shit without any of the stink."

"Don't see why them Hordlys don't stay down there in Florida or go all the way back up North where Nickle came from," Darnell said. "He's not our kind."

"They ain't so bad," Kimbell said, as he thought about the money Densley had supplied him with during the summers. They'd had some good time with Densley's money.

"That Nickel Hordly hain't got the sense God gave a frog," Markum told them. "A man such as that can be used mighty easy."

"His skinny old wife has peroxided all her brains out," Alvin repeated what he'd heard his mother say a hundred times before. None of the Korman women liked Phyllis Rainey when they were growing up together, nor did they like her any better now, even though they were kin. Their mother claimed that Phyllis' nose was always so high in the air she'd drown if she was caught outside in a rainstorm.

"That's a fact," Markum agreed. "Phyllis is one of them fake blondes who toots her own horn so much it blowed her brains all the way down into her bony ass. She's just like her brother, Enrick Rainey. Both of them are big enough assholes to shove a full-grown mule in."

All three boys agreed with a nod.

"How we gonna make 'em turn on the Barlows more than they do already?" Darnell asked.

"I aim to go home and get me a swallow of something wet while I think on it. All this here work has plum worn me to a frazzle," Markum told them.

Chapter 8

~~~~

Darkness was still good. Nothing hurt when the darkness had its claim on her. Yet, something kept telling her to make the darkness go away. It was time to open her eyes and let the light return. Catalena grunted and the sound alone hurt like blazes of fire. No, she certainly didn't want the light, not yet. She needed to hold onto the darkness until the pain went away.

Thankfully, she was able to bring the blessed darkness back.

The relieving darkness didn't last forever even though she tried to keep it with her. She was aware of time passing, of someone insisting she come out of the darkness and wake up. It was a woman's voice she kept hearing. It was a voice she didn't recognize and kept trying to make it go away.

"Open your eyes," the voice disturbed her again as something wet touched her face. "It's not good to be out this long." The voice was gentle, encouraging. Catalena listened to the voice and told herself she needed to trust it.

Still, she didn't want to open her eyes. When she did it caused her head to ache something fierce. Trying to listen to the voice made the ache hurt even worse. Catalena wasn't going to do it, didn't have to. She willed the darkness back and all was good again.

Catalena knew more time had passed. There was a vague memory of voices and movement, of something damp on her face and water touching her lips. The water was good but being lifted wasn't. It made her head hurt too much.

"All right," came a demanding voice. "It's time you wake up now or we'll have to take you to the hospital. They'll prod you and poke you full of needles and put stuff in your veins. If you don't want that, you'd best open your eyes. I ain't diapering you like you was a baby no longer. Time you get up and use the pot or go outside to the toilet. Do you hear me? Open them eyes or it's to the hospital you go."

Diaper? Was someone talking about diapering her? Prod? Needles? Veins? What had happened to her while she was hiding in darkness? Maybe it would be best after all if she allowed the light to return. Carefully, tentatively, she permitted one eye to open the slightest bit to test the pain. Okay, not too bad so far. She opened the other eye. There weren't sharp knives of pain any longer, just a dull throbbing ache, so she dared to open her eyes completely. She could handle a dull throbbing ache. She was made of tough stuff.

"Thank the lord," said a woman's voice. "You've finally decided to come around. I'd given up and sent for Homer to come take you to the hospital."

Catalena forced her eyes to focus on the face leaning over hers. It was the face of a stranger, a middle-aged woman with dark hair, graying slightly, pulled tightly back at her temples and fastened in a bun. The face appeared strict, almost forbiddingly harsh, but not cold. The woman's eyes were dark, emotionless. There should have been relief showing in them if she had wanted her to open her eyes so badly, but there wasn't. Catalena thought those eyes were filled with dread.

Looking at the woman drew Catalena farther away from the darkness. At first, she expected to recognize the woman, but she didn't. This woman was a stranger. "What happened?" Catalena rasped out through a sandpaper throat.

"You were in an accident. What's your name?" the woman asked.

The word accident stuck in her mind? What kind of accident had she been in? She wanted to ask questions, but her mouth felt like it had desert sand filling it. She tried to moisten her lips with a tongue she found to be dry and prickly. The woman noticed, crammed an extra pillow behind her back to lift her into a sitting position. She then picked up a cup and held it to Catalena's mouth. The water was wonderful. She grabbed the cup with both hands and tried to gulp, but the woman pulled the cup away.

"Easy. You can't have much at a time. It'll make you sick. You've been out three days."

Out three days? What did that mean?

"Out?" she managed to ask.

"Knocked out. Unconscious. You hit your head."

So that was why her head ached. "How?" she wanted to know.

"You wrecked your Jeep." The voice held no sympathy, sounded with nothing of love or even caring, only relief was present and maybe impatience. This woman really was a stranger to her or there would have been some stronger kind of emotion.

"Jeep?" Catalena said the word and tried to think. She didn't remember anything about a Jeep or about an accident.

"Where . . ." her throat closed up and she pointed toward the cup of water.

The woman picked the cup up and held it to her lips long enough for her to take another swallow before the woman pulled it away.

"Easy now. Don't want you puking all over everything."

"Where am I?" Catalena tried again.

"In my home. You've been here for three days."

"Am I hurt badly?"

A slight smile touched the woman's mouth at the question. "Not much, just a knot on your head. You must be soft-headed, or it wouldn't have done you harm."

"Soft headed?"

"Yeah, you landed on a tender spot and it knocked you out. Most people have a tender spot somewhere. Usually it's on the chin, but your chin wasn't hit. It was the back of your head."

Catalena tried to think, to remember, but there was nothing. She found herself longing for the darkness again, but her inside voice warned her against allowing it to return. It was time for the light to remain and for her to . . . to what?

"Diapered?" Catalena questioned at the revolting image that hit her again.

"A person's body keeps on working even when the mind doesn't," the woman told her.

"You diapered me?"

"Only me. Nobody else has seen your privates."

"I'm sorry," Catalena mumbled. "It had to be horrible for you."

The forbidding harshness on the woman's face eased slightly.

"You couldn't help it," she told her. "It was something that had to be done, and I did it the same as I always do what has to be done."

Still, Catalena didn't like the image. Diapering was diapering. "I'm getting up," Catalena told her as she tossed the thin cover aside and swung her feet off the side of the bed. The movement made the room swirl.

"Easy, you've been lying down a long time," the woman told her, as she placed a hand on Catalina's shoulder. "Don't try to stand yet. Sit on the edge of the bed for a while to see how you do."

The woman squeezed her shoulder in a comforting manner before she removed her hand.

Catalena didn't want to sit on the edge of the bed, but that was what she was going to do for a while, or at least until the room stopped swirling around.

"Can you tell me what happened? Why were you driving up that old road? You had to know it was dangerous considering how narrow it was," the woman asked.

Catalena looked at the woman ready to answer all questions. She even opened her mouth, but no words came out.

Confusion took hold. "What road?" she finally questioned. "What was dangerous?"

"The old loggin' road you drove that Jeep up. You had to know it was dangerous considering how narrow it was, not to mention that sheer drop off into the gorge."

"I drove a Jeep up a logging road? Why did I do that?"

"I don't know," the woman said as she put her hand on the girl's forehead to check for a fever.

Catalena was caught between jerking away from the woman's hand and allowing the comforting hand to remain. The hand gave her a degree of comfort, so she let the hand remain for the moments it took the woman to determine if there was a fever.

The woman frowned. "My name is Mazy. What's your name?"

"My name is . . . " she said, hesitated, and then almost panicked. "I . . . I . . . my name? I don't know my name." A new kind of panic took hold inside her. She wanted the darkness to return again. It was safe there.

"Easy," Mazy warned. "Don't excite yourself. You've just come to. Your mind's a little fuzzy, that's all."

"Come to?" she whined and was instantly angry at herself for making such a sound. She had a dislike for people who whined. She made a point of never doing it.

"That's right. Like I done told you before, you've been knocked out cold for three days. The Jeep you were driving went off the loggin' road and burned up. Thank the good Lord, you jumped out and landed on a rock ledge. My boy, George, found you and carried you to safety before you fell the rest of the way down the cliff." Mazy continued telling her what happened. "My boys found no sign of anyone else being in the Jeep. I take it you were you alone, right?"

Jumped out? Saved? Burned? Alone? Boys? No one else in the Jeep? Catalena was doing her best to think, to remember and understand what had happened.

"I'm always alone," Catalena told the woman with a degree of certainty. "Are you sure I drove a Jeep up a logging road? Why would I do a thing like that? I don't think I would never drive on a logging road.   Shouldn't I remember doing something such as that?" Catalena asked in one breathless gulp.

"You should. It was you in that Jeep, all right. Where did you come from? You don't talk like you're from around here."

Panic came again. "I don't know. I can't seem to remember."

"What can you recall?" Mazy asked gently as a touch of compassion softened her expression a bit more.

Catalena closed her eyes for a moment and then opened them rapidly. "Darkness and painful light," she told Mazy. "That's what I remember."

"That's all?"

"Just about all. I think I might remember your voice and maybe your hands touching me. You talked to me, didn't you? You touched me?"

"I talked to you and touched you. I was starting to get plenty worried when you didn't respond. I thought you should have come to a lot sooner." Mazy looked the girl's face over carefully, although she was certain the girl was telling the truth. "There's nothing else you remember? You ought to remember your own name."

Catalena shook her head. Tears came to her eyes as she gritted her teeth in an effort to stop the tears. She was certain she wasn't the kind to cry – well, hardly ever, and didn't want this woman or anyone else seeing her cry. But right now, she felt so very weak, helpless and not in control of herself. Catalena was almost sure she remained in perfect control of almost everything.

"Why can't I remember things?" she asked with a hated tremor to her voice. "I can't remember my own name."

"Can you remember your mother and father's name?"

Catalena tried to force her mind go back in time, but there was a huge wall of blankness, a wall of absolutely nothing. How could that be?

"Lay back down for a few minutes," Mazy told her. "I'll bring you a little chicken soup to drink before you try to get up. It'll give you the strength you need. You need to understand you've not had solid food in three days and that's enough to make you weak," Mazy assured her as she left the room.

Chicken soup? At least she knew what that was, and she wasn't particularly fond of it, but she was feeling slight hunger pains. As she watched the woman named Mazy leave the room, the room itself got her attention. The bedroom was small, with paneled wood on the walls and ceiling. She looked down at the floor to see if it was wood also. It was. There were two windows in the room that kept the small space from feeling dark and cramped. An old, worn dresser set against the wall with a small mirror above it. Places on the mirror were black spotted where the aluminizing was wearing off. The bedspread and curtains matched and were made out of white eyelet material with pink ruffles and tiebacks. The material was well worn but comfortable in a homey sort of way. It was obvious this room was for a girl.

Catalena had the strongest urge to see herself, see what her face looked like. Maybe that would make her remember who she was. She tried to get up again, but the room swirled and a strange kind of sickness took over, forcing her to lie back down. Don't you dare panic, she demanded of herself. Calm down and do as the woman said. Rest a few more minutes and everything will return to normal. She closed her eyes and allowed exhaustion to wrap itself around her like a cocoon. She drifted into a twilight sleep that helped ease her fears, but it didn't last long. Light insisted on overtaking the darkness again. She couldn't make the comfort of the darkness return for her to hide in.

~~~~~

Mazy heard heavy footsteps and then the creak of a rocker and knew Homer had set down on the porch. Since the accident that took Harm's life, Homer had slowly recovered from the accident physically, but Mazy knew he still blamed himself for his brother's death. Mazy also understood that Homer would rather been the one who had died. Harm had every reason to live, including a wife and six children who needed a father. Homer had no children and a wife who had died a few years before. He now considered it his duty to care for his dead brother's family, which alternately irritated Mazy and stirred her compassion.

Homer's limp had almost disappeared, except that he now walked hard, putting his weight on his heels instead of the balls of his feet. Mazy knew he was in pain a lot of the time, but he never complained, except for the fact that he was growing old. He was always complaining about that because it was a natural part of living, and he believed he was entitled to that much verbal dissatisfaction.

Mazy went to the kitchen and put a few sticks of kindling wood in the cook stove and pulled the pot of chicken soup over the eye so it would heat up fast. Then she went out to the porch where Homer was waiting for her.

"Say you're ready to take her to the hospital?" Homer said as she came out on the porch to stand beside his chair.

"No," Mazy leaned down and whispered near his ear. "She just came to."

Homer frowned as he saw the troubled look on her face. "You're not happy about that?"

"Oh, yes. It'll save us a lot of trouble," she continued to whisper near his ear.

"What's troubling you then?" he whispered back

"She doesn't remember anything."

Homer was stunned into silence for a moment as he let what Mazy said sink in. "Might be a lucky thing for the girl if she doesn't remember the accident. She had to be scared in an inch of her life when that Jeep tumbled down the cliff with her in it."

"No," Mazy was quick to set him straight. "It's not like that. She doesn't even know her own name."

Homer frowned. "Say what?"

"She doesn't remember much of anything. Not who she is or nothing."

"You're serious?"

"Afraid so."

"Well, I'll be a monkey's uncle."

"What are we gonna do? If she doesn't remember what happened, her folks can claim anything against us." Maybe we should have taken her to the hospital when the accident first happened and reported it to the law.

Homer rubbed the chin he hadn't had time to shave earlier. "Seems to me we won't have to be concerned about her folks until she remembers who they are. It's been three days, and nobody has come around searching for her."

"That could only mean they don't know where to look."

"Reckon I ought to take a look at her," he said as he eased himself up and followed Mazy into the kitchen.

Mazy dipped up a little chicken broth into a bowl and handed it to Homer. "Here, carry this and wait outside the door until I make sure she's in bed and is decent."

Mazy had watched over the girl like she was one of her own. Neither Homer nor one of her boys had gone into her room without her permission or her presence, not that she didn't trust them completely, for she did. It was simply the proper way things were done and she wasn't about to change what was proper.

The girl wasn't lying in bed. She was sitting against the headboard propped up by both pillows. The look on her face made Mazy halt a step as she entered the room. The girl's face was as pale as the bed sheets and her eyes were wide with fear.

"Honey, what is the world is wrong?" Mazy asked.

She turned those frightened eyes on Mazy. "I can't make myself remember anything. My mind is blank. I don't know my name. I don't know who my parents are or even where I came from. I can't remember one single thing other than you."

"There's no need to upset yourself. It's normal considering the kind of hit on the head you've had. You have to give yourself time to heal, that's all." Mazy wasn't sure if what she told the girl was true, but she hoped it was. She could only try to imagine what the girl was going through right now. It had to be horrible not knowing your own name much less anything else. When Mazy reached the bedside, the girl looked up at her with huge frightened eyes.

"What's to become of me?' she questioned in the most pitiful voice.

"You're going to eat your chicken soup and get well," Mazy told her gently as she looked at her empty hands. "Oh, Homer, bring her broth in here, please."

Homer came through the door carrying the bowl of soup as the girl watched every move he made. "You look familiar," she said once he reached the bed.

"I do? Well, that's unusual being you've never seen me before."

"Are you on television?" She asked as she took in his lean face and dark twinkling eyes. They were filled with a special kind of humor that made him seem to know secrets he wasn't about to tell. His hair was salt and pepper gray. His mustache was a shade darker, while his eyebrows were thick and jet black. He was an extremely handsome man considering his age. The woman was lucky to be married to him even though he was obviously older than her.

"Nope," he told her. "Unless you count the times, I sat down on that old busted one out back of my barn. Bessie, God rest her soul, used to love to watch television. Soap operas. She lived to see 'The Days of Our life.' I think that show was more real to her than her own life and a whole lot more eventful.

Once she died, the set went blank and I carried it out behind the barn."

"Stop talkin' nonsense. She doesn't want to hear about your dead wife," Mazy said to him as she took the bowl of chicken broth from Homer's hands. "Here honey, take a little sip of this." She shoved a spoonful of soup between the girl's lips.

She swallowed the liquid. She did want to hear about this man's dead wife. It meant the two of them weren't married and that fact stimulated her curiosity.

"I can feed myself," she insisted as she took the bowl and spoon from Mazy's hands. The smell of the chicken soup was almost nauseating, but she sipped it straight from the bowl anyway. If she really had been unconscious for three days, she obviously hadn't been able to eat, and she needed food to regain the strength she needed to keep from being this weak. She instinctively knew weakness of any kind wasn't something she could tolerate.

"At least you know what a television is," Homer said in his calming tone of voice. "I'd say your memory is coming back. That bump on the head had to be a solid enough to keep you fuzzy for a few days, but it won't last long."

Hope lit up the girls' face. It was easy to tell she was scared, and his words had comforted her.

"Did you help find me?" she asked as she looked into his dark brown eyes that gave a solid impression worthy of her trust.

"George was the one who found and rescued you from the rock ledge. He had you on solid ground by the time I arrived. My old legs don't move as fast as that boy's does."

"George?" she questioned.

"My youngest. I told you about him finding you," Mazy reminded her.

"Oh, yeah, I remember."

"See," Homer gave her a sideways smile he reserved for helpless little things. "You're remembering already. In a day or two everything will come back."

~~~~

Homer went to the woodpile to gather an armload of stove wood for Mazy to cook dinner for him and the twins. Mazy followed him.

"What do you think?" Mazy asked.

"Don't know what I think, but I don't like what I'm seeing. It ain't good that little gal don't remember nothing. We can't get her back home when we don't know where her home is."

"She certainly can't stay here," Mazy said with alarm.

Homer lifted his bushy, black brows. "Got a better suggestion?"

A confused look came to Mazy's face. "That girl has to remember and that's all there is to it."

"And in the meantime, how are we going to explain having her here?" A twinkle came to Homer's eyes. "I'd marry her but I don't think she'd go for that. Now take Rob or Bob . . ."

"Shut your mouth," Mazy told him firmly. "I won't have such talk as that around me and you know it. My boys aren't ready to take on a wife. Certainly not one we know nothing about."

Homer thought teasing Mazy was delightful. She had no sense of humor and took every word seriously. "Those twins are old enough to have half-grown kids of their own," he informed Mazy. "Don't know what's wrong with them that they ain't. Could it be you baby them too much, or maybe them being twins has made them kind of quare?"

"Don't you start in on that or I'll swarp your head with a stick of stove wood." Mazy warned.

Homer contained his humor because what he said was all too true – at least the part about Mazy babying her boys. Mazy didn't mind her girls getting married. Actually, she welcomed it. It was her twin boys, who looked so much like Harm, that she held onto with both hands. In his opinion, her possessiveness wasn't a good thing for the boys. That's why he had tried to step into their father's shoes – at least as much as possible. With those two hard-headed boys he couldn't provide much influence. They had each other to rely on.

George was a different matter. He was still young enough to need a dad to guide him and Homer was determined to give that boy the best chance in life possible – regardless of what it ended up costing him.

"There's gonna be a lot of talk regardless," Homer told her. "And we better have some answers thought up and practiced. It won't look good on us keeping her here and not reporting her or the accident to the sheriff."

"You know we were waiting for her to come around so we would know what to do," Mazy said in their defense. Folks living in their area didn't go running to the sheriff with every little thing. It had to be a major catastrophe for anyone to seek out the law. The law was considered an intruder that always made matters worse.

"The question will be why we waited so long."

"We'll tell everybody she is visiting us," Mazy said. "Or better yet, we can say she is a friend of one of my girls, maybe Willa's, who came for a visit and wrecked her Jeep. Could work, but will the girl agree? We've already told her we don't know who she is. Besides, she'll still be an unrelated female in the house with my boys."

"Can't be helped," Homer said.

"Lordy, Lordy. We shore don't need this right now. It couldn't have happened at a worse time." Mazy wrung her hands before she quickly picked up an armful of kindling wood.

"Can't change a thing now. We'll just have to do the best we can. Maybe we can keep the girl hidden until her mind comes back and we can get her where she belongs. Thing is there's a wrecked Jeep and an insurance company, but we'll handle that as it comes. We'll claim we were waiting for the girl to give us information, which is true."

Mazy didn't like leaving ends loose to flap in the wind, but she didn't know any way out of the situation they were now in.

Chapter 9

~~~~

"What do you make of all this? Bob asked his brother. "Pretty little gal like her don't just show up in a place like this without a reason."

"Nope," Rob said. "She don't."

"Then you think she had a reason for driving up that old logging road?"

"Don't know."

"Just doesn't make sense, her being a stranger and all. She's young too. Not old enough to be doing some type of government work."

"Young girl might be looking to buy a little weed." Rob said.

"You think she was hunting those Kormans because she wanted to buy some weed from 'em?"

"Could be. It's either weed or she's somehow connected with those Hordlys. She's sporting a good tan. Could be from Florida." Rob told him. "She has a rich-person air about her kind of like Phyllis pretends to have. Like she expects better than what we've got."

"She's not like us that's for sure. She's a lot nicer than those Hordlys are, but we never know how she'll be given a little time. There's a chance she might have gotten confused and drove up the wrong side of the mountain. That wacky weed does strange things to the mind."

"Yeah, it does."

"Could be what's wrong with her mind right now. Too much dope might have robbed her of her memory," Bob told him.

"Could, but most likely her condition was caused by the hit on her head. Can you imagine her fear when she realized she was going over that rock cliff? It would be a blessing for her not to remember how close she came to dying."

Bob frowned. "I don't want to imagine it. You know, she doesn't look like she's hooked on drugs. She seemed too nice and . . ."

"Plump," Rob finished for him. "Nice and sweet and plump."

"I wouldn't call her plump. Just well-rounded in all the right places," Bob insisted.

"Right," Rob said with a grin. "I'm surprised you noticed. She has good teeth too."

"Of course, I noticed. I always notice things like that."

"No, you don't, but I do," Rob admitted, "and so did George along with Homer. George has first claim on her," Rob taunted his twin. Rob thought it entertaining that his brother was more serious than he was. Rob always thought his brother had no sense of humor. Had to take back after their mother.

"George is far too young to be thinking about girls, and Homer is far too old," Bob said. "Besides George is going to be the first in our family to attend college. He don't need no girl messing that up. With his brains, he won't need to break his back being a sawmill man."

"That's a fact. He'll go to college if Homer has his way."

"Homer always has his way. He'd flat out die of a heart attack if he didn't get his way."

"Doubt he'd die, but he sure wouldn't like it," Rob said. "He's a tough old bird."

"Yeah, but he's getting old alright. You know how old men are."

"How are they?" Rob asked his brother just to see what he might say.

"Age takes a man downhill fast. Leaves him with little more than his memories, and with Uncle Homer that can't be anything to brag about. Makes me think we ought to start thinking about our future before we get old."

Rob tried not to grin at his brother's seriousness, but he couldn't resist poking at him just a little. "Are you starting to think about finding yourself a good woman and settling down? We've got several parcels of land we've timbered that you could build a house on. We could even saw you out a house pattern."

"At times, I do think about it, but I've not met anybody I'd want to marry up with." Bob admitted, still being serious. "How about you?"

"I've not had time to sow any wild oats yet, and I've got a mighty big sack full ready to pop open at the seams."

"What about that Lynn Johnson?"

"Didn't you know she's marrying Harold Ledford? She told me I'd dropped my candy and Harold Ledford picked it up and licked it off."

"No, I didn't know that. Her and Harold don't seem to be a fit for each other. Wonder if it will last? Guess she left you hanging high and dry though."

"I don't mind," Rob said. "She wasn't my type. Too bossy for me. Never did like being told what I could and couldn't do."

"I had my eyes on Katie Swift for a while, but I've turned sour on her," Bob admitted.

"Why is that?"

"She told me she wants to come first in a man's life instead of playing second fiddle to his twin brother."

"So, I'm a problem?"

"Nope. Finding the right woman is a problem. Maybe we should look for twins to court. They'd understand us better. Mom always told us we had to stick together. I'm thinking she was right."

"Know of any twin girls?" Rob asked.

"Heard talk about two sets of 'em. One set lives about an hour's drive from here, and the other set is clean in another state."

"Didn't know that," Rob admitted.

"Man at the lumber yard was talking about sets of twins hereabout when he discovered we were twins."

"We do look a lot alike," Rob admitted, except I'm better looking."

"Only in your own imagination. Think I'll either grow a full beard or shave my mustache, so I don't look so much like you," Bob told him.

"Good idea."

"Maybe we both should," Bob added.

Rob grinned. "Let's take a load of lumber to the yard and see if there's any talk going around. Buy us a newspaper. Might find out something about a missing girl."

"Okay, but let's make sure we don't mention anything about her until we do find out something. Mom doesn't want anybody to know she's staying with us."

"Always good to keep our mouths shut," Rob agreed.

"But those Kormans won't. They'll spread the word about her like it was a butter on hot bread."

"Doubt it," Rob said as he pulled the two-ton truck alongside the stack of air-dried lumber.

"Sure they will. Every single one of 'em has diarrhea of the mouth."

"Not where their farming operation is concerned. If they caused someone to wreck down that rock cliff, they'll not say one word about it and hope we won't either."

"Humm," Bob grunted in agreement. "You've got a point there. If they don't say nothing, we'll know they set the trap."

"We already know they did. I'd like to know more about her. She's not wearing a wedding ring, but that don't mean she's not spoken for. I'm guessing she's not though."

"Me too," Bob agreed. "Too bad she doesn't have a twin. Reckon we'll have to step aside and let George flex his muscles with her. That is unless she's not your type. I'd rather not show you up too badly if she takes a liking to me."

"You won't."

"What do you mean by that?" Bob wanted to know.

"The way I see it, she'll pick whoever she wants, and it might not be one of us."

"Of course, she'll go for one of us. Do you know anybody that would be a better catch than one of us?"

"Nope, can't say as I do."

Chapter 10

~~~~

Catalena was sitting in a chair on the porch beside Homer when she saw a young man walking up the path leading to the house.

"George is home," Homer told her. It's a long walk from the bus stop. There are several kids who get off the bus in that one spot because it's the last place wide enough for the school bus to turn around," Homer looked thoughtful for a few moments. "Most of them are Kormans. There are several families living up that hollow, but their kids seldom all go to school at the same time. Their folks try to keep them in school long enough for the truant officer to stay away, but no longer than that. The day a Korman turns sixteen is the day they stop going to school"

"Who are the Kormans?" Catalena asked, as they watched George getting closer to the porch.

"They're the folks who live across the hill," Homer told her. "Hate to talk belittling about anybody, but they're the kind you want to stay away from." Homer thought it was best for Catalena to be forewarned to stay away from the Kormans for her own safety.

"What kind of people are they?" she asked. Something about the way he'd spoken about the Korman's got her attention. It appeared there was a lot he didn't want to say.

"Don't like talking bad about folks, but they're a bad lot," he told her. "Bad lot of no accounts a pretty girl should avoid."

"Do I know them?" she asked.

Homer shook his head. "Don't reckon you know anybody around here. As far as I can tell, you come from someplace else."

If she didn't know anybody around there, then what was she doing here? she wondered. She didn't just drop out of the sky in this out-of-the-way place for no reason.

"Why did I come here?" she questioned out loud in hopes Homer might have some kind of solution to her question.

"That's the question we've all been asking. Don't reckon we'll know the answer until your memory returns."

He *had* to remind her about her memory loss. Surely, he didn't think she was pretending. Not having memory was like not having a previous existence.

~~~~

George had been thinking about the girl all day long. He and Brent Kilby were the only ones who took the right-hand fork of the road when they got off the school bus. All the Korman cousins took the left-hand fork. There was a long, tall ridge that separated the two tracts of land. The Barlows had bought the top of the ridge from one of the Korman heirs over a hundred years before. The Kormans still wanted to claim that tract of land as belonging to them regardless of who held the deed. "My great, great granddaddy owned that land," the Kormans were fond of saying. "It's a part of our heritage." Uncle Homer would always point out that it was a Korman who sold the land, and Barlow money that bought and paid for the land.

Brent was a slender, red-headed, fifteen-year-old boy who lived a quarter mile below the Barlows. He was an only child and had kind of a childish worship for George. He begged his parents for a set of weights to lift in hopes of developing his muscles the way George had. When his parents refused, Brent lifted rocks and logs when he wasn't begging to visit George's weights, which George kept in the barn loft. Several times

George often found him in the loft without his permission, but as long as nothing was disturbed or missing, he supposed it was all right. Had it been one of the Kormans, he would have put a stop to it. It never paid to have a Korman around. Their fingers were permanently sticky where other people's possessions were concerned. He was glad to have two brothers as tough as Rob and Bob, not to mention having an uncle like Homer. The Kormans were known to lean heavy on widows and children when there wasn't a grown man to protect them. Uncle Homer sometimes mentioned a widow woman the Kormans took advantage of, but that was before he could remember things.

He stopped in his tracks as he started to climb the steps onto the porch – couldn't help it. That girl was the prettiest thing he'd ever seen in his entire life. She was like a pink rose blooming in a briar patch. Her hair was long and brown with golden streaks of highlights, her face tanned, and her dark eyes flashing as she looked at him. When she smiled her entire face lit up. So did George's face as he rushed toward her as though he intended to grab her in his arms.

"Hot dang, you've come to," were the first words out of his mouth when he stood in front of her. "I mean . . . you're okay. You're not going to up and die on us." He hated the way he was ranting. Uncle Homer claimed his mouth worked before his brain went into gear.

"She came around this morning," Homer told him as he turned to the girl. "This is George. He's the one who hauled you up from the rock ledge. Do you remember seeing his ugly self?"

She ignored his question. "I'm alive, thanks to you," she smiled wider showing a perfect set of glistening white teeth. Ipana teeth, he thought. She probably never had to use baking soda and salt to brush her teeth with the way he did.

He already knew she was pretty but there was a lot of difference in an unconscious girl and one who was awake and looking at him with huge brown eyes with gold flecks shining.

"Uncle Homer said if I had moved even a few inches before you got to me, I would have fallen to my death. You really are my hero."

He felt his face flush red. She couldn't possibly know how much he wanted to be her hero, but he feared he couldn't live up to the rest of his family. He was used to it, and it really wasn't much bothersome. Uncle Homer? She was calling him that already? He had to give it to the old man; he knew his way around women, young and old. George envied that.

"I got to you before anyone else could or they would have saved you," he said as he shrugged his muscled shoulders. "You weren't much heavy to carry."

"You lift weights?" she asked, as she looked him over seeing how his arms and chest stretched the faded fabric of his shirt.

"Yeah, some. I do a little cross country running too."

"Running," she said the word as though it had a pleasant taste in her mouth. "I think I might like to run."

"Nothing to stop you around here unless you hate running uphill. It's a lot of fun running back down though. Course it'd be best if I run with you for a while. It'd be easy to get lost until you're familiar with the place. There are a lot of mountains around here including National Forest land," he said as though he intended for her to be there for a long period of time.

"Don't think she'll feel up to walking far, much less running for a good while," Homer added. "That hit on her head hasn't done her a bit of good."

"Right," George said. "A head needs time to heal, and you did take a right long fall down that cliff. By the way, I'm George," he added suddenly. "Oh, Uncle Homer already told you my name. What's yours?"

Her face changed, and her glow of happiness faded. "I don't know," she answered.

"I've been calling her Honey, but Mazy says her name is Lena," Homer said quickly. "That bump on her head has made her right forgetful for a little while. Have no doubt things will come back to her in a day or two."

Honey, George thought, sweet just like the girl herself. There were a lot more questions he wanted answers to, but the way Uncle Homer was looking at him told him to remain silent.

"Reckon I'll take my books inside and see if Mom needs any help," George said quickly. He wanted to ask his mother questions about the girl where she couldn't overhear him. He found Mazy in the kitchen sweating from the heat as she made a pot of chicken and dumplings for supper. He dumped his books on the kitchen table, went to her, and gave her a firm hug.

"Okay, what's going on with the girl?" he whispered as if he had the right to know.

Mazy drew in a breath of air and told George the same thing she had told Rob and Bob when they came in to eat their noon meal.

"She doesn't have any memory. That hit she took on the head must have knocked memory right out of her. She doesn't even remember her own name. We're going to tell folks she's a friend of Willa's who came to visit if somebody finds out she's here before she gets her memory back and returns to where she came from."

"Why not tell the truth about her?" George asked, sounding puzzled. He had already been warned not to mention to anyone about the Jeep burning or the unconscious girl for some strange reason. It seemed only them and the Kormans knew about the accident, and a Korman never told anyone anything that wasn't a lie. Most likely they'd come up with some big, hairy tale about the girl and the accident. On the other hand, if they were involved, they would probably want to keep her accident a secret.

"Cause we don't know nothing about her. Until we do, we have to be careful what we let folks know."

"Why?" George asked needlessly.

"George, you know good and well how folks talk about things that don't concern them. We sure don't want to add fuel to a flame when there's no need," Mazy told him with irritation. "No telling why that girl drove up that old logging road. Chance is it wasn't by accident, but we don't know that."

"But we can't hide her forever," George tried to use logic on his mother, which was useless. Mazy always kept her own logic ready and in fine working condition.

"We won't have too. Her memory will come back soon, and we'll know what to do. Until then, it's best to remain silent."

George frowned as he recalled the crumpled body lying on the rock ledge. It had been such a long drop he had feared she was dead. A drop of that distance would do damage, bad damage, but he didn't know exactly how far she had tumbled out of the Jeep before she hit the rock ledge. "She doesn't remember anything?" George questioned his mother again.

Mazy shook her head.

"Nothing at all?" he persisted.

"Nothing? Nary a thing."

"Humph," George grunted. "It'll be like starting over new for her. No bad memories or nothing." He thought about not knowing anything for a minute. "Well then, I reckon she ought to be happy."

Mazy slapped at him with her dishrag. He dodged, grabbed his books, and took them to his room. He had his own room. Rob and Bob had always shared a room. His mother's room and the spare bedroom were on the other side of the house. The sitting room and the kitchen were in the middle.

A girl without a memory. Now that was an interesting thing to sit back and watch unfold, especially when she was such a pleasure to look at.

~~~~

Catalena wanted to stay up and eat at the table, but Mazy insisted she lay back down in bed with a plate on the nightstand. Mazy said she didn't want her to overtax herself on the first day she'd finally come out of the coma. Mazy claimed bedrest was what she needed along with a few good meals of soft food. In Catalena's opinion, she'd already had enough bedrest, but she did feel weak and on the shaky side, so what Mazy said made sense.

Loss of memory didn't keep her from realizing weakness of any kind was something she couldn't tolerate – as was having someone wait on her. She might not remember anything about herself, but it didn't stop her natural instincts from working. Catalena realized she was an independent sort of person who liked doing things on her own. What she couldn't understand was what she was doing in a place like this to begin with? She had a feeling this area wasn't the sort of place she frequented. If these people didn't know who she was, then she had to be from a long way off.

She allowed her fingers to reach up and lightly touch the knot on her head. The knot wasn't huge, but it certainly was tender. She suspected she had suffered a concussion since there was memory loss, and a concussion could take a long time to heal. Odd, how she knew what a concussion was when she didn't have my memory? She consoled herself by thinking she couldn't be in critical condition if she was able to retain part of her memory. What did she know about the human brain? There was the cerebellum and the temporal lobe which related to memory. Okay, she also knew that certain areas of the brain had certain functions. She had obviously taken a hit on a part of the brain that held certain memories, but not instinctive memory, and perhaps not learned, or educational memory, if there was such a thing. As soon as that portion of her brain had time to heal, her memory would return. At least, she hoped she was sure.

But what if she was wrong?

"Don't panic," she told herself. "Rest. Take things easy for a day or two. Someone should show up looking for her soon. Surely, she had family who would realize she was missing and be wondering where she was by now.

Catalena closed her eyes and tried to force herself to remember something, anything. All she accomplished was becoming more frustrated. How was it possible for her to be here while not knowing who she was or where she came from? She didn't even know where she was at. It could be the far side of the moon for all she knew. And most important, what was she doing among strangers in the first place? She certainly wasn't from here, and these weren't the kind of people she grew up with. She knew that without a doubt.

These were . . . how should she put it? Poor people might be the right word, or perhaps backward in time was another description she could use in describing them. Perhaps living in a time that had long past would describe these people and their mountain setting. The big question was how she knew such as that without having memory?

Whatever their lifestyle was, it wasn't hers, although she did feel as though she was somehow familiar with it. Perhaps it came from reading about this kind of life in books. She instinctively knew she loved to read. She enjoyed studying and understanding different lifestyles along with the mysteries of life.

If only she could understand the mystery of being here in the first place. She closed her eyes and tried to think. Where could she possibly have come from, and why would she be driving a Jeep up a narrow, dirt road? As soon as she got a little more strength, she would check out the road and the place where she was supposed to have wrecked. That would surely bring her memory back. For now, Mazy was right, she needed to sleep and regain strength,

Chapter 11

~~~~

A day passed, and then two. Catalena's memory hadn't returned and she was becoming more afraid that she might not recover – or even have family searching for her.

"Shouldn't I see a doctor?" She questioned Mazy. The older woman appeared impatient if not irritated with the question.

"Folks around here don't go running to doctors like they do in big cities where you most likely came from. We've got enough sense to take care of our own. Besides, what good could a doctor do you? He'd just look at that knot on your head and ask if it was still tender. When you said yes, he'd tell you it was the swelling that's causing your memory loss. He'd advise you to give it time for the swelling to go down. Once it heals, your memory will return on its own."

Catalena hoped Mazy was right, but she was beginning to wonder if that was the case. Not only was her memory gone, but a life she had lived was also gone. Mazy had mentioned cities. That's obviously where she was from after comparing her accent to theirs. Living here with the Barlows felt like she was living in an alien world. She didn't need memory to know that. It was obvious. And yet there was some kind of familiarity tugging at her.

Nor did she need memory to realize Mazy didn't know what to do about her and that was one of the reasons Mazy didn't take her to the doctor. Also, doctors had to be paid and she had no money. The Barlows appeared not to have money to spare. Everything about the place had to be dated from a long-ago time. The age of things seemed to be something she still remembered. Even in her addled state, it was easy to tell the Barlows lived a meager existence.

Homer had explained the best he could about what happened after her accident. They hadn't known who she was, where she came from, or how to go about reporting the accident. They preferred not to get the law involved when they didn't know the reason she had driven up the narrow road. Homer explained they wanted to protect her until she was able to give them more information about herself. Trouble was, she still couldn't tell them a thing.

The lack of memory wasn't the only trouble she had. Her lack of money along with her lack of transportation were huge problems. She obviously had a Jeep and a driver's license when she arrived. Now she couldn't go anywhere or afford to buy one thing for herself. Her existence depended on the Barlows, and she was unable to alter her situation. Knowing she didn't even have an article of clothing was nothing short of tormenting.

Mazy explained how the clothes she had been wearing got destroyed by her fall down the cliff. They were so dirty and ragged Mazy burned them. Everything else she owned was also burned to a crisp along with the Jeep, including her identity. The clothes she was now wearing were left behind articles that once belonged to Mazy's daughters.

One thing went without question, her daughters were wise in leaving these clothes behind. They were the homeliest, homemade clothes imaginable, and sixty years outdated, plus Mazy's daughters were much larger than her. Catalena felt lost in the big, calf-length dress that didn't touch her body anywhere. Mazy had also provided her with a pair of baggy bloomers and something that might be called a bra that also appeared to be handmade. She realized Mazy was obviously overly concerned about her three boys getting too close a look at the female stranger. She longed to tell Mazy she didn't think she had ruined a boy's reputation yet, but dared not say such as that. Mazy might not take such a comment as humorous.

Catalena reminded herself she should be thankful for strangers who were willing to share what they had with her, and she truly was. But being thankful didn't bring her memory back or any of the things she needed for survival. She found herself wanting to beat her head against a wall and scream in frustration, but that wasn't an option.

Mazy didn't dress one bit better than she was dressed. Besides, what did it matter how she looked? What mattered was that she was alive, even without her memory, she assured herself repeatedly. But such assurance didn't do a thing toward satisfying her troubled mind in the least. Not knowing anything about herself was like being dead, or maybe worse. She was existing without ever having been alive.

Not having memory was a feeling helplessness, completely and totally panic, but she had no intention of becoming depressed and dejected. After all, she was . . . for a moment, her mind longed to tell her who she was, but only for a moment before the forthcoming revelation was gone. She still had no idea who she was, where she came from, or what she was doing in a place like this.

One thing Catalena did know was that she couldn't just lie in bed or sit on the porch as she was doing now. She had to get up and at least move about. She could see a walking path leading from the house, behind the barn, and disappearing into the woods. A walk along the path for a short distance would do her good. A little exercise after lying in bed so long might be the thing she needed to recover.

Her legs felt a little shaky after walking across the yard, but she chose to ignore their weakness. Maybe getting out and about would help regain enough strength to make it up the mountain where her accident occurred. Something had to help her. She couldn't imagine a worse horror than going through life not knowing who she was, where she came from, or if there was someone out there trying to find her. For all she knew, she could be a wife and mother.

Catalena hadn't walked far when she came to a small pond at the edge of the woods. There was a barbwire fence surrounding a green field of grass with a wooden gate that opened into the field. She opened the gate and slowly made her way across the field to the pond and sat down near the woods in a sunny spot. The warmth of the sun might ease her sore, aching muscles along with providing tranquility to ease her anxiety. She put her arms around her raised knees and laid her head on her arms.

"Good to see you out and about," A man's voice said from behind her.

She jumped and lifted her head to see Homer come out of the woods carrying a bucket in his hands.

"I thought a little exercise might help me regain strength if not my memory," She told him as a reason for sitting there.

"Mazy know you've left the house?"

"No. She was hanging a load of clothes on the line," she told him. Evidently, she wasn't accustomed to getting anyone's permission before she went on a harmless walk. She certainly didn't like the idea of having to do so.

Homer nodded as though he understood her silent thoughts. "In case you haven't noticed, Mazy is the worrying type. She worries about things that could happen twenty years from now, as well as things that did happen twenty years in the past. I've tried to coach her out of such foolishness, but it doesn't do no good. So, just to ease her mind, you might let her know before you take off somewhere."

"I'd only planned on walking through the yard until I saw this path. This place is so . . ." she hesitated while trying to find the perfect words to describe it.

"That it is," Homer agreed before she could find the description she was seeking. "Wouldn't want to live nowhere but here. Course, there are some disadvantages."

"Such as?"

"Isolation for the young. Freezing cold during winter. Perfect weather during the summer. I'm afraid our perfect summer weather brings in outsiders from off who want to take what little good we have and make our good theirs. You know, good things such as community and friendship, peace and quiet, being satisfied with what God gave you. Before outsiders started coming in this mountain was a peaceful and a quiet place where a body could rest without worrying about what somebody might do if you turned your back.

"We still have beautiful spring, summer, and fall weather. No cockroaches, fire ants, or alligators. Mostly good Christian neighbors to go along with the few bad ones. I mean no offence at you being from off or nothing like that, but to be truthful, we do have some folks over the mountain there," he pointed in the direction she'd wrecked in, "that I'd like to see go back where they came from. Along with a few locals whose leaving out would bring a whole sight of happiness to the rest of us folks."

"Who are they?" Catalena asked.

"The main outsider is Nickel Hordly. His name is right fitting if you ask me. He thinks the rest of us are poor ignorant hillbillies. Don't seem to have the slightest idea what we hillbillies think of them, not that they would care. One of the Norman relatives married him. Phyllis's folks left here when she was young. She was mainly raised up north, but she came back here to lord it over us. Wouldn't be so bad if they minded their own business and left the rest of us alone, but they won't. Think they own their place and everybody else's too. Got no respect for what belongs to others. Don't know why in this world a fine woman like Gertie Lee sold the place to the likes of them. She claimed her land would be passed on to her girl and grandchildren. Reckon when her daughter moved her away from here, it made her change her mind."

"Where are the Hordlys from?" she found herself asking.

"They're what we call halfbacks. Moved down from the North to winter in Florida, then only go halfway back during the summer. Seems no matter where they go, they have bad neighbors."

"Perhaps I'm one of those halfbacks," she told him, and wished again that she had memory.

"Could be," he said, "but I don't think you come from folks like them. You don't have their kind of attitude. That's not saying we don't have some mighty bad examples of bad neighbors who were born and raised right here. Those Kormans, who live over the hill yonder, are not what I'd call a Christian kind of people, to put it kindly."

"Kormans?" She said the name and for some reason it gave her a troubled feeling.

"Know of them?" Homer questioned as he looked at the expression she must be showing on her face.

"The name kind of sounds familiar. Seems like I've heard that name before."

"You might have heard it on television. Ever heard of Harvey Korman? He was on the Carol Burnett show."

How could she remember Harvey Korman or the Carol Burnett show when she couldn't even remember her own name? A sadness spread over her that she couldn't hide. A terrible feeling of aloneness and being out of place gripped her until she feared she might cry. She didn't want to be stranded in some place where she didn't belong. She wanted to go home so badly the ache inside her was a gut twisting pain.

"I don't know what I'll do if I don't get my memory back," she told Homer as tears stung her eyes. She tried desperately to hide them from him and almost succeeded. Not remembering anything was surely worse than being dead.

Homer looked out over the pond and started talking.

"See that spot in the pond right out there near the edge of the woods?"

She nodded.

"I had this here pond made years ago so the cattle would always have a place to drink, and our family would have a place to grow us some fish. Anyway, a bunch of young women showed up right here in this very pond a year or so back. It was on a hot summer day. Some came from the Kormans and others were visiting the Hordlys. Don't rightly know which was which though. Those Kormans and Hordlys have a strange type of relationship that goes beyond cousins. I've not exactly figured it out yet. The Kormans have always sucked up to them because they have money. Have you ever noticed how poor folks think sidling up to rich folks makes them become more important?"

Catalena shook her head in answer and wished she hadn't. Movement made her head hurt worse.

"That's one of the ways the rich have learned to take advantage of the poor folks."

"How's that?"

"Poor folks will work for just about nothing just so they can be associated with them. I've noticed when the poor folks send those rich folks a bill, the rich folks will try to beat them out of paying by claiming they didn't do the job right. They might even pay the first bill a worker gives them, if they need for the worker to do more work, but they'll never pay the last bills. They figure the poor people don't have enough money to hire a lawyer to get what's owed to them. I know of a rock mason down the road who built a nice rock wall for some rich folks. The bill, including the rock, was two thousand one hundred and ten dollars. The lawyer got the poor man's money, but the lawyer's bill was two thousand one hundred and fifteen dollars."

Catalena watched Homer as he leaned back on his elbows and continued talking as though he was telling her one of the most important secrets in the universe.

"The day those young women showed up the weather was mighty hot for these here mountains. I came down here to pick Mazy a bucket of early transparent apples and discovered that the whole pile of young women was skinny dipping in this here pond. I knew right off that Mazy would have a heart attack if she saw such as that. Her boys might have a heart attack too, but it would have been for an entirely different reason."

Catalena saw humor sparkling in his eyes, but she didn't find what he was saying offensive in any way.

"We try to discourage folks from fishing and swimming and the like because we have cows and a mean Jersey bull in this pasture. You'll have to watch out for the bull. We don't want folks messing around this pond in case somebody drowns or gets hurt. I've heard those Hordlys get their money from suing honest folks on some trumped-up charge. Anyhow, back to my story. I walked up to just about where we're setting right now and hollered at the girls to get out of the water and go home. One ole gal hollered back at me like a smart-aleck.

"We can swim where we want, and you can't stop us.

"Another ole gal hollered: We're not getting out of here until you're long gone. We've not got any clothes on."

"You're nothing but a dirty old man trying to get himself a look and see," another of them flung at me.

"Go get your jollies somewhere else". The first loud-mouthed gal yelled. "We're not getting out of here until we're good and ready."

"Then they hollered some things at me that ain't fit to repeat in mixed company. Mind you, I got right aggravated at their dirty talk, not to mention their attitude at trespassing where they didn't belong. So, I just held up my five-gallon bucket and hollered back.

"I didn't come down here to watch a bunch of stupid girls floundering about in the water naked. I lifted up my bucket even higher so they could see it nice and clear, I come down here this time every day to feed the alligators."

"Talk about peeling out of that water, they did it. Grabbed the clothes they'd left on the bank and headed for the woods. In my whole entire life, I've never seen such a variety of snow-white hind ends. Don't expect to see the like ever again. Haven't seen hide nor hind end of them back here sense."

Catalena laughed. "Is that a true story?" she had to ask.

"Pretty much. There're no alligators, though. Goes to show it's hard to outsmart an old man."

"I got an idea not many people can outsmart you," she told him.

He grinned. "There's been a plenty who has. You've heard the old saying, fool me once, shame on you; fool me twice, shame on me."

"Can't say as I have," she told him, "but it does sound familiar."

"You don't have a mountain accent, but there are times you say things similar to the way we say 'em," he pointed out. "I hope you get your memory back soon. I'd sure enough like to know who you are."

It wasn't possible for him to hope any more than she was hoping. At least she was no longer fighting tears.

"How's that pump-knot on your head feeling?"

"Sore. My head still throbs."

"Will for a while. Lord knows we've had our share of head-knocks around here. After the accident that crippled me, my mind was slow in coming back to me. I felt like . . . well now, I just don't know how to explain the feeling. I'd say you're feeling something akin to what I felt. Anyway, we'd best be getting on back to the house before Mazy becomes a one-person search party. She takes life mighty seriously. Like I've already told you, she's the worrying kind."

Catalena didn't want to go back to the house, but she might as well. Homer had already disturbed her quiet time. And he was right. Mazy would become fussy when she discovered she had gone missing. She owed the Barlows too much to cause them any more trouble than she was already causing.

"Mazy used to be the spunkiest woman who ever lived," Homer said as they walked side by side along the path. She laughed and sung songs all the time. Yes sir, Mazy was a downright feisty little thing until the accident happened. After that, she lost all her joy and laughter in life. Mind you, I'm not saying her children didn't give her joy, for they did. Losing

Harmon took that special and private kind of joy away from her. Don't think she's ever going to get it back."

"What accident?" Catalena asked after he became silent.

"Logging accident. It killed Harmon, who was her husband and my brother. Crippled me up. I blamed myself for the accident and so did Mazy. To this day, I'm afraid it was me who didn't get the logging chains cinched up tight enough on that load of logs. The loose chains allowed too much pressure to be put on one of the standards and it broke. A loggin' man is supposed to check everything twice. Don't remember if I was the one who left the chain too loose or if it was Harmon. A log kind of knocked some of my memory of the accident out of my head. To this day, I don't remember exactly what happened. I do remember hearing the standard crack and the sound of the logs rolling on top of us. I was told one log knocked me a considerable distance from the truck, but Harm wasn't so lucky. They all fell on top of him."

Catalena saw the sadness on his face along with hearing the pain in his voice.

"I'd give everything I've ever owned or hope to own if Harmon had been the one crippled and me the one who was killed. I didn't have children. Harm did. I do everything I can do to make up for Harm, but there's no way an uncle can replace a husband and father no matter how hard he tries."

Catalena didn't know what she should say as they walked around the barn, so she remained silent.

"That accident had a powerful effect on Mazy. It made her over-protective of her children. She fears something bad is going to happen unless she's right there preventing it. So, give her a little slack by telling her when you're going to wander off."

His words made her feel bad for not telling Mazy she was going for a walk, but no one had told her she was supposed to okay what she did with Mazy until now.

Mazy was coming around the corner of the house with an empty laundry basket as they came into the yard.

"I thought you were in bed taking a nap," she said to Catalena. "Here Homer has you out and about when it's rest you're needing. Lord have mercy on us for that man don't have the good sense of a goose."

"Her leg muscles will go weak if she doesn't use them a little," Homer told Mazy. "Can't have that, now can we? I know for a fact that weak leg muscles ain't good for nobody," he added as he slapped the leg that tended to drag a little behind the other one.

"You bring me any apples?" Mazy asked as though she had given up on fussing at him, but not her irritation.

"Nearly a whole five-gallon bucket full. I'll get you more when you're ready to can some apple sauce. These early June apples are still green enough to be on the sour side."

"I like them on the sour side," she told him. "Makes better sauce."

"And I like 'em sweet and tender enough to almost melt in your mouth."

She gave him an ill look. "You two can set down on the porch and peel the apples. I'll get kettles and knives for you."

Homer rolled his eyes and winked at Catalena when Mazy turned her back. "Happens all the time," he whispered once she'd gone inside. "Thinks I'm her own private workhorse, she does."

Catalena suspected she'd need to become a workhorse too if she earned her keep, and she intend to earn it.

Mazy brought out the kettles and two knives and gave a knife to Homer and one to Catalena.

"Homer will show you how to peel 'em," she told the girl and then went back inside.

Catalena thought it interesting Mazy assumed she didn't know how to peel apples. She didn't know if she had ever peeled an apple before or not, but it couldn't be that hard.

Homer handed her the knife. She took it in her right hand and picked up the apple with her left hand and started peeling.

It felt familiar, nothing awkward about peeling apples. She grinned like she had been given a gift.

"Appears you're used to peeling apples," Homer said.

"I used to try peeling the entire apple without the peeling breaking."

Homer nodded. "Who with?" he asked in a casual like way.

Catalena opened her mouth to answer, but nothing came out. Her mind became blank. She had no idea who she had peeled apples with, but she knew for sure that she had peeled them with somebody who made her feel loved.

"Don't get disturbed about it," Homer told her in his calm voice as though he was trying to sooth her. "The way I see it, when too many thought waves try to get through to your brain at the same time, they can become jammed up. It's when you are completely relaxed that memory stirs itself."

"It's infuriating. It's like I almost remember things and then I can't."

"I know what you mean. Sometimes I try to remember things and draw a blank, but mine is caused by old age along with the body and head trauma I suffered. My memory won't get any better, but yours will."

"I'm not sure about that."

"I'm sure," he said, trying to make her feel better.

"But what if it doesn't? What if I can never remember? What happens then?"

"You will, but let's just say you don't. What's the worst that could happen? I'll answer that one for you. You'll be stuck here with us until your relatives find you. If I do say so myself, being with us is a mighty good place to be stranded. Us Barlows are fine people, kind, dignified, and Godfearing. You'll have Mazy to mother you, George for entertainment and to keep you guessing at what he will come up with next. Rob and Bob are a girl's eye-candy, while they tug at your female heartstrings, and lastly, there's me. I'm sure you've already realized that I'm smart, witty, handsome, as well as being the

most intelligent man you'll ever come across. So, what would
be so bad about hanging out with us for a while?"

"I agree with all the things you just said, but there's the real
me – the me I don't know – the family I don't know – the place
where I belong. I could be married, have a half-dozen children,
have parents searching for their missing daughter."

"Mazy is right sure that you've never had children. She said
your belly is too firm and smooth without one teeny, tiny
stretch mark."

Catalena had an idea those were Uncle Homer's words
instead of Mazy's.

"As for a husband," he continued, "you don't wear a
wedding ring, not even an engagement ring and there's no sign
of one, such as a white streak or indention on your finger. The
twins said you were driving a really nice, recently restored
Willys Jeep. That tells me you're one of the hip, outdoorsy type
of young women with enough money to buy or borrow a
restored Jeep. The fact that you were traveling alone means
you're capable and independent. Most likely you held down a
job before you did what a bunch of other folks are known to
do. You went on vacation. A lot of folks are coming to these
mountains on vacation this day and time. Some have been
coming here for years. Did you know that Margaret Mitchell,
the woman who wrote "Gone with the Wind", spent summers
in Blowing Rock? That's not too far from here. Then there is
the town of Jefferson, the dead president, Thomas Jefferson
himself, used to spend time there. That's how the place got its
name. And then there was Daniel Boone who left a namesake
or two of his behind just about everywhere he went. I've heard
he was a right smart man with a lot of common sense, but I
can't verify that since I didn't know him personally, mind
you."

Catalena smiled because those names had a familiar ring to
them, and Homer expected her to smile.

"I do believe I'm a lone traveler," she admitted. "I also
know, or at least I hope, that someone will be searching for me

sooner or later. Surely, I'll be missed. I'm young enough to have parents, siblings, grandparents, and hopefully a few close friends."

"So, what is there to be uptight about? Relax, put your feet up and take it easy. Call this a vacation for your brain. When you don't remember a thing, you can be completely and totally happy, at least for a little while."

Homer had made a good point, or so she assured herself. She watched as Homer cut a chunk of apple off and stuck it in his mouth. He chewed it thoughtfully as she watched his Adam's apple moved up and down in his neck as he swallowed.

"Do you know what you get if you cross an apple with a shellfish?" he asked her.

"What do you get?" She appropriately replied.

"A crabapple."

She grinned. "That's corny."

"Okay, if you don't like that one, I'll tell you another one. Why did Eve want to leave the garden of Eden and move to New York?"

"I'm supposed to ask why again, aren't I?"

"You are."

"Okay, why did she move to New York?"

"She fell for the Big Apple."

"That's worse than the first one," she told him.

"Then just hang on a until I can come up with another one."

Catalena watched him pick up an apple and roll it around in his callused hand as though he was seeing it for the first time.

"Do you know why the apple stopped rolling downhill?"

"Why did it?"

"It ran out of juice."

She had to laugh at that one.

"You can guess why the apple went to the doctor, can't you?"

"Because it was feeling rotten to the core," she told him.

He shook his head in the saddest sort of way. "Dang, if you didn't beat me to the punch line on that one."

"Homer Barlow!" came Mazy's voice from the kitchen. "You stop aggravating her with your stupid jokes. You're not in grade school."

Homer rolled his eyes and grinned. "Hush-up in there, ole woman, and leave us be out here. We're busy peeling apples."

"Humph," she grumbled as her footsteps sounded. She closed the door to the porch with a firm click.

The expression on his face was pure delight as he gave Catalena a wink.

"When I was a young'un, we'd have to sit for hours helping Mom break bushels of beans for canning. I'd get so bored I thought I would die on the spot, as did Harmon. The only thing that saved us was that Mom would start telling tall-tales and making up riddles for us young'uns to answer. It sure enough helped keep our minds off the boring work we were doing."

Catalena had an idea she was going to get the privilege of experiencing exactly what he was talking about.

"Have you lived here all your life?" she asked him.

"That I have. Ain't hardly been nowhere else unless you want to count the four years I spent in the army when I was a young fellow. Don't like to think about that time though."

"Why not?" she asked.

"Vietnam," he answered after a minute of thoughtful silence. "It was a bad war."

She knew what a war was, and the word Vietnam was somewhat familiar, but her mind wouldn't put any kind of memory together.

"It would be a blessing if I didn't remember anything about those four years. That war either killed or broke many a man. It left many a woman crying. A lot of men who came back were a lot different than the men who left. In my opinion, it was a war for no good reason. Hope you don't mind me saying so, but Johnson wasn't my favorite president. He was bull-headed if not downright cruel when it came to getting his own way."

"President Johnson," She said the words and they meant nothing to her. By deduction, if he was president when Homer was a young man, he probably wasn't president at this time. "Who is president now?"

"Our president claims he made history. He's half white and half black. He's married to a black woman and has two daughters."

He stopped talking and waited to see if the information rang any bells with her, but it didn't.

"His name is Barack Obama," he said. "He used to be Barry Soetoro until he decided to use his father's name instead of his stepfather's."

Catalena shook her head. The names meant nothing.

"I kind of like to keep up with the presidents. You can tell a lot about American people by who they vote for. In reality, he's not the first president who had black ancestors. According to my understanding, there was at least seven presidents who were known to be of a mixed race. Thomas Jefferson, whom I mentioned earlier, was our third president. It's said his mother was a half-breed Indian squaw and his father was mulatto."

"Mulatto. That means he was part black and part white, right?"

"Right."

"Then this Obama is a mulatto."

"I reckon so, but I've heard he doesn't like being called that. He prefers being referred to as of African-American decent. It's kind of like us folks from the Appalachian Mountains. We're tired of being call hillbillies. From now on, we've decided to be called Appalachian-Americans."

He grinned as though he'd said something funny, but she didn't catch on to the funny part, so he continued.

"Our seventh president, Andrew Jackson, was born to an Irish mother who married a black man. You know folks talk about black slaves all the time, but they don't talk much about the Irish slaves that were brought to America. You see, black slaves were more valuable than Irish slaves, not to mention the fact that the Irish could blend in better. So, the slave owners bred the Irish women slaves to black African slaves so their offspring would sell for more money."

"That's terrible," she said.

"What's terrible?" he asked and waited for her answer.

"Breeding people against their will. Selling people is worse."

"Yeah, but both happened and still happens – in one way or another. There's still slavery and slave owners in all the uncivilized world. There's even slavery here in America, but it's kept hidden for most part," he added, shook his head in remorse, and got back to his story. "Then next came ole Abraham Lincoln. He was our sixteenth president. It's been told that he was the illegitimate son of a black man, which is kind of ironic as he is credited with the civil war, which ended up being a tool to set the black slaves free, even though slavery wasn't why the war was fought. And there was Warren Harding our twenty-ninth president. He was said to have black ancestors on both sides of his parents. Calvin Coolidge's mother was known to be a black Moor. Even our thirty-forth president, Dwight D. Eisenhower, was part black. So, Obama can't claim to be the first president who is part black and part white."

His story of presidents with mixed race didn't trigger any memories from her, but it didn't surprise her either. What did affect her was knowing there was a world of knowledge that she couldn't remember. Would she have to start from kindergarten and learn everything over again? Could she read and write? She had an overwhelming urge to jump up from the chair and find out. She looked at Homer and mentally spelled Homer Barlow. She then spelled Mazy, George, Rob and Bob. And her name? She spelled Lena, the name Mazy had given her for some reason. Again, she didn't find it familiar. She silently continued to spell the presidents names Homer had mentioned. She was somewhat relieved to discover she could correctly spell those names. She then spelled the word pneumonoultramicroscopicsilicovolcanoconiosis. It was a word that referred to a lung disease contracted from the inhalation of very fine silica particles, specifically from a volcano; medically, it was the same as silicosis. She instantly wondered how she knew such as that. Most likely she had looked up the longest word in the dictionary for some reason and then memorized how to spell the word. It was still a worthwhile feat, and a curiosity, to be able to spell such a long word correctly. At least she thought her spelling was correct, but she had no way of knowing unless she could find a dictionary.

"Do you have books to read?" she asked.

"George has his schoolbooks, and Mazy has her Bible. I have boxes of books in my attic. Truth is we kind of keep ourselves set-back from the modern world here on Nowhere Mountain. I read to kinda keep up with things. Why do you ask?"

"I wondered if I could read and write."

"I'm sure you can. I'd even guess you've been to college along with having a good deal of common sense. You've got intelligence shinning out of your eyes. Did I tell you that George wants to go to college? He'll be the first in our family to go if we can make it happen. Education is more important now than it was when I was a youngster. Wished I'd gone on to college after I got out of the army. They'd have paid for it."

"Why didn't you?"

"I was needed here at home. But then, I reckon you are already smart enough to know that time is the best teacher that ever existed. Unfortunately, time always ends up killing its students."

She was thinking on that comment when he continued.

"I liked math when I was in school, but my teacher told me I was average." When Catalena didn't respond, he said, "Okay, I'll try this one. When I was in school, the teacher told us if you said a word ten different times, you would own it for life.

An ole boy in the back row started saying Susan, Susan, Susan over and over again."

Catalena shook her head as she realized he was telling jokes. "Education is what is left after one forgets what one has learned," she told him.

"Albert Einstein came up with that one," he said. "See, you're starting to remember already."

"Who's Albert Einstein?" Her mind was blank again.

"An intelligent man without a lick of common sense. He couldn't find his way home, but he was considered a genius."

"Maybe I'll become a genius then."

"Something tells me you already are," he said without seeming to be joking.

She didn't believe there was anything genius about her, but it was true that she couldn't find her way back home. She didn't even have an idea which state her home was located in. She didn't know what state she was now in. Not knowing such things bothered her more than she wanted to admit.

"Where am I?"

"Siting right here beside me."

"No. I mean what state am I in?"

"North Carolina," Homer told her.

"What am I doing here?"

"Helping me peel apples," he said and grinned.

"Will you do something for me?"

"Such as?"

"Will you take me to where I wrecked?"

"We'll go Saturday when George isn't in school. Like I told you before, he's the one who rescued you from the rock ledge."

"Is it far from here?"

"It's a right smart over a mile up the logging road. It's a steep climb on a long, hard piece of rocky ground. You'll need all your strength to get there."

"The boys do their logging up that road?"

"No. It was logged over before I was born. The Whiting Timber Company logged these mountain forests a long time ago. Cut down virgin timber, they did."

"I thought Rob and Bob were sawmill men."

"They are, but they're logging a different section of timber than the Whiting Timber Company logged. There's no longer big, old timber like there was back then."

"Have you got those apples peeled?" Mazy asked as she opened the door.

"We've got 'em whipped. Lena is faster at peeling than I am."

"That's because you spend your time running your mouth when you ought to be peeling apples," Mazy told him.

Homer gave Mazy a wink and a grin that she obviously didn't appreciate.

Catalena heard him call her Lena and it didn't stir anything familiar in her. She didn't know what her name was, but she feared it might not be Lena if Mazy made the name up, which was likely since everything of hers burned in the Jeep.

"Meliva," she said out loud.

"What?" Homer questioned.

"That was Einstein's wife's name."

That was all she could remember, but even that small amount of memory gave her encouragement.

Chapter 12

~~~~

Saturday came, but Catalena's memory didn't. The person she had been before the accident was still a mystery to her. Interesting how she never for one moment thought about her past life and what it was like until she didn't know a past life. Her memory was still a blank slate. A desperate feeling came over her, but she did her best to hide it as she got up, made the bed, took off her baggy, granny-type nightgown, put on her faded, shapeless clothes and went to the kitchen in hopes of helping Mazy prepare breakfast.

"You can set the table," Mazy told her. "There's room for only one cook in my kitchen."

Mazy sounded grouchy, so Catalena found the dishes in the cupboard and set the table for six people. Homer was often there for meals, although he never spent the night there.

"Where does Uncle Homer live?" Catalena asked Mazy when she came into the dining room to inspect the place settings.

"Fancy aren't you," Mazy commented on the table setting where Catalena had put all the plates and silverware in their proper place. "Homer has a place of his own not far from here. He shows up for meals unless he's sick or pouting about something. Why do you ask?"

Uncle Homer pouting? She couldn't imagine such as that happening. "He's supposed to take me where I wrecked today in hopes it might help me regain my memory."

"Let's hope something does," Mazy said as she left the dining room.

Catalena frowned. Mazy was being unusually irritable this morning for some reason. Catalena wondered why, but she wasn't about to ask. Homer came into the dining room and gave her a wink as he sat down. He hadn't bothered to shave or change clothes, which was normal for Homer and the other men. Only George put on clean shirts for school.

Rob, Bob, and George came into the dining room wearing clean clothes and looking as though they'd all three had a bath. Catalena wondered where they could have washed considering there wasn't a bathroom in the house. The logical place was the creek that fed the cattle pond where the young women had gone skinny dipping. She closed her eyes for a moment and savored the thought of sinking into a tub of warm scented water. She could almost feel tension leaving her body for a moment – until reality hit. She had to use a washpan of cool water that Mazy brought to clean herself. She recalled how carefully Mazy pulled the curtains together before she left the bedroom. Did Mazy think someone would be a peeping tom? If so who? George was at school all day, and Rob and Bob were always away sawmilling. That only left Homer. Somehow, she couldn't imagine him peeping in a window.

She felt certain washpan cleaning of one's self was completely different than what she was accustomed to, still, she was familiar with the concept. The way the Barlows lived wasn't totally alien to her. Why, she asked herself. There had to be a reason she came here. Had to be. If only she could force herself to remember something – anything.

Mazy looked all three of her sons over and frowned. "Getting' ready for Sunday already?" she questioned. "Reckon you don't intend to work today."

"We're going to take Lena to the top of Nowhere," Homer answered for all of them. Telling Mazy the same thing Catalena had told her earlier. "We're hoping it might jog her memory if she sees where she wrecked."

"Pray to the Lord that it does. Don't see why it takes all four of you. Rob and Bob always work on Saturday. Besides, Saturday is the only time George gets a full day in," she added.

"There're for back up," Homer told her. "Never know when those Kormans will show up on top of old Nowhere in a fighting mood, not that it's likely with the twins there. I'd hate for them to get drunk and rowdy enough for me to have to shoot them. Been meaning to get the boys to help me put up a real good fence. Good fences make good neighbors and we need a humdinger on that mountain."

"Nothing will make good neighbors out of them," George was quick to say.

"They've been mighty quiet lately," Rob pointed out.

"Makes a body nervous," Bob added.

"I'd say they're staying out of sight until they see what comes of Lena's wreck. One thing is for sure, none of them wants the law snooping around. Oh, well. Let's say grace and get at all this good food. Hope you cooked up some of those early apples to go with those good biscuits you always bake."

"Course I did," Mazy told him. "Get on with grace and don't be talking foolish this time."

"I don't talk foolish," Homer mumbled as he bowed his head and closed his eyes. He said a respectable prayer of thanks, but ended it with *good food, good meat, good lord, let's eat*. Amen."

Mazy rolled her eyes at Homer but said nothing to him.

"Lena, help me carry the rest of the food to the table," Mazy said.

Catalena did not hesitate to follow her to the kitchen. Mazy gave the impression of being displeased with something. Catalena knew she was a thorn in Mazy's side, but what else could she do? Most likely she wouldn't be there if they'd taken her to the hospital.

"No matter what I say to that crazy old man he has to make a mockery out of it. Old age has rotted what little brains he was born with."

Catalena didn't respond. Mazy seemed to have been much more nurturing and protective of her while she was bedridden. Could it be that Mazy didn't believe she'd lost her memory? No one could pull something like that off – and even if she could, why would she want to?

Catalena quickly chastised herself for having such thoughts as she carried the apples and biscuits to the table. Mazy carried the huge bowl of gravy. A platter of sausage and scrambled eggs were already on the table.

"Sit down," Mazy told her. "I'll bring in the pitcher of milk and pot of coffee.

Catalena did as she was told, and the eating began.

She was surprised at the amount of food it took to feed four men. They ate in silence, but Rob, Bob, and George's eyes keep straying from their food to her. She pretended not to notice, but now had a better idea why Mazy wasn't pleased at having her around. Mazy didn't want her causing problems with her sons. Catalena understood, but what could she do about it? She had no way of leaving and no money. She needed to get her memory back in a hurry.

"Mazy, girl, that was a mighty fine breakfast," Homer told her as he scooted his chair away from the table. "Hope you don't mind if we steal Lena away for a while. It'll give you a rest to get rid of us fellows."

"How long do you plan on being gone?" Mazy asked with a deep frown and puckered up mouth.

"Most all morning, probably. Lena will have to go slow. It's a hard climb all the way to the top of Nowhere."

"Not for me, but it's always a hard climb for the old man," George said with a chuckle.

"I'm not old," Homer was quick to say. "I've finally lived long enough to be wise. It has always been for the best not to wear yourself out when you don't have to."

"Some excuse is better than none, and you're a man who's full of excuses." George continued.

"Hush up," Mazy told her youngest son. "No need to get you and Homer started this early in the day. I get mighty tired of listening to the two of you day in and day out."

Homer's grin widened. "It's a shame that a man can't get any sort of respect around this place. Come on, Lena, honey. Let's get started. Who all is going with us?" He'd up and called her honey without intending to. Mazy had asked him to call her Lena, and, for goodness sake, to stop calling her honey. She claimed it was disrespectful to the girl. Homer didn't see how it was when most all the old folks called people honey.

All three boys stood up. Mazy was still frowning. "Don't you get her over-tired," Mazy warned. "Don't want her having a backset and being bedfast again."

"We'll look after her," Rob assured his mother, but his remark did not seem to ease Mazy's concern.

"If those Kormans show up, don't get into it with them," Mazy said.

"They won't show up," Bob told her.

"They better not if they know what's good for them," George bragged as he flexed the arm muscles.

"Okay, now, don't nobody need to fret about those Kormans. My guess is they'll be minding their own business for a while. Let's get going," Rob added.

Homer put his hand on Catalena's back and gently guided her from the dining room.

Once they were a good distance from the house and the possibility of Mazy overhearing, Catalena asked: "What did Mazy mean by not getting into it with the Kormans?"

"Nothing to concern yourself with," Homer assured her.

"There's times when they like to fight with folks," George told her. "But only when they find somebody alone. They always try to make sure they have the odds on their side."

"They don't normally pick a fight with us Barlows," Bob told her. "Having them trespassing on Barlow land is something we can't tolerate."

"They like to sneak around and do things to spite us," George added. "They're a bunch of sniveling, no account cowards."

"Now let's not talk about the Kormans. It's too nice a day, and it's Lena's first outing. We don't want to scare her or anything like that." Rob pointed out.

"I would like to hear about them," Catalena was quick to assure them. "You've already got my curiosity up. What is it about them that you dislike so much?"

"It's a long story, and like Rob said, there's no need to ruin your first outing. Say, did I ever tell you about the time . . ."

"Don't start that," Rob and Bob said at the same time, but George was grinning from ear to ear.

"I was only going to tell her about the dancing frog. If you three don't want to hear it, close your ear holes. Have you ever heard of a dancing frog before, honey, girl?" Homer asked.

"Can't say as I have," she returned with a grin.

"Well, down in town there's this bar a lot of men go to have them a snort or two. One day I was in there and this man came in carrying a canvas sack. I've never figured out if the fellow was broke, or just stingy. Anyway, he asked the bartender if he'd give him a free beer if he showed him a dancing frog. The bartender decides to go along with the man and agreed. The man took a frog out of his canvas sack and sure enough, the frog stood on its hind legs and started dancing a waltz while the man whistled a tune.

"That's amazing," says the bartender and pours him a free beer.

"After the man finished drinking the beer down, he asked, can I have another free beer if I show you something even more amazing?

"That I'll do," said the bartender.

"This time he took a tiny piano from his canvas sack and set the frog in front of it. Then he pulled out a little, white mouse. The frog danced up to the piano and started playing a tune on the tiny keys, and the mouse twitched his nose a time or two, and then started singing a song in a beautiful bass voice.

"A stranger in a suit was sitting nearby watching closely what was going on. After watching for a few minutes, he got really excited and rushed up to the man. "I'll give you a hundred-dollar bill if you'll sell me that piano, dancing frog, and singing mouse," he said as he laid out the money on the bar

"I sure could use the money," the fellow said. "But I could never bring myself to sell my frog and his little piano. Tell you what though, I'll sell you the white mouse for that hundred-dollar bill."

"The man gave him the money, put the mouse in his pocket, and rushed out of the bar.

"I can't believe you sold him your singing mouse," the bartender said. "You don't come across many talking mice much less one that can sing."

"No problem," said the man as he put the money, piano and frog back in canvas sack. My frog's a ventriloquist."

Catalena frowned for a moment, before she rolled her eyes and chuckled.

"That's one," Bob told Homer.

"He's only allowed three jokes a day," Rob explained to her. "If he starts on a fourth one, we all run off and leave him."

"They do not," George said. "Besides, at his age he can't remember more than one joke at a time."

The thought of running tugged at something inside of Catalena. She had the strangest urge to stretch her legs out until she felt the tension in them ease. She longed to feel the sweat soaking her clothes along with the burn of her muscles.

"How often do you run," she asked George.

"Every day. The coach has the team run for about an hour around the track, Some Saturdays he gets us together for cross country running. I run a lot around here too. It's a tougher workout than the coach will ever give us."

"He uses running as an excuse to get out of offbearing at the sawmill," Bob told her. "Our little brother has a soft streak."

"I do not," George defended himself. "I offbear those heavy, green slabs of wood, plus I left weights, too. Weights and offbearing builds muscles and strength."

"You need long, flexible muscles for running," Catalena said. "Massive muscling can slow you down." She looked George over. "You're muscled just about right. Strong, without an ounce of fat on your body."

She also felt that her own body was strong and without unnecessary fat, but in the huge, bulky dress she was wearing it would be difficult for anyone to tell. Still, muscle memory made her want to stretch her legs until they were limber and then start running. The continuous throbbing in her head kept her from trying.

"Do you remember driving up this narrow road?" Bob asked her.

She looked at the narrow dirt road they were walking on with trees surrounding it on both sides. "No, but it doesn't look like a dangerous road. It looks more like a nice walking path."

"I figure that's why you kept driving. We're still on the relatively flat, safe part of the road. The farther up this logging road you go, the more dangerous it becomes," Rob told her.

"I drove to the top?"

"That you did. At first, we weren't sure you were alone. When the ashes cooled down enough for us to check, we knew you were the only one in the Jeep," Bob assured her.

"And I was driving a Jeep?"

"Right. It appeared to be one of those Willys Jeeps. The kind they don't make anymore."

"If it had been one of the newer models, it would have been too big to drive far up this old logging road," Rob added to what Bob told her.

"Back years ago, when I was a young fellow, a lot of folks around these parts drove Willys Jeeps. Roads were so rough and narrow those Jeeps were about the only vehicles that could get around. Didn't cost much back then," Homer pointed out. "But cash money was hard to come by. Folks bartered and traded with each other. They had to work hard for what little they got."

"Uncle Homer had to walk uphill in the snow to and from school in summer and in winter," George said in a serious tone of voice.

Homer swung a backhanded swipe at him, but George dodged easily. "You boys got it easy these days and don't know it."

"That's what . . . . "Catalena begin, and then frowned as her mind went blank. "That's what a lot of people say," she added attempting to finish her sentence.

All four of the men caught her hesitation and saw the disappointment that showed on her face.

"See," Homer was quick to point out. "Your memory is starting to return already."

"I hope so. Not remembering is like . . . like never having been alive."

~~~~~

Catalena was surprised by the number of times she longed to stop and rest. Rob had certainly been right when he told her the logging road would get steeper, but it wasn't only the steepness that bothered her. It was the narrow width of the road and the horrible drop-off on the right-hand side of the cliff. Even the rocky, sheer cut of the bank on the left-hand side of the logging road bothered her.

"See that scrape mark on the rock along with a little black paint?" Rob asked her. "We figure that's where your mirror started scraping against the bank. Right up there is where it hit a protruding rock and broke. We picked up most of the glass, but you can still see a little of the fine glass sparkling in the dirt."

Catalena rubbed the toe of her shoe over the glittering on the ground and tried to remember the mirror breaking but couldn't. She could feel a fearful kind of coldness clotting in her chest, making it harder for her to breathe. Her memory might be gone, but she thought her instincts were still in working order, and her instincts were telling her to get away from that road. As they climbed higher, she found herself clinging to the left-hand bank while refusing to look down into the drop off on the right side. She had to force herself to keep going and thought talking might ease the horrible feeling of fear.

"My shoes," she suddenly said. "Were these the tennis shoes I was wearing when you found me?"

George shrugged. "I guess they are. I wasn't much concerned about your shoes."

"What kind of clothes was I wearing?" she continued to ask.

"Shorts and a tank top, I think. Do you remember Uncle Homer?" George asked.

"Not particularly," he said hesitantly, as though he was trying to think harder. "You were kind of dirty, scraped, and banged up. We were paying attention to your condition instead of what you were wearing. The one thing we did notice was that you weren't wearing a wedding ring, so we didn't think you were married and had a husband with you."

"No husband to be missing me," she said as she looked down at her left hand. Not everybody wore a wedding ring, but she didn't think she was married. She wasn't even sure she had ever been in love, at least not romantically. She looked at both Rob and Bob and tried to stir up some sort of feelings. They certainly were handsome men with their dark hair, mustaches, and twinkling eyes. There was also a savvy intelligence in those eyes, not to mention a body that would be the envy of any man.

Yes, she could see having romantic feeling for someone, even for one of these Barlow men. If she was going to pick one, which one would it be? Homer was far too old. Yet, there was something appealing about the older man. She concluded it was his caring nature, his knowing attitude about life, and yes, even his sense of humor appealed to her. Too bad she couldn't have met Homer when he was forty years younger. As for George, he reminded her the most of his uncle, but he was still a child. She could only imagine what time and maturity would do for him.

As for Rob and Bob, they were both in their youthful prime, perhaps a couple or three years older than her. The outdoor life of sawmill men had made them both as tough as rawhide, but there was still some type of something that was lacking in them both. It was as though it took them both put together to make one whole man. She supposed that came from being twins.

If she had to pick one of the twins, who would she pick? she asked herself as she tried to keep her mind off the steep cliff below the road where she was supposed to have wrecked her Jeep. To think of driving up this road was becoming too much for her to conceive.

Rob, she decided, trying to force herself to think of something other than the narrow logging road, wrecking her Jeep, and her memory loss. Bob seemed to be a little more of a perfectionist. He was the kind who insisted everything had to be the way he thought it should to be. Bob had no play, while Rob had a tiny bit of Homer and George's type of play in him.

"What's it like to be twins," she suddenly asked them.

"Tough," they both said at the same time.

"You always have someone who's your equal to compete with," Rob told her.

"And someone who does everything so much like you do that it's irritating," Bob added.

"But you're never alone," Catalena pointed out.

"Exactly," said both men.

"You get to see all your flaws in someone else," Rob added.

"And you seeing the mistakes the person who is most like you has made, makes it mighty hard to live with yourself," Bob was quick to point out.

"Tell her the truth," George said. "They've always taken advantage of being twins. They flaunt it all the time. Makes me mighty jealous at times. And then I realize it took two of them, but it only took one of me to become an example of pure perfection."

"He's trying to brag and failing miserably," Bob said.

"He's still mighty young," Rob said, as though he was trying to make an excuse for his little brother.

"He's trying to grow up as tough as both of them put together, which is a might big ambition," Homer added. "The Barlow men have always been a mighty hard endeavor to live up to."

"I'm a Barlow man," George said.

"That's almost a fact," the Barlow twins said at the same time.

Catalena found herself smiling, and it sure felt good.

"Tell us something about yourself?" Homer prodded.

Her smile faded. "I can tell you that I'm starting to get tired and may have to stop long enough to get my second wind. I can also tell you that I don't think having to stop and rest is normal behavior on my part. I feel as though I've been deprived of my normal activity."

"Lying in bed for as long as you have takes a physical toll on a person. You'll be over that feeling after you've been up and going a day or two," Homer assured her.

"I long to stretch my legs and run, but the feeling is in my mind and not in my body."

"Good," George was quick to say. "I'd like nothing better than to have a running partner."

"Offbearing lumber ought to be enough exercise for you," Bob was quick to tell him.

"Offbearing builds muscles," George pointed out with a grin. "Running expands your lung capacity, builds endurance, stretches muscles and makes you more limber, not to mention more intelligent and better looking."

George's comment about running was familiar to her. Either someone said those words to her often or she had said them herself. A strong longing to run came over her again, but she remained silent. She was needing all the oxygen she could get to keep up with Homer.

"We can outrun you any day," Rob told his younger brother.

"No way," George returned.

"Without a doubt," Bob added.

George grinned and shook his head. "Put your money where your mouth is and put a dollar on it. Let's run to the top of Nowhere and see who wins. The winner gets the three dollars."

"Don't want to run off and leave Lena," Bob told him.

"Wouldn't be respectful," Rob added.

"Go ahead," Catalena encouraged, longing to slow down the pace the three young men has set. She was discovering determination alone were no match for a weakened body. Her pride was making her walk faster up the steep incline than she was physically capable of doing for much longer.

"Her and Uncle Homer can take their time catching up. We'll wait for them on top," George challenged with a toothy grin on his handsome, young face.

Neither twin responded.

"I'll even give you both a head start," he taunted. "Don't want to show you both up too badly. Can't stand the thought that I'm tougher and faster than you both, can you?"

Both twins hollered "GO!"

She and Homer chuckled as they watched them race each other. Rob and Bob altered back and forth at being in the lead.

"They'll out distance him in the short run, but George will pass them up from endurance training. The boys are sprinters. Their muscles and weight will hold them back. They're strong as a team of oxen, but not used to distance running. They'll tire out and be huffing and puffing about the time George gets his second wind."

Catalena could relate to that. "I'm already huffing and puffing, I didn't realize how weak I actually am." She didn't mind admitting her weakness to Homer the way she would in front of the healthy young men. It must say something about her pride.

"Do you want to stop and rest a while? If you do, I won't mind. This danged old leg gives me a fit."

She wanted to slow down and rest, but her obstinate pride refused to let her admit it – even with Homer.

"No, let's just slow down a little. This road is getting steep."

"Sure is, and it will get steeper the farther along we go. I usually have to stop and rest this leg of mine right often, even when the going isn't this steep."

Catalena was amazed at the unbelievable steepness of the narrow road. She didn't like what she was seeing. It made her legs want to tremble.

"Are you sure I drove up this road? Just thinking about driving it scares me. Somehow it just feels so wrong that I drove on this road."

"Yeah, we're sure. The boys searched for sign of another person. They would have found it if you hadn't been alone."

"Could someone have burned up? From what you've told me, the fire was terribly hot." And what if they had? How could she live with knowing someone was killed, someone she probably loved dearly? Perhaps that was why she couldn't remember. Trauma of loss could do strange things to a person – including taking away their memory.

"Nobody burned."

"How do you know for sure?"

"Several ways. The ashes would have been greasy. The boys put samples of the ashes in water and there were no grease bubbles floating up. Grease is lighter than water. It will float on top. There would also have been teeth and bone particles in the ashes, which there weren't. Plus, there was no smell of burning flesh. As you might have noticed, Bob doesn't have as full a head of hair as Rob. He singed his hair, along with his eyebrows and eyelashes while making sure nobody was in the burning Jeep."

"I hadn't noticed," she admitted. "He didn't get burned or anything, did he?"

"Nope. Bob is the kind that likes to get as close to the danger as possible. He thinks his determination can change the impossible."

"And Rob?"

"He's more level-headed. He'll stand back and study a situation before he jumps in with both feet. As for George, he's still a growing boy, but he seems to be somewhat on the level-headed side with a better sense of humor than his brothers."

She could tell he had a preference for George. That was surely why he spent so much time with the boy.

"Talking about level-headed. You had nerves of steel to drive around this bend in the road. If you'll look, you can still see your tire tracks right there in the loose dirt near the edge of the cliff."

Catalena looked. Tire tracks were mere inches from the cliff's edge. She shook her head and moved away from the drop off as far as possible.

"The boys tracked your footprints the rest of the way to the top. It appeared you stomped down rag weeds before you made your way back to your Jeep."

"I'm not sure I want to continue to the top of the mountain," she told him in a shaky voice. "I don't believe I'm ready for any more of this."

Homer gave her an encouraging smile along with a pat on the arm. "Of course, you're ready. I'm sure you've heard the old saying if you fall off a horse you best get right back up on it. In other words, face your fears and don't let them control you."

That advice sounded familiar, but her mind wouldn't tell her who had said those words to her before.

"If you don't mind me saying so, I'm thinking there had to be a mighty big reason for a girl like you to be driving a Jeep up our old rough road. The right fork leads to our place and the left fork goes to the Kormans' or Hordly's place."

"I must have taken a wrong turn," she told him what seemed logical.

"Folks don't often take a wrong turn onto a road like ours."

"How long have the people lived here?

"A mighty long time. Folks around here don't often sell their land. Only the Hordlys are somewhat newcomers. They bought Gertie Lee's place. The old woman who owned it moved away and ended up selling her land to them several years ago. Never would have thought Gertie Lee would have sold her land. Never thought she'd move away from these mountains, either. Reckon the freezing cold winters finally got to her rheumatism. Mine acts up a sight when the weather turns bad. Anyway, I'm thinking you were trying to drive over the mountain, made a wrong turn, and ended up on this logging road. My question is what brought a girl like you to this neck of the woods in the first place."

"A girl like me?" she questioned Homer's statement, not sure she liked the implication.

"Unless I miss my guess, you're more citified than countryfied."

She detected no intended insult to his words. "I think so, too," she agreed after she thought about it. "And yet, something seems familiar, although I'm sure I've never been here before."

"See, your memory is coming back, because you're thinking about familiar things. As soon as that knot on your head goes down, you'll be your old self," Homer tried to reassure her.

"Uncle Homer?" she said a little hesitantly, using the term uncle the way George often did. "Can I ask you something?"

"That you can."

"I know you don't want to talk about it, but what is it about the Kormans? Every time their name is mentioned Mazy gets upset and the boys' eyes get as hard as glass."

"Well now, you see, Mazy is a mighty religious woman. Reads her Bible and believes everything it says. It appears those Kormans do the opposite of what Mazy believes in."

"Such as?" she questioned when he hesitated to say more.

"Don't mean to talk too bad about anybody, but they don't go by the Golden Rule or any other biblical rule. But then you'll find people who are good, bad, and worse no matter where you go."

"Around here are the Kormans the worst?"

"Don't know exactly how to answer that other than say Kormans run a close second to the Hordlys and Raineys. But, then again, it seems there's times when good folks can be bad and bad folks can be good. It pays a body not to judge others too harshly."

She wasn't at all satisfied with what he told her. "What do the Barlows and the Kormans get into it about?" As for the Hordlys, she hadn't heard the Barlows talk much about them.

"Ah, well now, Mazy don't like it when folks get into a racket. Don't worry your head none. Mazy likes to worry over her family. Thinks worrying keeps them safe. Look down in the valley there. That valley is only a part of Barlow land," he said proudly.

"It's beautiful, but I'd rather not get close to the edge," she answered.

It didn't take her memory to realize Homer was avoiding answering her questions. She asked nothing else about the Kormans.

The rest of the trip to the top of the mountain was slow for them both, but they made it without her screaming in fear every time she glanced at the gorge down below.

When they got to the end of the road, the twins and George were waiting for them.

"Look down there at that ledge, George said with pride. "That's the place I rescued you from."

Catalena looked and wished she hadn't. She felt her stomach knot up and her heart race. A light headedness came over her causing her legs to wobble. It was Rob who grabbed hold of her and steadied her against his chest. She could feel his body's warmth through their clothes and welcomed it. Looking over the edge had made her feel like she'd been dipped in ice water.

"Easy does it," Rob's voice soothed near her ear. "You're all right. I've got you. You're not going to fall. I'll keep you safe."

Bob shook his head and frowned. "You've got to be a flat lander," Bob pointed out. "Not used to heights, I'd say."

"I , , , I . . ." she mumbled and then realized she didn't know what she was about to say.

"Can you stand on your own? If you can walk, I'm going to move you underneath the shade of that tree," Rob told her. "You're sweating but your skin is covered in chill bumps. Mom might have been right. Walking up this mountain could be too hard on you this soon."

"I'm okay," she mumbled. "Just give me a minute," she assured him, but she clung to his strong arms as he moved her several feet up the hill away from the spot where her Jeep had tumbled.

None of the laid rocks were there now. The Kormans had returned to push every loose rock down the cliff, but the ground was still slightly scuffed up where they had returned to make sure no signs of their deadfall of rocks remained.

"I can't believe I drove a Jeep over the edge," she did her best to keep her voice from shaking.

"I wouldn't say you drove it over the edge. From the looks of the ground, you were trying to turn around and the weight of your Jeep caused a rock slide," Rob told her. "With the loose rocks there, it didn't look as dangerous as it does now."

His intended comfort words didn't help her in the least.

"How's your memory?" George asked with boyish optimism. "Don't hardly see how anybody could forget tumbling toward that gully. If you ask me, something such as that would make a lasting impression."

Catalena felt her stomach heave as another surge of pure terror hit. Her mind did not remember, but her body surely did.

"I had to think I was dead," she managed to say. "Can we please leave."

"Are you up to walking?" Homer asked.

"I'd crawl to get away from here," she said, still clinging to Rob's arm.

Chapter 13

"**D**id you get a good look at that piece of ass?" Alvin Korman said to his brother Kimbell once the Barlows were long gone from the top of the mountain. They'd been searching the area in hopes of finding a little weed their pa had overlooked. Their pa had made them sell every single bit of what they'd grown and now they were feeling deprived and badly in need of a hit. Their pa didn't want to leave any leftovers behind on top of the mountain in case the law showed up. They'd even harvested the small stuff they had growing on Barlow property. They'd learned it was best to grow their weed in containers hidden in patches of giant ragweed. That way they were camouflaged, plus it could be moved in a hurry.

They'd warned the Hordlys about the possibility of the law showing up, but that Nickel Hordly was as hardheaded as his brother-in-law, Enrick Rainey. He didn't think the law would believe a crippled old man in a wheelchair would be growing weed and making meth. Alvin knew for a fact that was how the Hordlys got the wealth they thought entitled them to lord it over folks.

Alvin prided himself on being the intelligent one in the family. He'd kept an eye on the construction when Rainey and some of his buddies built a garage. It had a deep basement below the floor with a whole lot of overhead lights down in that hole. The planks underneath his feet felt too warm when he walked across the garage floor, which wasn't often. The Hordlys kept the garage doors locked. He'd picked the lock and sneaked into the garage one time when all the Hordlys were away from home. There was something down there heating the area. Alvin knew it was a sure sign strong lights were burning for a reason, and he knew the reason.

He had no doubt the heat came from grow lights. He wanted to sneak down there and get a better look, but he couldn't find the blasted entry. They'd done a right good job of hiding how to get down into that garage basement. Of course, he could have found it if he'd dared turn on the light and had a little more time to search.

He'd left Kimbell way down at the other end of the road with that old car horn they'd ten-fingered from some old man the last time they had gone into town. That old man didn't need that horn. It was out behind the man's shop and wasn't exactly being used. Kimbell had taken a shine to it. He liked things that made loud noises. He also liked taking things that belonged to other people. Alvin, his father, and his brothers felt the same way about ten-fingering things. They were just evening things up a bit. Folks had no business owning things the Kormans coveted.

He'd told Kimbell to lay on that horn if he saw a Hordly or Rainey returning. And he did. Alvin had gotten his hind end out of that garage in a hurry. Enrick Rainey was a mean devil, even meaner than those Hordlys. But Alvin wasn't worried, much. He had plans for Enrick just as soon as he could figure out a few things.

Today they'd been lucky enough to hear the Barlow boys racing up the logging road and hid in the same laurel hell they'd hid in with their brother and dad after that girl's Jeep had gone over the cliff.

"I sure enough got both eyes full of her. That's why I'm slobbering like a starved to death dog. My toes plum done curled up with want-to." Kimbell said with a twist to his mouth as he spit out particles of dead leaves. "Liked what I seen, too. Mighty glad the likes of that didn't get burned up."

Alvin gave his shoulder a shove. "Hands off, dummy. I saw her first, so I get first dibs on her."

"Hold on a minute, Alvin," Kimbell caught his balance and then drawled in his slow voice. "Seems to me we ought to share her fair and square. Besides, Pa done told you I hain't no dummy, so stop calling me that."

"Pa says a lot of things that hain't true, and you know it."

"I aim to tell Pa on you for calling him a liar. He'll give you a floggin' for certain for bad mouthin' him like you done."

"You hain't tellin' nobody nothing. If you do, I'll teach you what for, plus tell Pa what you've been doing to Jeanene."

Kimbell's fat lips went into a pout. "I don't do nothin' to her."

"Do too. I've watched you."

"Didn't do nothing you hain't done to Bendy."

"Bendy hain't little," Alvin told him. "Anyway, we'd best forget about squealin' on each other and go let Pa know we done set eyes on that girl."

"You gonna tell him how pretty she is?"

"Don't matter how pretty she is. What matters is who she is and if she goes to the law."

"Can't prove nothin' on us," Kimbell whined as though he was afraid someone might do exactly that.

"Reckon they can't, but you can never tell. Georgie boy and that old man got a good look afore we pushed those rocks down the cliff."

"They hain't never squealed on us afore. 'Sides, the trap was set on Barlow land not ours. They're the ones who'll get the blame."

"That girl might do some powerful squealing, She can't be one bit happy about her Jeep burning up."

She'll rack up on the insurance money for certain and sure. That ought to be enough to satisfy her."

"What had we ought to do?" Kimbell frowned in puzzlement. His round, pudgy face was greasy with sweat.

"Don't rightly know, but Pa will know what to do."

The boys didn't bother brushing the dirt and dead leaves off before they hurried down the back side of the mountain toward home. They figured they were running fast enough for the woods' trash to fall off.

Chapter 14

~~~~

Catalena felt like screaming to the high heavens. She wanted to beat and flail her own head until it told her who she was and what she was doing in this place. With each step she took her head throbbed. It felt as if a jackhammer was living inside her skull banging on tender flesh in hopes of forcing its way out of confinement. *It's my memory*, she told herself. Her memory was trying to throb its way to the surface. Instead, it had become trapped, unable to free itself. Her chest tightened up until it felt as though it couldn't possibly draw in another breath of air, while she had to force her legs to take another step. At least she was thankful she was now walking down hill instead of climbing up the steep logging road.

She drew in a deep breath of air in attempting to gain more strength, more determination.

"Want to stop for a minute?" Rob asked as he placed his hand on her back.

The warmth of his hand felt good. It also surprised her to realize how close Rob was standing next to her. He'd been gauging his steps with hers, and she hadn't even noticed until now.

"I'm okay," she answered.

"You might be, but I'm not," Homer stated firmly. "My old legs find it just as difficult to walk downhill as to walk uphill. See that rock right there beside the road? That's the exact spot where George had to sit down and rest a spell when he carried you home. Sit yourself down there, Lena, and see what happens. Who knows, it might strike a memory."

Catalena saw Rob look at his uncle and tried not to grin. Homer had trouble walking on level ground, but he also had too much pride to admit it. He was obviously trying to give her an excuse to rest – as well as himself.

"Maybe just for a minute," she said, as she allowed the hand on her back to guide her toward the rock. She eased herself down, trying not to jar her aching head.

Bob and George, who were a good distance ahead of the others, stopped and came back.

"Want me to carry you?" George asked with a twinkle in his eyes. "I can do it again if you want me to. You're not heavy in the least," George bragged. "You're not nearly as heavy as a couple sacks of cow feed."

"Thanks, but I'm okay." One thing she didn't want was to be carried or catered to in any way. The very thought of such was an insult to her capabilities.

"We're taking our time and enjoying ourselves. You boys go on ahead. Lena and I are in no hurry. We've got all day to mosey around in," Homer told them.

"Seems good to take a little time off from work," Rob admitted. "I'm in no hurry to get back at it."

Bob gave his twin brother an irritated look. "Fact is the less we do today, the more we'll have to do come Monday."

Homer wiggled his lips in an attempt not to grin. It was obvious Bob didn't like the attention his twin was giving the girl.

Homer turned to Catalena. "Let me tell you a story while we rest up a bit," Homer said. "The day after God created Adam and Eve and placed them in the Garden of Eden, he looked around and decided he needed to create some animals. So, he created a cow.

He ordered her to go into the fields and eat grass all day. The cow realized she would be the servant of the farmer, have to suffer under the sun all day, give birth to calves, and give milk to support the farmer. I'll give you a life span of sixty years God told the cow.

"The cow thought about it and said 'that's kind of a tough life to live for sixty years. Only give me twenty.' So, God agreed.

"On the second day God created the monkey. God said, 'Entertain people, do monkey tricks, make them laugh. I'll give you a twenty-year life span,' Monkey said, 'How boring. Doing monkey tricks for twenty years? I don't think so. I'll agree to entertain people for ten years. And God agreed again.

"On the third day, God create a dog to sit all day by the door of his master's house and bark if any stranger comes about. He told the dog he could have a life span of twenty years to serve his master. The dog thought about it and said, 'That's too long to sit at a door and bark. Give me ten years.' So, God agreed.

"On the fourth day God created man and said, 'you have twenty years of life to do nothing but eat, drink, sleep, play and have a good time. 'What?' said man. 'I only get twenty years? The cow gave you back forty years, the dog gave back ten, and so did the monkey. How about letting me have all those years they didn't want? I'll take the total eighty years.' So, God agreed.

"And that's why man does nothing for his first twenty years other than eat, sleep, play and enjoy life. For the next forty years he slaves in the sun to support his family. And then for the next ten years, man does monkey tricks to entertain grandchildren. For the last ten, he sits by his door and barks at everybody that comes along."

The boys moaned and shook their heads. Catalena smiled.

"When you get tired of listening to him run his mouth, you'll have to tell him to shut up," Rob told her.

"I like his stories," Catalena defended him.

"You wouldn't if you'd heard them as many times as we have."

"You haven't heard that one before. I just made it up while I was sitting here," Homer said triumphantly.

"I'm sure you realize he's in the last stage where all he does is sit at the door and bark," Rob added.

"And all you and your brothers do is play."

"George and Lena maybe, but Bob and I are in that cow stage."

"Don't think so," Catalena said. "I think I'm in the cow stage too."

"You don't look it," Rob told her.

"What makes you think that?" Homer eyed her closely.

"I don't know. I just feel old."

"No wonder, but it's not old you're feeling. It's exhaustion. Mom was right. We shouldn't have taken you up the mountain this soon. You're still weak," Rob said as he took in her pale face along with a fine mist of sweat on her upper lip.

"I can't lie in bed and do nothing. I don't think that is good for me. What I need is my memory back and I don't know how to get it." She didn't tell him she thought she should see a doctor, someone who was a specialist on head injuries and memory loss. She would seek out professional help herself if she knew where to go and how to get there. Until that time came, or her memory returned, she realized she was stuck right here accepting the care of the Barlows. At least, she believed what they were telling her about the accident. The goat-path of a road brought back strong feelings. The drop-off caused far worse anxiety.

"Would you take me to see where my Jeep burned?" she asked Rob.

"I will, but not today."

"Why not?" she didn't intend to sound peevish, but impatience came easily.

"We want you well as soon as possible," Rob told her.

"It's our job to take care of you?" Homer added.

Catalena didn't argue, but she wanted to.

Chapter 15

~~~~

"**I**djets!" Old man Markum slapped them both up the side of their heads. "I done told you to stay away from there. Don't want nobody seeing us up there on that mountain. If the law shows up, they can blame everything on them Barlows. It's their land."

"But . . ." Alvin begin.

"Don't you give me none of your buts, boy. I done told you them Hordlys are figurin' out how to work things. That crazy fart claims to be some big wig lawyer. Ask me, he's all brag and no brains."

"Why should we let 'em have their way?"

"So they'll get the blame, that's why."

"What blame?" Alvin asked.

"Idjet! The blame for anything that goes wrong."

"Since he's one of them lawyers won't he figure out how to blame things on us?"

"No doubt he'll try, but ole Markum hain't stupid. I know what I'm doin'."

"Can I have the girl?" Kimbell made a point of asking his pa before Alvin could. It changed his trail of thought instantly.

"Hell, boy. What you talkin' about?"

"I want her, Pa," Kimbell whined. "In the worst sorta way."

Markum swatted the back of his head. "If your brain was gunpowder, you couldn't blow a fart. Don't you never get close enough to that gal for her to set eyes on you. When the worst

sorta way hits, use your own two hands. Do you hear me, boy?"
Markum grabbed hold of his ear and gave it a hard yank.

"Yeah, Pa. I done heard you good and plenty," he said as
the pain brought tears to his eyes.

"Then you best mind me, or else."

Neither of the boys wanted to receive an *or else* from their
pa.

~~~~

Kimbell couldn't stop thinking about the girl who had
wrecked. She was the most tempting hunk of flesh he'd ever
set his two eyes on. Just imagining what her smooth skin would
feel like pressed against him was almost more than he could
endure. Anger flashed inside his head as he thought about that
know-it-all George carrying her all the way down that road. It
ought to have been him who found her. He started breathing
hard as he thought about what he'd have done with her. It
wasn't fair those no-account Barlows had all the good luck.

Alvin had told him the girl made him slobber like a starved
dog. Well, she made Kimbell ache all over like a case of the
bad flu. Hell fire, it was worse than having a case of the pukin',
runnin' off flu. The looks of that girl tormented his every
moment. He dreamed about her when he was asleep as well as
when he was awake.

His pa claimed God made a man to feel the things he was
feeling, otherwise he wouldn't be feeling them. Therefore, a
man was entitled to get relief wherever he found it. His pa said
those words came straight out of the Bible. He said women
were made out of a man's rib, which meant a man owned a
woman the same as he owned his own body. A man had the
right to do whatever he wanted with his own body.

His pa's warning to stay away from her along with his need
to see her again were having a fight inside his brain. He
recalled what his Pa had said. *Don't you never get close enough
to that gal for her to set eyes on you.* His Pa hadn't said that he

couldn't get close enough to *set his eyes on her*. Kimbell grew extra happy as his troubled thoughts left him. He knew exactly what he was going to do as soon as the opportunity showed itself – and he sure enough looked forward to it.

~~~~

"Get your fat ass outta bed," Markum yelled as he kicked Kimbell in the hind end with his dirty boot.

Kimbell scooted against the wall to get out of his pa's kicking reach.

"I'm sick, Pa. Got the belly ache mighty bad. Musta been them green apples I ate," Kimbell told a bald-face lie. He'd learned his lesson about eating green apples a long time before then. "I done got them Tennessee trots," he whined pitifully.

"Don't matter. You can shit in the woods. We gotta move some produce deeper into government land. Damn those do-goodin' Barlows. No tellin' what they'll do. Can't take a chance on leaving things where they are. Never know when the law might take a notion to snoop around. Damn that gal and her Jeep. She might even be the law for all we know."

Kimbell groaned as he rolled out of bed and made a point of letting off gas. His pa put his hand over his nose.

"Cut that fartin' crap out. You're stinking up the whole house. Get a move on. Don't have time to waste on the likes of your sorry ass," he yelled as he left the room

Kimbell lifted his middle finger when his dad turned his back. He didn't have to waste time putting on his clothes. He'd slept in them as usual, much to his ma's dislike. No reason for her to bitch at him about sleeping in his dirty clothes. She'd wash the sheets monthly regardless if they needed it or not.

He wandered into the kitchen to find out what cold breakfast might be left over. He couldn't get enough food to eat regardless of how much he stuffed in his mouth, and it was showing all over his body.

"Ha, Maw, I'm starved near to death," he called out as his mother came through the kitchen door from the outside carrying a bucket of water. "It's your place to feed me, he told her. You're my maw and you're supposed to take care of your baby boy."

His maw didn't bother to glance his way. "Breakfast's been over hours ago. Gotta get your sorry hind end outta bed early if you wanta eat before the others get at it."

"Damn your mangy hide, Kim-ball," his pa called him a name he meant as an insult. "Get your fat ass a movin'," Markum yelled from the back yard. "Else I'll come back in there and move it for you."

Kimbell grabbed a cold chunk of pone bread off the back of the stove and rubbed it in the congealed hog grease still in the skillet from where his mother, Letty, had fried eggs that morning. How he would have loved to have him four fried eggs, a big slab of side meat, and hot pone bread, but it was too late. He had to settle for what he could get and raced to try and keep up with his pa and Alvin, else his pa would give him a belt licking. Kimbell was getting mighty tired of his pa giving him a licking all the time. He considered himself a man. He already weighed more than his pa and Alvin, but that didn't make no never-mind. He was treated like a twelve-year-old kid instead of being nineteen, and he was getting sick and tired of such disrespect.

Markum had rigged a halter like contraption out of rope that fit over the back and front of him and his boys. It consisted of fourteen round loops that pots could fit in and be carried while being moved from one place to another. The only drawback was the plants had to be small. If they were tall, there was more of a chance they would get broken. Markum didn't dare use a wheelbarrow because it would leave tracks that were easier to follow than their footsteps.

"You boys walk careful," Markum fussed at them. "Break one of my plants and I'll take it out of your hides."

Both boys knew their pa meant it too. He used any excuse he could to give them a beating.

"I'm fed up with his shit," Alvin whispered to Kimbell when their pa walked out of hearing distance.

"Me too," Kimbell whispered back.

"I'm gonna do something about it."

"Such as?"

"I'm gonna join the army."

"The hell you say?" Kimbell said in disbelief.

"Can't be no worse than this," he whispered a little louder, which brought his pa rushing to them.

"Hesh up that mouthin'. Don't make another sound. You hear me?" he took a swipe at the boys. Alvin gritted his teeth and Kimbell cringed in hopes Markum wouldn't smack their heads a second time. "Sound carries on the wind and this here is a silent operation."

Chapter 16

~~~~

Catalena was restless. Another week had passed without her memory improving. She might not know her name or why she was there, but she knew there had to be a strong reason for her being in a remote place such as this to begin with. Ending up in these backwoods wasn't the result of a little afternoon trek in the mountains. She had surely come here on purpose.

What was that intention? If only she could remember.

"You're sure enough in deep thought," Rob said as he sat down on the porch beside her.

"Trying to make myself remember," she tried to smile, but it only added to her sad look. "Where's your twin brother?"

"He's out back in the Johnny house. I've been begging Mom to let us build a room onto the house and put in a bathroom. She's against it."

"Why would she be against it? I would think she'd welcome such a convenience."

"Mom doesn't want one thing changed from when Dad was alive. She's afraid change would wipe out some of his memory. She still wears the same clothes he liked, cooks his favorite foods. Has his clothes hanging in her closet. When she goes to bed at night, I hear her talking to him. She always whispers, thinking we can't hear."

"That doesn't sound healthy," Catalena couldn't help saying.

"Don't think healthy has anything to do with it. She simply can't let him go, so she keeps him with her in the only way she knows how. To my way of thinking, it shows a love so great that nothing can replace it."

To Catalena's way of thinking it showed a woman who wasn't willing to let go of the past in order to have a better future. She didn't share the thought with Rob.

"Why haven't you and your brother gotten married and built houses of your own?" she surprised herself by asking.

"You just stated the reason," he told her.

She gave him a questioning look.

"You said you and your brother. You didn't say you."

"What kind of answer is that?"

"We're twins. Folks don't see us as two separate people. The two of us are one."

"In other words, you're married to each other."

"I wouldn't go that far," Rob pushed his hat back on his head. "We've been with each other since the day we were conceived. It would be difficult if one of us fell in love and got married without the other one doing the same thing at the same time."

"Sounds like you're putting limits on yourselves that may never be met."

"It's difficult to split something in half and have two wholes."

"Do you ever want to try it?"

"Sometimes I'll see something I want and know I couldn't share it with Bob, so I'll make no attempt to get it. Know what I mean?"

"Not exactly."

"Let me just say, I wish you had a twin."

Catalena frowned, "Why?"

Rob lifted his brows and grinned. "I'll let you figure that out," he said as he saw Bob coming around the corner of the house.

"Let's get to work, baby brother. Time's a wastin'."

Bob gave his brother an irritated look, nodded his head toward Catalena and headed toward the truck a step behind his twin.

The truck had barely driven out of sight when George sat down beside her.

"Good morning," he said as though seeing her made the morning great.

She gave him a genuine smile. There was something about him that portrayed a light-hearted happiness.

"Good morning, George. Why aren't you in school?"

"It's Saturday. Uncle Homer says we're going into town today, so I'm not going to the sawmill with my brothers. Talking about my brothers, I overheard Rob making a play for you."

"He did not," she was quick to say.

He gave her his delighted laugh. "Won't do him any good. I've already told them I get first dibs on you."

Catalena didn't like that comment.

"Now, don't pucker up sour. I don't mean it literally. To be honest, you're too old for me."

She was still frowning.

"Don't take that literally either. What I mean is that I'm still a growing boy, while you're a beautiful grown woman."

Her frown lessened a little.

"You see, I'm the one who saved you. I'm sure not going to let my big brothers get in a fuss over you. So, if it's alright with you, I'm claiming first dibs."

Catalena didn't know what to say to a comment such as that. She wasn't up for dibs for anyone, especially when she was feeling helpless and ill at ease.

"Cat got your tongue?" George questioned her.

"You're a sweet and observant boy," was all she could think to say.

"Dang, that hurt. I was trying to be a brilliant and handsome man," he laughed again.

"Give yourself time," she was quick to return. "You might get there someday."

Homer came into the yard carrying two five-gallon buckets filled to overflowing with apples and sat them on the porch beside her.

"Mazy wants to can apples today. George and I have to go into town to get him a new pair of running shoes. He's worn holes in the bottom of his old ones. Reckon you'll be right busy with them apples."

She watched as Homer and George headed toward Homer's place. She wished she could go with them, but she owed Mazy for letting her stay there, plus taking care of her when she was unconscious. Maybe if she went into town, saw places she'd seen before, her memory would return. Somehow, someway, she had to return back to her normal self. She was certain she had never spent her previous life peeling apples.

Mazy came out onto the porch with pans and two knives. "Noticed how fast those men cleared out when there were apples to be peeled, didn't you?"

"Yes, I noticed," Catalena said with a grin as she took the knife and started peeling apples. "It would appear the male species have special privileges."

"My girls used to claim the same thing. Oh my, the jars we used to put up when my girls were home. Having girls to help made my work a lot easier."

"How many daughters did you say you have. I can't remember if you told me or not. My memory is a little faulty lately." Catalena intended to add a little humor, but Mazy took her comment seriously.

"Three. The oldest is Mary Ann, then Lily, and the youngest is Willa. The twins are my oldest and George is my youngest, but then you already know that. All my girls married early on. Marrying is about the only thing a girl can do here in these mountains. They have to move away if they want to find a good job at a factory or some kind of business. I'd rather they marry young than do that."

"Do they live close by?" Catalena thought Mazy had told her a little about her daughters, but she remembered little about them.

"No, not very close. Their husbands had to move away to find work."

And it made a difference if her daughters moved away to find a job, but it was okay if they moved away so their husbands could find a job? Catalena chose not to state what she was thinking.

"If they moved away after they were married, they weren't all alone. They had a husband to look after them," Mazy answered Catalena's question without being asked.

Catalena was almost keeping up peeling apple for apple with Mazy, but Mazy was talking, which might have slowed her down a little.

"Rob and Bob have never been too interested in marrying. Not that they haven't courted girls, mind you. I reckon they will end up married someday, but their wives would have to be mighty understanding. I'm afraid the twin bond could be stronger than the husband and wife bond. Now take George, he's bound and determined to go to college. Homer has been a big influence on him. Folks here about don't go to college. They're lucky if they finish high school."

"Why is that?"

"What good is a fancy education to folks here in these mountains? Teachers are the highest paid of anybody around here, except for those doctors over at the hospital. Can't nobody afford to go to them. They're downright rich compared to most folks."

"The children have no ambition to become teachers or doctors?" Catalena wanted to know.

"Only the teacher's children become teachers. Only doctor's children become doctors."

Catalena thought that was a feudal concept.

"Folks ought not to expect to get above their raising." Mazy said. "Did you get above your raising?"

"Wish I knew," Catalena told her.

"You appear to be of an upper class," Mazy told her.

"How can you tell?"

"You remind me a lot of those Hordlys"

"I hardly think that's a compliment."

"I meant no disrespect. I meant in the way you talk, and your level of education."

"Uncle Homer doesn't have a very high opinion of them."

"I believe in a rule Homer refuses to follow. I believe if you can't say something good about anybody, don't say nothing at all. I'm afraid I don't always follow it as much as I'd like. Especially where those Kormans are concerned."

"There is such a thing as telling the truth," Catalena couldn't resist saying.

"Just because something is true, doesn't mean you have to tell it."

"You've got a point," Catalena admitted.

"I'm trying my best not to say anything bad about those Kormans. The good Lord knows they've not had much of a chance at life. Who your parents are, and who you marry makes all the difference in a person's life."

Catalena didn't need her memory to agree with that.

"I'll warn you again, to stay away from them. I knew better than to allow my own children to be around them. I hope you listen to good advice."

"What about the Hordlys? Got any good advice about them?"

"Don't know 'em much. They hang with those Kormans a right smart. I'll say it again, it was a bad day when Gertie Lee sold that land to folks like that. I reckon her mind grew slack with age after she moved down to that hot country. That's where she met them, you know."

"Where did Gertie Lee move to?"

"Out in Texas somewhere. It was her daughter's idea. Bought her one of them condo things in a fancy retirement place. I went to school with her girl, Morene. I have to say that girl had ideas like nobody around here had. She had the drive and the ambition to go places, and none of those places was around here."

"Did she become a teacher or a doctor?" Catalena couldn't resist asking.

"No. Neither of those. She had looks and brains. She was mighty pretty, Lordy was she pretty. Your looks remind me of hers in a way. You're got darker hair and complexion than she had. Anyway, there was talk about some rich man buying a whole entire mountain in another county over from here. The word rich got Morene's attention. She got herself hired as something or other over at that rich man's house. She met a man at that place and married up with him. I heard he owned half of all creation. Oil wells in Texas, sawmills in South America, hospitals, hotels, and the likes.

"Gertie Lee was still living up here in these hills. She had a coal stove to heat with and a woodstove to cook on. She had chickens for eggs, and a milk cow for milk, and a garden to grow her food in. She had a good life if you ask me, but Morene didn't think so. She wouldn't give in until Gertie Lee up and moved away for here. Don't know what happened to her after that. Morene never came back once she left here. Sent one of them fancy cars with a driver to take Gertie Lee away from the only home she'd ever known."

"What about Gertie Lee's husband?"

"He died when Morene was little. That's one of the reasons they were on the poor side of life. It's hard for a woman to do everything by herself. Gertie Lee never married again. Survived all on her own. Hurt Morene's pride it did. Being the poorest and the richest in a place does something to people. Both conditions will make 'em or break 'em."

"Did Morene have children?"

"Don't know. All I ever knew about Morene was what Gertie Lee told me, and she wasn't much of a talker. I do know Gertie Lee watched after Morene like a hawk. She made sure those Kormans never got close Morene, same as my mother did with me, and I did with my girls."

"Why was that?"

"Don't like to talk about nobody, so I'll just say they didn't have the morals they needed to be Christian folks."

Chapter 17

~~~~

Mazy and Catalena had the apples canned by the time Homer and George got back home. They were both grinning like opossums who had just gorged on sweet, ripe persimmons. They had two small boxes of Stover's candy, one for Mazy and one for Catalena.

"What did you two do that you're afraid I'll find out about?" Mazy demanded when they handed her candy.

"Not a thing," Homer assured her. "We were just feeling generous."

"Foolish to waste your money on a thing like candy," Mazy told them. "Next time you're feeling guilty, bring me home a broom or a mop. Something that will last a while and I won't have to share with anybody."

George strutted around for a while. Pleased with himself for the candy, until Rob and Bob got home right before supper at their usual time. Both twins got out of the truck with a big grin on their faces. Bob's face was a little less happy. Rob was carrying something in his arms.

"Lena," he called out as his feet hit the front porch. "Come out here."

Never had Rob ever called out to her before. She and Mazy both came running out onto the porch.

"Good Lordy, Rob. What were you thinking?" Mazy told her oldest son.

"Brought something for Lena to pet," he said, showing a with-toothed grin.

"Oh," Catalena said as she held out her hands to take it. "How cute."

"A baby groundhog, Rob. Are you out of your mind?" Mazy continued.

"Nope. You and I both know they make wonderful pets."

"It'll eat up the entire garden."

"Lena can keep it out of the garden. She'll have to feed it on a bottle. We've got plenty of milk left over," Rob said.

"I'm not milking a cow to feed a groundhog," Mazy told him.

"You don't have to," Rob told her. "Uncle Homer milks his goat. That milk will make her pet grow big and strong."

Homer and George came out of the house to see what the commotion was about. Homer took one look at what Catalena had in her arms and laughed.

"Had me one of those when I was a boy. Made a mighty good pet," Homer told her. "Bob will have to climb a tree and get you a pet crow. Had those as pets when I was a boy, too."

Bob's face brightened at the idea. He didn't like his brother getting one up on him. Uncle Homer had the idea to even it up.

"Will you save enough goat's milk for it?" Rob asked his uncle.

"Sure will. They don't take much milk. It'll be big enough to fend for itself before long."

"Humph," Mazy snorted. "Looks to me like I'm the only one with good sense around here. What a groundhog won't eat up, a crow will take up."

~~~~

George wanted to go for a run. He was sitting on the porch strapping on his new shoes when Catalena, Rob and Bob came from around back. They had been in the barn fixing one of the corn cribs for Catalena to keep her pet groundhog in. Mazy had refused to let a groundhog stay in the house.

"Who's up for going for a run with me?" George asked.

"Not me," Rob and Bob said at the same time.

"How about you, Lena?" George asked. "We won't run hard. We'll just warm up a little until you get tired, then we'll walk back to the house."

"Wouldn't call that going for a run," Rob told his little brother.

"Don't want to run much in these new shoes. No need to chance blistering my feet."

"Yeah," Bob added. "We all know how sensitive your toes are."

George ignored him.

Catalena held out both sides of her shabby dress. This isn't exactly running clothes."

George thought of the shorts and top she had on when he found her. Those would be perfect, but he knew his mother had either hid them or burned them. He wasn't sure which. He did know that his mother wouldn't allow her to wear so little.

"I got an idea. I'll get a pair of britches and shirt I've outgrown from Mom's rag bag. You can tie a string around the waist to keep them up."

George disappeared inside the house.

"You don't have to go with him if you don't want to," Rob told her.

"I'm not sure you ought to be running so soon after your accident," Bob added.

"I think the exercise might do me good. I've been sitting peeling apples half the day. "My legs feel like they could use some exercise."

Rob looked down at his rough brogan boots. "Don't think I've ever owned a pair of running shoes."

"Me either," added Bob.

"Don't know if I could do much running in these heavy boots. They're more for working than running."

"Mine too," said Bob.

"George is the baby of the family. It's safe to say he's been spoiled rotten. Homer sees that he gets just about everything he wants."

"We make him behave," Bob added.

"Listen who's talking about me," George said as he came out the door. He handed a pair of pants and shirt to Catalena. "They're clean. Mom even washes her rags before she puts them in her rag bin."

"Where is Mom?" Rob asked.

"She wanted to look at the apple tree. She wants to see if there's enough apples ready to do a big canning. If there is, she wants me to climb the tree and pick some after church tomorrow, so she and Lena can have more fun canning them Monday."

Catalena cringed.

"Hurry up. Put these on before Mom gets back or she won't want you to go with me. She'll agree with Bob."

Catalena wasted no time in changing clothes. The clothes were a bit snug, but they had been worn enough until they were soft and more comfortable than the baggy dress Mazy had given her to wear. When she came out onto the porch all three boys looked at her.

"Dang," Rob said. "Those clothes never looked like that on little brother."

"Stop picking on her," Bob told him firmly. "He's the aggravating kind. They look just fine."

"Come on. Let those two nut cakes twiddle their thumbs while we're having fun."

Catalena didn't hesitate. She and George started out at a slow trot as they ran down the road. George was making sure they stayed on fairly level ground. All four of his family members would give him heck if he allowed her to overdo their exercise jog. They had jogged less than a quarter of a mile when George stopped.

"Why are we stopping?" She asked.

"To give you a rest."

"I don't need to rest. Actually, the jogging feels good. I keep wanting to speed up."

"Interesting," George said. "I'm guessing you are a runner. Your legs sure looked toned up when I carried you home."

"Looking at my legs, were you?"

"Me and Uncle Homer both. Had to make sure they weren't broken. We looked at your arms and head too. Mom checked your body out. Gotta say we've not been able to see much of your legs or arms since Mom put our sister's dress on you."

"Do you think that was intentional on your mother's part?"

"I sure enough do. She didn't want her four men ogling you. She's funny about things like that. She still believes all of a woman's body should be covered up. Heck, she wouldn't even let my sisters change clothes in front of each other."

"That's a lot different than where I came from," she found herself saying. "Wait a minute," she added happily. "I must be getting better if I remember something like that."

"Seems to me like you remember a lot, other than who you are and what you were doing here."

"Odd isn't it. I can't remember the most important things of all. It scares me when I think about it. What if I never remember?"

"No need to be afraid. If you don't remember, you'll get to stay with us forever. And I can promise you one thing, I'll grow up to be a brilliant and handsome man before much longer."

The both smiled and took off jogging again.

On their way back to the house, George stopped in the same place in case she needed to rest. He sat down on a grassy spot and insisted she do the same.

"While we were in town today, Uncle Homer and I went inside the soda shop to have us a chilly dog and root beer float. This bunch of women were sitting in the booth right behind us. I couldn't help hearing them talk."

"One woman said that Martha's friend Bertha promised Martha when she died, she'd do her best to come back and tell her what heaven was like. Well, she died and then returned last night."

"What's heaven like, Martha asked Bertha."

"I have good news and bad news to tell you. The good news is we have a softball team in heaven. Better still is that we're all young without a single ache or pain among us. Better than that is it's always springtime there. No snow or sleet or freezing cold, and we get to eat all our favorite foods without gaining a pound."

'Best of all is that all our old friends who died before I did are there. We can play softball all we want without ever getting tired."

"That sounds wonderful, Martha said. So, what's the bad news."

"You're pitching Tuesday."

Catalina laughed. "Rob is right. Uncle Homer has already ruined you."

~~~~

Mazy insisted on staying home with Catalena instead of going to church. Mazy claimed her absence was so she and Catalena could prepare a huge Sunday dinner. Catalena knew it was really was because she didn't trust her staying there alone. If they took her to church with them, Mazy didn't want to explain to the church crowd who Catalena was or why she was staying with them.

"Don't bring anybody home with you for Sunday dinner," Catalena overheard Mazy whisper to Rob. "Don't let Homer or George invite anyone. You know how they are."

Catalena eased what hurt feelings she had by imagining herself telling the congregation she was staying there to discover which of the Barlow twins she preferred to sleep with. She also imagined seeing Mazy die from a heart attack. It was probably best for neither of them went to church.

Good grief, Catalena thought, she was getting worse than Uncle Homer and George put together.

"You'll need to peel more potatoes than that," Mazy told her when she slacked up as her imagination roamed. "My boys fill up on Sunday dinner, so they can sleep it off in the afternoon."

"I thought George was going to pick apples."

"He will after the sun goes down. The Bible says men can do their work before the sun rises and after the sun sets on Sunday."

Catalena wanted to ask Mazy how they were keeping the Sabbath holy by cooking meals and washing dishes, but she knew better. She was learning Mazy's way of thinking. One thing was for sure, Catalena felt like she was working.

"Is Gertie Lee's house still standing?" Catalena had the urge to ask Mazy. For some reason, she found herself interested in the woman and her daughter.

"I think it is. I've not been that way in years. Back when Harm and I were first married, we'd pick wild strawberries back in that direction in the spring of the year and blackberries in the fall."

"You don't pick them now?"

"I still pick them, but not back in that direction."

"Why not."

"It's a far piece to walk."

"I'll go with you to pick berries," Catalena volunteered.

"Too late to pick strawberries and too early to pick blackberries. Don't worry though, we'll have enough apples to can tomorrow. The top of the tree is full."

That made Catalena feel a lot better. She almost rolled her eyes at the satire of that but knew better.

The table was set and the meal ready when Mazy's men got back from church. There was room for all of them to sit at the table. Uncle Homer bowed his head and gave thanks for the food and all their blessings.

Once they started eating it was almost a free-for-all to see who could out eat the other. They were full and enjoying the apple pie and homemade whipped cream, when Mazy asked how the preaching went."

Uncle Homer started talking.

"You missed a mighty good meeting today, Mazy. The preacher decided to start off by doing things a little different this Sunday. He stood right up in front of the congregation and said:

"This morning we're going to try something different. I'm going to say a word and I want everyone to start singing the hymn it brings to mind.

"The preacher shouted out cross. Every single person in the congregation started singing, 'The Old Rugged Cross'.

"Then the preacher shouted out grace. Sure enough, the congregation began singing 'Amazing Grace' how sweet the sound.

"Then the preacher said power. 'There's Power in the Blood', they sang.

"The preacher hollered out sex, and the entire congregation fell into total silence. Everyone was in shock. They nervously looked around at each other. All of a sudden, from the back of the church an old eighty-seven-year-old man stood up and started singing 'Precious Memories' how they linger."

There was total silence in the room. All eyes were on Mazy. Catalena was sure Mazy would hit Uncle Homer over the head with the gravy bowl.

"He's lying. It was no eighty-seven-year-old man." George blurted out. "It was Uncle Homer who started singing that song."

"Neither of you have one a lick of sense," Mazy said. and started laughing. She laughed so hard she had to wipe tears off her cheeks with her apron tail. When her bout of laughter was over, she looked at Homer and then George. "To pay penance for that bit of blasphemy at my dinner table, you two can clear the food and wash the dishes. During that time, you both best pray that God forgives you for your foolishness. Lena and I are going out on the porch to set and rest for a spell."

~~~~

It was Monday morning and Catalena wished she could go for a run, or at least a slow jog, but Mazy had other ideas for her. There were three bushels of early apples sitting on the porch waiting to be peeled and canned. The twins were at the sawmill. George was at school. Uncle Homer had disappeared off the face of the earth.

She smiled when she thought about the apple picking process. Rob and Bob held one end of a sheet while she and Uncle Homer held the other end. George picked apples and tossed them into the sheet. He shook the limbs of the apples he couldn't reach. Mazy busied herself by filling hampers from the caught apples. After the apple picking was over, Mazy put the sheet in a tub of water to soak.

Mazy didn't touch the apples until Monday morning. To do so would be working, and she believed in keeping the Sabbath holy.

"I'll wash and scald the jars while you peel," Mazy told her. "Make sure you drop the sliced apples in that bucket of saltwater, so they won't turn brown."

Catalena felt like saluting Mazy but refrained from action and comment. She sat down in the chair and silently started peeling the apples. She wondered if Mazy ever cooked those early transparent apples peelings and all? She remembered eating them like that before, but she couldn't remember where or when.

She had about half a bushel peeled when Mazy came back outside with another bucket of saltwater. She sat down in a chair beside Catalena. There were five twine-bottomed chairs on the porch, but they were seldom all used at the same time.

"Are you going to can all the apples on that tree?" Catalena asked with dread.

"No. There's probably ten or twenty bushels left. The deer, crows, squirrels, rabbits, and Kormans will get most of them. I tried once to give bushels of already picked apples to the Kormans, but they turned up their noses and told me they didn't want my no-account apples. During the night they slipped in and stole the apples."

"That doesn't make sense. Why would they steal what you were willing to give them?"

"It's the kind of people they are. They'll work a week to cheat somebody out of a dollar, but they won't work an hour to earn an honest dollar."

"Interesting," Catalena said. "Was Gertie Lee like that?" For some reason, her thoughts were always returning to Gertie Lee.

"No, she wasn't. Didn't I tell you before that she was the kind of person God ought to make more of. Her place joined the Korman land the same as ours.

"Joined?"

"Didn't I tell you she sold her land to those Hordlys."

"You probably did, but I tend to forget things lately," she said with a slight grin.

"That's right obvious," Mazy chuckled softly. "Is your memory getting any better at all?"

"I don't think so. It seems like the more I try to remember, the less I can remember."

"How's your head?"

"It hurts all the time."

"You don't complain."

"I do in my mind. If I complain out loud, it makes my situation scarier. I want my life back." Catalena felt her chin tremble. "I think I'm a runner," she blurted out to keep from getting emotional.

"You're a what?"

"Like George. I think I ran a lot. Running feels familiar. My body craves it."

"George claims he craves it, too. Wish that boy would settle down and get that college idea out of his head. But then, I don't want him working at the sawmill. It's dangerous work." Mazy drew in a breath of air and let it out. "Reckon just living is dangerous too. Look at you. You evidently took a wrong turn on the road and look what happened."

Catalena felt a tear slip from her eye and slide down her cheek.

"No need to haul off and cry about it," Mazy told her. "It'll all come back to you soon. In the meantime, you're living a good life right here."

Another tear slid down her other cheek

~~~~

When George got home from school, Catalena was still sitting on the porch peeling apples. The dress and apron Mazy had insisted she wear was covered in apple juice. Her hair hung in damp strands around her face. She looked an exhausted mess, a beautiful mess in George's opinion. If any girl he went to school with looked like that, it would be repulsive, but on Catalena it made George grin and wish he was old enough to kiss her. He was glad Rob wasn't there to look at her.

"Wash up and we'll go for a run," George said the magic words.

"I can't. I've got to finish peeling these apples so Mazy can put them on to can, while the stove is still hot."

"I'll put my books up, change into old clothes, and help you finish."

Those words were nothing short of beautiful.

A few minutes later, George came outside with a paring knife. Less than ten minutes later Uncle Homer showed up from the underworld of hiding out.

"You two need a little help?" he asked.

To Catalena, every apple down was a blessed reprieve.

"Always," George said.

"How's your groundhog doing?" Uncle Homer asked her.

"Great. I've fed it the bottle twice. It eats apple peelings too."

"That's good. In a week or so you won't have to give it the bottle."

"I like feeding it the bottle."

"It's fun for a while and then it gets old," he said, and turned to George. "How was school?"

"Same as always."

"Anybody bully Brent Kilby today?"

"No Kormans in school today."

"Not a one?"

"Nope."

"Wonder why?" Homer said.

George shrugged his broad shoulders.

"Brent is a neighbor who lives down the road. He likes to hang with George. Sometimes he runs and works out with George. Mazy doesn't like for George to run by himself, but he usually does," Homer said.

"Works out?" Catalena questioned.

"In the barn loft. George has him a little spot where he lifts weights. You didn't think he was born with all those bulging muscles, did you?"

She hadn't paid much attention to his muscles, but she knew he had them. Rob and Bob were both similarly muscled. She assumed it came from working at the sawmill.

"I must have," she told them.

Mazy came out onto the porch to glare at Homer. "Well, well. So, the dead has arisen."

"Now, now, Mazy. Let's not get cynical. A man has to do his own work once in a while."

"Humph. Like you ever work."

"Ah, mercy. Can't do a thing with a contrary woman."

"Hush your mouth, Homer."

"Run inside, Mazy, and bring out a tired old man a glass of cold water."

"You want water, get it yourself."

"Woman, can't you see I'm busy peeling apples?"

Mazy turned and marched back inside.

"Pay no attention to them, Lena. It's their way of having fun. They're at it most all the time. Gets right tiring after a while."

"Listen who's talking."

When the unpeeled apples were down to a dozen or so, Homer looked at Catalena. "Why don't you slip right quiet like into the house and change clothes so you and George can take off. I'll finish peeling the apples."

Catalena didn't need any persuasion. She moved as silently as possible. Fortunately, Mazy hadn't found the clothes she slipped between her bed cover and sheet when she and George had returned from yesterday's jog.

"Put those clothes back into my rag bag," Mazy had told Catalena. They're not fit to wear."

She hadn't.

Uncle Homer was in the kitchen getting his glass of water when Catalena slipped from the bedroom to the porch. She heard him and Mazy arguing with each other, but she couldn't hear what they were saying.

"Come on," George said, while Uncle Homer is giving us cover. Which direction do you want to run in?"

"I'd like to run by Gertie Lee's place. Your mom has been telling me about her." Catalena said as she jogged beside him.

"Why? She's been gone forever."

"How long is forever?" she asked as George led the way through the woods instead of taking the road.

"Don't know exactly. Seems like I can remember her a little, but I'm not sure. Don't know why you'd want to see her place. It's nothing but a fallen down shell. Don't know why those Hordlys don't tear it down. Of course, they wouldn't tear it down with their own hands. They'd hire somebody to do it for them."

"From what I've heard about the Kormans and the Hordlys, I don't think I'd be fond of them."

"Nobody else is either."

"What's wrong with them?"

"Who knows. Seems like some people are born bad and some born good. Mom says it's not Christian to talk bad about people, but I've been waiting to see some good in any of them."

"What makes them bad?" she persisted.

"All the things Mom won't allow me to talk about. She says it's up to God to judge and punish them, not us."

Catalena didn't agree with that. People were supposed to be punished for wrongdoing, otherwise they would not stop doing wrong. She wasn't about to argue with Mazy or even with George for that matter.

George slow jogged with her through the woods and slowly took an incline on top of a ridge to a fence where several goats were browsing.

"That's Korman land across that fence. This side is Barlow land. We'll bypass the Korman property. It's best we don't talk. Rather they not know we're about."

Catalena gave him a curious look, but she didn't ask questions as he'd said they shouldn't talk. Still, she didn't like the idea that George feared for the Kormans to hear them talking. Was George afraid of them? Were they dangerous?

When they went a bit farther, George caught her by the arm, leaned into her and whispered, "Down there is the Hordlys' log cabin. They claim they're roughing it when they come to the mountains on vacation."

They went a little farther to a wooded spot where a small house stood. The outside was a weathered gray with only a touch of once white paint showing. All the windows were broken out and the door sagged on one hinge.

"Those Kormans did all that damage," George told her. "They try to destroy what's not theirs."

"Let's go look inside," Catalena said.

"It's in worse shape that the outside."

Catalena didn't care what shape it was in. She wanted to see the inside of the house where Gertie Lee Smith lived. When they got close the lopsided door, they heard sobbing sounds, much like a child that had cried until all that was left were the sobs.

Catalena rushed inside before George could stop her. There in the corner of the room surrounded by trash huddled a thin girl who appeared to be about ten or twelve years old. Her arms were clasp around her legs and her face buried against her knees.

"Oh, honey. What's wrong?" Catalena burst out as she rushed toward the girl.

The girl's head shot up. The look on her face was a mixture of and hatred and fear.

"Leave me alone," she yelled as she picked up a broken plank and hurled it at Catalena's head. She dodged as it grazed her cheek. The girl was on her feet running out the back door before the plank ever hit the floor.

"Are you okay?" George asked as he came inside. He caught her chin in his hand and turned her face toward the light. "It's only a scratch. Good thing you dodged fast."

"Who was that little girl?"

"I think it was Jeanene Korman. I didn't get a good look at her. She's usually the one who's always hiding out in places. Folks say they see her running through the woods day and night. I found her hiding in our barn loft once. Folks claim she's not exactly right in the head."

"What was wrong with her?"

"Don't know."

"She was crying," Catalena pointed out needlessly.

"She usually is."

"Why?" Catalena persisted.

"She's a Korman."

"What kind of answer is that?"

"All the Korman girls cry a lot."

"Why?"

"Like I said, they're Kormans. I'd cry too if I was a Korman."

Catalena didn't like that answer in the least, but she knew it was all George was going to tell her. She was the type who wanted to find answers to all her questions. She was sure of that much.

"Have you seen enough of Gertie Lee's house?"

"For the time being."

"Don't you dare come back here without me," he told her firmly.

"Why shouldn't I?"

"It's not safe. There's several Korman and Hordly boys as well as men around here. They've got a bad reputation. Mom would never let one of my sisters get near them. We best go back."

"Do those boys ever bother you," she demanded to know.

"Nope. Uncle Homer said he and my dad established an understanding with Markum Korman, his brother, and his pa when my folks were first married."

"What happened?" Catalena asked as though she expected to receive an answer.

"Mom doesn't know we were told anything about it, but Uncle Homer let the twins and me years ago. If I tell you, you've got to swear you'll not mention a word about it to anybody. If you do, Uncle Homer might still get in trouble with the law, and Mom would die from having a conniption fit."

"You've got my word, I won't tell."

"Uncle Homer said he and Dad were coon hunting one night when Markum, his brother Jim, and their dad hid in some undergrowth and lay wait on them. All three jumped them when they weren't expecting it. They thought the three of them could whip two Barlows, plus they were all three carrying knives. Were they ever wrong. When they came out of the undergrowth with those knives pulled, the moon light reflected on the blades.

"Uncle Homer yelled out, they got knives. Dad caught Markum' knife arm and Uncle Homer grabbed Jim's knife arm. The both swung the Korman they had hold of at the old man who was coming at Uncle Homer with his knife. Uncle Homer was older and more experienced in fighting than Dad. They figured if they took him out first, Dad would be easier to handle. The old man went down. Dad and Uncle Homer worked at sawmilling and were as strong as oxen. They knew how to fight really well, both being trained in hand to hand combat during their time in the army. Their next move was to break both the Kormans right arms at the elbow. Dad and Uncle Homer finished them off by beating them into the dirt. Markum still has a crooked-up nose to remember Uncle Homer by.

"Dad and Uncle Homer left them where they lay moaning like they couldn't take a whipping. Come to find out the old man had fallen on his own knife and bled to death right there in the dirt. Markum and Jim lived. They swore that six huge men jumped them when they were coon hunting in the woods, but neither of the Kormans could describe a one of those men. They claimed it was too dark to get a look at them.

"Both Kormans staggered home in the dark of night without checking on the old man. When he didn't show up by the next day, one of the women went to look for him and found him dead in the woods and went after the sheriff. He determined the old man fell on his own knife since he still had the handle gripped in his hand with the blade stuck right into his heart."

"My goodness," Catalena said. "Why would they waylay your father and Uncle Homer?"

"Don't exactly know. Uncle Homer never told us. Don't mention this, but I expect it was nothing but meanness and jealousy. They always liked to gang up and beat on those weaker than them. Folks around here still talk about the time six strangers attacked the Kormans. They all figured the

Kormans deserved what they got. Even the sheriff said the same thing without ever trying to find out what happened.

"That really is a true story and not something Uncle Homer made up?"

"If I hadn't heard other people talk about it, I might think Uncle Homer exaggerated the story. You'll have to admit Uncle Homer always lets you know somewhere along the line that his stories are real if they're not. Some of his stories really are true. This story he told us boys as being a fact. He said we needed to know to watch our backs and especially watch out after our sisters. He figured those Kormans would try to get even someday. Of course, Jim died a few years back, and he doubts Markum ever told anybody the truth about that night. Markum is one of the biggest cowards that ever lived. Markum' brother, Jim, and his son, Kimbell, compete for coming in second."

"My goodness. And yet, you told me."

"You promised not to tell, plus I wanted to make sure you stay away from those Kormans along with the Hordlys. If you ask me, both bunches are pure evil."

"I thought the Hordlys moved here."

"They did, from somewhere down in Florida. Uncle Homer calls them half-backs, Flor-idiots. They moved to Florida from up north. Just because they aren't from here doesn't mean they're good people," George said, sounding a little put-out by her remark.

"I didn't mean that the way it sounded. I couldn't imagine an outsider being willing to buy a place next to the Kormans."

"Birds of a feather flock together regardless of what direction they fly in from." George quoted Uncle Homer.

"Something should be done about them," Catalena said with cold hard logic.

"What?"

"I'm not sure. I've always been told you can't arrest someone before they commit a crime, but they committed a crime when they attacked your dad and Uncle Homer."

"Uncle Homer will never admit to it and neither will Markum. One thing is for sure, Markum is afraid of us Barlows. So are his boys."

"A coward will kill you faster than a brave man," she told him as she slow jogged by his side. They were doing more talking than exercising.

"Say, who told you somebody couldn't be arrested before a crime was committed?"

Catalena opened her mouth to speak a moment before a puzzled look came to her face. "I don't know. I almost remembered, but then my mind went blank."

"See, you're making progress. By the way, make sure you don't say a word to Mom or Uncle Homer about us seeing Jeanene or being anywhere near Gertie Lee's old house."

"Why not?"

"Believe me, it wouldn't go over well, especially for me. Mom and Uncle Homer both forbid us kids to go on the backside of the hill unless Uncle Homer is with us. If either of them found out I went against their rules, I'd be grounded for the duration you're here. The upside is I might be a brilliant, handsome man by then."

"The downside is I'm starting to fear my memory is lost forever," Catalena was quick to tell him.

"Wonder if it's true that another knock on the head will cure the first one?"

"I would hardly think so."

"Me neither, but I'll give it a try if you insist," he gave her a mischievous grin.

"We'll save that cure until all other options fail."

~~~~

Mazy was not pleased when George and Catalena returned. Her youngest son was way too enthusiastic about having their unwanted guest staying with them. It was easy to tell George was brimming with happiness because he'd gotten to be alone with Catalena while doing something he loved. He had to be delighted to find someone who enjoyed running. Catalena was breathing hard and slightly damp with sweat. She also had a slight frown on her face. Mazy recognized it as being the same expression she wore when her head hurt.

"At least he didn't wear that little skirt in front of her," Homer told Mazy, only to receive a chilling look.

"She's wearing those clothes I told her to put back in my rag bag. They're indecent."

Homer had brought Mazy in another an armload of stove wood to use in canning the apples. One of the perks of owning a sawmill was having plenty of cook wood and heating wood.

"They weren't indecent when you had George wearing them."

"George never looked like her."

"That's a fact."

"Shut your filthy mouth, Homer Barlow."

Homer grinned. "Just agreeing with you Mazie darlin'."

"Don't call me darlin'."

"How about sweet thing?"

"I'll crack your head with this frying pan."

"No need to damage a good frying pan."

"True enough. She ought not to be running in her condition," Mazy declared. They were looking out the kitchen window at George and Catalena as they came fast walking into the yard and breathing hard.

"Not any harder on her condition than peeling apples all day."

"She was sitting during that time. She didn't break a sweat either," Mazy said defensively. "There's nothing wrong with busy work."

"Seems to me like you're giving her a lot of busy work."

"She might as well earn her keep," Mazy told him. "Like everyone else around here."

"What is it about the girl you don't like?" Homer asked.

"I don't dislike her," Mazy said defensively. "I do think she needs to know what it's like to work a little. I get the idea she's never done an honest day's work in her life."

"What makes you think that?"

"Her hands. When George first carried her in, her hands were soft and smooth. Her fingernails were long and all the same length. It was obvious she didn't know what hard work was."

"She doesn't have long fingernails now," Homer pointed out.

"I trimmed them off for her," Mazy admitted.

"Is that all?" Homer asked.

"She was all perfumed up like some kind of fancy hussy. Ivory soap took care of that."

"And?" Homer encouraged.

"The clothes she was wearing weren't fit to be seen in. She didn't even have on decent underwear."

"How's that?" Homer did his best not to grin.

"They were nothing more than a little scrap of fancy lace. Embarrassed me to look at her."

The girl mentioned that Mazy said her clothes were so dirty and ragged that she burned them. If he remembered correctly, her clothes looked to be in mighty fine condition to him. Homer hid his grin. She might as well tell him the truth. He already knew why she didn't want the pretty girl to be around. Even Rob and Bob had started taking a bath each day and sprucing up more than normal.

"Admit it, Mazy. What you don't like about that girl is her being around your boys. You're afraid one of them might take too much of a liking to her."

"That's true," she was quick to agree. "I told you that when she first showed up. She's the type . . . let's just say she's not our kind."

"What is our kind?" he continued to lightly pick at her.

"Common. That's our kind of people, and she's not common. When she gets her memory back, you'll see her looking down her nose on our kind of living – not that she isn't doing that already."

"If you ask me, she seems to be right content with our kind of living."

Mazy gave him a hateful look. "Homer Barlow, you'd spend all day arguing with a stump and get great pleasure out of it."

"At least the stump wouldn't argue back when it knows I'm right.

Chapter 18

~~~~

Catalena couldn't stop thinking about Jeanene Korman as she fed her pet groundhog from the bottle Homer had gotten for her. The girl had appeared to be in misery. Even her reaction at being caught crying was disturbing. She didn't know why she was feeling so strongly about the girl, but she was. If those Kormans were as bad as George said, why hadn't the neighbors gotten together to do something about them? There were laws to abide by even this far back in the hills.

Exactly how far back in the hills were they? And what was the name of the place? How far away was the closest town? What was the name of the town? Even more puzzling was why she hadn't thought to ask George important questions such as those. She knew he'd come a lot closer to telling her things she wanted to know than Mazy. Uncle Homer had told her what state she was in, and he usually tried to answer her questions. As for Rob and Bob, she never had a chance to talk to them for long. They worked from sunup until sundown, plus Mazy did her best to make sure they had as little contact with her as possible.

Catalena smiled at that. She supposed it was a mother's prerogative to think her sons were the most irresistible men in existence. She longed to tell Mazy she certainly wasn't interested in them romantically. The knock on the head may have caused her to lose her memory, but it hadn't caused her to lose her common sense. She knew she wasn't the marrying kind, or even the kind that fell for anyone at the drop of a hat.

She was independent and particular to a fault. Although she had to admit all three of Macy's sons, plus Uncle Homer, were good looking in a rough and rugged way. She would like to know what the boys' father was like, but she wasn't going to ask.

"Lena," Mazy said as soon as she came up behind Catalena. "You ought to turn that thing loose. Rob was plum crazy for bringing it here. He knows I don't like rodents."

"He was being considerate," Catalena tried to compliment him.

"He was being stupid," Mazy told her firmly.

"Have you noticed how firm its little body is? I love the way it stands on its hind legs and holds the bottle with its front paws."

"Nothing to love about that thing. When it gets bigger, it'll eat up my garden."

"I hope not. Maybe I can take her with me when I leave. Then it won't bother anything."

Mazy didn't comment further on the groundhog or her leaving. "Are you familiar with wash day?"

"Wash day?" Catalena questioned. "Washing what?"

"Clothes and such."

"Sounds familiar and necessary," Catalena grinned, but Mazy didn't.

"Familiar or not, I'm going to show you how we Barlows do our laundry."

"Sounds good," Catalena told her.

"Leave that thing be and strip the sheets off the bed you're sleeping in, while I get the washing machine ready. We always start with the sheets."

When Catalena returned with her sheets, Mazy had a wringer washing machine rolled in front of the kitchen sink.

"Where did that come from?"

"I keep it in the storage room until it's needed," Mazy told her. "I didn't think you'd ever used one of these. Probably never seen one before. I believe in using things as long as they work. Don't believe in wasting money on fancy do-dads."

Catalena remembered that Mazy refused to have a room added onto the house and a bathroom put in. She couldn't understand why any person would want to make something hard on themselves when there was an easier way. Still, she wasn't about to argue with Mazy on anything. She wasn't in a position to do so.

"Put those sheets in there on top of mine. I've got my underwear in there too. I've sewn up another pair one of my girls left behind for you. We'll wash ours first and then we'll wash the boy's bed sheets and shorts. You tote that canner full of water from the stove over here and pour it in, while I put lye soap shavings and cold-water in. If the water is too hot on white things it can set a stain in instead of washing it out."

Mazy had the washing machine's intake hose connect to the faucet of the sink. She turned on the water as Catalena carried the hot water from the stove with two dishtowels on the hot handles. She had wondered why Mazy had two canners full of water on the stove while they were cooking breakfast. She now understood it was to make the wash-water hotter.

"Pour it slow. Don't want you to scald yourself. Homer would never let me hear the end of it if I let you get hurt."

Catalena found herself thankful for Homer.

"Speak of the devil, and he shows up," Mazy said as Homer came through the kitchen door.

"We can't all be angels," Homer said sweetly to Mazy, which seemed to irritate her.

"Good morning, Honey," Homer said to Catalena.

"Good morning," she returned with a slight smile.

"See you're started your washing early today," he said to Mazy.

"That's because you're late."

"Nope. You're early, which is a good thing. It's gonna rain later on."

"How do you know?" Catalena asked. "They only had one radio in the house, which was never turned on."

"I feel it in my bones. Never fails me."

"He wouldn't know if something failed him or not," Mazy added

"You need you a television," Homer told her. "They have those romantic soap operas on there during the day. Last one I saw pert near curled my mustache."

"Don't you start with that dirty talk. Go fetch some more firewood in. I'm gonna heat water to wash the twins' britches. Those boys get everything under the sun on their clothes."

"That's how to tell you've got hard working men. Bankers and preachers keep their clothes clean."

"You're just busting at the seams with smarts today, aren't you?"

"Yeah, you've got that right. Say, what's turned you into such a grouch this morning?"

"Dirty clothes, dirty house, dirty men," she snapped at him.

Homer grinned. "Tell me, Mazy girl, which ones do you want to get rid of?"

Mazy opened her mouth and then snapped it shut. She stalked out the door mumbling, "I'll get my own wood."

"Don't pay any attention to her," Homer whispered to Catalena. "She gets this way once in a while. She's been thinking about Harm again. She's wanting what she can't have, and it tears her up inside. By the time the washing is done, she'll be over it."

"She gets this way often?"

"Just about every wash day. She hates washing dirty clothes."

"Why doesn't she get an automatic washer and dryer?"

"How do you know about washers and dryers if your memory is gone?"

"I don't know. There are things I know about and then things I don't know."

"Let's see here," Homer said as he reached out to feel of the knot on her head."

"Ouch!"

"Sorry. Didn't mean to hurt you. Your knot's gone down a little. That's a good sign. The swelling must be putting pressure on your memory spot."

Catalina grinned as she took the canner to the sink and filled it with water.

"Here, let me lift that. It's right heavy. I always lift heavy things for Mazy when I'm around."

"You don't work at anything?"

"Mazy claims I don't. I draw a little disability money each month since the accident. I've been trying to save as much of it as I can to send George to college. He's smart. I think he can make something out of himself."

"What does he want to major in?"

"He's not exactly sure. Did you go to college?"

"Seems like I did."

"What did you major in?"

"Wish I knew. When I think about myself, everything goes blank. It seems I have feelings about things but no definite answers."

"I wouldn't worry about it if I was you. Your memory will all come back when the swelling goes down."

That's what Catalena was counting on. He sounded sure about what he was telling her, and yet he'd said he couldn't remember if he'd tightened the chain on the logs. If his memory hadn't returned how did he expect hers to return?

"I tried to buy her one of those new-fangled machines, but she wouldn't hear of it. That woman is set in her ways."

Catalena could agree with that statement in the short time she'd been there, but she wasn't going to comment when Mazy was coming in the door.

~~~~

Catalena was surprised at how Mazy did the laundry. All the whites were washed in the same wash water and then run through the wringer. Then hot water was added to the water whites had been washed in and the men's pants were put in the water to soak. After poking the clothes with a stick and adding more lye soap, Mazy plugged the washer in and left it on until she determined the pants were as clean as they could be gotten.

"My folks used to boil clothes outside in a wash pot," Mazy told her. "But that is too much work for me. Harm bought me this General Electric washing machine right after the twins were born. It's hung with me ever since."

Catalena now had an idea why Mazy refused to give up the washing machine. Anything that was a part of her beloved husband was a treasure to be clung to – including his sons. She found herself wondering about Mazy's daughters.

"Do your girls ever come to visit?"

"Of course, they do," Mazy told her. "But they have families of their own and don't have time to galivant about."

Catalena wondered if Mazy was aiming a dart at her. Was she insinuating she wouldn't be in this predicament if she were married and had a family of her own instead of galivanting?

Homer came inside with more firewood and put it in the stove. He brought a metal tub from off the porch and drained part of the wash water from the machine and carried the water outside. It took three trips to drain the machine. Homer and Mazy then filled the machine with clean water and Mazy began the job of rinsing the white clothes. Mazy had Catalena feeding the clothes into the wringer. Once the first load of whites was wrung out, Mazy took the hamper of clothes outside to hang out while Catalena finished rinsing and putting the next load through the wringer.

"This is too much work," Catalena told Homer once Mazy was out of hearing.

"She likes it."

"Don't Rob and Bob make enough money at the sawmill to buy her a washing machine?"

"Sure, they do."

"Then have them do it without getting her permission. Maybe she'd accept it from them faster than she would from you."

"She'd be mad as a hornet."

"Not for long. She's not getting any younger. Like I said, this is hard work. No wonder she's cranky on wash day."

"You've got a point."

"Tell me a little more about the Kormans," she said suddenly.

Homer gave her a questioning look. "What do you want to know?"

"Do they go to school?" She was trying to think of a way to get information while keeping her promise to George.

"Some. They're not much on education."

"How many children are there?"

"Oh, let's see. The original Korman old folks are dead. The old folks had seven children. Four girls and three boys. Marie, one their girls and Markum and Burt, two of their boys still live here. One of their sons died, and the rest of the seven moved away. Markum has four children. Burt has three. Marie has four children."

"What about the Hordlys?"

"They have three boys that I know of."

"That's fourteen children."

"Some of them are grown or there about. The girls marry and move away as soon as they can. I don't keep up with them no more than I have to."

"Who else lives around here?"

"There's several houses below us."

"Do they have children?"

"They do. This place is like any other place. We're not isolated, but we do like to keep to ourselves while minding our own business. Why do you ask?"

"I'm trying to understand why I would come here. Surely I had a reason."

"I'm wondering the same thing. Knowing or not knowing doesn't change a thing. You're here now, and we have to deal with it until we can do better."

Mazy came through the door and they stopped talking.

"What were you talking about?" Mazy wanted to know.

"Lena was trying to figure out why she came here."

"We'd all like to know that," Mazy said.

"After we get your washing done, I'm gonna put her in my old truck and drive her about some. Seeing where she's at might help jog her memory."

"Yes," Catalena said eagerly. "It just might help." Even if it didn't help, she would know a little more about the place she was staying in.

Mazy frowned but didn't comment further.

~~~~

Once all the laundry was washed and Mazy was busy hanging the last load on the line, Homer turned to Catalena. "Let's take the path to my place. My truck is there."

Catalena followed him around the barn along a well-worn path through the woods. It felt wonderful not to be peeling and canning apples or doing laundry. "Do the twins make any money at sawmilling?"

"Enough to get by on."

"Enough to send George to college?"

Mazy and the boys think college is a waste of good money. The boys think George would be better off working at the sawmill rather than spending four years reading books and partying about."

"When my memory comes back and I have access to my bank account, I'll help send George to college, buy Mazy a washer and dryer, plus put in a bathroom in repayment for taking care of me."

"What makes you think you've got that kind of money?" Homer softly asked her.

"Something tells me that I do, and I don't think it's wishful thinking."

"Me either," Homer admitted. "After George carried you up that rock cliff and laid you on the ground, I swore you smelled like money."

She gave him a questioning look.

"You were wearing expensive perfume. Your hair was all fancied up nice and pretty. There was an expensive necklace around your neck, and you were wearing store bought clothes like city girls wear when they go visiting in the country. Even those sneakers you're wearing are expensive."

Catalena frowned. "If I was a rich city girl, what was I doing here?"

"Are you saying this place wouldn't be a place your kind would visit?" Homer prodded with a slight grin.

"No, not at all. I simply can't figure out why I was here, or why I would have driven up that horrible road."

"Do you smoke pot or indulge in meth?"

"Drugs? No. I'm positive I don't use drugs. Are you insinuating drugs are being sold around here?"

"Mind you, I didn't say that. I was just saying if a person was puffing on that wacky weed, it would be easy to get confused and take a wrong road."

"And drive off a cliff?" she added in a troubled way. "I don't think I'm a dopehead."

"Neither do I," Homer told her, as they came out of the woods. There was a small clapboard house with a front porch, a barn, and several small outbuildings. The grass was mown along with flowers blooming in profusion.

"What a lovely place. Look at all those flowers," she sounded surprised.

"Those purplish-blue ones are called money plants. They come up every year. My sweet wife loved flowers. Don't want her lookin' down from heaven and being disappointed cause I let 'em die."

"What's that strange noise?"

"That's my milk goat, Nanny. Want to see her?"

Homer led her through the yard to the barn. In the field was a large brown goat with floppy ears. Next to her was a medium sized goat with ears not as floppy.

"That's Nanny and her kid. Thought I'd better keep a baby from her this time. She's starting to get a little age on her. Nanny is a Nubian and her baby is half Alpine."

"Oh, how cute," Catalena said with a smile.

"You ought to see the babies when they're first born. Talk about cute. How's your groundhog doin'."

"Oh, I love her. That little body of hers feels so solid when I hold her. She's eating apples, grass, and vegetables along with the bottle."

"Won't be long until you can turn her loose, but you'd better do it at my place instead of at Mazy's.

"You're right. Mazy doesn't like her."

"Don't get Mazy wrong. It's not that she doesn't like things, she's simply cares about making sure everything turns out right."

"And my showing up here hasn't turned out right."

"Oh, I wouldn't say that. I've got an idea your showing up is a blessing."

Catalena disagreed. Neither having an accident nor losing her memory was anything near a blessing. She saw a tractor with a scrape blade on it as Homer led her to a shed where his truck was parked beside the tractor.

"Jump in," he told her as he opened the door and got into the driver's side.

She stepped onto the running board and then had to grab hold of a pull bar to pull herself up into the high seat. "That's one big step," she told him.

"Yeah. Old vehicles weren't made for comfort. This old truck rattles and knocks, but it's gotten me where I need to go for many a year."

"I miss not being able to drive. It's almost as bad as not being able to remember. I never realized how important it is to have a memory and a past. It's true a person doesn't know where to go if they don't know where they've been."

"Reckon that's true enough, but you'll remember."

Catalena was silent as they bumped over the rough dirt road. If he had a tractor with a blade on it, why didn't he use it to scrape the road smooth?

"Traveling salesmen," Homer said suddenly.

She frowned in question as she looked at him.

"If I were to have my driveway as smooth as a baby's butt, traveling salesmen would be sure to show up. If I leave it rough as a corn cob, folks won't show up unless it's mighty important."

"It's difficult for you to drive in and out."

"Exactly. A bad road keeps me from going anywhere I don't need to go." Homer turned his head away from the road long enough to glance at her. "You're lucky you're not blonde."

She frowned. "Why am I lucky."

"Knew a couple who lived in the city. They were both natural blondes. One week the newsman said six inches of snow was forecast. Folks needed to park their cars on the right side of the road so the snowplows could remove the snow. The good wife rushed to move her car to the right side of the road. The next week the forecast was eight inches of snow. Again, folks were asked to move their cars to the left side of the road so the snowplows could remove the snow. The good wife rushed to do so. Sure enough, the next week the forecast was ten inches of snow. Just as the forecaster was about to tell which side to move car on, the electricity went out. "What am I going to do now," lamented the good wife. I don't know what side of the road to move my car to. 'Honey,' said the good-natured husband. 'Why don't you leave the car in the garage this time?'

Catalena shook her head and grinned. "Must have been Kormans," she said, hoping to bring the conversation around to them. Jeanene was still troubling her and there was no one other than George she could talk to.

"They've done worse," Homer told her.

"Is it only the men who are odd or is it the women also?"

"I don't reckon stupid has a gender."

"What makes them stupid?" she asked with a degree of sympathy.

"Diarrhea."

"What?" she asked, puzzled.

"It runs in their genes."

"Are you trying to make a joke?"

Homer chuckled. "No, I didn't mean it to be a joke, exactly. You see, I've been a farmer for most of my life. One thing I'm sure of is what goes in the gene pool comes out of the gene pool. Sometimes inbreeding produces a good offspring and sometimes it don't."

"So, you're say the Kormans are inbred?"

"Nope. I'm not one to say something such as that. What I can say is back in olden times the kings and other royalty married family members. Produced some mighty peculiar offspring. With the Kormans, I see some mighty peculiar offspring."

Catalena knew exactly what he was saying without actually saying it. "I see. It's always best not to talk about people when you weren't an eyewitness, right?"

"You got that right."

"Did these kings and royalty have public weddings or secret weddings?"

"Both, but I'm guessing most of what went on was kept a secret."

Catalena felt a controlled anger rising in her. She wanted to correct a wrong, pass judgement on the offenders. Stop wrongs from happening.

"Right there is where the Kilby's live," Homer nodded toward a neat little house setting in the edge of the woods. "They're fine folks. The kind you want to have as neighbors.

Brent, their boy, goes to school with George. Brent likes to run and lift weights with George whenever he gets a chance. He helps his dad a lot on the farm."

It was obvious Homer had said all he was going to say about the Kormans and wanted to change the direction of their conversation.

She would let him.

"Brent Kilby lifts weights with George?"

Homer nodded. "Didn't George tell you he has a little place rigged up in the barn loft. Didn't want his brothers to out muscle him."

"Doesn't their muscles come from lifting heavy lumber at the sawmill?"

"That's a fact, plus George gets to earn a little money that way. He's saving to go to college. We're hoping he can get scholarships."

She started to say she would help with scholarships, but suddenly realized she was in a position of helplessness. At the moment, she couldn't help herself with her own name.

As Homer drove on, Catalena was surprised to see so many houses. She had gotten the idea the Barlows were living in a remote and isolated area.

"Want to see where the boy's sawmill?"

"I would like that," she told him. She had wondered where Rob and Bob worked.

"Like I told you before, Harm and I ran the sawmill until the accident. It set idle for a while. Mazy about panicked when the boys decided to put it into operation again, but it's been a blessing of sorts. They earn enough money to buy timberland, cut the trees, saw and sell the lumber, and then buy more timber land.

"Do they sell the land after the timber is cut?"

"They try not to sell it unless they get in a pinch for money. Land doesn't reproduce itself. Plus, it holds its value. The boys have planted white pine seedlings on most of the logged over land. White pine is one of the trees that might reach sawmilling size during their lifetime. If not, it'll be there for their grandchildren."

"How old are the twins?"

"Oh, let me think a minute. They'll be coming up on thirty years of age in a few months. They are Mazy's oldest."

"I'm surprised they're not married."

"They're the particular kind, plus they're hoping twin sisters will show up and get their attention. Those two have stuck together like glue on a plate. One of them wouldn't want to get married and leave the other one behind. They refuse to go out on a date and leave the other brother sitting at home."

"Sound like they're too close to each other for their own good."

"I agree, but Mazy doesn't. She thinks it's only right they stick together."

"How do the boys feel about being so close."

Homer frowned. "They'll do whatever suits them. If one of them falls in love and the other one doesn't, so be it. They are mighty adaptable. You have any brothers or sisters?"

"I . . ." she appeared confused. "I don't know, but I have a feeling I'm an only child."

"What makes you feel like an only child?" Homer asked gently.

She shook her head. "I think I always felt like I was alone. Like I had to struggle to be somebody special."

"Everybody is somebody special," Homer told her. "Could be you mean you had to struggle to be somebody of importance?"

"Maybe," she sounded uncertain. "It seems I always wanted to be more than what I am."

"Welcome to the real world, baby girl. That feeling is no big deal. A good portion of people want to be more than what they are. I still do at my age."

Catalena thought about what he said for a while. "Do you really?" she finally questioned.

"Oh, yeah. I want to close my eyes and wake up being eighteen again with my whole life ahead of me. But, and that a very big but, I'd want to know everything I know now, have knowledge about everything I've learned through the years. More important, I want to be able to avoid all the mistakes I've made during life."

"And right all the wrongs in the world," Catalena added.

"Maybe not all the world's wrongs, but at least all my own."

"But it will never happen," Catalena said sadly.

"That's right. We're left to do the best we can from where we're at," Homer said as he pulled the truck up to a huge mountain of sawdust and stopped.

Catalena got out of the truck and looked around with wide eyes. It was all she could do not to put both hands over her ears like a little girl trying to keep out an unpleasant noise. The sharp whining sound of a huge saw blade cutting through a log was deafening.

Both the twins were hard at work without so much as looking up. Both twins had their shirts off and were covered in sawdust. Even from a distance she could see the muscles rippling in their arms and back as one brother ran the saw, while the other brother picked up the slabs of freshly sawed wood and stacked them on a trailer.

"It smells wonderful," she said, but knew Homer couldn't hear her over the noise.

Homer looked at his watch and leaned into her until his mouth was only an inch from her ear. "They'll shut down for lunch as soon as they finish sawing this log. We might as well stick around and say hello."

Three more cuts off the log and they were finished. The end slab with the bark still on it was tossed into a different pile. One brother cut the machine off and the noise stopped. He turned to look at Homer and Catalena.

"They see us," she said.

"They saw us pull up," Homer told her.

Both twins came toward them pulling their earplugs out and beating the sawdust from their hair and body.

"What are you two doing here?" Bob was quick to ask.

"Just showing Lena around a bit. After helping Mazy with the washing, I figured she needed a break."

Rob smiled at her. "When I need a break, this is the last place I'd go."

"What do you think of our operation?" Bob asked.

"It smells good," was the nicest thing she could think to say.

"We're sawing white pine. It always smells rather fresh. Each type of wood has its own aroma. White pine is my favorite," Rob told her.

"Is it always this noisy?" she couldn't help asking.

"Always," Bob said. "We wear earplugs, or we'd be as deaf as Uncle Homer."

"What was that?" Homer lifted his hand to his ear.

"He only hears what he wants to hear," Rob said.

"Comes in handy. Say, you boys best eat your lunch and get back at it. Those logs aren't gonna saw themselves."

"I'll trade places with you," Rob was quick to tell his uncle. "Let you get back into the swing of things."

"Nope. Old age has its privileges. You boys will have to wait until you're as old as I am before you're allowed to escort a pretty girl about."

Rob winked at Catalena.

"He's delusional," Bob said. "He's not allowed privileges."

Homer crooked his arm to indicate Catalena was to take hold of it, and she did. "Let's get out of here," he said as he looked back at the twins. "See who has the pretty girl, don't you?"

Homer opened the truck door and made a big deal of helping her get in.

"They're eating their hearts out," he whispered.

"Do you always pick at each other?" she asked Homer as they drove away.

"Always," he said with a grin. "We're family."

Catalena felt envious.

Chapter 19

Catalena's head wasn't hurting nearly as bad as usual when she woke up. She could almost look forward to the day if she wasn't expected to get out of bed and help Mazy cook a huge breakfast for four hungry men. It wasn't that she minded cooking breakfast. What bothered her was the men expected her and Mazy to wait on them. Mazy had declared peeling potatoes, apples, carrying in firewood, and washing dishes her job. It was also her job to stand at the stove stirring gravy and making sure the biscuits didn't get too brown.

Homer also helped Mazy a lot, but her three sons did little around the house. Mazy treated the twins like royalty.

"Do the twins ever help you?" she made the mistake of asking Mazy, who obviously took offence to the question.

"They work every single day at that sawmill to pay the bills. If you ask me, that's more than enough to ask of them."

Mazy's tone of voice told her it was time for her find out who she was and return to her normal life. The question was how to go about it?

A mountain woman stands guard over her own territory.

Those words came to Catalena as clear as if someone was speaking them. Mazy was guarding her own territory, which meant she felt threatened by Catalena's presence.

"Hey, pretty lady," George said as he came into the kitchen. "Thought I might find you in here. Want to go for a run after I get home from school?"

"Yes," she was quick to say. "I'd love it."

"Good."

"She ought not be out running about in her condition," Mazy was quick to tell them. "It'll do her harm."

"Actually, it seems to help," Catalena told her. "I need the exercise."

"Try mopping floors, washing windows, and hoeing the garden if you need exercise," Mazy told her."

"Now, Mom," George said as he gave her a hug. "A body can't live on work alone. All work and no play drives a body crazy."

"Such are the claims of the lazy," Mazy was quick to reply.

George ignored her remark. "When's breakfast ready? I'm starving."

"Get yourself to the table, then. As soon as Lena gets the table set, we'll bring the food in."

Catalena forced herself to smile as she got the plates out of the cupboard.

"I'll help, if it will make eating come faster." George was quick to take them from her. Catalena got the silverware and glasses and followed George into the dining room.

"Homer said you lift weights," Catalena said.

"I do some. Too much lifting makes your muscles bunch and tighten. I do enough to be strong and yet allow my muscles to elongate so I can run fast."

"I know. I did the same," she told him.

George gave her a questioning look. "You remember?"

"I wish. It's more like some things simply come to me right out of nowhere. It's more like feelings rather than remembering."

"Don't go remembering too fast. I like having you around."

"The boy is wising up," Homer said as he came into the dining room. "He's finally figured out it's more fun to play with a pretty girl than it is to play with Brent Kilby."

"Brent can't run as fast as she can," George was quick with a reply. "We both know he's not as pretty."

"That's a fact," Homer said.

"You're late," Mazy told him as she carried a bowl of gravy into the room.

"Little stiff this morning, Mazy girl. A little stiff."

"That's always your excuse when you want to get out of work."

"Now, Mazy, you know I brought you in extra cook wood last night. Besides, there's not room for three in your kitchen. I become the human overflow in there."

"Where's the boys?" Mazy asked George, making a point of ignoring Homer.

"Out back washing up."

"Go tell 'em to get in here. Breakfast is ready."

When the twins came in, not only had they washed up, they had shaved. Shaving was something they did only on Saturdays. Washing up and shaving took too much time on weekdays. George grinned. Homer only lifted his brows. Not one of them said a word about the twins' new routine.

Once the meal was finished, Homer walked with the twins to where their work truck was parked. "Don't hardly think that little gal is woman enough for two men," he said, and then made a beeline for the path that led back to his place.

After the dishes were washed, the beds made, and the floor and porch swept, Mazy rubbed a rag handkerchief over her sweaty face.

"Don't tell nobody, but I think I'm gonna have to lay down for a while."

Catalena looked at her with concern. Her face was unusually pale. "What's wrong? Are you sick? Do I need to get Homer?"

"Good Lord, no. Leave Homer be. I don't want him around. I've just got a bad headache is all."

Catalena reached out and put her hand on Mazy's forehead. Mazy pulled away fast. It occurred to Catalena that Mazy seldom had anyone touch her.

"You feel clammy. Are you sure . . ."?

"Stop your fussing. It's just the change of life. It's been hard on me for the past week. I'll just rest a while. Promise you won't say anything to the men. This is women's business. They don't need to know nothing about it."

"If you're sure," Catalena told her.

"I'm sure. You go outside and sit on the porch or feed that ground hog of yours, while I rest up a little. You might want to take a little nap yourself. The rest could do you good."

Catalena had no problem with both of them taking a break. At least now she knew why Mazy had been so irritable for the last few days. She'd always heard that menopause was rough on a woman, and Mazy was the type who was too embarrassed to let any of the men know what was going on. She found herself wondering about Mazy's daughters. Where they as reserved about life as their mother? Had Mazy taught them they were to wait on their men without complaint? Did they believe it was their job to work from the crack of dawn until they dropped in bed at night? If so, no wonder all the girls were married, and the boys still stayed at home.

When she finished feeding the ground hog, Catalena slipped to Mazy's bedroom door and peeped in. She was on top of the cover with one sheet protecting the bed spread and another one covering her. Mazy's breathing was smooth and easy showing she was asleep. A feeling of relief swept over Catalena. She felt almost like a little girl left without her mother's strict supervision. She considered taking the path to Homer's place, but he'd be sure to ask how she got away from Mazy. Instead, she decided a short run would do her good. Better still, she could attempt to run up the goat path where she wrecked. Seeing that place again without anyone with her might help bring back her memory.

She ran up the goat path at a good speed until she came to the steep part where she slowed to jog. Mazy was right about not over-stressing her physical endurance. Running up that steep road was taking more strength and endurance than she'd thought it would. She was also getting rubber-kneed from looking over the rock cliff.

I drove a Jeep up this place? She thought with disbelief. No way! It was only too obvious she had taken a wrong turn somewhere, got on the narrow path and was afraid to back out.

She knew she wasn't any better at backing up than she was with heights. Before she got to the top, she slowed to a walk.

"Back in the mountains of home, the sky is so blue and the air so pure it feels like you're breathing in life itself. When you climb to the top of the mountain, it's so clear you can see for miles. It's not like here in the city where you're rebreathing air other people has huffed out of their lungs. You don't step outside into a tunnel of man-made buildings only to get a face-full of exhaust fumes. Back home you can hear the winds whispering through the pine trees, along with the singing of water as it rushes over rocks. Oh, how I want to go home, but I reckon I'll die right here."

Catalena seemed to hear those words as clear as if they were spoken to her right then. "When I'm dead, I want my remains to rest at peace in the hills of home."

Who said that? She questioned. Where had she heard those words, or had she read them in a book? She had a feeling that statement meant something to her, perhaps it still did.

"You've never known what it's like to chew on a mint leaf and then drink water from a spring. A-law," Homer groaned. "All you get here is chlorine filled water that ain't fit for a dog to drink," he added with a genuine ring of sadness.

When she reached the top of the mountain, she stopped and looked around her. "It's so clear I can see for miles," she said out loud.

She eased to the rock cliff where her Jeep had gone over. Down below was the charred, twisted metal of her burned Jeep near a stream of water. A strange feeling came over her. There were things she needed to do. Things that were important if only she could remember what they were.

"I had your grandpa's old Willys restored for you. He was proud of that thing. If only I'd learned to drive, I'd of drove it back home myself."

Again, Catalena heard those words and the sadness they were spoken with. Was the Jeep down below the same one

someone had restored? If so, whose? And, why was she driving
it?

She backed up away from the edge of the rock cliff and sat
down on a rock in the shade of a tree in hopes her memory
might return. She closed her eyes and breathed in deeply of air
pure enough to be life itself.

She opened them when she heard a slight sound behind her.

Something was thrown over her head a moment before she
was shoved to the ground face first. Someone heavy was on her
back, pushing her into the rocky ground as the hood tighten
around her neck.

Her first instinct was to scream. Her second instinct was to
fight. She did neither. Instead she lay perfectly still as though
she'd been knocked cold. The art of deception, she thought.
'Don't fight when you are at a disadvantage. Don't show your
skill before putting it to use. Surprise is a weapon in itself. Use
it to its fullest advantage.'

Sure enough, the man who was on her back lifted his body
up and rolled her over. He was straddling her and breathing
hard as his hands gripped her breasts. She didn't hesitate any
longer. She heel-handed him in the nose the same instant she
shot her knee into his groin. He squealed out in pain as she
rolled him off her. She yanked at the hood, but it was tied on.
She didn't take time to figure how to get the hood off. She
could barely see the faint image of her opponent rolling at her
feet. She remained squatted down, grabbed a rock in each hand
and started pounding at his head and face with all the force
brought on by fear and desperation. His pain-filled squalls
changed when she aimed the rocks at what she thought was his
Adams apple. The hood had loosened enough for her to see out
the bottom when she pulled on it. She saw his back side as he
got to his knees and start crawling away. She got to her feet
and started kicking at his groin area. His renewed pain was
incentive enough to make him lunge to his feet. It sounded like
he was trying to run away, while sniveling with pain.

Catalena chose not to go after him without being able to see. Instead she took time to untie the knotted twine holding a feed sack over her head. Once the sack was off, she followed him to the rhododendron hell that went down the other side of the mountain. She could hear him moaning and snapping limbs as he did his best to run through the underbrush. Her anger made her want to go after him, but her common sense stopped her. She might or might not be able to catch up with him. If she did, then what? Did she jump on him and try to beat him unconscious?

No, she told herself. It was best she go back to the Barlows house. She had no idea who attacked her or what would be waiting on her if she followed him. What she did know was that she was shaking with a mixture of fright and anger. Putting up a fight had come natural. It seemed she knew exactly what to do when being attacked. Her instinct had been to get away from the man. Once he was off her, a killing instinct set in. There was no way she was able to hurt him enough regardless of how hard she tried. Part of her still wanted to go after him, beat him to a pulp. The other part told her she needed to think this through.

"Cause and effect," she heard those words clearly. "Escape to safety first. Get revenge later," It was advice worth taking.

Catalena took time to brush the dirt of the front of her jogging clothes. Her hands and knees had been slightly skinned from where she was pushed forward. At least her knees couldn't be seen through the jeans she wore. If someone noticed the condition of her hands, she would say she fell. She slow-walked back toward the house, needing time to get herself under control. She now knew why she had been warned not to go far from the house alone. She had an idea the man who attacked her had also attacked Jeanene Korman. The poor little girl would not have been able to fight him off the way she had.

The question in her mind was what was she going to do about it? She couldn't continue to let the man go free. At the same time, did she dare tell the Barlows what had happened to her? As for going to the sheriff, from what the Barlows said, that wasn't the best idea.

Catalena neared the Barlow's house, shaking with a rush of fear and anger, she realized she'd felt those same feelings before. The more she thought about the attack, the more a hazy, unwanted feeling overcame her. She was young, in her early teens, scared out of her wits, and running as hard as she could run. There was darkness surrounding her, no safe place to go, no one to turn to. Someone was after her. She could hear her own struggled breathing, felt her legs stretching out in an attempt to run faster, heard footsteps overtaking her, getting closer and closer. A feeling of total fear gripped her. She didn't want to be helpless. She didn't want anybody or anyone to have control over her. She wanted to be as strong and capable as a girl could possibly become.

She wanted to protect herself, but there was no way. She could neither fight off an attacker, or outrun one. She was helpless, a tiny nothing in a big, bad world. A sinister shadow overtook her, grabbed hold of her hair, jerked her backward while her legs were still trying to run.

"Don't fight me." Those horrible words sounded in Catalena's mind. She knew she had fought, but it wasn't enough. A hand had clamped over her mouth stifling her screams.

Helpless – so very helpless.

And then there was another feeling that came over her, a surge of pain and then relief. Her hair felt like it was being ripped from her scalp. Someone had hold of the 'Don't fight me' man. He had been jerked away from her without turning loose of her hair. She had fallen backward, hitting hard.

She knew there had been pain, but she hadn't actually felt it as she jumped to her feet and started running again.

Right now, while walking on Barlow land, she felt that same fear as she felt back then, but she had been able to protect herself this time. Only protect herself. She hadn't been able to destroy her attacker, nor had there been someone who stepped out of the darkness to pull him off her.

There was no doubt in Catalena's mind, after the attack, she had started running and taking self-defense classes. She was able to save herself.

Chapter 20

~~~~

"**W**hat the hell happened to you?" Alvin asked Kimbell when he came upon him in the edge of the woods puking his guts out.

"Somethin' I ate," he mumbled.

"No, shit." Alvin said. "Looks like what you ate beat the hell outta you."

"No, she didn't," Kimbell made the mistake of saying.

"She? It was a girl who did that to you?" Alvin questioned before his puzzled look dissolved. "Oh, hell," Alvin said as the realization of what Kimbell had done. "You're a stupid idiot. It was that girl who wrecked her Jeep, wasn't it? You've been slobbering over her ever since you laid eyes on her."

As Kimbell thought of her and what she'd done to his balls, he puked some more.

"How did you run across her? I know you didn't go near the Barlow's house. You're too big of a fat-assed coward to go there."

Kimbell didn't like being called names, but he was too sick and hurting too badly to do anything about it. Shit, it was all he could do to breathe and talk at the same time. "I've been watching her for a while."

"So, that's what you've been slipping off doing. Thought you were hidin' from Pa to get outta work."

Kimbell shook his head causing another wave of sickness to overcome him.

"She get you in the balls?"

"Yeah, twice," Kimbell moaned. "It hurt like hell fire."

"Ah, man! You're up shit creek for certain. If those Barlows don't kill you, Pa will. He told you to stay away from her."

"She didn't see me," he gagged again. "I put a feed sack over her head."

Alvin sniggered. "You had a sack over her head and she still did all that to you?"

"She was like a wild cat, a kickin' and a clawin'. I couldn't do a thing with her."

"Looks like that wild cat did a few things to you. Your whole face and head are covered in blood."

"Reckon Pa will notice?"

"Yeah, you shitfaced idjet. Him and the Barlows both will notice unless you stick your head in a cow pile and pretend to be a shit-eating bug. There's no other way to hide how your face looks. There's even blood running down your neck. You've got a big chunk of meat missing outta your ear. The blood from it has already turned your shirt red. Pa will most likely take his razor strap and hide every inch of skin off a your back for going against what he told you not to do, but those Barlows will sure enough cut what she left of your balls off before they end up killing you."

Kimbell whimpered as he wiped blood mixed with snot from his nose onto his shirt sleeve.

A questioning look suddenly came to Alvin's face. "Say, where's the feed sack?"

"It was still on her head when I got away from her."

"Good going, shit for brains. Those Barlows will recognize the kind of feed Ma uses to feed her milk goats."

"I couldn't exactly take the sack off her head and let her see who I was, now could I?"

"You could have knocked her out cold and thrown her over the rock cliff again. She might not have been as lucky the second time around."

"How could I have done that when I was crawling on my knees with my balls all busted up like chicken eggs?"

Alvin chuckled with a morbid kind of glee. "Fool idiot. You're done got yourself in a fix, alright. You're gonna get bloody hell from all directions no matter what you do."

"What am I gonna do," Kimbell moaned, as tears ran down his fat cheeks leaving a mixture of dirt and bloody streaks. "I'll tell Pa me and you got in a fight, and you done this to me."

"Might work for Pa, but it won't work on those Barlows."

"They won't know it was me."

"You plan on hiding out from 'em until you're all healed up?"

"Yeah, I can do that."

"When those Barlows show up at the house and you're nowhere in sight, them and Pa both will know it was you without having to set eyes on you."

"I know what we can do. Let's me and you jump on Densley Hordly and beat the shit outta him. Then they'll think he's the one they're after."

"I'm all in for that, but it won't work. Him and his brother ain't here. They've been gone down to Florida with their Ma and Pa since yesterday morning. Don't know when they'll be back."

"How about Enrick Rainey? You and I both could take him if we snuck up on him from behind. That shithead deserves to have the Barlows after him."

"Might could, but that sneaky bastard would wait his chance and kill us for settin' him up."

"Once the Barlows think it was him, we can rat out his operation in the bottom of Nickle Hordly's garage."

"Could," agreed Alvin, "but then the Hordlys would help Enrick kill us."

"Not if they went to jail first."

"I like that idea, but I don't know how we'd pull it off in time to save your ass. Those Barlows will be here before you stop puking. If you ask me, that girl is tellin' them what happened right now."

"I can hide out for a while after we beat up Rainey," Kimbell suggested again.

"And leave me to lie to Pa? Sorry, bro, but you're onto nothing more than wishful thinking."

"Darnell can help us beat up Enrick Rainey," Kimbell continued hopefully.

"You know as good as I do that he won't strike a lick at a snake, much less fight."

"What am I to do, then?" Kimbell moaned.

"If it was me, I'd head into town and join the army like I've been wantin' to do for a spell now."

"Yeah, that'd get me away from here fast. You'd join up with me, wouldn't you?"

"Yeah, I've been thinkin' hard on it. Hain't no future staying here with Pa workin' my hind-end off when I get nothing outta it."

"Let's do it then," Kimbell begged.

"Stop pukin' and come on. We'll take Pa's truck and be long gone afore he catches us."

"You go get our clothes," Kimbell said.

"You dumb ass. We don't need clothes. The army gives us uniforms."

"Yeah, but we'll need some money to buy gas and things. If I'm gonna join up with the army, I want me a Pepsi and a moon pie first."

"You got a point there. I'll go to the house and sneak back with money from Pa's billfold and Mom's pocketbook. We best be a long way's gone from here afore Pa gets back."

~~~~

Rob and Bob pulled into the gas station in time to see Alvin getting back into Markum's truck like a biting bulldog was hot on his heels. When Kimbell saw the Barlows, he scrunched down in the seat until only the top of his head stuck up.

"Did you get a look at Kimbell's face?" Bob asked.

"Yeah, I did. By the looks of it, I'd say he lost the fight."

"Think Markum did that to him?"

"Probably." Rob said. "Alvin didn't look any worse than usual and we both know Darnell didn't have anything to do with it."

"Reckon those Hordlys and Raineys done it to him?"

"Heard the Hordly boys are in Florida with their folks. Most likely weren't them."

"What about Enrick Rainey?"

"To big a coward to fight by himself."

"Right about that. Where do you reckon they're going?"

"Wouldn't know."

"Look at the pump. They filled up the tank. They never get more than a few gallons at a time. Wonder why they're doing it today?"

"Don't know, don't care," Rob told his brother. "Toss you on who pumps."

"Okay," Bob said as he pulled a nickel out of his pocket, tossed it in the air, caught it, and slapped it on the back of his hand. "Call it."

"Heads," Rob said.

Bob moved his hand from the nickel. "Tails. You lose."

"Dang it."

Bob chuckled.

"I'm gonna tell Darlene I'm you, and set you up for a date."

"She can tell us apart. Bring me out a bottle of cold pop," Bob told him. "I'm right thirsty."

"Alvin Korman seemed in a rather big hurry," Rob said to Darlene, the check-out girl as he paid for gas and two bottles of pop.

She gave Rob her brightest smile. "He did at that. Bought a lot of cakes, crackers, cheese, bread, and a pack of bologna.

He's never done that before. I asked if he was going on a picnic. He told me to mind my own business."

"Interesting," Rob said.

"He appeared as nervous as a caged cat," she added. "No telling what he's been into. You're Rob, aren't you? I can always tell you apart."

"Bob," he said. "How much do I owe you?"

"Really? You're Bob?" She questioned and then told him how much he owed, as a hopeful look came to her face. "There's a good movie playing Saturday night," she added as she handed him change, while allowing her fingertips to slide over the palm of his hand.

"Hardly ever go to movies," he told her, as he pulled his hand away and put his change in his pocket. He didn't see the disappointment on her face as he went out the door, but he knew it was there.

He got into the driver's side of the truck and handed Bob the bottle of pop.

"She hit on you again?" Bob asked.

"Yeah," Rob answered. "Told her I was you. You've got a date for the movies Saturday night."

~~~~

Catalena wasn't sure how she felt as she walked back down the narrow road. She did know she was shaking inside and outside. Several emotions were churning inside her at the same time. For a moment, when the sack was put over her head, she was scared almost senseless. She hadn't known what to do until her training took hold.

Training, she thought.

What kind of training?

Had she been in the armed service? Was that where she was taught to fight? And she did fight. Somehow, she didn't think she was in the armed service. Like she knew she loved to run, she knew she'd been trained in self-defense. She knew how to fight off an attacker even when she was blinded by a sack. Right now, her anger was still pumping hot. She wanted revenge. She wanted justice. How was she to go about getting it? Did she dare tell the Barlows what happened? Did she dare not tell them? Whoever attacked her had obviously attacked poor little Jeanene Korman, plus who knows what other girls suffered a sack over their heads? According to what she'd been told, she had no doubt it was the Kormans.

Yet, if she told, the Barlows just might feel they had to defend her – by doing what? Going to the sheriff? She doubted that. There was a reason they stayed away from the law. If not, that would have been the first place they would have gone when she wrecked the Jeep. Was there a code of some sort in this place? Did mountain people deal out their own kind of law enforcement? An eye for an eye and a tooth for a tooth perhaps?

By the time she neared the house, she'd decided to remain silent until she knew more about what was going on – maybe even until she regained her memory. She was feeling as though her memory was slowly returning. If only she could remember who she was. It might help if she could see something familiar. Going up the goat path and seeing where she wrecked for the second time seemed to help a little. She might have remembered more, if it hadn't been for her attacker. Maybe if she went into the ravine and had a look at her Jeep more memory would return. She made a point of hiding the sack that was put over her head in the weeds at the edge of the woods before she went to the house.

Mazy was still sleeping when she got back. The twins had recently brought in a load of slabs from the sawmill. It was Homer's job to cut them into stove wood size sticks. She made a point of carrying wood from the wood pile to the porch and placing it on the ground. She didn't want to make any noise that might wake Mazy up. The poor woman needed all the rest she could get. After that, she pulled some grass and took it to her pet ground hog. She grinned as she thought of Rob and

Bob. If there had been only one of them, she might feel some strong appeal in the romance department. The two of them were one too many to even think about regardless of how good looking they were. Suddenly it hit her who they resembled. They were a cross between Sam Elliott and Tom Selleck in the movie "The Shadow Riders." Homer Barlow was an older Sam Elliott in looks, build, and actions. She wondered if Harm Barlow had been a Tom Selleck. If that was the case, no wonder Mazy couldn't get over losing him.

Stupid. She accused herself of being as the closed the door to the ground hog's cage. She was letting her imagination run wild. The thing she hadn't imagined were her skinned up hands and knees. They were still burning, and bruising was starting to show. It wasn't the first time her hands were bruised. It wasn't the first time she fought like her life depended on it.

"Yes," she whispered out loud. "I'm starting to remember. I'll know who I am soon. I know I will."

"Don't know if I like that idea or not?"

She whirled around to see Rob leaning against the frame of the barn door. "You startled me," she said.

"Sorry. Didn't mean to."

"Why wouldn't you like the idea of me regaining my memory?" His words had irritated her.

"If you regain your memory, you'll leave us," Rob told her. "I'm getting used to having you around."

His comment felt a little too personal. She tried to counter it. "I'm certainly grateful to your family for taking such good care of me. I don't think many people would welcome me the way your family has."

"Most folks around here would."

"Most folks?" she couldn't resist prodding him. "Who wouldn't welcome me? The Kormans? Perhaps the Hordlys?" If he answered, she could have more confirmation on who had attacked her.

"I'm sure they would welcome you, but in an entirely different way than the rest of us. How's little Pudgy doing? I see you brought her some grass to eat," he said, as he moved to the cage where Catalena was standing. He brought with him the aroma of fresh sawn lumber.

"She is growing fast and eating everything I bring to her." Catalena made a point of moving a step away from him. His closeness bothered her, and she wasn't sure why. "Where's Bob?"

"He's in the Johnny house."

"Oh. I'm surprised it's not a two-seater."

Rob grinned. "Once a twin, always a twin, right?"

"That appears to be the case."

"I'm afraid it is, to a point," he added.

He reached out and lightly curled a strand of her hair around his finger and gently caressed it with his thumb. "I'm anxious to see what happens when your memory returns," he told her. "I've got an idea you'll be gone from here faster than you showed up."

"You're probably right. Can I ask a favor of you?" she said without pulling her hair away from his finger. It almost felt like he was caressing her skin.

"What?"

"Can you take me to where my Jeep burned?"

"Why?"

"I'm hoping it might jar some of my memory back. I have a feeling that Jeep was important to me."

"Like I just said, I'm not looking forward to the day you to leave us, but I'll take you there. When do you want to go?"

"How about now?"

"Before or after Bob gets out of the john?" he asked.

"I wouldn't dream of separating the two of you."

"I was afraid you'd say that," he grinned and lifted his brows in a flirting sort of way.

"Are you testing the water, so to speak?" she questioned.

"I am. What is it's temperature?"

She grinned, willing to return his flirting - slightly. "Warm," she said, "but not boiling - yet."

"Good. I wouldn't like getting burned."

"Neither would I."

"What's this?" he questioned. "You've got some cracked corn and oats kernels in your hair. You been in the cuttin' room?"

"What is a cuttin' room?"

"That's where Mom keeps the feed for her milk cows."

"Oh, didn't realize it." She reached up and brushed at her hair.

He turned loose of her hair and took hold of her hand. She jumped with the sting it caused. He observed her knuckles before he turned her hand over and looked at her palm before she quickly pulled her hand away.

"What happened?" he questioned.

"I tripped," she said. "Caught myself with my hands."

Not only were her palms skinned, her knuckles were scuffed up and bruised from where she'd battered her attacker with both hands. Even holding the rock had bruised her. Never was forceful contact made that didn't hurt both the maker and taker. She wondered how her attacker fared? She had no idea how much damage she had actually done to him. She hoped there was some visual damage that marked him enough for her to recognize him.

Rob lifted his brows as Bob came into sight. "We'll discuss your fall later, okay?"

She didn't answer.

"There you are," Bob said. "I was wondering where you got to." He looked from Catalena to Rob, giving Rob a disapproving frown.

"Lena wants to see where her Jeep burned. She's hoping it might trigger some memory." Rob told his brother. "Let's take her before it's time to start supper."

"Okay," Bob agreed, but there was a reluctance to his tone.

"Aren't the two of you home early?" she asked as they walked toward the truck?

"Yep," Bob answered. "We sold lumber today. Brought Mom a load of slabs, and decided to take an hour or two break before we start sawing again in the morning. Why aren't you with Mom?"

"She's taking a nap. Didn't want to go in the house and wake her."

"Mom napping? That's odd. Why's she napping this time of day?" Bob wanted to know.

"She's not young," Catalena said.

"She's not old either," Bob was ready to argue his mother was nowhere near old.

"She's having some woman problems, right?" Rob was quick to question.

"Menopause," Catalena said.

Bob's cheeks turned red, and he shut up. Rob winked at her and stifled his grin.

Finally, Catalena found a marked difference in the twins' behavior. She also found herself in the seat of the lumber truck wedged between Rob and Bob. Her shoulders were touching the shoulders of both men. There was definitely a difference in her response toward the twins. She longed to move away from Bob, while leaning against Rob. Even the smell of their sweat was different from each other. For such a big truck, there wasn't as much room in the cab as she expected.

"Can I ask you a personal question?" she said hesitantly.

"Sure," Rob said.

"It depends on what it is?" Bob said.

"Spit it out," Rob told her.

"Do you earn enough money to build your mother a bathroom with a washer and dryer in it?"

"We've offered, but she won't have it," Bob told her.

"We probably could," Rob told her.

"Then why don't you?"

"I just told you why," Bob said.

"Mom doesn't like change," Rob told her. "It's her house and her wishes. We don't want to go against her."

"Do it anyway. Believe me, it's too hard on her. The last few days have proven that much to me, and I'm a lot younger than your mother."

"You're a timid city girl. Mom's not," Bob pointed out with irritation.

"She's making a good observation," Rob said. "Mom is taking a nap. Have you ever seen her do that before?"

Bob didn't answer.

"You think we should cut and kiln dry the lumber, bring it home and just start adding a bathroom onto the house?" Rob asked her.

"That's exactly what I think."

"Mom would have a stroke," Bob said.

"She's more likely to have one if you don't," Catalena told him. "If she complains, tell her you'd rather take a nice warm shower than trying to scrub sawdust off outback in the creek. You can also say soap kills fish if you want."

"You're a bossy little thing," Rob said with a grin. "But you might be right."

"She doesn't know a thing about our ways," Bob was quick to add. "Mom doesn't want to us to get too big for our britches."

"Your sisters have bathrooms in their houses," Catalena pointed out as she tried to hide her irritation at Bob.

"How do you know?"

"I've talked to your mother and Uncle Homer."

"You seem to have your mind stuck on this bathroom thing," Rob said.

"Plus a washer and dryer," she said.

Bob started to say something, but Rob was quicker.

"We'll see what we can do. We've always thought Mom knew best and stood back letting her do things her way. You're seeing all her hard work from an outsider's point of view. We'll take a closer look at things," Rob assured her.

"Good," she said, not sure all the harping she'd done while she was here would make any difference, but she tried.

"Are you taking Darlene to the movies Saturday?" Rob suddenly changed the subject by asking Bob.

"What are you talking about?" Bob returned.

"I told her I was you, and she asked you to take her to the new movie that was playing in town."

"Cut the crap, Rob."

"It's not crap. It's the truth."

"She's struck on you, not me."

"You've got that wrong," Rob told him even when he thought Bob was right. He also knew Bob liked her – at least a little bit.

"If that's true, she's finally starting to develop good taste," Bob was quick to add.

Catalena grinned. That remark sounded like something Rob would say – or their Uncle Homer.

"Besides, I wouldn't want to leave you home alone. What would people think if that happened?" Bob continued

"No problem there. We'd take Lena along and that would solve the problem. She needs to get out and about. It's not good for her to stay shut up all the time."

"So, that's your angle," Bob was quick to reply. "Lena, don't let him take you in on one of his schemes. Darlene has been after him for years. He's trying to dump her on me, while making her think you and him are an item."

Catalena didn't exactly know what to think of that remark, but she would like any excuse to get away from the house and all the work Mazy had her doing. Plus, she would like to be in Rob's company for a little while. See if the water would warm up or turn cold.

"Sounds good," Catalena surprised both men by saying. "I'd like to go to a movie again."

Rob grinned from ear to ear. "In that case, Bob, you'd best go by the gas station and ask Darlene what time she wants you to pick her up. Can't remember if she said a time or not."

"Can't all four of us fit in the truck," Bob pointed out with a touch of triumph

"No problem. You can drop Lena and me off at the movie house, and then go after Darlene. Look at this valley, Lena. Uncle Homer and Dad cut the timber off it years ago. Bob and I replanted the steep part in white pines a few years ago. We grassed the level land for hay to feed Mom's cows and Uncle Homer's goats."

"I like the river that runs through it," Bob told her.

"It's only a river in wet weather," Rob pointed out. "It's little more than a creek during a dry season."

"It's pretty," Catalena said, as she saw the crumpled-up clump of burned metal laying between the river and the foot of the rock cliff. "That's my Jeep?"

"That's it," Bob told her. "The gas tank hit so many rocks it exploded on the way down. I tried to put the fire out, but it burned too hot to get close it."

"He got singed," Rob said with a grin.

"I was trying to make sure no one was still in it."

"Are you sure there wasn't?" Catalena asked with concern.

"We're sure," Rob told her. "We raked through the ashes and found no bones or teeth."

"If there was an explosion, couldn't it blow someone out of the Jeep?"

"Could, but we'd have found them," Rob told her.

Catalena cringed. What if she hadn't gotten out of the Jeep? She tried not to think about that as Bob opened the passenger door and helped her out. His hand holding hers didn't have the same effect as Rob's had, but that didn't mean a thing.

"Want me to carry you across the creek so you can get a close up look?" Bob ask her.

"Goodness, no," she was quick to tell him. "I'll take off my shoes and wade it."

"You'll have to roll up George's britches legs or you'll get them wet. It's deeper than it looks," Rob told her.

"No problem," she said as she bent down and started rolling up the britches legs. She was surprised when Rob grabbed her up in his arms and splashed into the water.

"Hey, put me down," she said.

"Nope," he said as his arms tightened around her. "Not just yet," he whispered near her ear to keep Bob from hearing. "Had to see how you fit against me."

He was grinning when he set her down at the edge of the water.

"Thank you," she said politely as she rushed toward the burned Jeep. She wasn't sure if she fit in his arms or not, but part of her wanted to find out. She forgot all about finding out as she got close the Jeep. The words, "I'm sorry," came to her mind. She wanted to cry at the condition of the Jeep. She felt as though she had destroyed something special because of her carelessness.

"My purse was in there," she said. "Did you find it?"

"Whatever was in there burned to ashes," Bob said as he came up behind her.

"You found nothing at all left."

"A few pieces of broken pottery," Rob told her.

"Pottery?"

"Right. A flower vase or something like that," Bob added.

"Where is it?"

Bob pointed to a spot a few feet from the Jeep. "Right there. We raked them out when we were looking for bones and teeth. There might have been some color on the pottery, but the fire turned the pieces black. Clay doesn't burn up, but either the fall or the explosion must have broken the pottery."

A sadness came over Catalena as she picked the pottery out of the ashes. Something about the broken pieces made her want to cry.

"Are there enough pieces to glue it back together?"

"Why would you do that?" Bob asked her.

"To see what it was. It must have been important to me if I was carrying it around."

"She has a point," Rob said as he started picking pieces up from the ashes.

"Now that the metal is cold, we might ought to roll the Jeep over and see if anything is under it," Bob suggested.

"Good idea," Rob agreed.

Catalena cringed as she watched the twins grab hold of the charred metal making it clang as they moved it about. The frame without tires, top, and seats seemed so unsubstantial. To think this small amount of metal was all that protected the driver was an eyeopener.

She looked from the Jeep to the rock cliff where it had tumbled down, trying to see the outcropping she had landed on. No wonder she didn't remember anything. Going over that cliff would have scared the memory out of anybody, especially her, considering how afraid she was of heights.

"There's no wonder I don't want to remember that," she said, but neither twin heard her over the noise they were making. Looking up was almost as scary as looking down from the top. "I nearly died," she concluded. "But I didn't. I jumped out and hit my head on the rock." And that hit caused her memory loss. She lifted her hand and felt of the knot. It had gone down slightly. She remembered reading that a concussion could cause memory loss. Memory loss from a mild concussion usually returned after a week or so. Why did she remember that? Why would she have been searching for memory loss anyway? Had this happened to her before?

"There's a few more small pieces of pottery that we overlooked," Bob said as he came toward her from the Jeep. "We didn't find anything else."

She turned her attention to him. "No hinges or latch to a suitcase? Nothing such as that?" she asked.

"No, but the fire was mighty hot, plus the explosion scattered small stuff."

"Nothing that looked like a purse?"

"Nothing," Bob told her.

She wasn't surprised. A fire hot enough to warp metal was hot enough to burn a purse or suitcase. Unless there was no suitcase in the Jeep. What if she'd been staying in a hotel somewhere? If she wasn't from around there, if she was a city girl, then she would have to be traveling a distance. Most likely she would have a room at a hotel nearby.

"Have you seen enough? Mom will be worried if she wakes up and finds you gone," Bob told her.

Rob left the Jeep and came over to them. "You okay?" he asked her.

"I'm fine," she stretched the truth. She wasn't sure she would be fine ever again. "Bob's right. Mazy will be worried if she wakes up and I'm not there."

Bob grabbed her up in his arms with a laugh. "Beat you to it, brother," he was quick to say as he headed through the water. He'd gotten three feet when he tripped, dropped Catalena and fell on top of her causing her to drop the pieces she had in her hands into the water.

"I'm sorry, so very sorry," Bob said as he jumped up and tried to help her to her feet. Rob was bent over laughing.

Catalena didn't find anything funny about it – neither did Bob.

Once they were in the truck, Rob turned on the heater to warm them up a little. He didn't seem to mind getting slightly wet from Catalena sitting next to him. He actually grinned all the way home.

"What in blue blazes?" Homer asked as he watched them get out of the truck. "Who baptized who? And why?"

"Bob did it," Rob said with obvious amusement.

"I was trying to keep her from getting wet," Bob defended himself.

"Did a fine job of it," Homer grinned. "Best get those wet things off and hang them on the line to dry."

Catalena and Bob both disappeared through the door.

"She wanted to see the burned Jeep?" Homer asked Rob.

"Right. It bothered her some. Seeing the results of going over that cliff."

"What did she say about it?"

"Not much, but her face turned pale as she looked at the remains. Her hands were shaking."

"I can believe that. Say, I found a feed sack over yonder in the bushes next to the goat path. It was the kind of cheap feed Lettie Korman feeds her milk goats. Know anything about it?"

"Nope."

"Didn't think you would. Odd thing is there was a rock placed on top of it."

"Think one of the Kromans put it there?"

"Nope," Homer told him. "I found long strands of hair in it. Hair the color and length of Lena's."

"Any traces of feed inside the sack?"

"Some feed dust – showing the sack recently had feed in it. The sack hadn't been washed the way Lettie usually does."

"What do you think?"

"Can't figure it out yet. Anything unusual going on today?"

"Couple of things. Mom was having female problems and took a nap. That in itself is concerning. Plus, Lena's hands are skinned up and her knuckles are bruised. Kind of like she's been hitting something."

"Interesting. Walk up that road a little way and see if you can find any footprints. I was heading to do it when you drove up."

Homer watched as Rob disappeared. He went to the porch and sat down in his usual chair and waited for Bob and Catalena to come outside. He heard Catalena and then Bob go out the kitchen door to hang their wet clothes on the line. A few minutes later they came around the corner of the house.

"You both look a sight better after your baths," Homer said with a grin. "Come set down a spell before it's time to start the supper fire. Is Mazy still taking a nap?"

"She is. I peeked in on her," Catalena told him. "How do you know she's taking a nap?"

"What else would she be doing if she's not up going?"

"She's gotta be sick," Bob sounded concerned. "Mom don't take naps."

"Yeah, she does," Homer was quick to correct him. "She does it when she thinks no one is looking. She gets tired same as anybody else."

"You spy on Mom?"

"Nope, but I have eyes to see with," Homer told Bob. "As well as ears to hear with." Homer looked at the watch on his wrist, and then peered down the road. "Right on time. There comes George. You can set your clock by that boy."

"Where's Rob?" Bob asked.

"Moseying around somewhere, I suspect," Homer told him.

"Where would he go?" Bob persisted.

Homer ignored him as he turned to Catalena. "Seeing your burned Jeep stir any memories?

"It stirred my emotions," she admitted, but she didn't want to say more than that. What did one say when their world had been destroyed by a careless mistake. Without her identity she was nobody. A blank person filling up space.

"Talk about lazy," George said as he came up to the porch. "Sitting on the porch twiddling your thumbs. Never get anywhere in life by sitting on your rump," George repeated what his Uncle Homer had told him many times over.

"My guess would be that you didn't learn a thing at school today," Homer told him as George took his backpack off and sat down on the steps.

"Not enough to brag about. It's difficult to learn something new when you already know it all," he quoted Uncle Homer again. "Hi Lena," George said as he gave her a wink. "Wanna go for a run?"

"Can I take a raincheck until tomorrow," she told him. Running might help relieve some of her pent-up emotions but being attacked had also taken something out of her – as did seeing the Jeep she had been driving. Or maybe it had put something into her. Perhaps both.

"Whatever you want," he sounded disappointed. "Where's Rob?" he questioned Bob.

"Moseying around," Bob mocked Homer.

"Why's your hair wet?" George asked Catalena.

"Bob baptized her."

Bob rolled his eyes and shook his head.

Catalena grinned. "He dropped me in the water," she clarified.

"Okay," George drawled. "Do I ask anything further, or should I let it go?"

"Let it go until you get old enough to understand," Homer was quick to tell him.

"I'm old enough to understand all you got left is memories and that's going fast. As for me, I have a lot of fun to look forward to."

"Smart aleck kid," Homer mumbled.

"There was one thing I did find interesting," George said rather hesitantly.

"Spit it out," Homer told him.

George glanced at Catalena for a moment. "Jeanene Korman started crying and carrying on in class today. The teacher sent her to the school nurse. Never came back to class again, and she didn't ride home on the school bus."

"Wonder why?" Homer said.

"Wouldn't know," George told him.

"Speaking of the Kormans, Rob and I saw something interesting. Alvin and Kimbell were at the gas station when we were filling up. Kimbell's face was roughed up. When they saw Rob and me, they burned rubber getting out of there," Bob said.

"What about Alvin?" Homer asked.

"Looked normal."

"Markum must have laid one on Kimbell," George said.

"Could have. Somehow, I don't think so, but that don't mean it wasn't Markum," Bob added.

Chapter 21

~~~~~

Rob saw the print of Catalena's tennis shoes not far from the spot Homer found the feed sack. He figured Homer's hip and leg must be bothering him worse than usual for him not to have walked up the narrow road far enough to find the shoeprints. Her shoeprints were going up the road and coming back down. He walked farther up the road noticing that the prints were a much greater distance apart. She was running. She'd gone running. Running wasn't unusual for her. Yet, something didn't feel right to Rob. He continued tracking her to the top of the cliff where she wrecked her Jeep. The rocky ground had enough fine soil between rocks to tell him the story he sought.

Next to a large flat rock near a tree, the ground had been scuffed up considerably. He picked out Catalena's shoeprints along with larger footprints that surely belonged to a man. He followed the man's footprints into laurel hells where fallen leaves were scuffed up. It was much easier to track in soft woods dirt than it was on the rocky road. He continued tracking onto Korman land. At the edge of the woods near the Korman house, another set of shoeprints joined the first ones. The prints showed two men had stomped about in one place and then separated.

His first instinct was to rush to the Korman house and confront whoever had attacked Catalena. He had taken only a few steps when intelligent caution set in. There were four Korman men and perhaps several Hordly men, plus, the

women could be just as vicious as the men. It took a lot of
control for him to control his anger enough to backtrack to the
top of the knob where Catalena was attacked. On closer
inspection, he spotted a fist-size rock stained with dried blood.

"Good girl," he said with approval. She'd used whatever
weapon was available. Hitting him with the rock had helped
bruise her hand. No wonder she jumped when he took hold of
her hand. He stuck the rock in his pocket and took off running
down the road.

He was breathing heavy and sweating slightly by the time
he got to the porch where the others were setting. All eyes
turned toward him. He stopped at the steps in front of where
George set, took the rock out of his pocket, and held it out
toward Catalena.

"Best tell us what happened," he said to her.

Catalena sucked in her breath and then let it out slowly. Her
eyes were big with concern.

"What are you talking about?" she tried to sound innocent
even when she knew Rob figured out most of what happened.

"Who was he?" Rob questioned her. All eyes were on him.

Catalena realized she was caught, but she didn't know how
much Rob knew. Don't give away the evidence, she thought.
Find out what they know, versus what they suspect.

"Who was who?" she asked.

Rob gave her a bewildered look. "Who did you beat with
this rock?"

"I don't know," she told him.

"Why don't you know. Was he a stranger, or did he put a
feed sack over your head?"

Catalena gave all four Barlows a quick look. None of them
had so much as a scrape. It wasn't one of them. Rob had been
gone for a long time before returning from the direction of what
she called the goat path.

"Pretty good at reading tracks, aren't you?" she said.

"Real good," he answered.

"Okay," she said. "I thought going to where I wrecked by myself might help jog my memory." She stopped talking.

"And you set down on the rock to rest."

"Right."

"And the next thing you knew there was a feed sack over your head?"

"Yes, and then I was knocked on the ground face first. That's how I skinned my hands and knees."

"Know who it was?" Rob asked.

"No. I didn't see him. I beat him in the face and head with the rock and kneed him in the groin. He cursed and moaned a lot as he was hobbling away. He was gone by the time I got the sack off my head."

"Damn," Homer mumbled.

"Kimbell," Bob said.

"Let's go get him," George added.

"Hold on a minute," Homer said. "Lena, tell us again how you fought him off when you couldn't see."

"I told you I thought I was a runner. I also realized I'd been trained in how to fight off an attacker."

"No shit!" George said with a grin.

Homer smacked at him. "Watch your language boy."

"You're the one who did all that damage to Kimbell's face?" Bob started laughing.

Rob handed the rock to Homer. "See the dried blood on that rock. Kimbell looked a lot worse than the bloody rock."

Homer looked at the rock and then put it in his pocket. "What did he do after he shoved you down?"

"He was on my back holding me down until I couldn't get up. He was heavy, felt fat. I didn't move as I took hold of the rock. I was hoping he'd think I'd been addled if not knocked out, and he'd get off my back. He was still hovering over me as he rolled me over. I kneed him in the groin and pounded at his nose and Adam's apple with the rock and my hands. I kicked him in the groin again. He escaped and I took the sack off my head. I followed him to the woods."

"Why didn't you tell us what happened?" Rob asked. "You seemed rather calm."

"I thought you might retaliate, and I didn't want that to happen."

"Why not?" George asked.

"I didn't want any of you to get in trouble because of me. Besides, if I ever run across him when the sack isn't on my head, I intend to make him pay big time."

"Damn," Homer said again.

"Watch your language," George said as he smacked at him.

"That's why they took off so fast when they saw us at the gas station. They thought we knew what happened and were after them," Rob said.

"Let's go get 'em," George said.

"No," Catalena told them firmly. "You're not getting in trouble over me. I mean it."

Homer's eyebrows raised at the authority in her voice.

"I'm the one who'll see he gets what's coming to him," Catalena assured them.

"How?" George questioned.

"I'm not sure, but I know I will."

Rob started to say something, but Homer shook his head. "Let it be for a while, boys. Lena's right. Revenge is best served cold."

Those words had hardly left Homer's mouth when he saw Brent Kilby walking up the road. "Don't say a word in front of Brent. His maw is head of the local gossip grapevine. She works in maintenance at the hospital. Tell Brenda Kilby and it'll travel faster than the speed of light."

"Hey, boy. Come join us and rest your legs a spell," Homer pointed at the step beside George. Nice evening to set and jaw a little."

Brent set down beside George. It was obvious he was about to explode with what he'd come to tell them.

"How's your folks?" Homer asked as an opening.

"Mom just got home from work," he told them with excitement sounding in his voice.

"Is that so," Homer continued. "Anything happening at the hospital?"

"Oh, yeah," he said with shining eyes.

"Such as?" Homer continued.

Brent looked at George. "I found out why Jeanene wasn't on the bus."

"Why's that?" George asked.

"Don't know as I ought to tell. Mom said I might get in trouble if I did."

"Won't get in trouble by telling us. You already know that," Homer assured him.

"I know," he sounded hesitant. "The school nurse and some other folks sent the sheriff out to arrest Kimbell."

"Why's that?" Homer said in a calm, almost non-interested tone of voice.

Brent downed his head and his face flushed slightly, but he answered in a low whisper. "Seems she's in the family way."

"Did she say it was Kimbell's doing?" Homer asked.

Brett nodded. "Mom said she heard her screaming out, calling Kimbell every bad name in the book."

Catalena took in a deep breath but said nothing. She now knew why the poor girl was crying.

"How old is she now?" Homer asked.

"She's two or three grades below us, but she's in one of our classes. I'm guessing she's thirteen or fourteen," George answered.

"Thirteen. Mom said she was thirteen."

Catalena started to say she looked more like eleven or twelve, but she remembered her promise to George in time to remain silent.

They heard the sound of a car engine coming up the road. Brett jumped up and ran toward the barn.

"Sit still. Let's see who it is," Homer told George when he started to get up and follow Brent to the barn. "Lena, you hide inside."

Catalena didn't hesitate. Mazy made room for her as she stopped near the door where she couldn't be seen but could hear what was being said. She started to say something, but Mazy put her finger across her lips to warn Catalena to be silent. Catalena almost grinned. Mazy had been eavesdropping on them.

A black and white pulled into the yard and stopped on the grass in front of the porch. A pudgy man got out and swaggered the few steps it took him to reach the steps.

"If it ain't Herbert Waddell, never thought I'd be seeing you all the way up here. What can we do for you?" Homer asked in his most welcoming way. "Pull up a step and join us."

"Not got time for sitting on my hind end like some folks," he said pointedly. "I'm looking for Kimbell Korman."

"You're at the wrong house, then. Been some time since we've seen him. Why are you looking for him?"

"It's police matter and none of your business."

Homer's tone of voice became even more friendly and accommodating. "The Korman house is up the other road, Herbert."

"Hell, I know that. Want to know if you've seen him."

"Like I said. It's been some time since we've seen him."

"Is he speaking for all you boys?" Waddell demanded as though he knew they would lie.

"I've not seen him in some time," Rob said.

"Me neither," Bob added.

Waddell's eyes shot to George. "What about you, boy?"

"Don't hardly see nobody. Sure ain't seen Kimbell in a coon's age," George told him.

"You go to school with Jeanene Korman?" he demanded.

"She's in a few grades below me, but I sometimes see her if she rides the school bus."

"She on it today?"

"Seems like she was this morning. Don't recall seeing her on the bus this evening. She might have been. Why? Is something wrong with her?"

"It's my job to ask the questions, not yourn, boy."

"He answered your questions," Homer told him firmly. "Since Kimbell ain't here, you best be lookin' for him somewhere else if you aim to find him."

Catalena almost grinned at the way Homer was talking to the sheriff. Mazy poked her in the ribs to make sure she didn't make a sound.

"You know where he's at, or see him, you best be letting me know. Here's my card. You best call my office if you hear where he's at."

Homer took the card out of his fingers. "I'll do it," he said. "Most likely you'll not hear unless you've got mighty good hearing."

Sheriff Waddell gave him a challenging look.

"Folks don't have telephone lines this far back in the hills," Homer said. "Don't know for certain how far my calling will reach."

Sheriff Waddell gave him a scathing look. "Then send one of the boys in. That's an order from the law," he said as he turned and waddled back to the black and white. He spun up grass as he backed up and took off.

Once the sheriff was out of sight, Mazy stepped out on the porch followed by Catalena.

"He's as bad as the Korman's," Mazy said. "Kind of hope me and Catalena gets a hold of him before Waddell does. We'll do what ought to have been done at his birth."

All eyes turned to Mazy in surprise.

Mazy grabbed the card out of Homer's hand, tore it into pieces, marched to the kitchen with it, and tossed it into the stove's firebox. She looked Catalena in the eyes. "My boys won't get involved in this, you hear me?" she said firmly. "I'm not as timid as some might think. You beat the shit outta him, but I'll cut him slick as a boiled egg if I ever get a chance."

The men set on the porch in stunned silence. They'd never heard Mazy say something such as that in their entire lives.

Catalena grinned. "I'll tie him down and hold him for you," Catalena told her. "Poor little Jeanene."

"No wonder that girl has acted up all her life. If you ask me, every single one of those Kormans are inbred, and those Hordlys are worse. I never did understand why Gertie Lee sold them her land. She claimed it would go to her girl and granddaughter. She must have died, and her daughter sold it. I bet Gertie Lee rolled over in her grave at that."

Catalena frowned and rubbed at her forehead. There was something she was supposed to remember but she couldn't.

"Did I hear you right? Did you say you were trained to fight?" George asked as he came into the kitchen.

"Don't want to hear another word about it. Do you hear me, George? Don't you tell anybody a word of what went on."

"But . . ."

"It's nobody's business what goes on around here. We're not gonna be a part of anything."

In a way Catalena agreed, but in another way, she didn't agree at all. If a problem wasn't brought to the forefront, it might never get corrected. What Kimbell Korman was doing needed correcting in the worst sort of way.

Chapter 22

~~~~

Catalena spent a restless night. As soon as she fell asleep, nightmares came. She'd wake up not remembering what the nightmares were about. It seemed there were things she had to do before it was too late, but something was holding her back, keeping her from doing it. When she did manage to become fully awake, she realized the worse nightmare of all hadn't happened in her dreams. She was living it. She'd never felt so helpless in her entire life.

She was glad when it was finally time to get up and help Mazy with breakfast.

"You look as bad as I feel," Mazy told her when she looked up from the cookstove.

"I didn't sleep good."

"Me either," Mazy admitted and hesitated a few moments. "Did you really beat up Kimbell as bad as the twins said?"

"I don't know who it was or how much damage I did. I just know I was terrified and fought with everything in me."

"You did good," Mazy told her as she put more wood in the stove.

Catalena started toward the door to go to the woodshed for more firewood. As she opened the door, Homer was coming onto the porch with his arms full.

"At least you're doing your job today," Mazy told him without looking up as he came into the house.

"Yeah. I'm feeling plumb frisky this morning."

"Liar," Mazy came back at him.

"Now, Mazy girl, you don't know how I'm feeling."

"It's a no brainer, Homer Barlow. You've not been frisky in twenty years."

Catalena was surprised to hear Mazy use the no brainer term George often used. Mazy was a person who willingly held onto everything in the past.

Homer clucked his tongue sadly. "You do know how to hurt a man's pride," he told her. "Need me to bring in more firewood, or had you rather I milk your cow and do up the outside work?"

"Don't you dare milk my cow. The last time you got trash in it. I can't stomach seeing trash in milk."

Breakfast was almost ready and Catalena could hear the twins and George washing up for breakfast out on the back porch. As Mazy took the biscuits out of the oven, the sound of a car could be heard coming up the road.

"Reckon Waddell's coming back?" Mazy questioned. She scooted the sausage and gravy back from the hot part of the stove and followed behind Homer to her eavesdropping position near the door. She grabbed Catalena's arm to keep her from going outside. "Best we listen from in here," she said.

Catalena allowed Mazy to push her behind Mazy's back, but she didn't like it. She was used to being upfront without hiding behind a door or anything else. All four men were on the front porch waiting for what they assumed would be Sheriff Waddell showing up again.

It wasn't a black and white that showed up. It was a shiny new Cadillac.

"Who could that be?" Mazy whispered. "I've never seen that fancy car before. Nobody has anything like that around here."

Catalena was gripping the door frame. Her entire attention was focused on that car. It felt like a strange kind of warmth was spreading from the top of her head downward in waves.

"It's strangers. Look at that fancy dressed woman," Mazy said as she watched the woman open the door and get out.

Catalena's breath sucked in as a man wearing a cowboy hat got out of the car. She recognized him. She shot out the door so fast Mazy didn't have time to grab her by the arm.

"Dad," she called out in desperation. "Dad."

He opened his arms as she ran into them. Her arms going around his shoulders and hanging onto him as though it was a matter of life and death.

"Thank goodness you're okay," the man said, as the woman rushed toward them.

"We've been worried sick about you. Why haven't you called us like your promised? We've been worried sick about you," the woman said almost angrily as tears of relief ran down her cheeks.

"Mother," she said and burst out crying so hard she couldn't say anything else.

"What in the hell is going on here?" Tobias Gallaher demanded as he glared at the four men standing on the porch, his arms protectively holding onto his daughter.

"Morene Smith? Is that you?" Mazy said as she came out onto the porch before either of the men could do any explaining.

The woman looked away from her daughter to the woman who was coming toward her.

"It's me, Mazy. My goodness, Morene. I can't believe this. I should have known Lena was your daughter. She looks a lot like you did when we were young."

"My goodness, is it really you Mazy James? I didn't recognize you," Morene said before she caught herself. The drab little woman couldn't possibly be the girl she grew up with. This woman was not only old, she was wearing old woman clothes. The kind they used to laugh at when they were kids.

"It's really me. No wonder we had trouble recognizing each other. It's been over thirty years. People sure do change in that amount of time. These are my three boys and brother-in-law. Is this your husband?"

"Yes, this is Tobias Gallaher. What is Catalena doing here? Why didn't she call us like she promised?"

"Oh, it's a long story. Come on inside. It's too long a story to stand out in the yard telling it. I've got breakfast on the stove. We can eat and go over what happened at the same time."

Morene and Tobias shared a look that said they weren't sure what they should do.

"It's okay," Catalena wiped at her eyes with the back of her hands. "They took me in after the accident. Did you call me Catalena? My name is Catalena Gallaher?"

Both Morene's and Tobias's face showed both shock and puzzlement at their daughter's words.

"What accident?" Tom Gallaher demanded in his rough, loud Texas drawl.

"I wrecked the Jeep," Catalena told him. "I hit my head and couldn't remember who I was. I'm still have trouble remembering things."

"What the hell is going on around here?" Tobias' voiced raised. "Somebody needs to do some explaining right now."

"It was my fault. I drove up the wrong road," Catalena told him. "I tried to turn the Jeep around, but it went over a cliff. George saved me, but the Jeep burned along with everything in my purse."

Homer came down the steps to where they stood. "Come on inside and we'll catch you up on everything that happened to Lena."

"Homer Barlow." Morene said as she recognized him. "My goodness, Homer. Maturity suits you. You could be Sam Elliott's twin."

"Youth would suit me better," he told her. "You, Morene Smith, are more beautiful than you were growing up. Gertie Lee was proud of you. Talk about twins. Those two roosters standing on the porch are Mazy and Harmon Barlow's twin boys. George there, is her youngest."

"Gertie Lee Smith?" Catalena said with wide eyed astonishment. "She was your mother? My grandmother?"

"Catalena Gallaher, surely you remember your own grandmother," Morene told her.

"I didn't even remember who I was," Catalena explained. "No wonder I was so curious about her."

Morene looked at her daughter with renewed concern. "You really don't remember anything? Who you are? Why you came here?"

"No. I didn't remember anything at all right after the wreck. Small things are starting to come back to me now. Seeing you and Dad helped."

"I'll be damned," Tobias said. "What did the specialist say about your condition?"

"I've not been to a doctor."

Morene reached out her hand and gripped her husband's arm to keep him silent. "There are no specialists in this area. Really, there aren't many doctors."

"What . . ."

"Things are different here than where we're from, Tobias. We've talked about the differences in the way we were raised often enough. Let's eat breakfast as then decide what needs to be done."

It was obvious to Catalena her father didn't like what her mother was saying, but he graciously gave in.

~~~~

Mazy made fast work of cooking more eggs, and sausage. She added milk to the pan of gravy that had gotten too thick, while it sat on the stove. She always baked extra biscuits in case someone wanted a biscuit and jelly sandwich before dinner was ready, so she should have enough for two extra people. There was never anything wasted on a farm. What people didn't eat, the animals did. She set two more plates and had the boys bring in two chairs.

While they were all eating, George, the twins, and Homer added their parts to the story of the wrecked Jeep, leaving out the part about their suspecting the Kormans of wrongdoing.

"I remember that rock cliff," Morene said. "It's nothing short of a miracle that Catalena survived. I'm shaking at the thought of Mother's Jeep going over it. Thank goodness she was able to jump out and land on the crevice. Thank goodness George was able to get her to safety."

"I want to take a look at that rock cliff," Tobias said."

Morene reached out and took him by the hand. "Not right now, Tobias. It will be best to wait until all this trauma has settled down some."

"It's worse than the Grand Canyon. Remember challenging me to ride that donkey into the canyon, Dad. I rode it, but it certainly didn't cure my fear of heights."

Tobias smiled lovingly at his daughter. "She's petrified of heights, and yet she passed every challenge put before her."

"Tobias is a judge, and Catalena and I are attorneys. We're the good kind," she added with a grin. "Catalena is in the youthful stage of doing a lot of pro bono work for those who can't afford an attorney."

"Where do you live?" Homer asked.

"Texas. Can't you tell by our accent? Tobias was born and raised there as was Catalena."

"I'm the only one who has retained the slow Texas drawl," Tobias added. "Morene and Cat lost some of their native dialect in college."

"Dad calls me Cat. Mom calls me Catalena, and Grandma called me Lena," Catalena said with delight that she remembered. "My name is Catalena Lee Gallaher," she said triumphantly with boundless joy. Suddenly, the shock of sudden realization came to her face. "Oh, no!" she said as tears filled her eyes. "I failed."

"What's wrong, honey?" Homer asked as he patted her hand. "How did you fail?"

"Grandma wanted me to spread her ashes on Grandpa's grave. They were in the Jeep. Those pieces of clay we found was the urn that held her ashes."

"I see," Homer said as he squeezed her hand. "Seems to me like you did a mighty fine job of it. Your grandma's ashes are hovering all over the land that she loved. Not only that, but your Grandpa's old Jeep is right where it belongs, too."

Catalena's eyes suddenly grew wide as she turned to glare at her dad. "Those Hordlys! They built a house on Grandma's land. On my land."

"What did you just say?" Morene questioned.

"You heard her right," Homer told them. "The Kormans claimed they bought the land from Gertie Lee, sold it to the Hordlys, and they built a log house on it."

"My mother never sold that land to anyone. When Catalena was born, the doctor told us I would not be able to have any more children, so Mother made a deed to Catalena giving her all she owned. She kept a life estate. Mother never transferred that life estate to anyone and neither did Catalena. Mother died and that's why Catalena is here, to spread Mother's ashes as she requested."

Tobias raised his brows. "Appears we have a few legal matters to look into."

"No one is going to take Grandma's land away from me," Catalena said with defiance.

"No need to worry. I assure you, we'll find out what's going on," her dad told her.

"You can count on it," Morene added. "I wonder if the Hordlys were in cahoots with the Kormans?"

"Wouldn't know," Homer told her. "There's not much folks do that surprises me anymore."

"What has happened with those Kormans in all the years I've been gone?"

"The old folks died," Mazy said.

"They multiplied like rabbits," George added his two-cents worth to the conversation.

"Have they changed?" Morene asked, sounding hopeful.

Homer shook his head. "Not that I can tell. Don't reckon most folks can change what they're made out of."

"No cure for stupid," George said.

"If anything, they've gotten worse," Mazy told her. "One girl had enough sense to get married and move away, but her marriage didn't work out. She never came back though."

"They're one of the reasons I insisted Mother leave and move in with us. I was afraid she'd be taken advantage of."

"If I remember right, Gertie Lee could shoot a fox between the eyes when it was running full speed with a chicken in its mouth."

"You're right about that. Mother knew how to stand up for herself. She and Tobias get . . . got along just fine," Morene said with a sad smile. "Two peas out of the same packet of seeds."

"She was a mighty fine lady," Tobias added. "Smart as a whip. She never sold so much as a stick of wood off her land. I can assure you that much."

"Catalena took back after her far more than I ever did," Morene said.

"Why didn't Gertie Lee come back to visit after she left?" Mazy asked. "I kind of thought she would."

"Mother couldn't stand to come back here. It would have broken her heart to visit and not be able to stay. She and I both knew if she ever got back home, I'd never get her away again. She loved these mountains the way she loved life itself."

"She spent a lot of time telling me stories about life in these mountains. She wanted me to know the old way of living," Catalena said as memories of her grandmother rushed back to her. "Before Grandma died, she kind of regressed to where she was reliving her youth with Grandpa and Mother. Not that her mind left her or anything like that. She simply spent her time remembering the things she loved."

Chapter 23

~~~~

Catalena had the oddest feeling as she prepared to leave the Barlows and get into the car with her parents. Right now, the Barlows were more familiar to her than her own parents. Tear filled her eyes as she looked about at the people she was leaving behind. Seeing her parents had helped her memory return slightly, but she wasn't completely healed. Her memory was fuzzy at best, and she still had a dull headache most of the time. Seeing her parents had not brought back all memory. It appeared she was looking at her past life through a thick fog. She could see the outline but not the exact details.

"I can't stand for you to leave," George told her. "I won't have a running buddy after you are gone. At least not a pretty one," he added as he grabbed her in his arms and hugged her tight. "You can stay if you want. Mom will let you," he added.

Catalena laughed through her tears. "I can always come back and outrun you. I've got land adjoining you," she told him. "Don't forget you've got Brent."

"He's not pretty," George pointed out.

"You know you're always welcome here," Homer assured her. "You become one of our family."

"He's right," Mazy said, as she wiped at her eyes with her handkerchief. "You didn't get to stay long enough to meet my girls."

Bob gave her a slight hug before Rob stepped up to say his goodbye. There was an odd look in Rob's eyes as his gaze met hers. He opened his arms and clutched her to him tighter than any of the others had. "I knew this day would come, but I didn't want it to," he whispered in her hair as his lips lightly grazed the side of her face as he pulled away. She felt the ache in that brief contact all the way down her body to her toes. She held onto his arms for the few moments before he turned her completely loose.

Bob was quick to pat his brother on the back as though reminding Rob he was still there.

"Come back when you can," Rob told her. "We'll be right here."

"I will," she told him. "I'm the one who owns Grandma's land."

"Are you going back to Texas?" Rob asked Tobias.

"We'll be staying at a hotel for a day or two. Tomorrow will be a trip to the courthouse to check on Gertie Lee's land and see what the Kormans and Hordlys are up to," Tobias told him.

"I was staying at a motel," Catalena suddenly said. "My clothes are there. I was paying with my Visa card. I told them I'd be staying for several days," Catalena felt triumph at remembering those details. She wanted to laugh and cry at the same time. She was no longer lost in a world of unknown. Her life was starting to come back.

"We'll keep in touch. Thank you for the delicious breakfast. It made me miss Mother even more." Morene told them as they got into the car.

"What in the world are you wearing?" her dad asked as he turned the car around and drove away.

"They are clothes Mazy's daughter left behind."

"Where's the clothes you were wearing when the accident happened?" Morene asked her.

"Mazy said they weren't in fit condition to wear after the wreck. I think she burned them." Catalena thought of the rag pile Mazy always kept. Never once had she seen Mazy burn a scrap of cloth. She saved ever little piece to make into quilts and other things.

"Were the Barlows good to you?" Tobias made a point of asking.

"They treated me like I was one of their own." She chose not to mention being attacked. She wasn't sure how her parents would react to such knowledge.

"They didn't get you medical attention," Tobias pointed out.

"It's the way of people here, Tobias. They don't go to the doctor unless they're dying," Morene told him.

"I don't like the fact that my daughter's health was neglected. Being hit on the head hard enough to cause memory loss is serious."

"I'm fine, Dad. I really am. My memory is returning. Besides, what good would going to a doctor have accomplished?"

"As soon as we get you to the motel and into some decent clothes, we're taking you to see a doctor – a reputable specialist."

"I'd rather go to the courthouse right now and find out what's going on," Catalena told him. "I want my Grandmother's land."

"You needn't worry. We'll get Mother's land cleared up as soon as we're convinced you're okay." Morene assured her.

"Where is the road that goes to the Hordlys' house? I'd like to take a look at it, while we're here. It will give us a better idea of what we have to deal with."

Morene told him which road to take. It was a narrow dirt road filled with potholes. At the end of the road, two dirt driveways forked. One rutted driveway led to the several Korman houses and the other fork went to Gertie Lee's land. Morene gasped to see a log cabin and a garage not far from the entrance of her mother's land.

"That was Mother's garden spot. She doted on that piece of ground. Each fall she would gather leaves to work into the soil. Every speck of cow manure was precious to Mother. To see earthworms in the soil made her happy." Morene said.

"How long has that place been built? Mother gave me power of attorney the day she left here. I certainly didn't sell anything. I couldn't if I had wanted to. Mother deeded it to Catalena retaining a life estate."

"Grandma's house is in shambles, but it's still there," Catalena told her mother. "I had George take me there."

"I thought you didn't remember anything," her father said.

"I didn't remember, but I still had feelings. You might call it intuitions. I was curious about Grandma's place even when I didn't know she was my grandmother. Actually, Mazy mentioned you, Mother. She said I reminded her of you."

Morene's face took on a strange look. "Let's go," she told her husband. "Mother loved this place, but I never did. That's why she deeded it to Catalena instead of me, but then you already know that."

Tobias turned the Cadillac around doing his best to miss potholes. "This road is horrible," he said. "What kind of people don't fill the potholes when there are plenty of rocks along the side of the road?"

"The Kormans were the type of people who wouldn't toss a rock in a pothole if the rock was already in their hand. I doubt the Hordlys are any better. Dad was the only person who tried to maintain the road. He used to say the Kormans were quare in the head. Dad didn't believe in talking bad about anyone, and quare was the kindest word he could use to describe them."

"There's a regular little community packed together. I've counted five houses," Tobias said with disapproval.

"There was only one house when I was growing up. Kopie Rainey Korman was the woman's name. James Korman was her husband's name. Everyone called him Little Jim. Kopie had two sons and four daughters. My parents made sure I was never alone with any of them. Mother warned me not to associate with the Korman's even when we were at school. Kopie wasn't exactly right in the head. There were a lot of rumors going around that most of her children belonged to her brother instead of Little Jim. Mother always felt sorry for poor old Kopie. That poor woman never went out in public. Seemed she always had bruises on her face and hands. The rest of her she kept covered up, even during the summer months."

"As a judge I've be subjected to the fact that incest happens more often than people realize, and not only in remote mountainous areas. A lot of elite families go to great lengths to keep such secrets hidden. There are a lot of well-known celebrities who have gone public with their own stories. One of the wealthiest women on television today is one. Her grandmother helped raise her, while her uncle molested her. The story is she miscarried her uncle's baby when she was still a child. She is now one of the richest women in show business. She is a well-known success story who overcame all odds," Tobias said. "I'm sure you know her."

"Yes, she came from rags to riches being a television host." Catalena was certain she knew her, but she couldn't remember her name at the moment.

"Jeanene Korman is thirteen or fourteen. Kimbell, her uncle, was raping her. She miscarried," Catalena told her parents. "George said she was crying at school and the school nurse sent her to the hospital. The sheriff came by the Barlows looking for Kimbell Korman. It seems he and his brother, Alvin, took off."

Morene drew in a deep breath and then let it out slowly before she spoke. "Now you understand why I left this place and never came back."

Catalena understood only too well why her mother left the area. Her mother had more ambition than the mountains had to offer her.

"People like the Kormans are the exception, not the rule," Morene made sure to point out. "However, I knew of three other families I went to school with who had a lot of gossip being spread about them. Unfortunately, I'm afraid such gossip was mostly true. Back then, in these isolated mountainous backwoods, husbands and fathers thought they owned their wives and children and could do whatever they pleased with them. Which I fear held a lot of truth in my mother's time.

"I want you both to realize most mountain people are like the Barlows. They are good, God-fearing people who mind their own business, while taking care of their families in the way they should. They are even willing to help a stranger when that stranger is in need," Morene said pointedly. "I don't want either of you to get the wrong impression of people who live here. It took me moving away to realize there is a mixture of bad and good no matter where you go, and the good in these mountains cannot be beat. Oh, well. Let's stop philosophizing and see what we need to do. What hotel did you check into, Catalena?"

"I don't remember. I'm guessing it would be the closest one near here."

~~~~

Tobias knew his daughter's taste and habits. She wouldn't go for the most expensive hotel nor the cheapest. She liked her comfort at the same time she enjoyed roughing it in the great outdoors, but not when it came to hotels. Most likely she would have checked in at the nearest Holiday Inn which was in Boone.

"That's the place," Catalena said as her dad pulled up in front of the hotel. "At least, I think I recognize it."

"Your memory is coming back then?" her mother asked with a mixture of hope and concern for her only child.

"I didn't remember anything at first, but here lately I've been having something like flashbacks in feelings or memory. I wasn't sure which. Once I saw you and Dad, I recognized you both. It was horrible not knowing who I was. I felt like I wasn't a real person." She still didn't feel whole. It was like she went to sleep and woke up in a different world populated with different people.

"I imagine the fright of going over that rock cliff was traumatic enough to make you want to forget," Morene cringed at the memory of standing on the rocks and looking down in the gorge when she was young. She'd even gone there once with Harmon Barlow. He was one of the most handsome young men she had ever known. She could have easily fallen for him, and him for her. There was enough chemistry between them, but the thing was she decided in grade school she would never marry a man from the mountain, and she hadn't. She didn't want to spend all her life stuck on a rocky, mountainous, black dirt farm, barefoot and pregnant. She wanted to experience a few pleasures instead of all hard work that wore a woman out before her time. Personally, she thought Mazy Barlow looked twenty years older than she looked. She placed her hand on Tobias' leg and let out a thankful breath that she had escaped a bullet. Had things been different, she could have been the widowed mother of Harmon's children.

~~~~

It felt odd getting out of the backseat of her parent's car. She had ridden in the back seat for years as a child, but not recently. She had always been independent and capable. She was sure of that fact.

"What do I normally drive other than Grandma's Jeep?"

"You have your own car," Morene told her as they walked toward the motel.

"Where is it?"

"Back in Texas. You drove Mother's Jeep ever since she had it restored for you."

"I wish I had it back."

"I'm sure you do," Morene said. "Unfortunately, we don't always get what we wish for."

Catalena was certain she'd already had lessons in that area. She said nothing else as they followed her dad inside the hotel.

"I'm Tobias Gallaher. I would like a room beside my daughter's room," Tobias told the desk clerk. "Catalena Gallaher." As a judge. Her dad had learned to come right to the point fast.

"We do have one available," the woman smiled at Tobias and then Catalena. "We were wondering when you would return. The maid reported you hadn't used your room in a while, but your things were still there," she said as she eyed the clothes Catalena was wearing but didn't comment on the worn, faded dress that hung from her shoulders like a giant sack.

"You made no attempt to contact anyone about her being missing?" Tobias questioned.

"She told me her grandmother had a house in the area and she was going there and wasn't exactly sure when she would be back. We assumed she was staying there," she said as she looked Tobias in the eyes. "We mind our own business unless we have a reason not to," she told him. "How long will you and your wife be staying with us?"

"Two or three days. We're not sure yet," Tobias said as he handed over his credit card.

"And you, Miss Gallaher?"

"The same," Catalena said, although she wasn't sure she wanted to return to Texas with her parents, at least not yet. Thing was she needed a vehicle and a new visa card. She also needed to know if she had money in the bank – and how much.

While Catalena showered and changed into her own clothes, her father made a phone call to the Brain Injury Association to find the nearest doctor who specialized in head trauma. He also made a call to his own personal attorney to have him fly in from Texas. Her dad believed in doing everything right the first time.

"Do something half-assed and you'll regret it," was what he always told his wife and daughter.

"You'll have to lick your calf all over again," was how her grandmother described a poorly done job.

Catalena concluded that her grandmother's words had helped turned Morene into an attorney who always double checked to make sure all her i's were dotted, and all her t's were crossed. Catalena took pride in knowing other attorneys cringed when they went up against Morene Gallaher.

Catalena was proud of her father and mother. She hoped she could surpass her mother someday as an attorney, but she had no drive to be a judge. She didn't like sentencing people even when they had done wrong. What she liked to do was defend the innocent – bring justice to the unjust.

"You have an appointment at Duke Hospital tomorrow at ten o'clock," Tobias told her after she had showered and dressed.

"Okay," she agreed. She'd do anything necessary to make the fog in her memory disappear. "What about Grandma's land? Can we go to the courthouse now?"

"You and your mother can stay here and rest, while I do research," Tobias told them with his usual demeanor as a judge who thought he knew best.

"No," they both said at the same time. "Three people doing research will be faster than one."

"Probably, but I don't want either of you exhausted."

Catalena grinned as Morene lifted her brows. Catalena knew for sure her mother was a whirlwind on the go, and Catalena was sure her own energy was usually equal to her mother's. Besides, the Hordlys had stolen her land and she wasn't about to sit back and do nothing, while letting her dad handle things, which he preferred.

Chapter 24

~~~~

"**D**o you think they saw me?" Kimbell asked as Alvin pushed the gas pedal of the old truck to the floor, spinning slick tires as they left the gas station.

"Don't know for certain. Think they might of," Alvin said. "One of 'em got his eyes full of me. Damn, if I don't hate those Barlows. Think they're better than everybody else."

"Hain't no better than us," Kimbell said as he wiped his snotty, blood streaked nose on his shirt sleeve. "They's two of us same as they's two of them. They following us yet?" Kimbell wanted to know as he tried to sink lower in the truck seat instead of lifting his head enough to see out the back window.

"No. One of 'em went inside."

"If you ask me, they're flaunting their money after selling a load of lumber," Kimble whined. "Gotta take a bundle to fill that tank up."

"Outta be a law against cuttin' the woods down the way they do," Alvin said. "Don't got no respect for nothing."

"How long afore we get to where we sign up for the army? I'm wanting to wash up and get all settled in comfort now that we've decided to do it."

"I done checked on that recruiting place. It's way off the mountain in Wilkesboro."

"How far away is that?"

"Don't know exactly. Two or three hours I'm guessing considering how slow this old truck goes. If we had the money them Barlows have, we could afford us a big truck."

"Ought to go right fast if you put 'er outta gear and let 'er coast being it's all downhill. It'll save on gas too," Kimbell said.

"Can't do no coasting. Brakes ain't no good no more."

"Oh. I forgot about that."

"Besides, it's best not to go fast. Don't want to get stopped by the law, being you ain't got no driver's license."

"I ain't the one driving," Kimbell pointed out.

"Don't matter. If the law gets me, they'll take you to jail cause you can't drive without a driver's license."

"What would they do with Pa's truck if they hauled us in?"

"Take it to a lot and auction it off."

"The law can take a body's stuff like that?"

"Just like that," Alvin said. "Law can do whatever they want to a body, and there's hardly a thing to be done about it. Once we get joined up in the army, we can do most what we want cause the army has their own law. That's why solders can kill without going to jail for it."

"No, shittin'. You're saying we'll be able to kill them Barlows without going to jail?"

"No, you idjet. You can only kill foreign solders, and a few other folks the army wants you to kill."

"Oh," Kimbell's hopes fell.

"They'll give us our own gun though, and all the ammunition we can carry."

"Sounds better all the time. Free guns, ammunition, clothes, boots, clothes, along with a bed and all the food we can eat three times a day."

"Plus, we get paid good money. And that's not all, once we get out, we can claim disability like Pa does and draw a check each month for the rest of our lives."

"Pa ain't disabled. He's stronger than me and you put together," Kimbell said.

"He never claimed physical disability. He claimed mental disability. Can't nobody prove Pa ain't crazy. No doctor can see into a man's brain like they can see your body."

"Hot dang. Why ain't we joined up sooner?"

"You know why. Pa wouldn't hear of it."

"Pa joined up himself."

"No, he didn't. He was drafted. Don't get drafted no more."

"Why not?"

"Cause it's such a good deal everybody's wantin' to sign up, even women."

"No shit?"

"No shit."

"Say, look under the seat. Pa ought to have a jar of shine under there."

Kimbell got down in the floorboard and searched through the trash until he found his Pa's quart jar. It was over half full. "Yeah, man. Wish I'd a found this afore we started out. Wouldn't be hurting nearly as much."

"That's a fact. I'm the one who does the thinking. Everybody knows I got all the brains."

Kimbell wasn't about to argue with him on that point even if he did disagree. He was too busy unscrewing the lid and taking a big swallow. Fire hit the back of his throat taking away his breath as the big swallow went down. He coughed and heaved for breath as tears streamed out of his eyes and made streaks through the dirt and blood on his face.

Alvin laughed. "Pa always did keep the good stuff for himself. We ain't never got nothing but watered-down shine."

"Hell fire," Kimbell blurted out once he finally drew breath. "A man needs a chaser after that stuff."

"If it wasn't for wasting good shine, I'd say you need to wash your face and head in it afore we go inside that recruiting office, but I don't reckon it'll matter none. They ought to have enough sense to know a bloody man is already a fighting man. Hand me that jar."

~~~~

Sgt. Gary Berk was sitting behind his desk, relieved it was almost time to go home when the door opened and two young men staggered in. The odor of liquor and sweat preceded them. One looked like he'd already been in a recent fight. The other one looked fairly normal – well, maybe normal compared to the bloody, overweight one.

"Can I help you gentlemen?" he asked with reluctance. If he had his way, he'd shove them out the door and lock it. Over the years he'd gotten good at judging young men and their potential.

"We came to sign up," the non-bloody one said as he staggered to the desk and sat down in the only vacant chair. The bloody one held onto the back of the chair to aid in standing.

"What is your name?"

"Alvin Korman."

"And yours?"

"Kimbell Korman."

"So, you both want to join the army?"

"Yeah," Alvin answered.

Kimbell remained silent.

"Okay," Sgt. Berk said as he opened a drawer and pushed two enlistment forms in front of them. "Fill out these requirement forms."

Both of them looked at the forms as Sgt. Berk handed Alvin a pen. "I take it you're both over seventeen years old."

"Both boys nodded."

"How far did you go in secondary school?"

"We quit when we turned sixteen. We had more'n enough education by that time. We're as smart as whips, I tell you," Alvin said with pride. "Both of us."

"How's your physical fitness?"

"Our what?" Alvin questioned.

"Are you strong?" Sgt. Berk asked, as a touch of amusement came to him. If he had to sit here and waste time with these two, he might as well have a little fun to ease his boredom.

"I'd say we're mighty strong," Alvin bragged.

"Can you lift two hundred pounds?"

"We can lift it," Alvin's voice was slightly hesitant.

"How far can you carry that much weight?"

"Live weight or dead weight?" Alvin wanted to know.

"Dead weight."

"Depends if the ground is downhill, level, or uphill."

Sgt. Berk nodded. The fellow had a point. "Level. Across a wooden floor."

"Don't know. Never tried it," Alvin told him."

"How much does your brother weigh?" he asked Alvin.

"Never weighed him," Alvin smarted off as though he was getting irritated with the questions.

"How much do you weigh?" Sgt. Berk asked Kimbell.

Kimbell licked at a split place on his lip. "Enough to get by on."

"Whatever you weigh now, you won't be weighing that amount for long. You will go into basic training fat and sassy, but you won't come out that way.

"Who did you get in a fight with?"

"That's my business," Kimbell told him.

"Son, once you join the Army you've got no business. It is all the Army's business. You got that?"

Alvin and Kimbell both tensed up but said nothing. The man in the uniform gave off too much of an authoritative air.

"If the Army accepts you, and I am saying if, you will be doing what you're told, how you're told to do it, and when you're told to do it until the day you're discharged. You will have no say in any matter – none whatsoever. Both you boys got that, or do I need to repeat it?"

Alvin couldn't stay silent any longer regardless of how authoritative the man appeared. "I thought we got clothes, food and board, plus a paycheck if we join up. Ain't that no longer so?"

"That part is true, but in return the Army gets you to do with as they deem appropriate."

"We're both crack shots with a gun," Alvin bragged.

"How are you with a shovel, running ten miles with fifty pounds pack on your back, crawling on your bellies through two foot of mud, wading up to your neck through cottonmouth infested swamps with leeches sticking to your body, burning those blood-suckers off, sleeping on the ground during an ice storm, or sweating your guts out in a hundred-twenty degree weather while insects you've never seen before feast on your flesh?"

Kimbell's mouth came open as he looked down on the top of Alvin's head. "I ain't signing up for that kind of shit," he said.

"Me neither," Alvin said. "I want the good life them Army posters promised. I want to travel the world while getting paid for it."

"Chances are you'll get to travel the world while fighting to stay alive in the conditions I just described."

Alvin jumped up from the chair so fast it turned over, knocking Kimbell backward. Alvin grabbed hold of him to keep him from falling, and they both staggered out the door, leaving it wide open.

"Some boys just can't stomach the truth no matter how good it is," Sgt. Berk said as he stood up, went to the door, looked out to see what they were driving before he closed and locked the door. He grinned all the way back to his desk where he put things back in order. He looked at the phone on his desk, thought about his options and exactly how much the arrogant driver had drunk. Was he over the limit? Was he a safety threat to other drivers? Should he call the sheriff's department with the make, model and license plate number of the old truck?

~~~~

Markum Korman was pacing the floor in a rage. "Why the hell did you let 'em take off in my truck," he yelled at Lettie, his wife.

She downed her head in her usual subservient way. She'd learned a long time ago never to argue with Markum regardless of how wrong he was. When he was mad, he wanted someone to take his anger out on. She was the handiest. The kids had learned to run and hide."

"Talk to me," he yelled as he grabbed hold of the loose bun of hair in the back of her head and jerked her head up until she was looking in his furious, bloodshot eyes. "Why did you let 'em take my truck?"

"I was down yonder hoeing the garden when I heard the truck start up. I hollered at 'em to stop, but they was gone afore I could do anything."

His hand slapped her across the face so hard she hit her back against the hot cook stove. She tried to catch herself to keep from falling. Her arm hit the hot stove. Her flesh singed. She didn't make a sound, knew better as she tried to regain her balance. When Markum was in a rage it was best to remain silent no matter how much she hurt. She felt blood trickling down her chin as she tried to ease some distance from her and the hot stove. Burns were worse than bruises.

"You're nothin' but a worthless piece of shit. Knowed better than to marry a thing like you who done nothing but spit out a bunch of brats. All of 'em as stupid as you are. I ought to kill every last one of 'em along with you."

Lettie looked at her feet and tried to make herself appear small. His fist flew out hitting her in the side of the head. She banged against the wall, slid down it, landing on the wood box and stayed down. He kicked her in the leg, called her a slew of names, and went out the door.

Lettie was thankful.

Several minutes later Darnell slipped into the kitchen. "Are you all right, Ma? Did he hurt you bad this time?"

"Is he gone?" Lettie whispered.

"I seen him go toward the Hordly place."

"They ain't home," Lettie still whispered.

"I know it. He aims to crosswire their truck so he can go after the boys."

"Help me stand," Lettie lifted her hands toward Darnell.

"What we aim to do, Ma? He aims to kill us all dead as a door nail. You heard him say it," he told her as he pulled on his mother's hands.

"He ain't changed none since the day we married, and we're all still living," Lettie tried to make an argument she could believe.

"You call this living, Ma? How many days have passed in all these years that he hasn't hurt you? Can you answer me that, Ma? How many times have you seen him beat us with his belt? It's slavery, brutal slavery for every single one of us."

"What's the alternative, son? Can you tell me that?"

~~~~

"What's the alternative, son?" Those words haunted Darnell's mind almost as much as seeing his ma's bruised and bleeding face. It wasn't like he hadn't seen her looking this bad, if not worse, through the years. Somehow, she'd managed to survive and so had they. But his ma was getting older and his pa was getting crazier and meaner. The shine he drunk and the weed he smoked had warped his brain big time. Darnell knew it was far too late to remedy anything about his pa and the things he did. He'd never change. Marcus Korman would only get meaner, and that was something he didn't want to witness.

The words his mother said lingered in Darnell mind and begged for a solution. He did what he usually did when he had some deep thinking to do. He took to the silent woods, seeking the shadows that brought a kind of tranquility to his soul.

One thing he and his brothers had been taught was how to be silent and sneaky. His ears had been trained to pick up the slightest sound, the slightest disturbance. Birds, squirrels, especially crows acted different when someone was near. He knew how to blend in with a large tree trunk and wait in silence.

He had gone into the woods and sat hidden in the same spot when his brother had attacked the girl. He thought of the previous time, he'd been there. He'd seen Kimbell sneaking along as though he was on the stalk for something. In Darnell's opinion his youngest brother had a lot to learn about remaining silent and unseen in the woods. He was too reckless and impatient. But then Kimbell didn't care about the little things that mattered and neither did Alvin. Both of them took back after their pa, while he took back after his mother. He and his mother wanted to live in a gentle peace – something that was unlikely to happen as long as his pa was alive.

He had followed behind Kimbell to see what he was up to. He watched from the woods as Kimbell sunk down behind a clump of weeds like a rabbit hiding from a cat. Right there in the wide open sat the girl on a big rock. Her shoulders were hunched, and she seemed to be in torment about something. It was obvious that her mind was on something that had her in its powerful grip. He figured she was thinking about her pretty little jeep that had gone over the cliff and burned. If she hadn't been able to jump out, she'd have experienced a taste of hell before she died.

Much to his surprise, Kimbell moved forward slow and easy. He'd watched in silence as his brother sneaked up on the girl and put a sack over her head before the girl had a chance to look up. Fool girl. She ought to pay more attention to her surroundings. It was easy to tell she was a dumb city girl who wasn't used to mountain ways of hunting prey. He felt right sorry for her as Kimbell's heavy bulk knocked her face first on the rocky ground. There was no question as to what Kimbell had in mind doing to the pretty girl.

He was deciding what to do about the situation when Kimbell rolled her over, groping at her. Thankfully, he didn't have to do a thing. The girl exploded and went fighting crazy. Her hands and feet were moving like a whirligig in fast motion. In a matter of seconds, she put a whipping on Kimbell he sure enough hadn't expected.

Darnell laid hidden in the leaves and grinned as he'd watched his baby brother hobbling away in an all too familiar busted-ball creep. Busted balls were nothing new to Kimbell or any of them. They'd all taken hits in that sensitive area far too many times.

The last time their pa had gotten him in the balls, he'd gone down, but had kicked his right foot straight and true. His pa hadn't expected to receive the kind of pain he was always dishing out.

"You ever touch me again and I'll kill you," Darnell threatened, speared on by his pain and fed up by his pa's continuous beatings. Darnell managed to get to his feet and left his pa rolling in the leaves, puking all over himself.

His pa had left him alone since then, partly because his oldest son was bigger than him, and partly because Darnell was smart enough to remain absent when his pa was around.

Darnell had watched the girl work the feed sack off her head and run down the narrow road. He'd wondered how long it would take for the Barlows to come after Kimbell? Couldn't rightly blame them.

He'd followed Kimbell as he stumbled and puked his way toward home. He had no intention of showing himself when Alvin intercepted Kimbell. He continued to hide in the woods listening to Kimbell and Alvin's plans to join the army. He thought that was the best idea they ever had, if they could pull it off. He'd do the same thing if it wasn't for the idea of leaving his ma and little Jeanene to the mercy of his pa. On second thought, that wasn't exactly true. He wouldn't join up with the Army if it meant killing people. He was kind of sensitive about things such as that.

Then there was that movie he'd seen once about Sargent York, the sharpshooter from Kentucky. Once Sargent York got

religion, he didn't believe in killing either, but he killed the
enemy anyway. When asked why, York had said it was better
to kill one person than let that person live to kill a lot of people.
Darnell knew Sargent York was a lot stronger man than he was,
but even a weak coward had some responsibilities toward
doing what was right.

~~~~

After sitting there a while, remembering what his dad had
done to him, his brothers, his sister, and his mother, Darnell
got up enough nerve to leave his hiding place and put one foot
in front of the other. He made his way to the trash dump out
beyond the Hordly place on Barlow land. The Barlows didn't
believe in dumping trash down a bank, but the Hordlys and
Kormans did it partly to spite those high and mighty Barlows
and partly because they were too lazy to haul their trash to the
county dump like they should.

It didn't take Darnell long to find an old car battery the
Hordlys had thrown away. Stupid rich Hordly's. Didn't care
about the little amount of money they could get on trading it in
on a new battery.

He picked up the cleanest jar he could find, and cleaned it
better with his shirt tail before he put all the battery acid he
could in it. He tried not to do any thinking as he left the dump
and made his way back home. He kept thinking Sargent York,
Sargent York, Sargent York as he eased though the silent
woods. He wondered what life would be like if there was no
longer any fear of being hurt by his pa.

He checked to make sure the Hordly's truck wasn't back.
It wasn't. That meant his pa hadn't found his brothers yet, but
he was sure to come back before long regardless if he found
them or not. His nervousness of what he was about to do caused
him to break out all over in a wet sweat, He tried not to think
as he made his way to his pa's private jug of shine. He and his
brothers knew better than to ever get into their pa's private jug.

He carefully uncorked the jug and poured some of the liquor into the jar. He swirled the liquid around and around for a long while making sure he had it mixed really good. There was some trash floating in the liquid which would never do. He pulled his long shirt tail out of his overalls, poked some of the material in the jug with his finger, and strained the liquid back into the jug. He was precise in placing his pa's jug in the same exact position. His pa watched for little things like that.

"This is the only alternative, Ma," he whispered as he left his pa's hiding place and disappeared into the comforting silence of the deep woods. He didn't want to be a witness to whatever happened next.

~~~~

"Join the Army, you said. It'll be a piece of cake you said. All we'll have to do is sign up and we'll get free food and clothes and guns and ammunition while drawing a paycheck. You've not got the brains of a Guinea fowl."

Quick as a striking snake, Alvin hit Kimbell in his already busted mouth with his fist. Kimbell drew the almost empty quart jar of shine back and bashed Alvin's in the side of the head. The force of the hit drove Alvin's head against the side window. Alvin's hands unwittingly jerked the steering wheel hard. The truck skidded off the road and landed on its side in a ditch.

"You've gone done it now. You dumb-ass wrecked Pa's truck. He'll kill you for real and certain," Kimbell yelled at his brother once he realized they were both alive and not hurt more than a few bruises.

"It was your own fault. You busted Pa's private jar of shine on my head. I oughta beat the shit outta you right here and now." Suddenly he stopped talking and drew in several sniffs of air. "Do you smell gas?"

"Hell! It's leakin' outta the truck. That's what you get for filling it up. Wasted money, I tell you. Let's get outta here before it catches on fire." Kimbell said, as he grabbed the window crank and rolled down the door window on the up side of the truck as fast as he could, while Alvin pushed and cursed at him for being too slow. They crawled out the window and looked about them trying to decide what to do next when they saw two men coming down the bank toward them.

"Put both hands in the air," one of the men said.

Alvin stopped cursing Kimbell long enough to take a good look at the two men. Shit! They were both wearing uniforms. Even worse, a black and white was parked on the bank with its blue lights still flashing.

~~~~

Markum drove the Hordlys' truck down the dirt road faster than he'd ever driven his own truck. He didn't much care if it did damage to the truck or not. Those fool Hordlys didn't deserve a truck like this or anything else of value. They were nothing but a bunch of crooks. That Phyllis Rainey was nothing more than a cheap two-bit piece of tail who'd latched onto a no account idjet from up north Chicago way. She'd screwed him into marrying her and moving down to Florida during the cold winters, but it was way too hot for them come summer.

Thing was, he had cheated so many people up Chicago way, it wasn't safe for them to go all the way back up north during the summer months. It was those no-account Rainey's who came up with a plan and paid him to go along with it. He'd done it to get easy money in his pocket, while it being no skin of his nose. That old Smith woman was either dead or long gone. As for that girl of hers, that uppity bitch thought too highly of herself to ever come back to a place like this.

He'd driven the truck almost empty of gas without seeing hide nor hair of his truck or those no-account run-away boys of his. He'd either have to buy gas or head back home. He had no intention of putting a dollar's worth of gas in that truck.

"Those damned boys will be back sooner or later," he said out loud. "Got no choice in the matter. No other place for 'em to go."

Luckily for his old woman, she had a good supper cooked for him when he walked in the kitchen door. If she hadn't, she'd have looked worse than she already looked. She didn't say one word as she took up the food and set it on the table. He'd worked up a mighty powerful hunger.

It was just him and her at the table. Not a one of the kids were there, which was mighty unusual.

"Where's Darnell and Jeanene?" Markum demanded of his wife.

She bowed her head as she looked down at her plate containing a few spoons full of soft food. Her mouth was too hurtful to chew. "Don't know."

"What you mean you don't know? Did they take off in my truck with them two other idjets? If they did, they're in for a hiding like they've never seen afore."

"Looked to me there was only Alvin and Kimbell in the truck when I ran to try and stop 'em."

"Good job you done of stopping 'em. Never have done nothing right and never will, if the truth be told."

She knew better than to respond unless she had too. It wouldn't take much for him to turn on her again.

He wasn't halfway through eating his supper when a black and white pulled into his yard. The sheriff got out holding Jeanene by the arm as though he was helping her walk.

"If that girl got into trouble, I'll thrash every inch of hide off her with my belt," Markum told his wife as he got up from the table. He met the sheriff at the door.

Jeanene jerked free of the sheriff and hobbled into the house all bent over.

"You this girl's father?" Sheriff Herbert Waddell asked, when he knew good and well he was.

"What business is it of yourn?" Markum demanded.

"It's plenty of my business. I just brought that little girl home from the hospital where she miscarried her brother's baby. I've come to arrest Kimbell Korman."

"What tha hell!" Markum spat out. "You're outta your freakin' mind."

"Afraid not. Where's Kimbell Korman?"

"That's what I'd like to know. Him and his brother took off in my truck a long while ago. Don't know where they went or when they'll be back, not that it's any of your damned business."

"Mind if we look around." The sheriff motioned toward his deputy standing at the open passenger door as though he was expecting trouble.

"You're damned right I mind. I know my rights. You'll not set another foot on my place unless you've got one of them papers signed by a judge saying my God given rights are being taken away from me."

"Have it your way, then," the sheriff said in a threatening way as he turned and got back in the black and white. "We'll be back, and it won't be so good for you or your son. There's laws on the books now that you don't know about. Laws that will get you and your boys in big trouble."

Markum stood his ground glaring after the sheriff until he was out of sight.

~~~~

Jeanene was still hurting bad from the whipping her pa had given her after the law brought her home from the hospital. He'd yanked off his belt and left raw welts on her legs and hips for bringing the law to their place and setting the sheriff onto Kimbell.

She had aborted the baby, but not in the way she had planned on doing. What she hadn't expected was for it to happen while she was at school.

Her Ma had told her pennyroyal, tansy, angelica, black and blue cohosh, cotton root bark, mugwort, parsley, and even the somewhat poisonous yellow fruit of mayapple aided in abortion. She'd picked every one of the plants she could find, mixed all the plants together, mixed in a little water, and crushed all the plants until their juices run out. Late Friday evening she drank all the horrible liquid and even forced herself to swallow as much of the crushed mixture as she possibly could. She gagged a lot, but finally forced it to stay down. When nothing happened by Saturday morning, she found her ma's bottle of Caster oil and drank as much of it as she could get down.

On Sunday she'd set in the outhouse for hours, but nothing more than a powerful cleanout happened. When morning came, she claimed she was sick and stayed home. Still, nothing happened. The next morning her pa forced her to go to school. He'd never been for going to school longer than it took to learn how to read and write, but he made her attend for what she thought was pure spite cause she hated school so much. It did something to a girl when all the students looked down on her.

"I feel sick on my stomach, Ma. I need to puke," she'd pleaded. "Please don't make me go."

"It's best to go on to school," her ma told her. "He's in one of his moods, and you know what that means."

She knew all too well what it meant. When he was in one of his moods, he was itching to go after somebody so he could beat on them. If he couldn't get hold of his children, the beating landed on their mother. At least she'd be safe from one of her pa's belt whippings while she was at school. There was also a chance he'd wear out his mood on Alvin or Kimbell if he caught one of them unaware. Darnell got beat on the least. He was the oldest, biggest, and strongest, but he had a way of not being around much. He kept himself off in the woods both day and night. He only showed up when he was hungry, and never during mealtime. If her pa didn't take his mood out on the boys, she'd come home to see what condition her mother was in.

She hadn't expected the cramps to hit her the way they did after time had passed. It was like her guts were being twisted into knots, and then being jerked tighter the longer she sat at the school desk. When the big one hit, she doubled over and let out a moan. By the time the teacher got her to the nurse, her moans had turned into muffled screams.

She had started bleeding by the time she got to the school nurse. The nurse wasted no time in wrapping a blanket around her and rushing her outside to the car. By the time they got to the hospital, the pain was nonstop, as was her screaming and cursing Kimbell.

There was no question as to whom she was blaming for her condition.

She remembered her pa's warnings once she was put in a wheelchair and wheeled into the emergency room. She was *'telling nothing to nobody'*, but she couldn't stop her screams of pain, or shut the school nurse up.

The school nurse answered the hospital's questions the best she could. When a deputy arrived, the school nurse continued to answer questions Jeanene refused to answer.

"What's the girl's name?" was the first question.

"How old is the girl?" was the second question.

"What happened to her?"

"Did the girl say who the father is?"

"She said her brother, Kimbell Korman, was the father. She called him every bad name she could think of, and then screamed out a few of her own making.

Jeanene listened in silence as the school nurse then told the deputy the same thing she'd told the hospital staff about the teacher bringing her into the nurses' office and the actions she took.

Finally, the stretcher she lay on was rolled out of the room, and she didn't see the school nurse again. They kept her in the hospital against her will to make sure she was going to be okay after the miscarriage. The sheriff was the one who drove her home since he was to bring Kimbell in for questioning. Seemed like the hospital had gotten right picky about things that didn't used to matter much. Neither the school nor the hospital wanted to have problems, so they dumped everything in the lap of the law.

She never told anyone about the mixture she had prepared and drank.

~~~~

When Markum got through teaching his daughter a lesson, he kept his leather belt wrapped around his fist twice with the long part hanging down and went to look for his wife. This was all her fault. She ought to have known better than raise a tramp of a girl, one who lied about everything. No telling what she told the sheriff and that hospital bunch. He decided he would beat more sense in her after he taught her ma a good lesson. A woman ought to do better raising a bunch of bratty kids than Lettie had done. She'd find out in a hurry that he wasn't putting up with it.

She was nowhere in the kitchen or in the living room or bedrooms. She was surely out in the barn somewhere. When he got to the barn, she wasn't there either. He cocked his head sideways to listen better. He heard her in the outhouse making a kind of humming, grunting noise. That's where she tended to hide when he was disciplining one of the kids. If she'd done her job with those brats, he wouldn't have to. He'd see to her when she came out of the toilet. In the meantime, he'd worked up a right good thirst.

He made sure the jug was exactly how he'd placed it – with a straw leaning against the side. He picked the jug up, took a few long swallows, coughed a little, and wiped his mouth on his shirt sleeve. Damned if that stuff hadn't gotten more powerful as it sat there percolating. He turned up the jug and took a few smaller swallows. He felt the burn from his mouth all the way down into his gut. Even his nose started tingling.

He took a few more swallows to see if the liquid would ease the burning. It didn't.

"Damn," he said out loud. "That's some mighty fine shine. It's gotta kick like a mule." But he was man enough to take it. He downed a little more and was unable to get his breath for a minute or two. He put his jug back and headed for the spring house to see if some cold water would ease the burning of his insides. It didn't. If anything, the water made the burning worse. He grabbed a quart jar of milk and downed it. It didn't seem to help one bit. The hurt in his belly felt like a fire had been lit inside him.

He rushed back to his jug, uncorked it, and poured some in his hand to see if the clear color had changed. The palm of his hand had too much stain on it to tell, but there was a burning sensation to his flesh.

"Hell-fire and damnation," he screamed as he busted the jug of liquor against a rock. Somebody had put something in his liquor. He'd heard of moonshiners toping of their run of liquor by putting in a car battery, but he was the one who'd run the batch off from his own still. He'd even drunk another jug from the same run. It hadn't hurt him none.

Somebody had put battery acid in his liquor.

He was a dead man for certain.

But he wasn't going out of this world alone.

"I'll kill every damned one of you," he shouted to the top of his lungs.

~~~~

Darnell was hiding, watching for his pa to drink the liquor. He had imagined his pa dying a somewhat silent, painful death without ever knowing what killed him. When his pa busted the jug, he realized his pa knew what he'd done – or what somebody had done. When he yelled out that he'd kill them all, he knew his pa meant it.

He saw his ma come out of the toilet and run for the woods. That left his little sister in the house. He tried to keep cover between him and his pa as they both headed toward the house. He heard his pa going into the bedroom and knew he was after his shotgun. Darnell jerked the bedroom window open.

"Quick, Jeanene. Come here. He's gonna kill you

Jeanene was still sobbing, but she heard him and ran the few steps from her bed to the window. Darnell grabbed hold of her arms and dragged her out like she was a sack of goat feed.

"What . . ."

"Shhh,"

He tossed her over his shoulder and headed for the woods. He'd made it behind the trunk of a large poplar tree when the first shot was fired. Bark from the tree flew in several directions. Jeanene whimpered.

"Hush," Darnell told her. "Can you run?"

"No-o," she whined. "I'm hurting bad."

Darnell judged the angle from the bedroom window to the tree and decided to make a run for it before his pa could shoot again, but his pa wasn't shooting right then.

"I'll kill you all," Markum Korman yelled as he tumbled out the window, hitting the ground screaming and cursing as he got to his feet, took aim, and shot more bark off the poplar tree.

Darnell wasn't sure if the screaming and cursing came from pain or rage. Most likely both. Screams were for pain, and cursing was for anger.

Jeanene was heavier than Darnell thought, but the adrenalin and fear surging in him spurred him on. He had to get to a hiding place before his pa got within shooting distance. At least the trees offered some protection as well as camouflage. He was younger and faster, but his pa was driven by pure hell fire and brimstone rage. How long would it take for the acid to do its job? Why hadn't he thought to get his ma and sister out of harm's way before his pa went crazy? But how could he have known how his pa would react once he realized he was a dying man? If he was a dying man. Exactly how much liquor would he have to drink for the battery acid to kill him? What if he'd only tasted the shine and knew right off what he'd put in it" There was also a chance the acid had lost some of its potency laying there in the dump. Why hadn't he thought about that too? He'd been dumb, just plain dumb, and now they were all going to pay for it – unless they could outrun his pa and the gun shots.

Chapter 25

~~~~

Catalena was relieved to finally have the specialist's diagnosis. She had received a concussion, but no sign of significant brain damage. Her memory loss could have been the results of the concussion, her extreme fear when she realized she was going off the cliff, or the swelling she had endured. The fact that she was now regaining her memory was a plus. Most likely her remaining brain fog would clear up with time.

She saw the relief on her mother's face as they drove away from the doctor's office. "It's a miracle you are still alive," Morene told her. "My suggestion is that we go home immediately."

"What about Grandma's land?"

"Let your father and his attorney handle it. They will see that the Hordlys and the Kormans pay for their forgery."

A streak of Catalena's independent nature came to the forefront. "No, Mother. I'm staying here. Grandma's land is now my land, and I'm not leaving until those people get what's coming to them for forging the sale of it."

Morene let out a sigh. "Surely you've seen enough already to know this isn't the land of opportunity. It's a land of stagnation, a land of poverty. A land where children get stuck in the same unhealthy rut as their parents are in. I grew up hearing the term 'don't try to get above your raising'. Where would people be if they didn't get above their raising? Wearing animal skins and carrying a wooden club, is where they would be."

Catalena looked at her mother and wondered why she hated the place she was born and raised so much when Grandma Gertie Lee loved it. During the time she had spent with the Barlows, she'd grown fond of the land and suspected that given time she would love it as much as her grandmother did. What she didn't love was the man who attacked her. She certainly wasn't going to tell her mother about that. If she did, most likely her parents would hogtie and drag her back to their home, regardless of her age.

Yes, Catalena remembered how her mother and she were always butting heads with each other. Morene was one of the most stubborn women she had ever come across. Much more stubborn than her grandmother, maybe even more stubborn than her Texas judge of a husband. She supposed that was why her mother made such a good attorney. She never gave up on anything and was willing to go to any lengths to prove herself right.

"This isn't the place where I want my daughter to be," Morene told her firmly.

"I understand completely," Catalena said. "What I don't understand is how such a place could produce such an outstanding person and attorney such as you."

"Don't you get sassy with me," Morene warned her.

"Mother, I'm not being sassy. I am being serious. You are exceptional. Grandma was exceptional. The Barlows are exceptional people."

"There are also people like the Kormans, Hordlys, and Raines."

"We both know those kinds of people are everywhere regardless of the location."

"Some locations have more of those kinds than other places," Morene pointed out.

Catalena didn't want to argue further. What she wanted to do was rest enough to completely heal. The knot on her head was still sore, as were several places where the attacker had knocked her to the ground. She was vaguely starting to remember taking self-defense classes sinse she was a child. Her mother had wanted her to take ballet lessons and signed her up for them at the Parks and Recreation center. It didn't take long for her to become more interested in karate lessons also being taught there. She asked her father if she could take karate instead of ballet lessons. He told her that learning to defend herself would prove far more valuable than learning how to dance on her toes.

"Now that I know you are okay, I'll be flying back home. I have an important case coming up and I need to prepare for it. I'm hoping you'll fly back with me and help with the research before it goes to trial."

"Is Dad flying back with you?" She was hoping if he did, he might leave the car for her to drive.

"No, he and his attorney will be here for a while until they get Mother's land fraud settled."

"Good. Then you won't worry about me staying here as long as Dad is here too."

Morene shook her head. "I should have known I'd have a child just as stubborn as her father, one who won't listen to good advice. I blame my own mother for deeding you that land. I'm sure she did it to spite me because I made her move away from the place. She simply wasn't able to stay there and take care of herself. She wasn't a young woman. I did what was best for her."

Catalena smiled as she remembered her grandmother saying, "Morene might be able to take her away from the mountains, but she would never take away her love for the mountains." There was no doubt in Catalena's mind that her grandmother dreamed of her beloved home until the day she died. That was why she had the old Willys Jeep restored and requested Catalena promise she would take her ashes and spread them *back home* and scatter them on her dear husband's grave.

That was what she was doing when she wrecked her grandfather's old Jeep. How she wished she could salvage the crumpled metal and turn it back into her grandpa's Jeep. That, she realized, would be almost as difficult as bringing her grandmother back to life.

A sadness gripped Catalena. Some of those memories she longed to have returned could make her cry.

~~~~

Homer Barlow was heading into the barn when he ran into Rob coming out. He was carrying Catalena's pet groundhog in his arm.

"What are you doing with her?" Homer asked him.

"I'm going to set her free," Rob told him.

"Why?"

"Lena isn't here to take care of her," Rob told him.

"Why don't you take care of her yourself?" Homer asked. "You're the one who caught her and put her in a cage."

"That's why I'm setting her free. I don't want her to be kept in a cage any longer."

"Then why did you put her in a cage in the first place?"

"I thought Lena needed something to take her mind off her own troubles, at least for a little while."

"I take it you don't need anything to take your mind of things?"

"Nope, I don't need a thing. Work takes up all my time."

"That's a shame. If you ask me, a man who works all the time is kept in a cage as easily as that little groundhog was kept in a cage."

"There you go again. Philosophizing when nobody wants to hear you airing your brain."

"Now ain't you the crabby one. Looks to me like your pouting lip is hanging below your chin. If you miss her that much, why don't you go after her?"

"What are you talking about?"

"As if you don't already know. You're pouting because you missed the best chance you had to do a little courting with the girl when she was here."

Rob ignored his uncle as he walked out of the barn.

Homer shook his head as he continued his way through the barn and out the back door. He didn't feel like eating supper with the family, especially when all three boys were down in the jaws about Lena not being there. He suspected even Mazy was missing her, or more correctly missing her help with things.

He knew he missed having her pretty face to brighten up the place. He wasn't sure she would keep her promise to come back. He hoped she would since she claimed Gertie Lee had willed her the land the Hordlys now claimed. That was going to be interesting, especially since her father was a judge and her mother an attorney. He grinned. Those better-than-thou Hordlys just might get what was coming to them – but one never knew how the law would rule on a thing. A lot of times the outcome was the result of who had the best attorney.

Homer had almost reached the front porch of his house when he heard his name being screeched out. He turned to see Lettie running toward him.

"What in the world is going on, Lettie?" he asked as she grabbed hold of his arm with both hands.

"It's Markum. He's gone plumb crazy and run Darnell and Jeanene off to lord knows where. I heard him in the woods screaming like something was killin' him. He was rollin' in the dirt beggin' for me to get him water when I reached him. I tried to help him to his feet, but there was no way I could do it. I ran back to the house and fetched him a quart can of spring water. He drunk it all and started puking up blood. He needs a hospital bad."

"Why don't one of the boys take him?"

"Alvin and Kimbell are gone in the truck."

"What about the Hordlys?"

"They's down in Florida."

"What about his cousins living up that hollow near you?"

"Don't know where they're at. You know they're gone more than they're home. There ain't nobody about but me and Markum. I tell you he's dying unless you're willing to get in your truck and haul him to that hospital in a mighty hurry."

Homer considered going after Rob and Bob, but he thought it best not to get them involved in whatever was going on with the Kormans. One thing was for certain, Lettie wasn't torn all to pieces about nothing. If she claimed Markum was about to die, he figured she was telling the truth.

"Get in my truck and I'll drive to your house. It'll be quicker than walking."

Lettie nodded, turned loose of his arm now that he was doing her bidding, and followed him to the truck.

"Has he been beating on you again?" Homer asked as he turned the truck around and headed up the rough road. She couldn't get away from his question if she was sitting in the seat beside him. Poor Lettie. She wasn't a bad woman, but she'd made a bad decision when she married Markum Korman, one she hadn't been able to escape. When a woman married bad, it wasn't only her that suffered. Every child she gave birth to was forced to suffer from the mother's mistake.

"No, oh no. Markum wouldn't do a thing such as that to me," she told him without a moment's hesitation.

"If it wasn't him, who was it?"

"Nobody. I fell face-fomas, that's all."

Homer knew falling face foremost wouldn't do the kind of damage that was showing on Lettie's face, but he wasn't going to contradict her story. She had enough on her plate without him calling her a liar.

"Tell me what happened with Markum?"

"He didn't beat me or whip Jeanene with his belt," she told him firmly. "He'd never do a thing like that to us."

"I mean what has caused him to be almost dying? I need to know as much as I can before we reach him." Homer let his arm brush his overalls to make sure he still had his pistol in his pocket. Never paid to trust a Korman when a man was all by himself with no back up. Carrying a little insurance was always a wise thing to do even if you never needed it.

"Don't know. I was in the toilet when he kind of went crazy. He took off runnin' through the woods yelling. There was silence for a spell, and then he come back yelling some more. When he kept yelling but didn't come on to the house, I went to look for him. I done told you how I found him."

She wasn't about to tell Homer Barlow that Markum had his shotgun out trying to kill Darnell and Jeanene, or anything else about what happened that might matter where the law was concerned. If Markum lived, she'd get a bad beating for going after Homer. No need to add the law into her problem with Markum. Theirs was a family matter.

Homer only nodded. He knew she wasn't telling him the entire truth, not when the blood on her face was still fresh and oozing. He'd never known a Korman to tell the whole truth to anybody, even when the truth was easier than making up a bald-faced lie.

It didn't take ten minutes to go down his driveway and turn up the rough road to reach the Kormans' place. He could see the Hordlys' place along with a few of the Korman relatives' places, but he couldn't tell if anybody was home or not.

Lettie jumped out of the truck as soon as it was stopped and ran toward the woods where Markum's screams were coming from. He was rolling in the dirt puking blood when Homer reached him.

"What the hell?" Homer said.

"You gotta help him," Lettie begged. "I don't want him to die. I truly don't."

"Has he been drinking liquor?" Homer asked even though Markum and his puke both had the faintest smell of moonshine. Good corn liquor didn't have the same odor as beer or whiskey.

"No, no. He never touches the stuff," Lettie fell easily into telling the same lie she always told. "How're you gonna get him to your truck. Don't think he can walk. You'll have to tote him."

"There's no way I can tote him. He weighs more than I do. Besides, he's rolling around, kicking and fighting like crazy," Homer said as he thought on it for a few moments. "Tell you what, I'll grab one of his hands if you'll grab the other one, and we'll do our best to drag him to the truck. He's kicking so much I don't think we can get a hold on his feet. At least, it's downhill from here."

It wasn't easy getting hold of his flailing hands, but they finally managed. Dragging him down the hill to the truck was even more difficult considering he fought them every step of the way. There was one thing for sure, Markum wasn't able to stand on his own two feet or even his own two knees. Homer had seen many a drunk man but not one in this sorry condition. If his puking wasn't bad enough, the blood coming up was a sure sign he swallowed the wrong batch of shine.

"Grab that piece of tin roofing that's blown off the barn," Homer told her. "We'll have to use it to slide him up into the truck bed once I back up to that bank. If I put him in the cab, he's flailing and fighting about so much he'll cause me to wreck." Not to mention the smell of puke and liquor he'd bring into the cab.

"Stop fightin' us. We're tryin' to get you some relief," Lettie told him. "Act like you've got some sense about you for a change."

"Water," he screamed out. "Fetch me water." He tried to raise himself up but couldn't.

"Don't get him any water," Homer told her. "If he'd drunk poison liquor, water will only make him puke more. Bringing the poison up will burn his insides more, making the bleeding and puking worse."

His thrashing about hadn't eased up much since they dragged him out of the woods, but they finally managed to get him up the bank and slid him along the tin roofing until he was in the bed of the truck. Both Lettie and he were wet with sweat and heaving for breaths from the effort.

"You'll have to ride back there with him, Lettie. Otherwise he might manage to climb out," Homer told her as he took his handkerchief out of his hind pocket and wiped the sweat from his face.

"No way. I ain't goin' to no hospital. I'm stayin' right here where I belong."

"You don't have a choice in the matter. Somebody has to watch out for him."

"Tie him down," Lettie told him.

"I'm not going to do that, Lettie. You came to my house to get me to take him to the hospital. You can now help me do it or watch him die right here." Homer was almost positive Markum had a belly full of the fore-shot, which was the first small amount runoff of poison liquor from a still. By the smell of him, and the way he was acting, there wasn't much use in hauling him to a hospital, but he'd do it for Lettie. She'd need to know she had done all she could to save him. He'd never seen anyone poisoned, but he'd heard stories about a man who drunk the first fore-shot off a run and the horrible way in which he'd died.

He watched as it took every bit of Lettie's determination for her to crawl in the back of the truck bed with her husband, but she did. Homer got in the cab, started the engine, and drove down the road as fast as he dared. He didn't have much hope for Markum, but he rather he died at the hospital than in the back of his truck.

It took a while to reach the hospital. As soon as he pulled the truck up to the emergency entrance and stopped, Lettie jumped out of the back and ran into the bushes to hide. Homer figured she didn't want to answer questions about her husband, or have people see her face and know of the beating she'd had to endure. Lettie never did like being in public sight.

"Get a gurney out there," Homer told the nurse setting behind a desk. "I've got a man in the back of my truck I think has been poisoned on liquor."

It was a lot easier getting Markum out of the truck than it was getting him in. His struggles were now mighty weak at best. His clothes covered in more puke and blood than when they started. Homer felt kind of guilty for being glad he wasn't one of the men who was lifting him onto the gurney. They'd have to wash and change clothes before they helped other patients.

"Pull your truck out from in front of the emergency door and come inside. We'll need some information," one of the men told him.

Homer did as he was told, making sure he took the truck keys with him. He wasn't sure if Lettie could drive or not. He took time to lock both truck doors. Lettie would slip in the cab once he started the truck. Otherwise, she'd have to walk for hours to get back home.

It seemed to Homer that he had to answer at least a thousand questions that ranged from giving Markum's name to if he had any insurance or not. He had to explain over and over that he didn't know a thing about what happened to Markum. All he knew was that his wife showed up at his place begging for him to drive her husband to the hospital.

"Don't know," Homer answered the question of where Markum's wife was at.

No one asked why Markum was in the back of the truck instead of being in the cab, not that it would have made any difference to Markum. By the time he had answered almost all their questions, a doctor came out.

"Are you a close relative of his?" the doctor asked.

"Nope. Only a neighbor."

The doctor asked him several questions he'd already answered for the woman to write down on the admission form.

"It'll probably be best to leave his body here until we discover exactly what killed him. I've called the sheriff. He'll be here any minute to ask you questions.

Homer nodded his agreement and the doctor left. "Mind if I get me a swallow of water outta the water fountain?" he said to the woman. She didn't bother answering, only nodded her head.

He didn't take time to get that swallow of water. He'd done all he could do, and he certainly didn't want any contact with the sheriff. Just as he thought, Lettie jumped into the cab of the truck as soon as he'd reached across the seat and unlocked the passenger door.

"Is he all right?" she asked.

"Nope," Homer told her. "He's dead and the sheriff is on his way here. Do you want to stay here and talk to him?"

"No."

That was one thing she and Homer agreed on. The sheriff could drive out to the Korman's place and ask Lettie all the questions he pleased. Homer was already more involved than he ever wanted to be, not that he could escape being questioned about his part in what happened with Markum.

Lettie never said a word or shed a tear as Homer drove her home. When he stopped the truck near her front yard, she opened the door, got out, and disappeared inside the house. The words thank you never came out of any Korman's mouth. He drove part of the way back to his house and stopped at a creek. He found an old bucket he kept hid in the bushes when he needed to dip up water for whatever reason. He used a stick and clumps of grass to scrub his truck bed over and over until it was clean enough to get by on. He didn't want any smell or remains of Markum Korman lingering. He wished the pitiful image of the dying man wouldn't linger, but he knew it would stay with him for a while.

He didn't know what to make of what had happened to Markum. He always took a sort of pride that he could outdrink any man in the mountains and remain standing. Homer was only surprised that he hadn't gotten hold of bad liquor sooner – either by accident or on purpose. He did know he'd best get on home and tell the others what had come about before the sheriff showed up strutting his authority, while trying to find something somebody did wrong.

~~~~

Why didn't you come after us?" Rob wanted to know when Homer told them what had happened.

"Yeah," Bob chimed in. "It could have been a setup."

"I didn't want nobody else involved. Besides, by the way Lettie's face looked, plus the way she was torn all to pieces, told me it was for real."

Mazy shook her head in sympathy. "Lord only knows what Lettie had to endure all these years, not to mention those poor little children."

Homer started to point out that only Jeanene was little now but decided not to. Markum Korman was dead now, and that was that.

"Did you say his body was left at the hospital without Lettie staying with him?" When Harm died at the hospital, they had to physically drag her away from him. She remembered holding him tight in both her arms and screaming "No! No! No! You'll not take him from me," while someone pried her arms and hands loose.

"Lettie never went into the hospital. As soon as the truck stopped, she jumped out and hid in the shrubbery until I started to leave."

"You're telling me she never went inside with him?"

"That's right."

"Do tell," Mazy mumbled. "She doesn't sound normal."

"What will happen now?" George spoke up for the first time.

"The sheriff was called to the hospital, and the coroner will declare him dead. Then the sheriff will show up to talk to Lettie to find out exactly what happened. After that, he'll come to my place to ask me questions. Most likely they already drew blood to check for alcohol. I'm thinking he drank the fore-shot and it killed him, but I don't know nothing."

"What's a fore-shot?" George asked.

"That's the first pint or so of alcohol that drips from the condenser of a still. It contains the most methanol, which can be deadly to drink."

"Didn't know that," George said.

"Hope none of you boys ever need to know it, but it might be worth remembering."

~~~~

Homer knew the sheriff would want to question him, but he hadn't expected the black and white to be sitting in his front yard when he walked back home. Sheriff Waddell was standing on the front porch with the deputy standing by the open door of the patrol car.

"Can I help you, sheriff?"

"There you are. I want to ask you a few questions."

"Concerning what?"

"Concerning Markum Korman's dead body that's cooling off in the hospital morgue."

"Ask away," Homer said as he leaned against the porch post without inviting Sheriff Waddell to take a seat in one of the chairs. The sooner the man was gone the better.

"You're the one who brought him to the hospital, weren't you?"

"I was. Lettie Korman, his wife, was with me, but she didn't go inside."

"Why not?"

"You'll have to ask her."

"Okay, I'll do that when I find her. She wasn't home. In the meantime, I want you to tell me exactly what happened."

Homer told him exactly what happened, except the part about Lettie's face being beat up and her hiding in the shrubbery at the hospital.

"Do you know what happened that killed him?"

Homer could have laughed at that question, but he didn't. "Nope. Figure either the doctor or the coroner is the one who will answer that question one for you."

"Where does – did- Markum get his liquor from?"

"Wouldn't know."

"I'm thinking you do."

"Then you're thinking wrong."

"Everybody on this mountain knows what's going on with everybody else, so you might as well talk before I haul you in."

Homer didn't like being threatened, but he made sure he didn't show a response. The sheriff loved nothing more than to rile people into some kind of reaction. "Then you best ask everybody on the mountain, cause I don't know a thing. I mind my own business and let others mind theirs."

"You're the only person who hauled him in to the hospital. Seems to me like you know a lot about his death."

"Done told you everything I know. I kind of doubt even you would refuse to take a man to the hospital if his wife came running up begging you to, but then I could be wrong. I've been wrong a few times in my life."

"Don't get smart-mouthed with me, Homer Barlow."

"Just telling you the truth, that's all I can do. Figuring out why he died is up to you and the doctors, not me. I can be a good neighbor, but I can't be a doctor or a sheriff. Wouldn't want to try."

"I'll be going now, but don't think you're in the clear just because I'm leaving. There's a lot more questions I expect you to answer truthfully."

"I'm always truthful, Sheriff. You already know that. By the way, Sheriff, do you know what the tallest building in the world is?"

Sheriff Waddell gave him a 'you've got to be crazy' look.

"It's a library because it has so many stories. Just want you to know I'm not a library. I've only got one story, and I've already told it to you."

Sheriff Waddell marched to the black and white in a huff. It was obvious he wanted to pin something on the Barlows, but he'd never been able to do it – and Homer intended to keep it that way.

It was just like a Korman to cause trouble even after they were dead.

~~~~

Morene did everything in her power to convince Catalena she should return to Texas with her, but Catalena had always been able to out-stubborn her mother.

"I'm not leaving here until Grandma's land is settled."

"That could take months, even years. You know how slow the courts operate."

Yes, Catalena knew, but she wasn't about to leave. The land had meant a lot to her grandmother, and now meant a lot to her.

"It's obvious there's fraud involved," Tobias told his wife and daughter. I can stay here for two more days helping Jackson do the research needed to find out what came about, and then I'll fly back. I'll leave the car for Cat to drive. while hoping it doesn't have the same ending as the Jeep."

Catalena knew he was trying to lighten the mood with a joke, but neither she nor Morene thought it was funny.

"You always give in to her," Morene accused her husband. "She needs to be home where we can look after her properly."

"No," he said. "I don't give in to her or anyone else. That's why I'm a judge. I do respect the fact she's twenty-six years old and has the right to do what she thinks is best for her."

"She's been injured. As her mother, it's my job to make sure she's safe."

"We both heard what the specialist said. She's going to be fine. Her memory has already returned along with her usual stubbornness."

Catalena didn't bother to tell them her memory was still hazy, or that she suffered from dull headaches most of the time. She intended to pretend she was well until she actually was.

"Don't go into your litigation mode, Mother. Dad is right, and I'm not leaving yet. Besides, Jackson will still be here after Dad leaves, if Dad wants Jackson to get to the bottom of things. I could probably find out all by myself, but I would be considered prejudiced, which is true." She almost grinned when she said that, because she was prejudiced. "It's not like either one of you are leaving your helpless little girl alone with a head injury. I'm not helpless and my injury has healed."

"It hasn't healed completely, and you know it. I'm not comfortable leaving you with a head injury," Morene pointed out.

"She'll be fine," Tobias assured his wife. "Like she said, Jackson will be here in case something arises that she needs assistance with."

Morene threw her hands up in the air. It was impossible to win a case with her own family. She didn't know why she wasted time and breath trying.

~~~~

Alvin and Kimbell were in separate jail cells where they couldn't communicate with each other. Alvin had been charged with driving while intoxicated, and reckless driving resulting in an accident. However, by the time a blood sample was drawn, the driver's alcohol level was slightly less than borderline. Kimbell had been charged with having an open container of alcohol in a moving vehicle. To which, both boys claimed the container wasn't open but got busted during the accident. Since the lid of the jar was still screwed on, the boy had a reasonable claim. The vehicle that was wrecked received little to no damage. It had been towed in. Both men had sobered up quickly and shown a creditable amount of remorse after a night in jail and two meals in their stomachs,

The sheriff had made a phone call to Sheriff Waddell in their county to find out more about the two young men he had locked up in his jail. Sheriff Waddell said he was seeking the youngest for questioning concerning a family matter, but there were no warrants for their arrest, and this was their first offence. The sheriff could tell that Sheriff Waddell didn't have a high opinion of the two young men, which didn't come as a surprise. He was the kind of sheriff who liked his position of power a little too much. Sheriff Waddell also said the boys' father had died at the hospital about the same time the boys had been arrested.

All things considered, and the fact that traffic court was in session, the sheriff agreed that the boys' court appointed attorney ask the prosecutor and judge to dismiss the charges. Which was done. No one told the boys about their father's death. That was a family matter and not something any of them wanted to become involved it.

"I can't believe they let us go," Kimbell told his brother as they drove away in the truck.

"Had to. We ain't done nothing wrong."

"You wrecked Pa's truck."

"You busted Pa' private jar over my head."

"He'll beat our asses big time for taking his truck, wrecking it, getting arrested, not to mention busting his private jar."

"That's a fact. Least ways, he'll give it a try, but I ain't willin' to take a beatin' no more from Pa or anybody else."

"What ought we to do? No chance of us joining up with the Army. Don't want to," Kimbell told him.

"We don't have to go back home. We could just keep on driving to somewhere else."

"We got enough money to go somewhere else?"

"Lucky I knowed to hide my stash, else those cops would have stolen it from us. No way of provin' it belonged to us and didn't belong to 'em. Our money looks like everybody else's money It's enough to buy us gas to get us somewhere else and find us a paying job."

"Pa ought to of had a lot of money. Hording it the way he went and done."

"Didn't have time to find his stash. All I got was his little bit of emergency spending money."

"Let's not go back home," Kimbell said.

"You're thinkin' straight for once."

"Where we gonna go?"

"Tennessee, Texas, Montana. No tellin' depending on where we find that we like."

"You're doing some sound thinking, if you ask me."

"Didn't ask you. Fact is, I'm the only one what does some sound thinking. I know what's best. Going back to where Pa can get hold of us ain't what's best. If Pa don't put a hurtin' on us, Enrick Rainey will."

"Why would Enrick do that?"

"I knowed where he stashed his sister's half of the drug money he took in while they were in Florida. I got it hid in the lining of my boots. Those cops took my boot strings, but not my boots."

"He'll for certain and sure kill us dead," Kimbell whined.

"Not if he don't know we done it."

"He'll know."

"Done got that figured out," Alvin bragged.

Kimbell rolled his eyes. "How?"

"I aim to stop at the next gas station, get a dollar's worth of change, and call him from a pay phone."

Kimbell gave him a skeptical look.

"I aim to tell him the law's onto them and us. I'll tell him the girl what gave you a whippin' was a plant sent to find out about our operations. He'll think she took the money."

Kimbell nodded eagerly. Telling Rainey that sort of thinking suited him just fine.

~~~~

When Darnell had gotten a far enough lead in front of his pa, he hid Jeanene under a small rocky overhang and ran in a different direction making a lot of noise to get his pa to follow him. Jeanene had gotten too heavy for him to carry and dodge shotgun pellets at the same time. He hadn't gone far when he noticed his pa was getting farther and farther behind him. Before long, his pa stopped chasing him, turned around, and headed toward the house. He waited a few minutes and then followed. Markum Korman started staggering, and then stumbling. Finally, he went to his knees at the edge of the woods. His squalls of painful cursing and begging for water echoed throughout the woods. His cousins, who lived on up the hill a way, didn't so much as open a door to look out. They'd all gang up on an outsider, but they wouldn't lift a finger to help one another.

Darnell wasn't about to go to him. A man in pain was a sight meaner than one who wasn't in pain. Besides, his pa still had his shotgun. Darnell hunkered down and watched. He wasn't entirely sure how much battery acid his pa had drunk or how it would affect him. He'd always heard battery acid would do a number on animals and people, but he'd never seen it at work before.

It took a while for his ma to get up enough nerve to go see what was ailing her husband, but she finally did. He knew his ma would do her best to get him to the house and ease whatever was wrong with him. Ma was like that. She always did want to ease a hurt. He'd always wondered why she'd married a man such as Markum Korman, but she never told him a thing. Ma was more of a silent type. Darnell always thought he was the only one of the bunch who took back after her.

He didn't know what to think when his ma took off running toward Barlow land. Surely, she wasn't seeking help from one of them. Homer Barlow might be a man with enough smarts about liquor to figure out what he'd done. His worry grew for a spell as he silently watched his pa get worse and start puking harder. If he got so bad, he couldn't tell 'em what happened before he up and died, nobody would ever know. Darnell didn't think his pa would ever tell anybody anything if he did live, but he might get well. If that happened, Darnell might as well start running right now and never stop.

He continued to watch as Homer Barlow showed up in the truck with his ma in the cab with him. He stayed put without offering to help as the two of them dragged his pa out of the woods and loaded him in the truck. His ma got in the truck bed with his pa and they drove off.

Darnell hid for a few minutes longer as he listened to the truck engine go down the road out of hearing. He drew in a long breath of air, got to his feet, dusted the leaves and woods dirt off, and made his way through the woods to where he'd hidden Jeanene.

"Is he gone?" Jeanene whispered when she saw her brother. She had buried herself in leaves and twigs the best she could in hopes she would be more difficult to spot.

"Yeah, I think he might be."

"Is it safe for me to crawl out?"

"It's safe, for now."

"Don't think I can walk."

"I'll carry you."

"I don't want to go to the house if he's comin' back. He'll beat me again."

"Why did he beat you?"

Jeanene downed her head, refusing to answer.

"I saw the sheriff's black and white bring you home. What kind of trouble did you get yourself into?"

"Weren't nothin' I done wrong," she whimpered. "It made no difference to Pa. He blamed me just the same."

"He used to blame me for things I didn't do. Weren't nothing I could do but let him," Darnell said as he reached down and picked her up. "I stopped being a coward today."

Jeanene was in bed asleep by the time their ma returned in Homer Barlows truck. Darnell was hiding in the barn waiting to see what happened next. When he saw that his pa didn't return with her, he followed his ma in the house. She stood in the kitchen floor, looking out the window, seeing nothing.

"What happened, Ma?"

Lettie continued staring, saying nothing.

"Ma? What happened?" he asked as he took her by the arm.

She looked at his hand on her arm, and then up at his face. His touch was gentle, not hurtful like Markum' always was.

"It's over," she whispered through her busted lip.

"What's over, Ma?"

"Markum. He's over."

"What do you mean by that?"

"Go get the shovel. He'll need burying."

~~~~

Enrick Rainey was in his sister's house making use of her place while her useless tribe was gone. She had three pansy-assed boys that were too soft to ever be any account. Took back after their father and his people. Everybody knew the Rainey's were a hard-assed bunch, and he was proud of it. Nickel Hordly was nothing more than a loudmouth, strutting excuse of a man. His sister didn't have a lick of sense for marrying a wimp like him. She thought he had money, but when the truth came out, he was nothing but a penniless blowhard. Phyllis had come to him crying because her husband was drowning in debt and taking her down with him. He'd come up with a plan to make them both a lot of money, while being able to blame it on those stupid Kormans if things went wrong.

Nothing went wrong.

Not even those stupid Kromans got busted for selling land they didn't own, or for growing a little weed in the laurel hells on somebody else's land. The law never showed up in that god forsaken place. Everybody appeared to be too piss-poor to be doing anything illegal. It was the perfect location to produce meth as well as grow weed. Didn't take long to have enough money for him to have his sister add on a garage with a secret hide-away down in the bowels of the earth. He wasn't even concerned about that Korman bunch. If they ever gave him and his sister away, they'd give themselves away as well.

He only had one problem with his sister and her tribe. She'd forbidden him to cook his meth in her place. Too dangerous, she claimed. Set you up a place in the woods, she told him. If it's found, nobody can prove you are guilty. He'd told her the woods were too open for what he had in mind. Don't want to smell the fumes, she said. Too volatile, she said. Well, she wouldn't be smelling fumes or doing any forbidding if she wasn't there.

He had a large batch going when his phone rang. He'd let it ring. They'd call back if it was important. It stopped ringing just to start right back up. He let it ring. The third time it started ringing, he answered.

"Why the hell hain't you answering your phone?"

"Who the hell is this?"

"Alvin. You gonna owe me a big time for lettin' you know what's coming down."

"What-the-hell are you bothering me about?"

"Me and Kimbell has done picked up our feet and left that place behind in Pa's truck. We ain't comin' back either."

"What's it to me? I don't give a damn what you do or where you go."

"You'd best be givin' a damn and then some. I only aim to warn you once."

"About what?"

"That girl what wrecked her Jeep is a plant. The law sent her undercover."

"Like hell, you say."

"It's a fact, and you know it is. She's been snooping about ever since she's been at the Barlow's place. They're in on it, you know. Pa had us watching her. Kimbell saw her break in your sister's house and garage. He said she left there carrying stuff."

"What stuff?"

"How the hell is Kimbell to know what stuff? Anyhow, there's gonna be one of them raids. Me and Kimbell done cleared outta there. Hain't taking no chances. You owe me big time for giving you a heads up."

Enrick heard the operator come on the line and ask for more money to be put in the phone. That meant Alvin was calling from a pay phone. When the phone went dead, he hung up. The Kormans were not willing to spend money on getting a phone. Markum claimed telephones were government devices designed to spy on people. What in the hell was he to make of that phone call? Was it possible Alvin was telling the truth for once in his life. If so, why would he do it? Alvin never did anything that wasn't a benefit to him.

He rushed to the secret place where he'd hid his sister's share of money. It was gone. That damned girl had taken it, or one of the Kormans. He wasn't sure which was guilty. It wasn't like the Kormans were known for truth telling. But then the girl had shown up out of nowhere to stay at the Barlows for a while. They'd sure enough tried to keep her hidden and silent. That alone was suspicious.

He heard the sound of a vehicle and rushed to the window to look out. Hell fire! If a black and white wasn't pulling into the Korman's yard. Two men got out and swaggered toward the house.

Alvin Korman hadn't been lying.

Enrick Rainey wasted no time going out the back door and heading into the woods. He seldom drove to his sister's house. He always came through the woods on foot when he was going to cook a batch. That way no one could prove he was the one involved. Those Kormans would get the blame, since his sister and her tribe could prove they were way down there in Florida.

~~~~

Lettie opened the door before the sheriff had a chance to knock.

"Morning, Mrs. Korman," Sheriff Waddell said. "Sorry about your husband's death."

"Is that why you're here?" she asked as her backbone stiffened and her chin lifted.

"It is. The coroner has declared his death to be from alcohol poisoning. Thought you might want to know that."

"That's what I figured all along," Lettie said with a forlorn nod of her weary head. There was no question in her mind it was the liquor that killed him. "He got hold of that fore-shot. Reckon folks get right greedy now adays."

"Do you know where he got his liquor from?"

"I don't. He never told me nothing. Didn't figure it was woman's business in knowing such matters."

"Are you sure about that?"

"I am." Her chin lifted a bit higher. She took offence at having her word questioned. "Is there airy other thing you be wantin'? If not, I'd be obliged for you to leave me to my grief. Death is a difficult thing to wrap the mind and heart around."

"What happened to your face?" he finally asked, although he'd been staring at it for several minutes.

"Been having quare spells lately. Took one and fell face fomas in the stove wood pile out in the woodshed."

"If I was you, I'd be a might careful of those quare spells."

"I aim to be mighty careful from here on out."

"Oh, before I go, where's your sons at?"

"Don't rightly know. Took off in the truck some time ago and ain't come back yet."

"When was that?"

"Yesterday."

Sheriff Waddell nodded. "And your girl?"

"She's in bed resting up since you brought her home."

"Have you talked to her about what happened to her?"

"So much has happened, I ain't had time for much talkin'."

"You two best be having a long talk. You do know there are laws concerning underage children, don't you?"

"Folks on this mountain have our own laws," she told him firmly.

That was a fact, and he wished he never had to set foot on that mountain. Did his best not to, but there were times when things came up when he was forced to look like he was doing his job.

"I hate to bring this up, being your boys and truck are gone, but the hospital wants you to come get your husband's body out of their morgue. They've got a limited amount of room in their cooler."

Lettie started to nod again but didn't get the chance. The ground shook with the loudest noise she'd ever heard in her life. She had to grab onto the door frame to keep from being knocked off her feet. The sheriff went to his knees right there on the porch, while the deputy grabbed hold of the open car door as he ducked down. Pieces of wood and lord only knew what else went flying through the air for what seemed like neigh onto forever.

"What the hell?" the sheriff shouted as he stood up, looking around to see what happened.

"That log house exploded," the deputy yelled out as his head popped above the car door he was gripping for dear life. "It's on fire. Want me to radio in for a fire truck."

"Hell, yeah," the sheriff yelled back as he stumbled off the porch and around side of the house to see what had happened. Sure enough, it was the log house several hundred yards beyond the Korman's place. What was left of the log house and garage, that hadn't been blown all over the mountain, was on fire. A truck was on its side a ways from where the garage once stood. He watched as the cabin's gas tank exploded and fire shot into the air.

Hell fire, if those Kormans weren't ruining his easy life. He'd always known he ought to stay away from that hellhole of a mountain. Now, he wished he had sent his deputy without him. There would be a shit-load of questions asked along with two bushels of paperwork to fill out. Sheriffing wasn't what it used to be. Sometimes a sheriff couldn't catch a break.

~~~~

Darnell was on top of the ridge digging a grave for his pa in the Korman family graveyard when the black and white pulled into the yard. He stopped digging and hunkered down to watch. He saw Enrick Rainy shoot out the back door of the Hordlys' cabin and take off running for the woods. He must have thought the black and white had come after him. The sight brought a grin to Darnell's face. He liked to see Enrick Rainey scared and running in hopes of saving his own sorry hide. There was no question he was up to no good while his sister was gone. Not that his sister and her bunch were any better than Enrick. Didn't matter how many times snakes shed their skins, they were still snakes. Those Raineys were a sorry den of copperhead snakes without doubt. They were by far the meanest and most dishonest bunch he'd ever come across. They were even worse than his own relatives.

Darnell was glad he was hunkered down. If he hadn't, he'd have been knocked flat as a flitter. That Hordly cabin exploded right before his eyes. Made him think of a cherry bomb going off in a little wooden match box. Pieces of wood and everything else went flying through the air like paper confetti in a windstorm. At least his folk's house was still standing. He continued watching as the sheriff ran around the corner of his ma's house all in a tizzy. Reckon the sheriff finally had something to get excited about, not that there was a thing he could do. Enrick had done blown the Hordlys' place up.

Chapter 26

~~~~

Jackson was staying at the same hotel as Catalena and her father were staying. For two days straight, they were at the courthouse the minute it opened and didn't leave until it closed. The best way to find out what happened was to research the paper trail. From the time a land grant was given until present day ownership should consist of a well-established paper trail to be followed. In some cases, it required time and effort to pick the bones of documents and transactions in order to get a clear picture of transfers that would stand up in a court of law. Land was one thing that held firm and did not change, but rightful ownership did. Since land was continual and ownership an all-important right, laws were strict and consistent.

They also had private investigators on the job. Soon, they would know more about the Hordlys and Kormans than their own mothers knew.

During the time Gertie Lee Smith was supposed to have sold and signed the deed to the Kormans, she was in a hospital in Texas with a case of pneumonia. It would have been impossible for her to have sold her land.

Another factor was a money trail. No signs of monetary value had been shown in any transactions between Markum Korman and Gertie Lee Smith.

There was no question the documents had been forged – first to Markum Korman and then a few days later the land was transferred to Nickel and Phyllis Rainey Hordly. Two years later the log cabin was built. No attorney had been used in the transference of land, nor had there been a title search. If there had been, it would have shown the deed to the land had been in Catalena's name since she was one year old and put on record at the courthouse long before Markum Korman claimed to have purchased the land. North Carolina was a race state which meant the deed put on record first held the lawful title. Not only that, but records also showed taxes were always paid by check from Gertie Lee Smith to present time.

They had Markum Korman and the Hordlys by the short hairs.

~~~~

Catalena pulled up information at the courthouse on Markum Korman to find a recent death certificate. The coroner's report stated his death as accidental alcohol poisoning. She and Jackson were still there gathering legal information to take Markum Korman and the Hordlys to trial for fraud resulting in thief of real estate. She wasted no time bringing Markum Korman's death to Jackson's attention.

Catalena got in her father's Cadillac and drove the same road she had once driven in her Jeep. Memories she hadn't expected came flooding back to her. Her grandmother's face as she told her stories about the mountains she had loved and how age had forced her to move away from. She remembered his grandmother's words.

"Morene tried to get me to sell the land after my Sanford died, but I could never do that. It's my life, part of my and your grandfather's life together. I remember the day we bought the land. It was rough mountain land, not fit for doing much farming on, but we made do. Sandford always longed for some of the bottom land down along the river where the grass grew green and tall, but he died without ever affording even an acre of it.

"After he died, I had to make do on my own. I knew there were people who'd try to take advantage of a lone widow woman. So, I went ahead and put the deed in your name and kept a life estate for myself, being you were still a baby. I figured the land would be safe from Morene selling it off if you couldn't legally sign over the land until I died, and you came of age. I even paid a lawyer to make sure everything was set up nice and proper. He had a fancy name for the way he set up your inheritance, but I don't recall it.

"You see, I didn't exactly trust Morene to do as I wanted. She always believed she knew what was best for herself and everybody else. She would argue until the cows came home until she got her own way. Our Morene always had a spirit that differed from mountain people. She had dreams of prosperity along with an easier lifestyle. Sanford used to say no hoe handle was ever made that would fit in Morene's hand.

"I have only one request of you in return for the place me and Sanford loved so dearly. When I die, I want you to take my ashes back home and spread me over my dear Sanford's grave."

A soul gripping pain shot through Catalena's chest. She had failed her grandmother's only request of her. The urn containing her grandmother's ashes had been sitting in the passenger seat when she wrecked the Jeep. Instead of being scattered over her husband's grave, her ashes had been scattered down the rock cliff into the valley below. She didn't even know where her grandfather's grave was located.

Homer would know. That man seemed to know just about everything concerning the people and the mountain he grew up on. What did he know about the Kormans, the Hordlys and her grandmother's land? Why hadn't he told her more than he had? It dawned on her that he had no reason to tell her any more than he'd already told her. He hadn't known she was Gertie Lee Smith's granddaughter and neither had she. Her questions would be different now that she had her memory back, or at least most of it back.

This time Catalena turned into the Barlows' driveway instead of continuing up the old logging road she referred to as a goat path. Just the thought of driving up that narrow road made her knees grow shaky. She almost wished she could forget how afraid she'd been. She remembered how her father had tried to cure her fear of heights by encouraging her to ride a donkey down into the Grand Canyon, and even traveling the Road of Death in North Yungas, Bolivia. Neither had worked.

She smiled, remembering her father's encouragements and her mother's protectiveness. Her grandmother had always seemed more reasonable where she was concerned. Her grandmother always believed she was intelligent and capable enough to do what was right.

"I'm doing what I think is right, Grandma. Even more important, I'm doing what I want to do – what you always thought I would mature enough to do.

She parked the Cadillac and got out. She walked onto the porch and knocked on the same door she had entered not long ago as freely as though she belonged there. No one answered.

"Mazy," she called out. "Are you home?"

Still no answer.

Instead of going inside, she went to the barn thinking Mazy or Homer might be there. This time of day, George would be at school and the twins at the sawmill. Odd though, the big lumber truck was parked beside the barn.

"Mazy. Homer," she called out as she entered the barn.

Still no answer.

She went to the groundhog's cage only to find it empty. Disappointment surged. She felt as though something of importance was no longer hers, but then she had left it behind. She had no right to expect it to still be there – waiting for her return. Slowly, she turned around and made her way back to the house. She considered leaving but couldn't make herself do so. She went to the porch and sat down in the chair she had set in many times before. It felt as though she had come back home.

Only a few minutes passed before she heard the sound of a vehicle coming up the road and turning into the driveway. Uncle Homer stopped his truck beside the Cadillac.

All three young men jumped out of the back and came toward her with a smile on their faces, wearing their Sunday best.

She stood up.

"You've come back," George shouted as he got to her first and grabbed her in a bear hug.

She laughed and hugged him back. Homer was next, then Mazy, and Bob. Rob hung back watching her as the others did their welcoming. Their eyes met and held as he slowly moved forward. Instead of giving her a welcoming hug, as the others did, he held out his hand to her. She took it, held on tight, and continued to hold on until it was past time to let go.

"Welcome back," Rob said, and their hands relunctly lost their grip on each other.

She was sure the others had spoken words of greetings and welcome, but it was only Rob's voice that penetrated all the way to her heart.

"Why are you all dressed up on a weekday?" she finally came to herself enough to ask.

"Sit back down and we'll catch you up on what's happened since you've been gone."

Catalena set back down, feeling like she'd been gone years instead of days.

"You look different," George was quick to say. "You're already dressed for a run. I'll change clothes and we can take off. I want you to see what's left of the Hordlys' cabin."

"Hold on, boy," Homer told him. "Let's get her caught up a little before you run off with her."

"What happened to the Hordlys' place," she asked George as he got up from where he always sat on the porch steps.

"It exploded and burned. Uncle Homer thinks Enrick Rainey was cooking meth. The explosion blew the garage up too, exposing an underground room under it. Uncle Homer said there was scorched weed all over the place."

"Hold on a minute, boy. Go change your clothes. Let's tell her what happened in the order it happened."

George reluctantly went inside, along with Mazy. Uncle Homer was seated on one side of her and Bob on the other side. Bob had made a point of seating himself between her and Rob. Homer and Mazy had both noticed but pretended otherwise.

"Is it true that Markum Korman died of poison alcohol?" she blurted out.

"Yeah," Bob was quick to answer. "Uncle Homer took him to the hospital where he died."

"We just came from his funeral," Rob added.

"Lettie asked us to be there," Homer told her. "She's been right tore up about all that's happened. Poor woman has had a rough life. I hope things get better for her now that Markum is in the ground, and her two youngest boys, Alvin and Kimbell, left out to parts unknown."

"Alvin and Kimbell are gone?" she questioned. "What about Jeanene. Is she still there?"

"She was with her mother at the funeral."

"Did she seem okay?"

"Far as I could tell,"

"If you ask me, Markum being dead and those two being gone is the best thing that could have happened for Lettie and Jeanene. Darnell's not got good sense, but he's not as bad as those three," Bob said.

"Darnell takes back after Lettie and her people," Homer said. "George already told you about the Hordlys' place blowing up. Now that we've caught you up on the happenings around here, tell us about yourself. Are your parents still here?"

When she caught them up on her parents flying back to Texas, and everything they had discovered about the forged documents of her grandmother's land, she stood up to leave.

"You're still staying in a hotel?" Homer asked with disapproval. "You know Mazy will let you stay here, don't you?"

Catalena wasn't so sure Mazy would be as welcoming as Homer indicated. Although, she did seem happy to see her. The only one who didn't appear very happy at her being there was Bob.

"Yes, for a while longer. My dad's private attorney is still here. I need to let him know what has happened with the Hordly place. I think things will be less complicated with the cabin gone. There was no question about the land being mine, but the cabin could have been in question. They might have been able to claim squatters' rights, and brought in other legalities related to time," Catalena said, not willing to go into further details that were complicated at best.

"Wait," George burst out. "You can't leave yet. We've not gone for our run."

Catalena wasn't interested in going for a run right then, but she was interested in exactly where the corners of her grandmother's land, now her land, was.

"I don't suppose you know where the corners to Grandma's land are, do you?" She asked Homer.

"Sure do," Homer told her. "Rob knows where they're at, too. Why don't you change out of your church clothes, Rob, and show Lena where the boundaries are?"

"George can show her," Bob was quick to say, but he didn't hesitate to follow Rob inside to change clothes.

Homer grinned. "It might be best if all of us fellows went with you, considering what all has happened. We don't want to take a chance on you beating up another man. Darnell Korman and Enrick Rainey are still roaming about. You might get in trouble with the law considering how often the law has been up the Korman way lately."

"Are you serious or making a joke?" she asked him.

"Both," he told her. "There was some out of town investigators called in about the explosion. Right off hand, rumor is a meth lab blew up. There was also an underground drug operation going on under the garage," Homer told her without sounding surprised at the turn of events. "One thing is for sure, you're one tough little gal."

"Tough?" Catalena questioned that word. "Trained would be more like it. My father had me taking self-defense classes instead of the ballet classes Mother thought I was taking. I'm actually a tenth-degree black belt in Karate. I also ran eight miles a day until I came here." She didn't comment on the explosion and pot operation. If Jackson didn't already know about it, the private investigators would inform him soon. She grinned to herself. People on this mountain already knew more than investigators would ever turn up.

"Yeah," George was quick to say as he came out of the house. "Tough. That's my kind of woman."

He was ignored.

"So, your memory has returned completely?" Homer questioned.

"Yes, it has," she answered, although the word completely was stretching it slightly.

"Has the knot on your head gone down?"

"Almost. My parents insisted I have a specialist examine me. Seems I have nothing to be concerned about."

"Mind me asking why you didn't go back home with them?"

"I want to get the theft of Grandma's land cleared up. That's why Mr. Jackson is still here, diligently working on a resolution."

"And when it's cleared up, will you return to Texas or stick around here?" Rob asked.

"I'm not sure. Both most likely. It will likely take considerable time to get the cloud on the land cleared."

"You got a fellow waiting on you back in Texas or some other place?" Homer made a point of asking.

"No."

"Why not? You one of those men haters?"

She grinned. "No, I'm not a man hater. Actually, I've spent most of my time getting an education – both in the classroom and in traveling. I'm thinking about settling down some."

"Good," George told her. Once I turn eighteen, we can do some courting. Ma won't allow me to spark a woman until I'm of legal age. Claims she's protecting me from having my future ruined."

"I'm too old for you," Catalena told him with a light-hearted laugh. Her grandmother had used the term spark every once in a while.

"Nope. You're just about the right age for me. Ma ought not to object now that she knows you really are one of us instead of an outsider."

So, Mazy had disapproved of her because she came from somewhere else. Being Gertie Lee's granddaughter changed thing in Mazy's way of thinking, or had it?

"Ma doesn't think a person can be happy if they marry outside their own kind," George continued to rattle on.

"I see," she said.

"Go see what's keeping your brothers and stop putting words in Mazy's mouth that she never said," Homer told him.

"What's the boy up to now?" Bob asked as he and Rob came outside.

"Being full of himself as usual," Homer told him. "The boy is making a play for Lena. Can't say as I blame him."

"Boy?" George mocked. "You know the seven stages of a man are? No? Then I'll tell you. They are spills, drills, thrills, bills, ills, pills, and wills. Rob and Bob are in the bills stage. Uncle Homer is in the pills stage. Me, I'm still in the thrills stage."

Homer swatted at him with the back of his hand. "Hush up and let's get going if Lena wants to walk around Gertie Lee's entire boundary. It's a right good-sized piece of land."

"Aren't you gonna change out of your Sunday clothes? George asked his uncle.

"Nope. I'm old enough not to get dirty." Besides, he'd have to go all the way to his house to change. Mazy forbade him to keep clothes at her place.

"Might not look right," she'd told him.

~~~~

Catalena stood on the ridge and looked down at the remains of what was once a log cabin. She'd seen pictures on television where bombs had blown up houses. This was a prime example. Logs, tin roofing, and other debris were scattered everywhere.

"Have the Hordlys returned?" she asked.

"Not that we've seen," Homer told her.

"Do you think they will come back?"

"I'd say they will, sooner or later."

"I'd rather they not know who I am or that my parents were here until Jackson gets our case prepared and them served with a warrant."

"I can understand how it'd be best until you get things straightened out. You did hear her, didn't you George?" Homer added.

"I know how to keep my mouth shut. Think they'll go to jail?"

"Mr. Jackson is handling the legalities," Catalena told him.

"Once you get things settled, and if you want to sell the land, I hope you'll let us Barlows know. We'd kinda like to have a choice in who our neighbors are," Homer said. "Bad neighbors are a misery to decent folks."

"Would be mighty fine to have you as a neighbor," Rob said as he took a few steps closer to her.

Bob tried to inconspicuously get between her and Rob, causing Homer to turn his back to keep the twins from seeing him grin.

"Let's walk back up the goat path. There's something near there I think Lena might want to see that we failed to show her."

"Are you talking about the three-way corner?" George asked.

"Right. Barlow land, Korman land, and your Grandparent's land meet near the place your Jeep went off," Homer told her.

Once they reached the spot, Homer went to the tree she had sat under when she first walked up the goat path. Right over there is your grandma's land, and right here is your grandpa's grave. He always told your grandma that he wanted to be buried right on this spot in a wooden box with nothing but big, flat rocks for a head and foot stone. He liked the view from here. Gertie Lee honored his wish."

Catalena walked to the tree where she had first set on the large rock that was her grandpa's head stone.

"I don't believe it," she said as tears came to her eyes. She'd actually brought her grandma's ashes, along with her grandpa's Jeep, back to him without knowing it. They, along with her grandpa, would forever be a part of this mountain at the end of a goat path.

It was Rob who went to her side and gave her his clean handkerchief. She took it as his other arm slipped around her waist. It felt good to finally have a firm body to lean against.

Chapter 27

~~~~

On Saturday Catalena found herself sitting on the right-hand side of Rob, while Darlene sat on the left-hand side of Bob as they watched a movie at the theater. Rob and Bob were sitting next to each other, which seemed to ease a little bit of Bob's possessiveness over his brother. Catalena could tell Bob didn't like the idea of his brother paying so much attention to her. Darlene was doing her best to keep his attention focused on her. She had supplied him with candy she'd bought at the service station and slipped into the theater in her purse. The theater had a rule against taking food and drink into the movies unless they were bought there at three times the normal price.

Once the candy was gone, Darlene held his hand and caressed his fingers as she pretended to be watching the movie. Occasionally, she stole a glance at Rob with a kind of regret showing in her eyes. Catalena could understand Darlene's disappointment. Catalena also preferred Rob to Bob, and she didn't know exactly why. There was a chemistry about Rob that reached out and touched her soul when Bob's didn't.

Right now, Rob's arm was on the back of the seat with his thumb gently caressing the back of her neck. His eyes were watching the movie, and at the same time it felt as though he never looked away from her face.

He leaned over and whispered in her ear. "I thought you were never going to pay any attention to me."

"How could I do such as that when I didn't even know who I was? You weren't spilling over in the romance department," she whispered back. "You hardly talked to me."

"For all I knew, you had a husband and a dozen kids waiting for you to return home."

"Point taken for both of us."

"Would you like to have a dozen kids?"

"No," she told him firmly.

Disappointment came to his face.

"Four or six maybe, but not a dozen."

He grinned. "I'd like to help you get them."

"I think you'll have a better chance at it than most," she added in a teasing tone of voice.

"Shhh," Bob whispered as he punched his brother in the ribs with his elbow.

Rob grinned and so did Catalena.

Darlene made a point of lifting Bob's hand and rubbing the back of it against her cheek. Bob was a flat-out idiot if he didn't start paying more attention to Darlene. She was attractive enough and willing to work a convenience store to earn herself a living. Even Mazy told Bob Darlene was a good girl who came from an honest, hardworking family. Plus, Darlene was pure mountain woman.

Catalena knew Mazy still wasn't completely sure about her – and with good reason. Catalena had spent years of hard educational work to become an attorney like her mother. She wasn't sure she wanted to give it up. At the same time, she was fast becoming attached to Rob – almost as possessively as Bob had been attached to his brother.

After the movie was over, Darlene and Catalena managed to get the brothers separated long enough to take them on a walk through the town. Darlene was smooth as silk in handling Bob, although it was evident, he didn't want to be handled.

"It's obvious Bob doesn't want you to be alone with me," Catalena told Rob.

"He's always been possessive over just about everything, It's in his nature," Rob told her. "Darlene will get his focus turned onto her before long. She's kind of wily that way."

"You and Bob two are too close," she'd told him.

"Naw," he said with a grin. "We're just brothers who stood up for each other. We discovered early on we could get by with a lot more if we did."

"What about George? Do you stand up for him as well?"

"Of course, we do. We're family. Uncle Homer took him under his wing. He became the child Uncle Homer never had. Mom never much liked it, but there wasn't a thing she could do about Uncle Homer. He's a part of our lives as solid and everlasting as these mountains."

"What will happen if one of you decide to get married?"

"You're referring to Bob and me instead of George or Uncle Homer?"

"You know I am."

"If one of us is lucky enough to fall in love and get married, I suppose the other twin will do the same – or not," he added with a touch of humor as he stopped at a little park bench next to a statue. They both sat down. He looked into her eyes as his hand gently buried into her hair. His fingers moved gently as he eased her face toward his. He lightly let his lips brush against hers.

She felt the tingle all the way to her toes.

"There you two are," said Bob. He was definitely displeased at what he was seeing. "We'd best be getting back home. Mom will be worried."

Darlene rolled her eyes in her bewilderment at Bob. Obviously, things hadn't gone as well as she'd planned on their walk.

"Mom wouldn't be herself if she didn't have something to worry about," Rob told her, as he took her hand and stood up.

They walked back to Catalena's car. Bob and Darlene got in the back seat, while Rob got behind the wheel. They had met

Catalena at the hotel and driven her car since there wasn't room for four in the truck seat.

Catalena didn't wait for Rob to open the car door for her once they arrived at the hotel, although he tried.

"Thanks for an enjoyable evening," Rob told her, as he slipped her car keys into her hand.

"My pleasure," she said.

"We'll do it again, soon," he said as he leaned forward and brushed a kiss on her forehead.

"Yes," she whispered, again feeling the tingle.

She locked the car as she watched Rob walk away. Bob and Darlene were getting in the truck. Double dating with the twins reminded her of double dating during high school. Adolescent was the word that came to her mind. The dates she had in Texas were nothing like this date, and yet there was something touching about it. She was smiling as she went inside the hotel.

~~~~

Catalena was still in her night gown drinking a cup of coffee, when a knock sounded on her door. She checked the peephole to see Jackson standing there. She opened the door and let him in.

"Want a cup of coffee?" she offered. "At least this hotel provides a tiny coffee pot and packets of coffee in each room."

"I've already drunk several cups while eating the hotel's complimentary breakfast. I take it you've not eaten breakfast yet."

"Not yet. Have a seat."

Jackson sat down in one of the two chairs and laid his briefcase on the tiny table.

"What discoveries have you made?" Catalena asked as she sat in the other chair and finished drinking the strong coffee.

"I was contacted last night by one of our investigators. He found several shady deals Nickel Hordly has been involved in. Hordly was hired to build government-backed public housing in Chicago. He had a crew of legitimate employees, plus two fictional workers that he wrote checks to each week. The fictional workers cashed the checks and gave Nickel ninety percent of the cash. He also used inferior building materials while getting kickbacks from sub-contractors. When his shady deals started being brought into the light, he left Chicago behind and headed for Florida. He tried rubbing shoulders with the good ole boys down there, but it didn't last. It didn't take the good ole boys long to discover what type of man he was and would have nothing to do with him."

"Why am I not surprised?" Catalena said.

"I haven't gotten all the investigator's reports back, but it appears Hordly pulled fraud scams with a number of older women. He's scammed them out of homes, land, and their bank accounts. His practices were usually a *get-it and run* scam. Since Phyllis, his wife, was from the area, they chose to build a summer cabin on your grandmother's land. They forged a deed to Markum Korman from your grandmother and then bought the land from Markum.

"Unfortunately, Markum is dead and can't testify against the Hordlys. Fortunately, the cabin exploded and burned to the ground before the fire department arrived. Fortunately, for us, the Hordlys' had an active meth lab in their house which caused the explosion. Plus, they were also growing marijuana in an underground section of the garage."

"Can we use that against them in our case of fraud?"

"I believe we will be able to come up with something in our favor since they have a history of fraudulent behavior. I have an idea Nickel and Phyllis Hordly just might be taking an out of the country vacation for an extended period of time. It seems they drew all their money out of several bank accounts on the day of the explosion, and their Florida house is now empty. Phyllis' brother, Enrick Rainey has also gone missing. It is believed he was operating the meth lab when it exploded. Darnell Korman admitted to the FEDs he saw Rainey running from the house minutes before the explosion happened. The

Hordlys could claim innocent on the meth lab since they weren't home at the time, but the underground growth chamber in the garage is evidence of their guilt."

"I want the deed cleared on Grandma's land as soon as possible," Catalena told him. "I'm going to build a place of my own. I've already got the exact spot picked out."

Chapter 28

~~~~

Rob drove the truck with Darlene sitting between him and Bob. She made a point of not to letting her shoulder touch Rob's, while pressing herself against Bob as she gripped his arm with one hand and played with his fingers with the other hand. She was actually doing everything short of crawling in his lap. Bob didn't seem to know what to do or say.

"I love the feel of big calloused hands," she said. "It shows you're a hardworking man. You wouldn't believe how many men come into the service station with hands softer than a woman's. Even my own hands aren't as soft as theirs."

Bob didn't seem to know what to say, so Rob decided to help him out a little.

"Yeah, Bob sure enough has big, strong, calloused hands. He'd make some woman a mighty fine, hardworking husband. Wouldn't you, Bob?"

"All sawmill men have calloused hands," he said. "Even George does, and he only works on Saturdays."

"I've heard sawmilling is dangerous work, is that true?"

"Not so much, if you know what you're doing," Bob told her.

"I'm sure you always know what you're doing," Darlene all but cooed as she blinked her eyes at him.

Rob gritted his teeth together to keep from grinning. She was putting on some sort of overdone show, but he wasn't exactly sure why. Unless she was trying to make him jealous, which wasn't working. Of course, she might just be trying to encourage Bob to show her more attention. Rob hoped that was the case because he didn't have a thing for Darlene. He didn't think Bob did either, but a man never knew what might happen to turn him around.

Take him for instance, he sure hadn't planned on having feelings for a city girl, especially when she was a lawyer. The fact that her grandmother had been a mountain woman helped a little. Still, he wasn't sure there was a chance of them having a relationship that would grow into anything other than good friends, regardless of how much he wanted it to happen.

Actually, she and George got along much better than she got along with him. Not that they didn't get along. They simply hadn't spent enough time together to find out if they were compatible. He planned to remedy that if she stuck around long enough.

When Rob stopped the truck in front of Darlene's parent's house, Bob had the door open and his feet on the ground before the truck came to a good halt.

Darlene grabbed hold of his hand in a near death grip. "A gentleman always walks a lady to her front door," she told him.

It was more like Bob was being dragged than walking her to the door of his own free will. When they reached the door, she turned loose of his hand to clasp both arms around his neck. "Thank you," she said, "for a wonderful night." She laid a kiss on his mouth that had him gripping her shoulders with both hands. When she turned him loose, his eyes bugged, and his mouth hung open. He wanted to say something, but not one single word came to mind. "Uh," he finally mumbled.

"I'll be expecting you next Saturday at six-thirty, or maybe sooner, depending," she whispered in his ear when she finally drew her mouth away from his. "Without your brother." she added before she slipped inside, leaving him standing there in total awe.

Bob slow walked to the truck and got in without looking at Rob or saying a word.

"That girl grew up siphoning gas," Rob said.

"What do you mean?" Bob finally came around enough to ask.

"Had to by the way she put a suction on your face."

"That's not funny," Bob told him.

"Nope. I'd say it was right pleasurable."

"Uncle Homer is bad enough with his jokes. Don't you start too."

"If you're not the touchy one tonight. I thought Darlene would turn you into a happy man."

"Did Lena turn you into one?"

"She sure enough did," Rob admitted.

"Then ain't you the lucky one. Just like always."

"Okay," Rob said. "What's eating at you?"

"You," Bob told him.

"What about me?"

"You always get what you go after, and I have to take your leftovers."

The way he said that surprised Rob. "Darlene is not my leftover."

"I wasn't talking about Darlene. I'm talking about Lena. You knew I had my eyes on her, but you didn't care. You snatched her away from me the first chance you got."

Rob's eyebrows raised and his mouth all but gaped open as he looked away from the road to stare at Bob. "You've got to be joking."

"I'm not joking. I'm mad as a hornet. If I can't have Lena, you can't either."

"Hang on a minute there, brother. I didn't know you had your eyes on her, nor did I snatch her away from you. She said yes when I asked her to go to the movies. The same as Darlene said yes to going with you."

"Both of them wanted to go with you," Bob said in a pouting manner.

Rob burst out laughing. "I don't believe it. You're jealous of me. Shit, brother. We're so much alike the girls can hardly tell us apart, and you're jealous of me. I'm willing to stand back and let you make your move with Darlene and Lena all on you own. I'll even take off hiking for a week and let you have free reins at 'em."

~~~~

Rob spent Sunday thinking about Catalena and his threat to take off and going camping. The more he thought about things, the more he believed going camping alone was a good idea. A man needed to breathe his own air once in a while without having to share it with his brother. As for Bob, they really were too close to each other. Their closeness had pushed everyone else aside. Shit, time was flying by. They already had wrinkles and gray hair in their beards.

Rob got up Monday morning at the crack of dawn. He didn't wake Bob sleeping in the other twin bed. He needed the quiet time as he drove all the way into town before anyone else got up. He found a store that opened at six o'clock in the morning, and bought ten cans of pork and beans, a box of raisins, a water canteen, a backpack, and a sleeping bag. He was going to do exactly what he told his brother he would do. If Lena wanted to ditch him for Bob, it was time for her to do it. If she didn't go for Bob, then she would be his free and clear. As for Darlene, she was a nice girl, but he had no interest in going down that path.

"Where have you been? You missed your breakfast," Homer said as Rob got out of the truck and walked to the porch where Homer was sitting.

"I decided to take off work for a few days and go camping," he told Homer.

"Good idea. All work and no play makes a man have the temperament Bob had this morning. Why didn't you tell Mazy where you were going and take Bob with you?"

"It's a long story. Where is Bob?"

"He headed for the sawmill on foot as soon as he finished eating breakfast. If you ask me, he was right put out because you took off without him."

"He's right put out because Lena went to the movies with me instead of him. He thinks I charmed her away from him."

"I thought he went with Darlene."

"He did. He also claimed Darlene preferred me to him. So, I told him I'd go camping for a week so he could court them both without having me around as temptation."

"You're joking," Homer said, grinning like a possum.

"Nope."

Homer reached up and scratched his head. "If that don't beat all. Reckon you might have a good idea there about taking off camping alone. You two never was Siamese twins, even though Mazy tried to keep you both permanently connected to her umbilical cord." Homer frowned and took a closer look at Rob. "You say Bob's gone sweet on Lena?"

"That's what he told me last night."

"Who is Lena sweet on?" Homer wanted to know.

"Reckon that's for her to decide."

"If it's gonna be a Barlow it'll have to be George. Although, I know she's got a right big hankering for me. Reckon she'll have to get over it. I'll be too old to do her much good in about ten years from now." Homer laughed at his own joke, stood up and headed along the path home. He'd let Rob handle this sudden camping trip on his own.

~~~~

"You're going to do what?" Mazy questioned.

"Take a few days off from sawmilling," Rob told her as he ate a cold breakfast of leftovers. "I've always wanted to try my hand at camping, but never got around to it until now."

"Why didn't Bob go into town with you?"

"Because he's not going camping with me."

Mazy gave him a dumbfounded look. She didn't believe she heard him right. "What did you two get into a disagreement about?" she demanded to know.

"We didn't disagree on anything. We're just taking a week off from work. He'll do his thing, while I do mine."

"My goodness, I never thought I'd see this day. You two are brothers, and brothers are supposed to stick together. It's over her, isn't it? I knew it would happen the day that girl showed up. That girl is no better than her mother was. They'll lead a man on and then dump him because he's not and never will be rich enough to give 'em all the things they want."

"Mom, what are you talking about?"

"Her. That Catalena girl. She's already causing trouble between you and Bob."

"No, she's not. The way I see it is that Bob believes I have life a tad bit easier than he does. You know how he takes what you used to call fits when things aren't going exactly as he wants them to go. He and I both are old enough to get on with our lives separate of each other, don't you think?"

"Where you going camping at?" Mazy asked. She wasn't about to tell him any more about what she thought.

"Nowhere special. Just going to hit the woods and let my feet take me wherever."

"How long will you be gone?"

"Until I decide to come back home."

At least he knew where home was and so did she. Unlike Morene Smith, she had stayed home to marry Harmon Barlow.

She and Morene might have been friends years ago, but they never really liked each other much. Part of it was because of Harmon Barlow. The other part was because they were so different. She was willing to stick to her roots and accept what little life had to offer. Morene wasn't willing to accept less than what she dreamed about having. She ought to be thankful Morene wouldn't settle. If she had, Harmon Barlow would have married Morene instead of her.

Chapter 29

~~~~

The sound of the truck engine woke Bob. He felt both left out and angry when he looked out the window to see Rob driving away without him. It was as much his truck as it was Rob's. He had no right to take off in it without his permission. Come to that, Rob had no right to take off without him. They had shared everything since the moment they were conceived. Didn't Rob realize they were more important than a couple of girls? Surely Rob wasn't going to do what he threatened and stop sawmilling for a week. It would cut into their bank account. They had separate savings accounts with exactly the same amount in each one. Every time they sold lumber, they paid themselves a portion and deposited the rest in a business account. Neither of them ever touched their savings.

On another thought, maybe he should let Rob take off by himself. How better to teach a man a lesson than to let him find out for himself what's important and what's not? A soft bed to sleep in, three meals a day without having to lift a finger or build a fire, no dishes to wash, a good, nice-smelling job, nobody to boss you around, unless Uncle Homer counted. Yeah, might as well let Rob have at it. Chances were, he'd learn when he was well off and forget about Lena. He might forget about her to.

Bob wasted no time in eating his eggs, sausage, gravy and biscuits. Once he'd finished eating, he decided he'd walk to the sawmill. Check things out. He didn't need to hang around waiting on Rob to come back. If he stayed around the house his ma would find something for him to do.

It felt right good walking through the woods when he wasn't in a hurry to get anywhere. Without the sound of the engine and saw blade whining he could even hear a few birds singing and squirrels chattering in the trees. Things he had never paid any attention to before because he was always in a hurry to get things done.

Once he reached the sawmill, it was a whole different feeling showing up without the intention of firing the engine and getting at it. The silence of the place was almost deafening. It kind of felt like something important had died, but it hadn't. Rob would be back soon, and things would go back to normal. It wasn't like he really wanted Lena instead of Darlene. Truth was he didn't want either one of them. He didn't want Rob to have one of them either. Having each other was enough, and he didn't want things to change from the way they were. Change scared him. A silent sawmill kind of scared him too. It wouldn't be silent long.

Much to his surprise, he heard the sound of a car – not the truck Rob was driving. He stepped between two stacks of freshly sawed lumber where he couldn't be seen and waited. Much to his surprise, it was Darlene in her old Ford car. She parked, got out, and looked about as though undecided about what to do next. He could see her take in a deep breath of the sweet-smelling air. They had been sawing white pine lumber again. He did like the aroma white pine gave off and Darlene obviously did too. She looked kind of content as she started walking among the stacks of lumber. She'd even reach out her hand and touch a board as though she liked its feel. A crow flew overhead, and she looked up toward it.

Bob had to admit she was a right pretty girl. She didn't look a thing like Lena, which wasn't entirely a bad thing. Lena kind of had a sissified fragile look about her – a city girl look. Darlene was as country as a lilac bush in bloom in spring – and just as welcome a sight.

When she was only a couple feet from the stacks he stood between, he stepped out.

"Oh, my gosh, Bob. You scared five years off my life," she said as one hand went to her throat and the other over her heart.

He was pleased she had known him instantly.

"Sorry," he said, but he wasn't sorry. He was amused at her reaction.

"I had no idea you were here. I didn't see your truck, so I thought I would get out and walk around in hopes you would show up."

"You needing something?" he asked, being she had never been there before.

"I was needing to see where you worked. You know, see for myself how dangerous sawmilling really is."

"Why would you want to see such as that?"

"Oh, just wanted to make sure you would be safe."

"No kidding?"

"No kidding," she said with a smile. "I just happen to have a jar of lemonade and a couple slices of pound cake in the car if it's time for you to take a break."

"Break? I've not started work yet."

"Oh," she said.

"Don't need a break, but I could sure eat some cake and drink some lemonade."

"It tastes twice as good when you're eating it with somebody you like."

"You like me?" he sounded surprised.

"I thought you already knew I liked you."

"No," he admitted. "I thought you liked Rob."

"I do. He's friendly and more talkative than you are, but you've always been my pick. It's just that I thought you didn't like me. You never talked to me or anything."

"I talked to you Saturday night," he told her as they walked toward her car.

"Seems to me like I did all the talking."

"Didn't much know what to say. I never really dated a girl before."

She laughed. "Have you dated a boy before?"

"Ah, Darlene. You know what I mean."

"Yeah, I think I know. Deep down inside you're still shy."

"You're right about that."

"Know how to get over being shy around girls?"

"How?"

"Like this," she said as she leaned against the fender of her car and pulled him against her. Her arms latched around his neck, and her lips met his.

This time his arms clutched her against him, and he pretended his lips were siphoning gas.

"Damn," he whispered when they finally pulled apart.

"Not bad," she said as her lips brushed against his neck and lingered to nibble a little.

"Right. Not bad, but I think we need a little more practice."

"I agree," she said as she lifted her face slightly.

Five minutes later they were both hot and bothered and in need of some lemonade to cool them off long enough to decide what to do next. Neither of them had expected to feel the burning need passion brought to them.

"That was kind of like eating a potato chip," Darlene finally got her breathing under control enough to talk.

"How's that?"

"It's hard to stop with just one."

"You're saying we have to stop?"

"No, but we should."

"Why?" Bob asked.

"No need to rush what we have a lifetime to continue doing."

Bob liked the *continue doing* idea.

~~~~

Rob was packing things in his backpack when Catalena drove into the yard. She got out, closed the car door, and walked over to the porch where Rob was.

"Hi," she said.

"Hi," he returned with little enthusiasm.

"What are you doing?"

"Putting things in a backpack."

"Why?"

"I'm going camping."

"You're joking."

"What makes you think I'm joking?"

"The man who works six days a week without ever taking a day off, is going camping on a Monday. I find that hard to believe."

"I need a vacation."

"With Bob?"

"Nope. Alone."

Catalena took a closer look at his face to make sure he was serious.

"Why without Bob?"

Rob frowned. "Seems you're plumb full of questions today."

"I do seem so, don't I?" she smiled. "I used to go camping a lot. I love being out in nature. Haven't been in the last two years. I've missed it."

She didn't tell him how much traveling she did, or that she regretted not spending more time with her grandmother during her adult years. Her early years were spent at her grandmother's side. Even when she was away at college, she made a point of visiting her grandmother before her own parents.

Rob gave her a questioning look but remained silent.

"How long do you plan on being gone?" she asked.

"Not sure."

"Where are you going?"

He pointed to a mountain slightly higher than the one they were on. "Up there. Hiked to the top once or twice when I was younger."

"With Bob?"

"With Bob and my dad. Thinking about those hikes have filled me with good memories."

"Memories are always better when they are shared with someone who is important to you."

"Sometimes. It's also good to have some alone time. A time to think and let your confusions disappear."

"I've had a lot of alone thinking time since the accident. You can't imagine how alone you are when you don't remember anything."

"I tried to imagine what you were feeling. Hurt to see what you were going through."

Catalena looked him in the eyes. "I'd like to take a camping trip. It might help me think straight about a few decisions I need to make."

Rob lifted his brows in question but said nothing.

"Of course, you wouldn't be alone if you had a camping companion. That's probably why Bob's not going along. I must say I'm surprised at that," Catalena told him.

Rob grinned. "Call it a trial separation."

"Does it have anything to do with us going to the movies?"

"I think it has more to do with sibling rivalry. Bob and I were slower than average getting there."

"I always wanted an older brother and a younger sister. Mother was in her thirties when I was born. She had a thriving career as an attorney and didn't want to give it up. She had a combination housekeeper, babysitter until I got old enough to stay by myself. I learned to take care of myself along with doing household chores. When I was old enough, I got a part time job as a waitress. I was able to save most all of my tips. Dad paid for my college education. As soon as I graduated from law school and passed the bar exam, I took a year off to travel and get myself on track. Until I came here, I worked for a small law firm."

"Alongside your mother?"

"Nope. My mother owns her own law firm. She insists I blaze my own trail into my future."

"Interesting, but let me tell you some truths. Having older and younger siblings isn't all it's cracked up to be. You never come first in a large family. You're only one in a crowd of needy kids."

"I can see that. What I want to know is, are you're going to ask me to go camping with you?"

Rob was saved from answering when his mother came around from the backyard. She was carrying an empty laundry basket in her hand.

"Thought I heard talking," Mazy said. "If I'd known you were here, Lena, I'd have got you to help me hang out the wet sheets."

Catalena was glad Mazy hadn't known she was there. She had no desire to wash or hangout laundry ever again. The convenience of a washer and dryer was more her speed.

"What have you got there?" Mazy asked her son.

"It's a backpack. Like I said earlier, I'm going to take off and go camping."

"Why anybody wants to go camping so they can sleep on the hard ground is beyond me. I like a soft place to lay my body down at night."

"It's mostly a man thing," Rob told her.

"A soft bed is a soft bed regardless if it's a man thing or a woman thing," Mazy told him as she stepped onto the porch. "If you're gonna be here a while, you can help me get dinner on to cook," Mazy told Catalena.

"I thought Homer might be here," Catalena was quick to say.

"Reckon he went back to his place after he freeloaded breakfast. If you're determined to find him, you can follow the path he's made around back of the barn to his place."

"I'll probably drive."

"Suit yourself."

Both Rob and Catalena watched Mazy go inside.

"I'll walk with you to Uncle Homer's place, if you want," Rob told her.

"I'd just as soon drive," she said again. "That way I'll not have to walk back to get my car."

Rob picked up the backpack with one hand and walked beside her to the car. "Follow me to the sawmill," he told her in a voice low enough for Mazy not to overhear. "I'll leave the truck there for Bob in case he wants to load lumber on it."

"Okay," she agreed, as she watched Rob toss his backpack on the seat, start the truck, and drive away. She turned her car around and followed. She looked in her rearview mirror to see Mazy watching them leave from behind a lace curtain.

When they reached the sawmill, Rob parked the truck in a grassy spot to allow Catalena room to turn her car around. She stopped beside him and got out.

"Interesting," Rob said as he reached her.

"What's interesting?"

"Those tire tracks leading closer to the sawmill."

He followed the tracks a few dozen yards to where it stopped and turned around. One thing about a light coating of sawdust blown on the ground, it was easy to read tracks.

"Look there," he said. "There's a woman's shoe tracks along with Bob's boot tracks. We both wear the same kind of boots."

Why was she not surprised at that bit of information?

"Dang! Their footprints are only inches apart. Looks like her feet were standing between his. They had to be leaning against the car. Their feet moved about slightly. Look at that. The woman must have gotten in the driver's seat and Bob walked around the car and got in the passenger seat. Appears he went willingly with her."

"Who do you suppose the woman is?" Catalena asked.

"Darlene. I recognize her tire prints. She had a flat and put the spare on. I noticed it when we picked her up Saturday and again when we dropped her off."

"Might not be missing your company too badly right now," Catalena couldn't resist saying.

"Looks that way."

"Suppose the two of them decided to go camping on their own? You know, making trial separation easier."

"Smarty pants," Rob said with a grin. "Walk back and lean against your car, if you don't mind.

Catalena did, noticing there was also a slight amount of sawdust on the ground where their vehicles were parked. Rob followed, put his hands on her shoulders and kissed her long and hard.

"See," he said after he regained enough breath to talk. "We made similar footprints."

"So, that was only an experiment and not the real thing?"

"That was only an experiment alright," he said as he took her in his arms and kissed her the way he'd always wanted to kiss her.

When he finally eased his lips away from hers, he said: "That, Lena, was the real thing."

"Does it mean I get to go camping with you?"

"It means we dang well better not be alone for long. I've got an idea about what will happen."

"You think your idea is a bad one?"

"I doubt my idea would be bad for either of us, but we would stir up a lot of gossip."

"I don't mind gossip if you don't."

Rob gave her a questioning look. She grinned and opened the rear door of the Cadillac and slipped herself inside.

"Well?" she questioned. "Are we going to try the real thing again or not?"

~~~~

The Cadillac's windows had steamed up when they realized they heard the sound of a car engine heading toward the sawmill. They were straightening clothes that had become oddly displaced when the car stopped. Rob opened the door and got out the same time as Bob did. Rob thought his brother had to be drunk as a skunk. His face was red, his eyes bugged, and he was actually dancing a jig around and around.

"What the Dickins do you think you're doing?" Rob asked.

Bob reached across the car seat and pulled Darlene out. The girl looked as though she had won the big prize at church bingo.

"Congratulate us," Bob said as he hugged Darlene with one arm and Rob with the other. "We've been to the justice of the peace."

Rob waited, holding his breath.

"We're married," Darlene crowed.

"No shit?" Rob said as he looked his brother in the eyes.

"Sure enough. I'm now Darlene Barlow."

"I've done got me a wife," Bob said with slightly less enthusiasm that he was showing before.

"Does Mom know?" Rob's words cooled things down a little.

"Nope. That's why we came to find you. We're going to take off for our honeymoon and let you tell Mom the good news. She likes Darlene. Mom will have time to get used to me being married by the time we get back."

Rob was getting ready to tell him he'd lost his freaking mind, when Catalena grabbed hold of him.

"Congratulate him, Rob," she said as she squeezed his arm a little too tight.

He looked at Catalena and then back at Bob. "Congratulations. I'm kind of speechless right now."

"I'd a lot rather be going on a honeymoon with Darlene than going camping alone," Bob said triumphantly.

"You've got a point," Catalena smiled at both of them. "May I add my congratulations to Rob's. I'm sure you'll be both be very happy."

"Thank you," Darlene beamed as though she had personally outsmarted Catalena.

"You tell Mom how happy I am, and don't let her get too excited. You know how she can get when unexpected things happen."

Rob knew only too well. "Don't you think you should tell her yourself?"

"No way."

"See you later," Darlene said as she pulled Bob back in the passenger seat. She was grinning so big all her teeth were showing as she turned the car around and drove away.

"If that don't beat all," Rob said.

"Darlene knows how to go after what she wants," was all Catalena knew to say. In her opinion, Darlene knew she'd never get Rob, so she had gone after second best – and snared him when he was most vulnerable.

"I'm gonna have to sit down a while," Rob told her. "Might even need a swallow or two of Uncle Homer's pick-me-up tonic. I'll need a whole glass full before I'm brave enough to tell Mom what Bob has gone and done."

"Maybe Homer should tell her."

"No way. Mom would kill him on the spot. Chances are she'll only break one of my legs if I'm able to dodge fast enough."

"If neither he or you show up, she'll think you went camping together. That will give Bob time to show up with Darlene and tell her himself."

"Good idea. I'll have to think on it a while. Perhaps run it by Uncle Homer while I'm getting a tad of his liquid courage."

"I'll drive you to his place and bring you back for your truck."

He didn't argue.

~~~~

Catalena was surprised when Homer burst out laughing. "I'll be a monkey's uncle," he said between bouts of laughter. "Never thought the boy would beat you to it. Got any idea how to get tranquilizers down Mazy before you break the news to her?"

"Nope," Rob said. "I was hoping you'd come up with something."

"Then you'll have to give it to her straight and fast. Make sure Lena is with you when you tell her. She doesn't like to make a scene in front of anyone other than her own family. On second thought, why don't you go get the preacher to tell Mazy Bob and Darlene are married."

"They got married by the justice of the peace."

"Don't matter. Tell the preacher she'll take it better coming from him. He knows Mazy good enough to help you and her out a little."

"That's a good suggestion," Catalena told Rob. "The preacher might save you a broken leg, or worse."

"You've got a point."

"Say, while you two are at it, why don't you go to the courthouse, get yourselves a marriage license and have the preacher marry you? Mazy might as well choke on a full-grown horse as on a pony."

Both Rob and Catalena were speechless.

"Hold on a minute," Homer said as he got up from the porch chair and went into the house. He came back outside and handed Rob a plain gold band. "This is the wedding band I gave to my darling Bessie on the day we were married. I'd be proud for Lena to wear it until you get her something better."

Rob didn't move. Homer stuck the ring in his shirt pocket. "If it's not needed, bring it back to me. Sometimes at night, I'll wear it on my little finger."

Chapter 30

~~Epilogue~~

Eight years came and went before Lettie heard from Alvin and Kimbell. Alvin sent her a letter saying he was in Texas working on oil rigs. He said he expected to be a rich man as soon as he could afford to buy an oil rich section of land. If she had any money, she should send to him because he'd become rich sooner and be able to pay her back faster.

He also wrote that Kimbell had found a woman to marry him after she had the first baby girl by him. Her pa and brothers hadn't hurt Kimbell too bad before they dragged him in front of the preacher. He was able to stand on his crippled legs and say his I do regardless of missing teeth. Kimbell and his woman now had two girls. Kimbell was thinking about moving on to Montana or maybe even California, but he was afraid his in-laws would find him and drag him back the same as they did every time he tried to run away. It appeared those Texas men were right tough to deal with, but Kimbell kept hoping for a better day to arrive.

Lettie didn't have any money she was willing to send Alvin or anyone else, nor did she even write a letter back. The last eight years had been the best she'd ever spent, and she wasn't willing to bring troubles back into her life.

She had sold all her goats to some fool and her land to Rob Barlow. She kept only a life estate to the house and a half acre of land to grow a garden on. The old house was falling down around her, but she didn't care and neither did Rob.

Darnell had gone off on his own and worked for a construction company. He had bought himself an acre of land and moved a trailer on it. He never married. Never wanted to.

Jeanene was married for the third time and had three children – one by each husband. She made a point of telling everyone who was willing to listen what her brother had done to her when she was little. She called Kimbell and her pa a lot of names they both deserved. She claimed if she ever saw Kimbell again, she'd bob his male parts off as slick as a ribbon. As for her pa, she hoped he was in hell being beaten with the devil's belt the same way her pa had beaten her.

Lettie had taken part of the money she got from the land and paid the funeral home in advance for the best burial plot and funeral plan they offered. She didn't want to go out of this world knowing she would be buried in the same place where her husband had ended his existence. She wanted to be as far away from Markum Korman and the Korman graveyard as she could get.

As for Mazy, she had slowed down a little. She still hung her clothes outside on a clothesline when the weather was good. When it wasn't, she did her laundry in the fancy laundry room Rob and Bob had built for her. She even gave in and soaked her aching bones in the bathtub she claimed she'd never use. She now had a new electric stove to cook on, but she liked using her wood cookstove most of the time. What she liked best was fussing at Homer to carry in more wood for her to burn.

The secrets she kept best were the skimpy clothes she kept between the mattress and bedsprings, and the necklace hidden in the back of the drawer with the word *Lena*. Why she hadn't returned them to Catalena, she didn't know. It simply seemed right that they should remain where they were – along with many of the things that happened in the past.

Homer still lived alone in his house. Sometimes at night, he still wore his Bessie's gold wedding band on his little finger, although he never admitted to doing so ever again.

Bob and Darlene lived in a house close to her parents. Her mother was a great help in looking after their five children while Darlene worked at the service station. Rob and Bob were both still sawmill men working at Harm and Homer Barlow's sawmill. They had made a few improvements, but they clung to the old ways because it was the way they liked it.

Just as Homer had feared, Rob and Catalena chose not to have the preacher marry them. Rob did take her on the camping trip with him. They stayed the entire week, returning with poison ivy and chigger bites, along with great big smiles.

George went on to college and became a doctor, of all things. Not a single one of his kin folks had expected him to take up that profession, least of all George. He simply discovered he loved babies so much he became a pediatrician. He and his wife had two babies of their own.

As for Catalena, Jackson had little problem removing all clouds on the title to her grandmother's land. She had a nice little farmhouse built on top of the ridge near her grandfather's grave. She claimed to dabble a little in being an attorney, especially in real estate law.

As far as Catalena knew, the Hordlys and Enrick Rainey never returned to Nowhere Mountain. She didn't know where they were. She hoped they remained there.

As for Rob, he was the father of two sets of twins. One set of twin boys and one set of twin girls. Catalena said it was just her luck to have twins almost exactly like Rob and Bob. Even worse, she had two twin girls who were the spitting image of her in both looks and feistiness. She figured both of them would end up becoming judges like their grandfather. Both of them thought they knew exactly what was right more than anyone else.

All four children loved to run down the old logging road to spend time with their grandmother. They seemed to have mellowed Mazy up considerable.

As for Uncle Homer, he filled both sets of twins' heads with farfetched stories, along with every joke he could think of or make up. He especially liked to tell them about the little skirt their Uncle George was wearing the day their mother's Jeep tumbled down the cliff and burned. He claimed seeing George in that little skirt scared their mother so badly she passed out cold and didn't come to for three days.

Much to Catalena's amazement, Mazy agreed with Homer's story.

Sometimes Catalena would go to the rock cliff and look down, get the chills, and then sit on the big rock that marked her grandfather's grave until the chills left her. She'd wonder about the plans God had for people and the crazy way he had of allowing them to happen.

www.ingramcontent.com/pod-product-compliance
Lightning Source LLC
Chambersburg PA
CBHW031100260626
47172CB00001B/148